T0129246

The Somerset sisters, three beautiful, headstrong debutantes in Regency London, are discovering that a bit of scandal is a delightful thing ...

For the sake of propriety, and her younger sisters' reputations, Iris Somerset has kept her rebellious streak locked away. But though she receives a proposal from Phineas Knight, Lord of Huntington, Iris can't marry a man she knows isn't truly enamored with her. In fact, Iris no longer wants to be chosen—she wants to choose. Under the clandestine tutelage of "wicked widow" Lady Annabel Tallant, she'll learn how to steer her own marriage prospects—and discover her secret appetites...

What kind of debutante refuses a marquess? Finn is surprised, a little chastened—and thoroughly intrigued. This new, independent version of Iris is far more alluring than the polished socialite she used to be. Finn believed he needed a safe, quiet wife to curb his wilder impulses. But the more Iris surprises him, the more impossible it becomes to resist their deepest desires...

Books by Anna Bradley

LADY ELEANOR'S SEVENTH SUITOR

LADY CHARLOTTE'S FIRST LOVE

TWELFTH NIGHT WITH THE EARL

MORE OR LESS A MARCHIONESS

Published by Kensington Publishing Corporation

More or Less a Marchioness

Anna Bradley

LYRICAL PRESS
Kensington Publishing Corp.
www.kensingtonbooks.com

First Electronic Edition: February 2018
eISBN-13: 978-1-5161-0532-8
eISBN-10: 1-5161-0532-X

First Print Edition: February 2018
ISBN-13: 978-1-5161-0535-9
ISBN-10: 1-5161-0535-4

Printed in the United States of America

Prologue

London, late April, 1817

An honorable gentleman would never be so callous as to wager a lady's future on the turn of a card. Most of the time, Phineas Knight, the Marquess of Huntington, was an honorable gentleman.

This wasn't one of those times.

"Disgraceful, Huntington." Lord Derrick, who was a gentleman *all* the time, sat next to Finn at the gaming table, his lip curled with disgust. "Disgraceful, and unworthy of you."

Finn didn't argue the point. God knew the whole business was despicable enough. Unless he happened to win, of course. Then the wager simply became a neat way to rid himself of a troublesome rival.

Neat, and quick. A card turned, and the matter settled.

The economy of the thing appealed to Finn. As far as the winnings themselves were concerned, they were a secondary consideration, and a distant one at that.

Either of the two young ladies in question would do.

"It's too late for regrets now, Derrick. The game has begun." Finn drummed his fingers on the table, one eye on his cards, the other shifting back and forth between his two opponents.

Lord Harley, as usual, was grinning like a fool. One didn't like to lose to a half-wit like Harley, but men like him were much like rookery vermin— disgusting enough, but so common one hardly gave them a second thought.

Lord Wrexley, however, was another matter. Of the two men facing Finn across the table, Wrexley was the one who'd slide a blade between his ribs the moment he turned his back. Wrexley bore watching, because there was nothing more dangerous than a reckless man who didn't have a thing to lose.

"You'll regret it soon enough, Huntington. Harley has the devil's own luck at cards. Damn it, Harley." Lord Derrick raised his voice. "Why can't you wager over bank notes, like every other scoundrel in London?"

Harley peered over the edge of his cards, his infuriating grin widening. "We *are* wagering over bank notes. If you recall, Lady Honora has fifty thousand of them."

"Miss Somerset has forty thousand, and eyes so deep a blue she's brought half of London to its knees." Lord Derrick shot a contemptuous look across the table. "But I suppose that isn't bloody good enough for *you*, is it, Harley?"

Harley laughed. "What a romantic notion. But if forty thousand and a pair of blue eyes were enough to tempt any of us, we wouldn't be in the middle of this wager."

"Quite the opposite, Harley. Why bother to wager for a lady who doesn't tempt you?" Lord Wrexley curled his fingertips over the edge of his cards, his lips stretching into a provoking grin as his gaze met Finn's. "I'd sink lower than my knees for Miss Somerset."

Lord Derrick snorted. "So low you'd wager over your own cousin's future, as if she were a prime bit of horseflesh at Tattersall's? Lady Honora deserves better from all of you, but especially from you, Wrexley."

Wrexley shrugged, and rapped a knuckle on the table. "Finish it, Harley."

Lord Harley tossed a card across the table to him, then looked at Finn. "Well, Huntington? Another card, or will you hold?"

Finn glanced down at his hand again. They were playing *vingt-et-un*, and he held fourteen points. It didn't look promising.

He tapped the table once. Harley passed him a card, then placed the deck face-down beside him, without taking a card for himself.

Another bad sign.

"What the devil have you got against Miss Somerset, Huntington?" Lord Derrick's scowl was turning blacker with each card tossed across the baize.

"She's well enough."

This terse answer didn't satisfy Lord Derrick. "She's as lovely a lady as I've ever seen, and you don't give a bloody damn if her fortune is ten thousand shy of Lady Honora's. Why not just court Miss Somerset, and be done with it?"

For any other gentleman, Miss Somerset was a tempting option. She'd been raised in Surrey, and still had a tedious whiff of the country in her manners, but even so she was undeniably a diamond of the first water.

Despite her success on the London marriage mart, however, she wasn't Finn's first choice. She did have beautiful eyes—that much was beyond dispute—but there was occasionally a flash of willfulness in those blue depths Finn didn't quite like.

"Too lively for my tastes."

Lady Honora Fairchild, on the other hand, was the type of young lady who'd never give him a moment's concern. She was as docile and sweet-tempered as a new spring lamb, and thus the perfect choice for a wife. She'd make a splendid marchioness.

Lord Derrick crossed his arms over his chest and lapsed into a moody silence.

"Well, Huntington?" Harley was licking his lips like a man who already tasted victory. "Are we to sit here all night while you ponder the vagaries of fate? Look at your bloody card."

Finn turned over a corner of his card.

A five.

He flipped it face up, then tossed all his cards to the middle of the table. "Nineteen."

Not a flicker of emotion crossed Wrexley's face, but Finn could see right away his hand wouldn't beat Harley's. A man with losing cards didn't wear such a gleeful smirk.

Harley slapped his cards down. "Twenty. Bad luck, Huntington."

Finn frowned at Harley's cards, scattered on the table in front of him. Well, that was it, then. Harley would snap up Lady Honora at once and get to work straight away on squandering her fortune.

"Well, Wrexley?" Lord Harley could hardly contain his delight. "Is Huntington to remain a bachelor until next season, or not?"

Lord Wrexley flicked a careless gaze over Harley, then Finn, and tossed his cards into the pile. "Twenty-two."

"Damn shame, Wrexley." Harley was more amused than sympathetic.

A shame, or potentially ruinous. The present Lord Wrexley, like every Lord Wrexley before him, had an inconvenient fondness for wagering, and his fortune hadn't survived his latest run of bad luck. He still had his title, of course, but little else aside from his handsome face and charming manners to recommend him. He'd aimed rather high with Miss Somerset to begin with. If he'd had hopes of her, she must have encouraged him.

Not very discerning of her, particularly since Wrexley didn't appear to return the sentiment. If he was devastated by his loss, his face didn't reflect it. He merely shrugged, and pushed his chair back from the gaming table. "There are other heiresses. But you look glum, Huntington. Not at all like a man who's just secured a chance at forty thousand and London's most celebrated blue-eyed belle. Don't say you're in love with my cousin."

In love, with Lady Honora? Hardly. If he was in love with the chit, he'd never marry her. A man didn't want to lose his head over any woman, but especially not his wife. It would only complicate things, and Finn didn't care for complications. "Love hasn't got a damn thing to do with marriage."

"Well, what's the trouble, then?" Harley gathered up the cards and slipped them into his coat pocket. "One would think you were being forced to marry a lady with empty pockets and a face like a sheep. If you don't fancy Miss Somerset, leave her to Wrexley. He seems keen to have her."

Finn leaned back in his chair and studied Wrexley's face. Losing a wager brought out Wrexley's vengeful tendencies, and he'd never been as good at hiding them from Finn as he was the rest of London. "Is that so, Wrexley?"

"I only think it's a pity to see such a lovely lady wasted on a man who doesn't have a proper appreciation for her. But perhaps you'd care to make another wager on her, Huntington?"

Given that Finn had already wagered on Miss Somerset once, he didn't have much right to be offended by Wrexley's crass offer, but irritation made his lips tighten. "Make another wager on her? Now, Wrexley. That's no way to talk about my future betrothed."

Wrexley shrugged again, then shoved his arms into his coat. "Let me be the first to offer my congratulations, then." He nodded at Harley and Lord Derrick. "I wish you a pleasant evening, gentlemen."

Harley watched him go, then turned back to Finn. "A friendly word, Huntington. Wrexley can be vicious when he wants something, rather like a highwayman after a gold pocket-watch. If he's made up his mind to have the lovely Miss Somerset, he might sink to questionable stratagems to get her. If you do decide to court her, you'd do well to keep an eye on him."

Finn had long since made it a point to keep an eye on Wrexley, but he merely nodded. "I'll bear that in mind."

"You'd be a fool not to court her, you know. It won't be a hardship to bed her." Harley grinned like a man who'd given the matter a good deal of thought. "I'd wager she's a spirited one."

Lord Derrick, who'd remained silent during this exchange, slammed his fist down on the table. "No, you won't. Haven't you two disgraced yourselves enough for one night? No more bloody wagering."

"Yes, if it's all the same to you, Harley," Finn drawled, "I'll decline that wager, for Miss Somerset's sake."

"That's good of you, Huntington, but it's a bit late for chivalry now. I can't help but feel sympathy for the lady, to be wasted on such an indifferent husband. Rather like being married to a block of ice, isn't it? Once she's done her duty and squeezed out an heir or two for you, she may have a mind to take a lover, and I'll take care to be in her way when she does."

Finn gave Lord Harley a sour look. "If you're so enamored of her, why did you wager for the right to court Lady Honora?"

"Money, of course. What else? Besides, I don't think Miss Somerset cares for me, despite my many charms. I have a suspicion she'd refuse me if I offered for her."

"If she wouldn't accept you as a husband, Harley, she won't accept you as a lover."

Harley laughed. "Marriage has a way of lowering a lady's expectations in that regard."

"A gentleman's, as well." Though if boredom was the only challenge he faced in his marriage, Finn would count himself fortunate enough.

Harley pushed back his chair and rose to his feet. "That's what mistresses are for. But you already know that, don't you, Huntington?"

Lord Derrick waited for Harley to leave before he turned a disgusted look on Finn. "Bloody waste of time. You were a damn fool to let Harley talk you into that wager."

"No real harm was done." Harley was right. If Finn couldn't have Lady Honora, he'd settle for Miss Somerset. She'd do well enough. Willfulness could be tamed, after all.

"No harm to *you*, but what if Miss Somerset should hear of it? It will hurt her feelings, and she might just decide to discourage your courtship. What then, Huntington?"

"Don't be absurd, Derrick. There isn't a lady in London who'd discourage a marquess. In any case, she won't hear of it. Wrexley and Harley can't say a word without implicating themselves. None of us will speak of it."

Lord Derrick frowned as Finn rose and plucked his coat off the back of his chair. "Now you've settled the question of a wife, it's off to see your mistress?"

"I may as well enjoy her while I can."

He'd end it with her once he was betrothed. He was the Marquess of Huntington, after all, and despite his occasional lapses into the wickedness he'd inherited from his mother, he was a man of honor, like his father before him.

But he wasn't betrothed yet, and Lady Beaumont was just a short carriage ride away, waiting for him, her lush body warm and eager.

As for Miss Somerset...

He'd have preferred Lady Honora, but Miss Somerset was nearly as pliable as her rival, and her grandfather had been an earl. Once the question of lineage was settled, what difference did it make which lady became his marchioness?

When it came to wives, one of them was as good as another.

Chapter One

Three months later

"Lord Huntington won't kiss me."

Iris Somerset drew in a deep, cleansing breath, then heaved it back out again in such a long sigh her lungs flailed in protest.

Goodness, it felt good to say that at last.

It had been weeks since she'd drawn a full breath. She'd been dangerously close to suffocation since the start of the season, when the Marquess of Huntington had singled her out as the fortunate recipient of his exalted attentions.

Of course, she hadn't meant to blurt out her confession *here*. One didn't speak of kissing in the middle of Lady Fairchild's rose garden. It was considered a great honor to be invited to her ladyship's Hampstead estate for her annual scavenger hunt, and a certain level of decorum was expected.

But she'd come this far, so she may as well finish it. "I've tried everything I can think of to lure him into an indiscretion, but it's like trying to coax a fish to hang itself on the hook."

Iris crossed her arms over her chest, eyed her two companions, and braced herself for the inevitable uproar.

As usual, Lady Honora broke first. "Hush, Iris! He could be right on the other side of this hedge!" She darted a panicked look around the garden to make certain they were alone, then swung back to Iris, a scandalized expression on her pretty face. "What do you mean, he won't kiss you? Of course he won't kiss—"

"Why don't you just kiss him, then? He'll succumb to his savage desires the moment your lips touch his, and that will solve the problem in an instant." Violet snapped her fingers.

At any other time Iris might have found it amusing they'd each reacted just as she'd predicted they would, but Lord Huntington's lack of interest wasn't a laughing matter. "As far as I know, he hasn't *got* any savage desires. That's the problem, Violet."

Lady Honora winced at the word *desires*. "My goodness, Iris. What do you expect? He's an honorable gentleman."

Violet frowned. "Honorable gentlemen don't have desires?"

"No! I mean, yes, of course they…oh, how should I know?" Lady Honora turned on Violet. "If they do have desires, they keep them well hidden out of respect to their betrothed."

Iris couldn't deny Lord Huntington treated her with the utmost respect. He was unfailingly solicitous and polite, just as one would expect from a gentleman of such impeccable character. No proper young lady could complain of such treatment.

How disconcerting to find, mere weeks before she was to become the Marchioness of Huntington, that she wasn't, after all, a proper young lady. "He's *too* respectful, if you ask me."

Violet wiped her tears of laughter on the sleeve of her gown. "Well, you'll have him all to yourself soon enough. Can't you wait to lure him into a kiss in the privacy of your bedchamber after you're wed?"

"I can wait, yes, but *he* shouldn't be able to."

"Oh, dear." Lady Honora was wringing her hands. "I'm sure we shouldn't be discussing kissing. Or luring. Or bedchambers."

"Perhaps not, Honora, but who else am I meant to talk to if not you and Violet? Do you suppose I'll discuss kissing and bedchambers with my grandmother?"

The idea Iris would have such a discussion with Lady Chase, their elderly, cantankerous grandmother, sent Violet off into fresh gales of laughter.

Iris glared at her younger sister. "You may laugh all you like, Violet, but you'd do well to keep in mind you'll have to manage your own troublesome suitors soon enough. Now, what am I meant to do to encourage, ah…a physical expression of affection?"

"Do?" Lady Honora gasped in horror. "Why, nothing at all. How can you ask such a thing, Iris?"

"How can I *not* ask it, Honora? If anyone bothered to show young ladies how to subtly indicate to a gentleman a kiss would be welcome, I wouldn't need your advice at all. For pity's sake, all that time spent practicing the quadrille and pounding away at the pianoforte, but not a word about how to orchestrate a seduction."

"*Seduction?*" Lady Honora looked ready to swoon. "Have you lost your wits?"

"Well, what have you done to encourage him so far?" Violet had overcome her fit of hysteria, and she clapped her hands together with her usual practicality, as if preparing to marshal her troops.

Iris gave a helpless shrug. The truth was, she didn't have the faintest idea how to entice a gentleman into a kiss. "Whatever I could think of. Gazed into his eyes, brushed his hand with mine when he takes my arm— that sort of thing. We've walked alone in Grandmother's garden several times, once in the moonlight, even, but Lord Huntington is immune to every amorous overture."

Immune, or oblivious. Iris hadn't yet decided which. The latter could be overcome easily enough, but the former...

That was a bit more worrying.

Violet tapped her bottom lip with her finger, considering. "Have you licked your lips? I read somewhere glistening lips make gentlemen think of kissing."

Iris stared at her sister. Wherever did Violet get such notions? "I haven't tried *that*, no."

Lady Honora let out a little moan of distress and covered her face.

"Oh, do stop moaning, Honora. It's a kiss, not a ruination, and they *are* betrothed, after all." Violet paused, her gaze narrowing on Honora's flushed face. "You're betrothed too, come to that. Has Lord Harley kissed *you?*"

Lady Honora's flush spread to the roots of her hair. "Well, I—that is... oh, for goodness' sakes, Violet. Very well. Yes, he managed to corner me into it once, in this very garden. He's quicker than he looks, you see."

Lady Honora's voice quivered with distaste. She didn't care at all for Lord Harley, but Lady Fairchild insisted on the match, and Honora wouldn't dare to question her mother's wishes.

Violet's brows drew into a puzzled frown. "Well, perhaps the glistening lips would help, but otherwise I can't account for it. Lord Huntington is quite...well, he's a vigorous sort of gentleman, isn't he?"

They all paused for a moment to consider the question of Lord Huntington's vigor.

A moment was all it took.

Lady Honora let a tiny sigh escape, and Iris and Violet responded with breathless sighs of their own.

Physically speaking, Phineas Knight, the Marquess of Huntington, was utter perfection.

His presence was enough to set feminine eyelashes fluttering across every ballroom in London, and for good reason. But it wasn't just his broad shoulders, his cool hazel eyes, or his thick golden-brown hair that made every bosom in London heave with delight. It wasn't even his ancient title, or the impressive fortune that accompanied it, though any one of these things was more than enough to recommend him to a young lady.

No, it was the man himself. He was the quintessential English gentleman. Honorable, handsome, and intelligent, fashionable without being a fop, skilled with the sword and pistol, and an accomplished whip, Lord Huntington was what every lady sighed for, and every gentleman aspired to be, and if he was a bit too cold and grand for some tastes, fashionable society didn't blink at it.

The man *was* a marquess, after all.

Lady Honora sighed again. "His face is perfect in every regard."

Violet rolled her eyes. "No one is flawless, Honora, not even Lord Huntington."

"Well, what's his flaw, then? I defy you to identify one."

"It's that tiny dimple in the center of his chin," Violet declared without hesitation.

"But that dimple is charming. Don't you think so, Iris?"

Iris had grave concerns about Lord Huntington's frigid propriety, but his face was beautiful, and it was nothing short of heresy to remain silent while her sister maligned that lovely dimple. "I've always been rather enamored of it. How is it a flaw, Violet?"

Violet gave them a triumphant look. "Because, any lady who dreams of kissing him—and that's every lady in London, by my reckoning— must decide whether to start with his delicious lips, or that distracting little dimple."

There was a brief silence, then Iris and Violet burst into laughter.

Even Lady Honora couldn't resist a smile. "How did you come to be so wicked, Violet?"

"We're discussing Iris's wickedness, if you please, Honora. Though I don't know if it's so *very* wicked for her to want an innocent kiss from her betrothed. It's not as if she expects him to drag her off into the bushes and ravage her."

"No, but when I try to lure him into a kiss, I do expect him to cooperate." Iris glanced at Honora. "I only want to see if I find it acceptable. Is that so shocking?"

If she could judge by the tingle of anticipation in her belly every time she looked at his lips, she'd find it quite acceptable, indeed, but what use were his handsome lips if he kept them to himself?

Iris hesitated, then swallowed down the last bitter remnants of her pride. "Do you suppose he doesn't *want* to kiss me?"

The humiliating truth was, she'd suspected for some time he didn't have any true affection for her. His courtship had been utterly correct, but Iris had nevertheless been surprised when he came up to scratch. He could have whoever he wanted, after all. Every young lady in London had spent the entire season sighing over him.

Once he did take his suit to her grandmother, he'd been given approval readily enough. Indeed, no one would think to refuse Lord Huntington anything, including Iris, who'd accepted him as a matter of course, and perhaps just the tiniest flash of guilty triumph at having secured the one gentleman every lady in London yearned for.

But it wasn't long before a distressing voice in her head began whispering Lord Huntington wasn't all that enamored of her, and no matter what she did, it wouldn't be silenced. She didn't expect him to make some elaborate declaration, or attempt a seduction. He wasn't a demonstrative sort of gentleman. But an innocent kiss would go a long way to relieve her doubts about his affections.

But the kiss was not forthcoming, and Iris couldn't quite hide her unhappiness as she looked at Violet and Honora. "Perhaps he regrets making an offer, and wishes he were betrothed to another lady."

Honora rushed to wrap an arm around Iris's shoulder. "Oh no, Iris. I'm sure that's not it. No one is lovelier than you."

Violet, who refused to hear a disparaging word about any of her four sisters, looked offended at the very suggestion. "Every eligible gentleman this season has been angling for your hand, Iris. Lord Huntington is fortunate to get you, and I daresay he knows it. You're everything the belle of her season should be."

Lady Honora squeezed Iris's arm. "Violet's right, Iris. Social custom, habit, propriety—all conspire to keep you from becoming familiar with each other before you're wed. Lord Huntington's behavior is utterly correct. As a gentleman, he can't breach decorum, even if he wishes to."

Iris drew in a shaky breath. Perhaps they were right, and she was fretting over nothing. "I hadn't thought of it quite like that. It's just…I thought courtship would be different. More romantic, somehow. It's foolish of me, I suppose."

"I don't think it's foolish at all. It's a simple kiss, for goodness' sake, and little enough to ask. Surely between the three of us we can come up with a way for Iris to tempt Lord Huntington into a kiss. Now let's see—she's tried moonlit walks, a touch to the hand, gazing into his eyes, and she'll try the glistening lips." Violet was ticking points off on her fingers. "It's a good start, I daresay, but there must be more she can do. Help me think, Honora."

A long silence ensued as they each considered the possibilities, and it continued to stretch until at last Violet made a disgusted noise in her throat. "For pity's sake. I can't think of another thing. You're quite right, Iris. Once a lady is betrothed, what good does it do her to know how to flirt a fan? The accomplishments expected of a young lady on the marriage mart are utterly useless once she sets foot outside Almack's."

Lady Honora shook her head at this. "Well, Iris's accomplishments worked well enough to secure her an enviable suitor. She *is* betrothed to the Marquess of Huntington, after all."

"Yes, but what am I meant do once I'm married to him? No one says a word about that, do they? Indeed, no one seems to care much what happens to a lady after she's secured a proper husband, unless she does something scandalous."

"My goodness, Iris. What a depressing thought." Violet took her by the shoulders and gave her a gentle shake. "You'll give yourself the vapors. Come now, I know just what you need to cheer you up."

"You do?" Iris gave her sister a hopeful look. "What is it?"

"A kiss from Lord Huntington, of course."

Iris deflated again. "I've tried everything I can think of, Violet—"

"No, you haven't. You haven't tried to kiss him." Violet seized her arm with one hand, and pointed toward a pathway that led to the back of the garden, her face flushed with sudden excitement. "He just went down that pathway. Quickly. Go after him, and kiss him!"

Lady Honora grabbed Iris's other arm. "No! She can't go chasing Lord Huntington all over the garden. It isn't proper. What will my mother say if she finds out?"

"She won't find out unless you tell her, Honora. There's no one about in this part of the garden. Go on, Iris. It's a scavenger hunt, after all." Violet's lips turned up in a grin. "Surely a kiss from Lord Huntington wins you the game."

Iris took a hesitant step forward, but then stopped. What if she should look into those cool hazel eyes of his and see nothing but indifference? "What if he...what if he rebuffs me?"

To her surprise, Lady Honora released her arm and gave her a gentle push in the direction Lord Huntington had gone. "He won't, Iris. He never would have made you an offer if he didn't care for you, but if a kiss will ease your doubts, then it's worth the lapse in propriety."

Iris took a few stumbling steps forward, then a few more. Her heart rushed into her throat at the idea of kissing Lord Huntington, but when she looked back, Violet and Honora both smiled reassuringly at her.

"Go on." Violet waved her forward. "We'll wait for you on the terrace."

Iris plunged blindly into the foliage until she saw him ahead of her, hurrying along the twisting pathways. She would have lost him entirely if she hadn't caught occasional glimpses of his dark green coat among the brighter greens in the garden.

"Lord Huntington?" She was a bit breathless from chasing after him, but she was only a few paces away when she called out. There could be no doubt he'd heard her. Yet he hesitated before turning to face her, and once he did...

Oh, dear God.

It took every bit of bravery Iris could muster not to flee back into the safety of the garden. He never fell into spasms of joy when he saw her, but he was looking at her now as if she were an offensive bit of garden fungus.

"Miss Somerset." His smiled was strained. "I suppose you're on your way back to the terrace?"

Iris gave him a puzzled look. It was an odd question, since she was walking in the opposite direction. "No, my lord. I still need to find the red rose petals for the scavenger hunt, and Lady Honora sent me this way. She said all the nicest red roses are at the back of the garden."

"I'm sure I saw some closer to the house."

His tone was polite enough, but a frown played at the corners of his lips. Even so, Iris's foolish heart began to pound with anticipation when she met his gaze. His hazel eyes were changeable, and this afternoon they were more golden than brown, with just the faintest hint of green.

A little sigh escaped her. If a lady *were* to kiss a gentleman, she could do a great deal worse than Lord Huntington.

"I'm sure you must be fatigued after so long a time in the sun. Allow me to escort you back to the terrace."

He offered his arm, and Iris took it, but she held back when he tried to take her down a path that led to the house. "No, I'm not fatigued. I'm very well, and it's a lovely afternoon, isn't it? Such beautiful light."

"Yes. Lovely." But he didn't look as if he were enchanted with the garden, or with her. His frown deepened until it was almost a scowl, and his arm tensed under her fingers. "But I'm certain your sister must be looking for you, and I believe Lady Fairchild was about to serve tea."

Iris hesitated, puzzled at his curt tone. Lord Huntington hadn't ever been romantic with her, but he'd also never been anything other than scrupulously polite, and his tone at the moment bordered on rudeness. He seemed agitated, as well, as if he expected someone to jump out of the bushes at any moment.

"Just to the far end of the garden, my lord, to see the roses." She cast him what she hoped was an encouraging look from under her lashes. "They're in bloom, and there's a bench there where we can rest."

She gave his arm a gentle tug, but he didn't move. "Why should you need a bench, Miss Somerset? You just said you weren't fatigued. If you feel the need for a rest, I beg you'll let me escort you back to the terrace."

Iris drew in a long, calming breath, and tried again. "It's not far. Just on the other side of the hedge." She slid her hand down his arm and let her fingertips rest on the inside of his wrist. "The flowers are especially fragrant when they've been warmed by the sun, as they have this afternoon."

"I'm sure they are, but our friends and your sister are waiting for us, and it's hardly proper for us to be alone here, out of sight of the house."

Iris knew very well Violet wasn't waiting for her, but for some reason Lord Huntington was determined to take her back to the terrace. He was fairly vibrating with impatience, and she couldn't imagine a less auspicious moment to steal a kiss than this one, but she found herself clutching at the sleeve of his coat before he could stir another step.

Was it propriety holding him back, as Lady Honora suggested, or was he as indifferent as he appeared? He didn't seem to find anything about her alluring, or even mildly interesting, and she couldn't bear it a second longer.

This kiss was no longer about passion, or even affection. It was a kiss born out of desperation.

"Wait, Lord Huntington." She didn't say anything more, but darted her tongue quickly over her lips to make them glisten and then raised her face to his, her heart pounding with fear and hope. It was clumsily done, but surely the glistening lips would move him this time.

She let her eyes drift closed, and prayed with every breath in her body his firm, sensuous lips would settle over hers.

They didn't.

Iris's heart was thrashing in her chest like a trapped bird, but she'd come this far, and she knew she'd never have the nerve to try again if she gave up this time. She drew in a deep breath, rested her hands against his chest, and rose onto the toes of her slippers, but he was so tall she still couldn't reach his mouth. After another shaky breath she slid a hand up to his shoulder and around to the back of his neck and tugged gently to bring his face down to hers.

It was like trying to bend the trunk of a tree.

He didn't move. "What are you doing, Miss Somerset?"

Iris's eyes snapped open, and mortified heat raced into her cheeks. "I—I was...surely it's not so very improper for a betrothed couple to—"

"Betrothed, Miss Somerset, not married. You're aware there's a difference?"

His voice was sharper than she'd ever heard it, and Iris drew in a shocked breath, as horrified by his rebuke as if he'd slapped her. It took her a moment to gather herself, and when she did speak, she couldn't quite disguise the tremor in her voice. "Yes, I—shall we go back to the house, then?"

He blew out a breath, and when he spoke again his voice was gentler, and he patted her hand as if she were a child who needed soothing. "Yes, that would be best."

He tried to hide his relief as they began the walk back to the house, but Iris saw it, and her chest flooded with misery and humiliation.

What had just happened? Had she done something awful? Violet hadn't seemed to think a kiss between a betrothed couple was so scandalous, but they'd been raised in Surrey, not among the *ton*. Lady Honora had been hesitant, but even she'd admitted Lord Harley had kissed her. But Lord Huntington...

He seemed angry, as if she'd done something inexcusable.

Iris darted a glance at him, but he wasn't looking at her. His gaze was focused straight ahead, as if he'd forgotten she was there at all. When they neared the house, he paused. "You're quiet, Miss Somerset. I'm afraid you're fatigued, after all."

Iris looked up into his handsome face. He smiled at her, but it didn't reach his eyes, and she could see he only waited for the moment when he could escape her company. "Yes, I—I believe I am."

"Come, then. I'll escort you to the terrace."

"No, thank you, my lord." She withdrew her arm from his and took a step away from him. The sun was warm, but Iris rubbed her hands over her arms to chase away a sudden chill. "That is, I'll come after I fetch my wrap from the house."

"I'll fetch it for you. Where is it?"

Her shoulders moved in a listless shrug. "I don't remember. The drawing room, perhaps, or—"

"Never mind. I'll find it." He hesitated, then to Iris's surprise he reached forward and slid his warm fingers under her elbow, cupping it briefly. "I'll join you on the terrace in a moment."

He bowed and turned toward the house.

A large party of young people were arranged on the terrace, where Lady Fairchild was serving tea, and Violet and Lady Honora looked up hopefully when Iris joined them, but the moment they saw her expression, both their faces fell.

"There you are, Miss Somerset." Honora's mother, Lady Fairchild, gave her a gracious smile. "Tea?"

"Yes, thank you, my lady." Iris accepted the teacup, but her hands shook, and the teacup rattled in its saucer. She took care not to look at Violet or Honora, but she could feel their sympathetic gazes, and her face burned with shame.

"What's become of the rest of the party, I wonder?" Lady Fairchild set her teacup aside. "Lord Wrexley's been gone for an age. Have you seen your cousin, Honora?"

Iris glanced toward the door that led out onto the terrace, and panic made her throat close. Lord Huntington would be back at any moment, and she'd have to sit here and pretend he hadn't just dashed her every hope—

"No, Mama, but I suppose he's in the garden somewhere, with the rest of the gentlemen."

"Well, bother. We won't wait for them, will we? How did you all do with the scavenger hunt? Come, let's see what you've brought back for me."

Iris lurched to her feet with a jerk that made her tea slosh over the rim of her cup. "Oh, dear. I've lost my rosebuds, and I forgot the red petals. I'll just run back to the garden and fetch them, shall I, Lady Fairchild?"

"Yes, all right, dear. Do hurry back."

"Yes, I will, my lady."

Iris stumbled toward the garden, half-afraid she'd run into Lord Huntington on her way, but she made it to the rose arbor without encountering a soul and sank onto the bench. She'd just gather herself together before she had to face Lord Huntington again. She'd only stay a few moments, just long enough for her knees to stop shaking, then she'd paste a pleasant smile on her face and do her best to keep it there until this wretched afternoon was over, and—

"Good afternoon, my lady. What are you doing here?"

For a single moment Iris thought she'd imagined his voice, but only one gentleman had such a low, slightly mocking drawl. What was Lord

Huntington doing in the garden? She'd seen him walk into the house not ten minutes ago.

"Oh, Huntington!"

Iris froze. The second voice was high, feminine, and ringing with despair.

Lord Huntington wasn't in the house anymore. He was here, in the garden, on the other side of the arbor, and he wasn't alone.

Iris staggered to her feet. Every instinct urged her to flee before she heard anything more, but she was already moving, her slippers silent on the gravel pathway. There was a gap between the thick, thorny rose branches, just large enough for her to peer through. She pressed her face to it, and glimpsed the folds of a dark red gown fluttering in the breeze, and long, black curls resting against delicate white shoulders.

Lady Beaumont.

Iris knew her at once, and her heart shifted in her chest, but not in the pleasant way it always had before whenever she looked at Lord Huntington's lips.

No, this was a shift into panic.

Where in the world had Lady Beaumont come from, and what was Lord Huntington doing alone in the garden with her?

She soon had her answer.

Iris watched through the gap in the branches as Lady Beaumont threw herself at Lord Huntington, and his arms closed around her.

Chapter Two

Half an hour earlier

"What's the matter, Derrick? Couldn't find a rosebud?"

Lord Derrick was striding across Lady Fairchild's lawn toward Finn, a grim look on his face. "You have a problem, Huntington."

Finn yawned. "I can't think what, unless you mean my poor showing in the scavenger hunt. Not a rosebud to be had, but if I can bear the shame of it, surely you can."

Lord Derrick wasn't amused. "On the contrary, your humiliation for the day has just begun."

"Well, what is it? Do the ladies require my assistance?" There were few things Finn loathed more than a scavenger hunt. He would have done the gentlemanly thing and escorted Miss Somerset into the garden despite his aversion, but she'd hurried off with her sister and Lady Honora without a backward glance at him.

"No, Huntington. It's Lady Beaumont. She's in the garden."

Finn blinked. Lady Beaumont? What the devil would his former mistress be doing in Lady Fairchild's garden? "I think the sun has addled your brain, Derrick. That's impossible."

"One would think so, but she's there. I saw her with my own eyes behind the beds of red roses, and she looks as if she's ready to claw the petals off every one of them. I've never known a woman with a nastier temper. You did say she didn't take it well when you broke with her, didn't you?"

"She cracked my carriage window with her riding crop, Derrick. I think we can both agree she didn't take it well. But how would she get into the garden? There's no chance a high stickler like Lady Fairchild would invite a woman of Lady Beaumont's reputation to her scavenger hunt."

"No doubt she bribed one the servants to let her in."

"Jesus. Do you think she'd go that far?"

"I think she *has* gone that far. Do you suppose a lady who'd crack a window with her riding crop would hesitate to bribe a servant? And she's here, isn't she?"

"Damned clever plan." Ugly, but clever. He should have expected something like this from her. She never did anything by accident, or by halves. Whatever her reasons for being here today, she'd do a thorough job of it.

"Clever enough to work. I'd advise you to go into the garden and fetch Miss Somerset at once, while I escort Lady Beaumont off the property."

"No, Derrick. Fetch Miss Somerset for me, will you? Say her sister wants her, and escort her back to the terrace where she's out of the way. Lady Beaumont will refuse to stir a step out of the garden until she sees me and says whatever it is she's come to say. Christ, what a bloody mess."

Finn dragged a hand down his face. Lady Beaumont might very well snatch the petals off every rose in the garden, but they weren't her primary target. If she managed to get her claws into Miss Somerset, she'd rip her to shreds.

"Yes, all right. *Go*, Huntington, before she catches up to Miss Somerset, and it's too late."

But Finn was already gone, rose petals drifting to the ground in his wake as he ran through the garden. Short of stuffing her into a burlap sack, he hadn't any bloody idea how he'd get Lady Beaumont out of here without anyone seeing her, but he'd have to find a way—

"Lord Huntington?"

Finn froze, his eyes squeezing shut.

Not Miss Somerset. Not now, and not here—

But of course it was her, because one way or another your sins always caught up to you, and now his latest sin was about to catch up with Miss Somerset, as well.

Finn sent up a quick plea for mercy, turned to his betrothed, and offered her his arm. "I'm sure you must be fatigued, after so long a time in the sun. Allow me to escort you back to the terrace."

But Miss Somerset wasn't fatigued, and she wasn't of a mind to leave the garden. No, she was in the mood for a romantic stroll among the roses. His betrothed, who'd never been anything other than politely accommodating, had chosen this moment to assert herself. That flash of willfulness he'd glimpsed in her dark blue eyes had come back to haunt him.

She resisted his every attempt to escort her back to the terrace. First she wanted red rose petals, and then she wanted to admire the light, and sniff the roses, and rest on a bench, and then...

Then, dear God, she wanted to kiss him.

All this while Lady Beaumont was nearby, likely in fits of malicious laughter over Miss Somerset's awkward attempts at seduction and ready to leap from the bushes like an avenging fury and rain misery down upon Miss Somerset's head.

It was the longest ten minutes of Finn's life.

He did manage to lead Miss Somerset out of the garden at last, but despite his best intentions, he'd done a damn poor job of it. He'd snapped at her and hurt her feelings. She'd tried to hide it, but there was no way Finn could miss the humiliated flush on her cheeks. She'd lapsed into complete silence after that, and she hadn't looked at him again.

By the time he returned to the garden and found Lady Beaumont hidden like a stinging nettle among the red roses he was ready to wring her lovely neck, but if he hoped to end this scene quietly, he had no choice but to play her childish games. "Good afternoon, my lady. What are you doing here?"

She flew at him in a whirl of red skirts. "Oh, Huntington!"

Finn forced himself to catch her in his arms, but beneath his icy control, his temper was gathering like a tempest in his chest. He hadn't intended to see his former mistress again, least of all here, in Lady Fairchild's garden, where his betrothed could get tangled up in one of her devious intrigues. Before she took her leave today, he'd take care to make Lady Beaumont understand he wouldn't tolerate any further surprises from her.

"I'm afraid you're rather late for tea, my lady."

"Tea, with that crowd of simpering misses? No, indeed." She tore herself from his arms with a dramatic flourish. "I came to tell you I despise you, Huntington!"

"You didn't need to sneak into Lady Fairchild's garden to tell me that." Finn flicked his eyes over her, already bored with her antics. "You've said so many times before."

Lady Beaumont spent a good deal of time and energy despising him, but since her deep disgust hadn't ever prevented her from taking him to her bed, he didn't trouble himself much about it. Occasional moments of abhorrence were common enough between lovers, and it wasn't as if he'd gone to her for adoration.

Her pretty red lips twisted into an ugly scowl. "How can you forsake me in such a cold manner, Huntington, when you know I love you so?"

"You just told me you despised me. Which is it, then? Love, or loathing?"

Her lower lip trembled. "It's ever been love, and you know it well, my lord."

"How flattering. I always imagined your affection for me was based on commerce, not emotion."

Lady Beaumont let out a howl of rage. "Oh! You dare to doubt my devotion, even as you leave me heartbroken? Your cruelty knows no bounds!"

She swung her open hand at his face, but Finn turned aside before her palm could connect with his cheek. Her tantrums had grown more extreme of late. He'd seen dishes, crystal vases and mirrors all fall victim to her frenzied rages, but she'd never tried to strike him before.

It was a mistake to try now.

He moved quickly, trapping her wrists behind her back before she could swing again. "Let's not resort to violence, my lady. Now, I'll let you go if you promise not to do yourself, or me, an injury."

A calculating look flashed in her eyes, and she squirmed against him, pressing her body close to his. "Oh, Huntington! Losing you will destroy me. I'm near-crazed with despair, and not myself."

"On the contrary. I think you're very much yourself."

Even more so when, predictably, her large dark eyes filled with tears. But then he'd expect no less from her. Lady Beaumont's first concern was always herself, and she'd be a fool to let him slip through her fingers when a few tears and seductive wiles might lure him back to her bed.

Their liaison had been an advantageous one for her. He was a generous protector, and perhaps one of only a few lovers who was a match for her insatiability, and...creativity. And if he occasionally had an appetite for the darker side of desire, she'd been an enthusiastic participant.

Their time together had been amusing enough, but he was weary of her dramatics, and in any case, a man couldn't indulge his more exotic tastes too often before they ruined him. Neither could a woman, come to that. He'd seen for himself the toll unchecked debauchery could take, and there was nothing uglier.

"I'll do myself an injury if you leave me. Indeed, I will!" She wriggled closer to him, pressing her lush breasts against his chest.

Finn watched her performance with detached interest. She wept so prettily. Her plump lower lip quivered, and sparkling drops hung from her feathery lashes. It was an affecting scene, and he didn't doubt her manipulative tears had been used to great effect with her former lovers.

Fools, every last one of them.

He took hold of her shoulders and held her away from him. "There now, sweetheart. Are you quite finished?"

She caught the last of her tears on dainty fingertips. "Yes, I—I'm sorry. Forgive me, my lord."

"Of course I forgive you." He stroked a careless hand over her silky dark hair, even as his muscles tensed with the effort it took not to drag her from the garden, bundle her into her carriage, and send her on her way. The drama would only encourage her, and he didn't have any more patience for her tears and theatrics. He'd left Miss Somerset pale and shaken, visibly reeling from his harsh words to her in the garden, and he needed to set it right again.

Betrothed, not married. You're aware there's a difference?

Finn cringed as he recalled the look on her face when he'd said it. She'd flinched away from him as if he'd dealt her a blow. As soon as he rid himself of Lady Beaumont he'd return to her at once, and beg her pardon, preferably before she realized he'd abandoned her to sneak off into the bushes with his mistress.

Former mistress.

He sighed. For a former mistress, Lady Beaumont was troublesome, indeed. "Now, suppose you tell me what this is all about, my dear."

He already knew, of course. She'd been in a jealous frenzy over his courtship of Miss Somerset for weeks now. He'd expected an explosion when he broke with her the day after Miss Somerset accepted his suit, but Lady Beaumont had held back in favor of making her sentiments known today.

Here.

In the middle of Lady Fairchild's garden, during a scavenger hunt, with the *ton* lurking behind every rose bush.

How like her. She'd always had a flair for the dramatic, and now she was ready to perform her closing act.

"Miss Somerset is quite lovely, isn't she?" Despite her sweet tone, Lady Beaumont's dark eyes glittered with malice, and her plump lips curved in a satisfied smile. She knew Finn's tastes didn't run toward innocent young maidens, and she couldn't resist reminding him of it.

It was true enough Miss Somerset didn't send him into a panting froth of lust, but he preferred it that way, and besides, the girl was well enough. Even if she hadn't been, he had no intention of discussing her shortcomings with Lady Beaumont.

"She won't be able to satisfy you. You know that, don't you, Huntington?" Lady Beaumont moved closer, her clever hands slipping inside his coat to stroke his chest. "You may think you can resist your darker nature, but you're not the kind of man who can ignore your desires. Oh, you might do so for a little while, but your insipid blue-eyed bride won't interest you for long."

Miss Somerset didn't interest him *now*, and he doubted it would change once they were wed, but he was a gentleman, and he'd never disparage his future wife to his former mistress. He looked down at Lady Beaumont, a slight smile on his lips. "Ah, but my bride is none of your concern, and neither I am. Not anymore."

"But you will be my concern again, I think, and soon, Huntington. Your sweet little bride may amuse you for a time, but once the novelty of innocence wears off and she starts to bore you, you'll come back to me."

Finn took her hands in his, removed them from his chest, and lowered them to her sides. "No, I won't, and you'll only be disappointed if you expect otherwise."

She didn't touch him again, but a feline smile drifted across her lips, one that said she knew him better than he knew himself. "I don't think so, my lord. You see, I've known men like you—men with the same dark needs you have. Those needs don't go away if you deny them, they simply grow stronger, squirming under your skin until you go mad from it. Once that happens, you'll come back, Huntington."

He gave her an amused smile. "Men like me? I beg your pardon, but there *are* no men like me. I may have spent the past few months dallying in your bed, but that doesn't mean you know me, my dear."

She knew only one side of him—the wicked side—but the rest of London knew him as the perfect English gentleman, and he took care to keep it that way. Whatever debaucheries he and Lady Beaumont might have shared, he left them behind as soon as he walked out of her bedchamber, and now he was walking away for good.

Lady Beaumont stood on her tiptoes to croon in his ear. "Oh, but I do know you, and when you come to me, I'll see you on your knees before I'll have you back. I'll make you beg for me, and you'll do it, *my dear*. You'll do anything I ask."

"I don't beg. Not for anyone, or anything."

"No? Shall we find out?"

Finn stood still as she unknotted his cravat and trailed her clever fingers across the bare skin of his throat. Lady Beaumont fancied herself a dangerous seductress, and it couldn't be denied her plump red lips and sleepy dark eyes had reduced more than one gentleman to a quivering mass at her feet. She'd cut quite a swath through London's noblemen, leaving a trail of broken hearts in her wake, and she'd no doubt expected to add him to her list of conquered swains.

This scene between them was inevitable. She wasn't one to rest until she'd exhausted her every option, and she wouldn't be satisfied until she'd tried to seduce him, and he'd refused her.

"You know, my lord, many gentlemen keep their mistresses when they marry, and a *passionate* gentleman such as yourself may find the marriage bed lacks certain intimacies you've grown accustomed to indulging."

The corners of his lips lifted in a cynical smile. Dear, avaricious Lady Beaumont, so reassuring in her predictability. "Do they, indeed? But a gentleman who would do such a thing can't be an honorable gentleman, can he?"

"Honorable?" She shook the word off, like so much dust from her boots. "Why, I'd rather say he's a wise gentleman, to anticipate his needs with such foresight, and what is honor in comparison to wisdom, my lord?"

"The two are not exclusive, my dear. Honorable men are invariably wise, and wise men invariably honorable." Finn let her push him toward the bench behind him, and within seconds her warm body was writhing between his sprawled legs.

"Never mind honor or wisdom, Huntington. I've always preferred foolish, amorous gentlemen, and while you may not be the first, you are most assuredly the second."

She sank to her knees before him, the corners of her lips turning up in a smug smile when he slid one hand into her dark hair. Well, it stood to reason she'd smile. After all, he'd never before taken hold of her hair to pull her *away* from him.

But before he did pull her away, perhaps she needed a reminder of how generous he'd been to her when he ended their liaison. "The jewels suit you." He traced the ruby and diamond necklace glittering around her slender neck, then ran a finger over the earrings dangling from her ears. "Not quite the thing for afternoon tea, but pretty all the same."

Nothing made Lady Beaumont happier than jewels, and his parting gift to her was a handsome one. He'd chosen the deep red rubies because he thought they'd complement her dark coloring, but her pleasure in the gift had far more to do with the fact that every one of the fifteen rubies in the set was as big as the tip of his thumb, and each of them surrounded by a cluster of twelve diamonds.

"Yes. They're lovely." Lady Beaumont's tongue darted out to lick her already slick lips. "Do you recall, Huntington, when you gave them to me? You said you wanted to see me draped in the red stones, and nothing else."

He gave her a faint smile. "You were nothing if not obliging, my dear."

"I could hardly refuse after receiving such a generous gift. But indeed, Huntington, you're not the kind of man one disobeys, are you? Particularly when you're intent on having your way. If I recall, you were intent on having your way quite often, and with the mildest provocation." A throaty laugh followed this statement. "I've never know a more insatiable man. Not many women could satisfy you, either in frequency or tastes."

She didn't say Miss Somerset wouldn't ever be able to satisfy him, but then she didn't need to. Her eyes gleamed with triumph as she stroked her fingertips over his thighs. "You looked quite wild when you clasped the necklace around my neck. You were so savage, I was almost frightened of you."

Or willing to pretend she was. "Oh, I doubt you've met the gentleman yet who could frighten you, my dear."

"Ah, but if I *were* to be frightened of a gentleman, it would be you, my lord. You're rather intense when you're aroused." Her voice dropped to a low, husky murmur. "Why, you stripped my gown from my back right there, and took me against my dressing table. Why, I had half a mind to run away to my bedchamber and bolt the door behind me, but then you like a bit of a chase, don't you, Huntington?"

Her busy fingers went to the buttons of his falls. He didn't want her anymore, but Finn was a man of strong urges, and his hard cock sprang readily enough from the crumpled fabric of his breeches. She made a low, approving sound in her throat, and lowered her head to his lap.

He'd never before denied himself the pleasure of her mouth, or her decadent, unapologetic debauchery, but dependence led to weakness, and Finn didn't tolerate weakness.

Especially in himself.

Before her plump lips could close over his eager flesh, he tightened his fingers in her hair and pulled her back. "No, my lady. Not now, and not ever again."

Their time together was over.

He set his breeches to rights, then rose from the bench and fetched his coat, which had fallen to the ground. "The jewels were a parting gift. But perhaps you've forgotten that?"

She rose to her feet and ran brisk hands over her skirts. Now her attempt to seduce him had failed, she dropped her game at once. Lady Beaumont was nothing if not practical. "Not at all." She ran her fingers over the gems at her throat. "Such a generous gift, too, but then you always do things handsomely, don't you?"

He did, because he was the Marquess of Huntington, and an honorable gentleman didn't dismiss his mistress without a generous gift, no matter how troublesome she'd proved to be. "Always. You wouldn't have had me otherwise."

She didn't bother to dispute this assertion. She looked him over as carefully as she had the jewels when he'd given them to her, and gave a regretful shake of her head. "Certainly not, but I don't deny I've found other aspects of our arrangement nearly as rewarding as your gifts."

He shrugged into his coat. "It was a satisfactory arrangement for both of us."

"Satisfactory?" Her mouth turned down at his choice of words. "As I recall, Huntington, there were a number of times you appeared to find it a great deal more than satisfactory."

Finn regarded for her a moment, considering. He hadn't ever found it more than satisfactory, but he might have said he'd miss her, just to soothe any hurt feelings on her part. Perhaps he even would miss her, for a short while.

But he didn't say it.

It was past time for him to turn his attention to the suitable young lady he'd chosen as his bride. He'd transform Miss Somerset into a marchioness, get a few heirs on her, and raise a family that would do honor to his name.

And Lady Beaumont would fade from his mind sooner rather than later.

She'd been watching him with a sulky expression, and now her eyes narrowed to angry slits. "Miss Somerset is beautiful, isn't she? So innocent, with those wide blue eyes, and such beautiful fair hair. Angelic, rather like a child. I wonder what she'd think if she knew what you hide under those gentlemanly manners of yours? Those dark proclivities, Huntington, that need for control—however will you explain it to an innocent like your betrothed?"

"What makes you think I'll explain it at all?" He'd settled for Miss Somerset for one reason—nothing about her brought out the savagery he hid under his gentlemanly veneer. She was sweet, dull, and predictable, and he'd never think to expose her to his darker desires. Once he no longer indulged them, they'd cease to trouble him.

Eventually.

Lady Beaumont drew closer, sensing an advantage. "Oh, you won't have a choice. You're a man of strong appetites. I'll grant you have remarkable control, Huntington, and manage to suppress them a good deal of the time, but you can't do so forever, and when you do let yourself go, you're quite…demanding."

Finn's smile was frigid. "Of my mistress, yes. Not my wife."

"So you tell yourself, but just think of it, Huntington. No more blindfolds, or binding your lover with silk scarves? No more games? That chit you're betrothed to—she's a sweet young thing, and rather pretty, too." Lady Beaumont's voice dripped with scorn. "But she's not at all to your taste. You'll lose interest in her within a fortnight."

He'd never been interested in Miss Somerset—not in the way Lady Beaumont meant—but then that was rather the point. "She's naïve, docile, and predictable, my dear. In other words, precisely to my tastes. What more could a gentleman ask for in a wife?"

Lady Beaumont gave a light, tinkling laugh that nevertheless managed to be ugly. "She wasn't even your first choice, Huntington! Such a pity you lost Lady Honora to Harley, but then it's not quite the thing, is it, for a gentleman to wager to win the right to court a lady? Poor Huntington. Luck wasn't with you that night, and Lady Honora would have made such an ideal marchioness. But as you said yourself, one aristocratic young lady is very much like another."

"Much like a mistress is, I suspect." Finn wasn't proud of that wager, and even less pleased he'd been foolish enough to confide it to Lady Beaumont, who'd been far too amused by it for his tastes. "But the less said about that wager, the better. It would be too bad if Miss Somerset should hear of it." He ran a fingertip down Lady Beaumont's cheek, but his voice was cold. "I'd be quite displeased if she did."

He turned to leave her, but she gripped his arm. "Miss Somerset is from the county, isn't she? Surrey, I believe? A little country miss who'd no doubt be shocked at what a wealthy nobleman gets up to when no one's watching."

Finn's expression didn't change, but cold anger made his jaw tense. Not at her threat—Lady Beaumont knew there were limits to how much nonsense he'd tolerate from her—but because she knew quite a lot more than he'd realized about Miss Somerset. It seemed she'd made it her business to find out about his betrothed, and Finn didn't like it.

He didn't like it at all.

He took her chin between his fingers, his touch gentle. "I could almost imagine from your words, my dear, you mean to threaten me somehow. I don't mind it for myself, but as for Miss Somerset..." His fingers tightened almost imperceptibly, but he could see by the way her eyes widened she noticed it. "I'm afraid I'll have to insist you stay far, far away from her. Do you understand, my dear?" He swept his palm down her throat, and felt her nervous swallow. "Ah, yes. I see you do. That pleases me, my lady."

Another swallow. "Yes, you do look pleased with yourself, Huntington."

He gave her a polite smile, but his narrowed gaze held hers until her eyes skittered away. "I believe your visit is over. I'll escort you to your carriage, shall I? I wouldn't want you to get lost in Lady Fairchild's garden. Who knows where you'd turn up?"

"Who knows, indeed?" She took the arm he offered with a resentful sniff, but Lady Beaumont had played her last card, and she was wise enough to know it.

Finn led her around the outskirts of the garden, relieved when they made it to a gate in a far corner that led into the mews. Her carriage was there, waiting, and Finn handed her in.

"Goodbye, my dear. I'll remember our time together with fondness."

Until I forget it entirely.

"Oh, one more word before I go, Huntington?" Lady Beaumont propped her gloved hand against the door before he could slam it closed. "You might want to keep an eye out for Lord Wrexley. I hear he's rather taken with Miss Somerset, and you know his lordship isn't one to easily relinquish a plaything, no matter how dull it might be."

Finn's mouth went as dry as dust. "Is there something you wish to tell me, my lady?"

She shot him a poisonous smile. "Now I think of it, my lord, there is. I believe I saw Lord Wrexley today, when I came into the garden. Yes, I recall it perfectly now. He was lingering there this afternoon. He said he was looking for someone. Do you think it was Miss Somerset? It's a trifle worrying for her, perhaps. I hate to say it of him, but Lord Wrexley occasionally forgets he's a gentleman."

Finn's nerveless hand fell away from the door of her carriage.

Lady Beaumont pulled it closed with a satisfied slam, her eyes gleaming as she took in his tense face. "I wish you a pleasant day, Lord Huntington."

Chapter Three

Iris squeezed her eyes shut and pressed her hands against her ears. A strange numbness stole over her, as if she'd been standing in icy water for hours, and her blood had frozen in her veins.

She stood there helplessly as their words got uglier and uglier, until at last Lady Beaumont said something that made the blood surge again in a dizzying, painful rush, and she fled, the gleeful hiss of laughter ringing in her ears.

She wasn't even your first choice, Huntington.

Iris ran until a pain in her side forced her to a wheezing halt, her only thought to get away before she heard another word. When she came back to herself at last, she was slumped on a stone bench in a remote corner of the park, surrounded on all sides by silence, under a copse of trees whose spreading branches obliterated the sun.

Her arm stung, and she looked down to find the sleeve of her gown was torn, and a long, bloody scratch stretched from her wrist to her elbow.

She didn't remember how it happened.

She pressed her forehead to her knees and sat there for a long time, listening to the sound of her own gasping breaths.

When she managed to raise her head and look about her, her first thought was she'd been gone for far too long, and must return to the terrace at once. But when she did, she'd be obliged to flirt and smile, and pretend everything she knew and trusted hadn't just collapsed into a pile of rubble at her feet.

Lord Huntington would be waiting for her there, his handsome mouth full of lies.

She shrank against the bench as panic rolled over her again. Soon—she would go back, very soon, yes, and when she did she'd take his arm, and send admiring glances his way, and flirt with him, and behave as if she were besotted and believed herself London's most fortunate lady to be honored with his attentions, because it was what everyone expected of her.

But not yet. Not while she could still hear Lady Beaumont's high, cruel laugh in her head. Not while every hurtful word was still reverberating in her chest.

So angelic, rather like a child...

Of all the awful things Lady Beaumont had said, there was no reason these should be the words that kept echoing in Iris's head.

No reason but one.

They were true.

She *was* like a child, with her naïve attempts to inspire a kiss. She even looked like a child, with her fair hair and wide blue eyes, in her sweet pink frock with the itchy lace sleeves.

No wonder Lord Huntington was bored with her.

Whereas Lady Beaumont...well, whatever else the woman might be, she was no child. She wasn't naïve, docile, or predictable. She was beautiful, tempting, wicked—she was everything proper young ladies like Iris were cautioned not to be, with her wild dark hair, her glittering jewels and her revealing red gown.

Red.

Iris had never worn a red gown. Every item of clothing she owned was either pale pink, pale yellow, or pale blue. She'd wanted royal blue, and Pomona green, bright primrose, and Parma violet, but her grandmother insisted a proper young lady didn't wear dramatic colors, and that a lady with Iris's coloring could never have too many pink gowns.

Iris hadn't argued. She'd worn the gowns her grandmother chose for her without a word of complaint, and she couldn't deny each was more beautiful than the last, trimmed with yards of costly Belgian lace and endless lengths of satin ribbon.

All that sweet pink silk and satin, wasted.

This, then, was what came of doing what you were told. To be ridiculed by her betrothed's mistress, laughed at by her, to be called dull and insipid without her betrothed speaking a word in her defense. This was to be her reward for becoming everything a proper young lady should be.

Iris drew, painted, and played the pianoforte. Her quadrille was without compare, and she was an accomplished equestrienne. She was well read, well-spoken, well-dressed, and possessed of a smile that made gentlemen rush across crowded ballrooms to reach her side. She spoke French, German, and Italian with perfect fluency, her fair coloring was fashionable this season, and the filmy French gowns that were all the rage made the most of her gentle curves.

Useless, all of it.

Her engaging smile, her proper gowns, her many accomplishments—none of it made the least bit of difference, because compared to a woman like Lady Beaumont, Iris faded into insignificance.

She looked down at her hands, ashamed of this somehow, though she couldn't explain why. She hadn't done anything wrong. On the contrary, she'd been careful to follow every rule, and she was on the verge of making a brilliant match, just as her grandmother wanted.

On the surface, she and Lord Huntington made perfect sense. Or they had, until today, when he'd rushed her out of the garden so he could steal away to meet his mistress. Iris might be the very image of maidenly perfection, but looking back at their courtship now, she couldn't think of one instance where Lord Huntington had shown any real interest in her.

The truth was, she might be everything he *should* want, but it didn't change the fact that he *didn't*. He wanted Lady Beaumont. If not her specifically, then another woman like her.

Rose Beaumont.

Rose was a fitting name for her. She looked like a lush, extravagant flower, with her mass of silky hair and that creamy skin she took care to display at every available opportunity. Iris had seen her at the theater just the other night, wearing a dramatic primrose-colored gown, with two delicate wisps of black lace for sleeves. Her shoulders and neck had been bare, revealing a daring expanse of décolletage, and she'd been wearing enormous teardrop-shaped rubies clustered among circlets of diamonds, flashing at her throat and in her ears.

The jewels were a gift from Lord Huntington, apparently. A generous one.

Iris had always been rather fascinated by women like Lady Beaumont, though only from a distance, as there could be no question of any kind of acquaintance between them. Iris was the granddaughter of an earl, and thanks to her grandmother, a young lady of fortune. Lady Beaumont was part of the demimondaine, the kind of scandalous widow proper ladies went out of their way to ignore. Lady Fairchild would fall into a nervous fit if she knew the woman was skulking about behind her hedges.

Yet here she was, cool as you please, staking a claim on Lord Huntington, as if she had every right to him, and perhaps she did, because despite his bored drawl, he'd been utterly distracted by her.

But then Lady Beaumont had plenty of practice distracting gentlemen, and there was no question she knew how to look after her own interests.

Lord Canard had been her first protector, an elderly, wealthy gentleman who quite lost his head over the seductive young widow. The gossips claimed the old fool went mad when Lady Beaumont dropped him for the younger, wealthier Lord Dorsey, but then poor Lord Dorsey had been set aside in favor of Lord Huntington, who was younger and wealthier still, and blessed with a face and figure so perfect even a hardened businesswoman like Lady Beaumont wasn't prepared to relinquish him without a struggle.

Iris looked down at the skirt of her pale pink gown, and a raw laugh tore from her throat. It wouldn't be much of a struggle, would it? Had it only been an hour ago she'd thought she wasn't a proper young lady because she wanted to tempt Lord Huntington into a kiss?

It seemed ludicrous now. Laughable.

"Lord Huntington doesn't care for me."

It was a whisper only, but Iris said the words aloud, because if she heard them, perhaps it would help her decide whether or not she could tolerate the truth behind them. If it was only her pride that was damaged, and not her heart, then it made no difference in the least whether Lord Huntington cared for her or not. She would become a marchioness, and according to the rules of London society, that was more than adequate compensation for his lack of affection.

"He has a mistress."

Or he'd *had* a mistress. He'd sent Lady Beaumont away with hundreds of pounds in rubies to compensate her for the loss of his company, but even if he hadn't broken with her, Lord Huntington's having a mistress wasn't sufficient reason to jilt him. Many gentlemen had mistresses, especially gentlemen of rank and wealth. A wife might not like it, but she was expected to look the other way.

No matter how awful that mistress was.

"He wanted Lady Honora."

Iris couldn't deny this stung. No lady wanted to be a gentleman's second choice, but in the end, even that made little difference. He must have deemed her an appropriate choice for his marchioness, or he never would have offered for her at all.

After he wagered away the chance to offer for the lady he really wanted.

Iris's hands clenched until she'd crushed the folds of her pink gown between her fingers. Dear God, she despised this gown. She wished she could squeeze it hard enough to make it bleed.

Not that it would do the least bit of good. The damage was done. Now it was just a question of how to manage it.

Iris took a deep breath and forced her hands to relax. Very well, so he'd wanted Lady Honora. It hardly mattered. He was betrothed to Iris now, and every other young lady in London had spent this entire season wishing she was Iris Somerset. She was one of the lucky ones, and it was nothing but selfishness to sit here and whimper over it. Lord Huntington was a wealthy marquess, who, despite the mistress, had a character beyond reproach.

The mistress, the blindfolds, and something to do with silk scarves, that is.

Blindfolds. Dear God. An image of Lord Huntington with a cravat stretched taut between his hands rose unbidden in her mind, and an unwelcome shiver of...*something* shot down her spine.

Not desire, of course. Fear? Shock, perhaps? Or was it disgust? No, not quite that, either, though Iris would have been far more comfortable if it had been.

But this was all nonsense. Huntington's disgraceful wager, his lack of affection for her, his mysterious dark desires...what did any of it matter? Her grandmother wanted the match, and that was reason enough for Iris to want it, as well.

She rose from the bench, threw her shoulders back, and raised her chin. There. It was settled. She was betrothed to Lord Huntington, and despite the deep ache in her chest—an ache that would surely fade—she hadn't overheard anything to make her change her mind about marrying him. She shouldn't have been eavesdropping at all. She should have remained on the terrace with Honora and Violet and quietly drank her tea like a proper lady, instead of running about the garden like a wild animal.

Really, this entire episode was her own fault—

"Don't tell me you got lost in the gardens, Miss Somerset."

Iris whirled around, her heart rushing into her throat at the thought of having to face Lord Huntington so soon, but it was only Honora's cousin, Lord Wrexley, his lips curved in the charming, careless smile she knew so well.

Relief rushed through her, so profound an answering smile rose at once to her own lips, despite the crushing weight of misery on her chest. "I've been in the garden on dozens of occasions. I'd have to be an utter half-wit to get lost in it."

"Are you calling me a half-wit? Every time I come out here I lose my way. I've taken to dragging Honora with me whenever we plan to go further than the rose garden, just to be certain I make it back safely."

Iris's smile widened. *Dear Lord Wrexley.* His amusing nonsense never failed to cheer her. "You ventured well beyond the rose gardens today. Quite a risk, my lord."

"Yes, well, I came in search of you, and you're worth the risk." He swept her a gallant bow, then straightened, and gave her another artless grin. "It's a lucky thing I found you. I may never have made it back otherwise."

"I suppose my sister is wondering where I am." Iris sighed, but there was no point in putting it off. She'd have to face Lord Huntington at some point, and it may as well be now.

Iris reached to take the arm Lord Wrexley offered her, but before she could, his hands landed on her shoulders and he turned her to face him, his smile fading as he searched her face. "You look distraught. Has something happened?"

Iris hesitated. She'd spent as much time with Lord Wrexley as she had with Lady Honora, and he'd become a friend, but even so, she couldn't discuss Lord Huntington with him. "No, nothing. Just the headache, likely from too much sun this afternoon."

"But you're bleeding." He hooked a fingertip under the sleeve of her gown and tugged it away from her arm. "Right here."

Iris held her arm out to get a closer look at the cut. "Oh, it's nothing. I must have scratched it on a tree branch."

He moved closer, his brows drawn together with concern as he traced a gentle finger over the cut. "If you're unhappy about something, you can tell me, you know. Perhaps I can help."

"You can't." His offer made tears press behind Iris's eyes, but she blinked them back. "It's kind of you to be concerned, but—"

"Miss Somerset!" The deep voice came from behind her, and a large hand caught her elbow and pulled her away from Lord Wrexley. "What are you doing way out here, so far from the house?"

Lord Huntington stood there, his lips white, a look on his face Iris had never seen before. Shocked at his low, furious growl, she stuttered into a reply. "I—I was about to return to the terrace…"

She trailed off into silence, because Lord Huntington wasn't listening. He wasn't even looking at her anymore. He was staring at Lord Wrexley.

"She got lost, Huntington. No harm done."

"Not from lack of trying, I'm sure." Lord Huntington's voice was soft, but threaded with cold menace that made no sense to Iris and left a nervous knot in her belly.

Lord Wrexley didn't seem to notice it, however. He turned to her with an easy smile. "I believe Lord Huntington wishes to escort you back to the house, Miss Somerset, so I'll leave you to him, but do let me know if you change your mind about that talk."

He bowed, then sauntered down the pathway, whistling.

Lord Huntington watched him go, his face as hard as carved stone. Iris couldn't imagine what had made him so furious, unless he was put out he'd had to abandon his mistress to come and search for her. Quite put out, if his grip on her elbow was any indication.

Perhaps she should be grateful he didn't have a silk scarf to hand.

A rebellious little laugh tickled her throat at the thought, but Iris choked it back down. Oh, dear. She couldn't say *that*. Though it was tempting enough to go ahead, just to see the expression on his face—

"Well, Miss Somerset? Have you had a nice frolic in the gardens this afternoon?"

Frolic? For pity's sake, he *did* think she was a child, or perhaps a small woodland creature. "Well, I wouldn't call it a frolic, my lord. I believe it was more like a wander. One does tend to wander when they're lost, you see."

His hazel eyes widened with surprise at her clipped tone, then darkened to a mossy green. Goodness, what an unusual color. Perhaps she should have attempted to annoy him before now, because that was a lovely shade of green. Why should Lady Beaumont be the only one who ever got to admire it?

His scowl deepened. "What have you been doing out here all this time?"

All at once Iris recalled why she was out here in the first place, and her nervousness evaporated on a wave of righteous fury. "I believe Lord Wrexley told you already, Lord Huntington. I got lost."

Lord Huntington recognized this for the blatant lie it was, and he wasn't at all satisfied with it. "You got lost."

"Yes." Iris didn't offer another word of explanation, because she was afraid if she opened her mouth again, every word she wished she could say to him would spout from her lips like water from a fountain.

Words like *wager*, and *blindfold*, and *mistress*.

"If you were concerned about your direction, perhaps you should have brought your sister with you. She made it back to the terrace easily enough."

It took everything Iris had not to snatch her arm from his grasp. "I told you I got lost, my lord. I believe the word *lost* implies it was done by accident. The word *accident* implies I wasn't aware it would happen before I left the terrace."

Iris blinked, surprised to hear such an ill-mannered speech burst from her lips, and yet she couldn't regret it, either. Ah, well. Docility was tricky that way, wasn't it? One never knew when it might disintegrate into open rebellion.

He raised an eyebrow at her, a curious look on his face, something between surprise and impatience, as if she were a normally obedient child who'd stamped her foot and refused to go to bed when ordered. "You've been gone for nearly an hour."

Only an hour? Was that all? It didn't seem to Iris an inordinate amount of time to take to recover from her betrothed's cruel betrayal. Considering what she'd overheard, he should be pleased she hadn't asked Lord Wrexley to take her back to her grandmother's house in Bedford Square.

"Was Lord Wrexley with you the entire time?"

Iris frowned at his harsh tone. "No. I met him not five minutes before you found us. I suppose my sister sent him out after me."

He searched her eyes, then let out a long, slow breath, but his face remained hard. "It's not proper for you to be wandering the gardens with him."

Proper? Iris stared at him, dumbfounded. It wasn't proper for her to be in a garden because Lord Wrexley, who was her friend, and who'd never been anything other than a perfect gentleman to her, might be here, too?

And this from Lord Huntington? He'd blindfolded Lady Beaumont and bound her with silk scarves, for pity's sake!

Iris bit back a wild little laugh. It wasn't at all amusing, of course, but his insistence on the strictest propriety struck her as hysterically funny, given his mistress had been on her knees before him less than one hour ago, her long fingers expertly lowering his falls, as if she'd done it a hundred times before.

Iris's face heated at the thought. It might have been best, after all, if that gap in the branches hadn't been *quite* so wide.

But it was too late now, and now she'd seen…well, *that*, she was hard pressed to stand obediently while Lord Huntington lectured her on improper behavior. But she thought of her grandmother and her sisters, gritted her teeth, and forced her lips into a stiff smile. "I beg your pardon if I've worried you."

"Come. Your sister is anxious for your return."

He held something out to her, and Iris realized with a start it was her shawl. Despite the drama with Lady Beaumont, he'd fetched it for her, after all.

"Thank you, my lord." Iris took it and draped it around her shoulders, then tucked it into the crook of her elbow to keep it from dragging on the ground, but before she could stir a step, his hand snaked out and jerked the wrap away again.

Iris's eyebrows shot up. "My lord, what are you—"

"What happened to your arm?" He tugged her closer, so close the arm he held brushed against his chest. "Your sleeve is torn."

"Oh, it's nothing. I—"

"Don't tell me it's nothing. You're bleeding."

His voice emerged in a low growl, and Iris froze, too surprised to say a word. What was he so agitated about? She raised her gaze to his face, but as soon as she saw his eyes, she wished she hadn't. They'd gone so dark with fury they'd turned a rather terrifying black.

He was…dear God, he was frantic. Whatever was the matter with him? It wasn't an amputation, for goodness' sake. It was a scratch, nothing more.

"Tell me what happened."

The injury was so inconsequential Iris didn't even recall how it had happened, but his voice was strained, and every muscle in his body coiled with tension, and she saw at once this was no time to trifle with him. "I—I was hurrying, and—"

"Why were you hurrying? Were you running away from someone?"

Yes. You.

But she couldn't say that. Even if she'd wanted to she couldn't, because his gaze was fixed on her face with such furious intensity she couldn't say a word, and had to look away from him.

What was happening?

"Miss Somerset? Did Lord Wrexley touch you?"

"No! Of course not."

He grasped her chin between his long, firm fingers and tipped her head up so he could look into her face. "Then why is your sleeve torn? It looks as if someone grabbed you."

His eyes were still flashing with fury, and she had to drag in a breath to calm her thrashing heart. "No, my lord. No one grabbed me. I was hurrying, and not paying attention to where I was going. I caught my sleeve on a sharp branch, and when I tore it loose, I scratched my arm."

He searched her face, then let out a long, slow breath. After a moment he gathered her wrap and tucked it around her elbow, careful not to brush against the scratch on her arm as he did, but even as he took care to touch her gently, his next words sliced into her like a whip.

"Your carelessness in guarding your safety perplexes me, and that's to say nothing of your reputation. I trust you'll be more vigilant in the future."

For a moment Iris was sure she'd misunderstood him, but as his words sank in she could only stare at him, shocked into speechlessness. Not two hours ago he'd left her on the terrace so he could rush off to meet his mistress in the garden, and yet he dared to stand here and calmly accuse *her* of improprieties?

"I can see I've distressed you. May I call on you tomorrow, to offer my apologies? You're to become my marchioness in a few weeks, and I don't like for us to be at odds."

Iris tried to say something, to offer a polite smile, but all she could manage was a stiff nod. How ironic he should speak of her as his marchioness now, when all her anticipation over their betrothal had hardened into cold dread.

"May I escort you back to the house? Your sister has been waiting for you on the terrace for quite some time, and I'm sure she's concerned."

He held out his arm, like a proper gentleman.

She took it, like a proper lady. The belle of her season.

You'll lose interest in her within a fortnight, Huntington.

Phineas Knight, the Marquess of Huntington. An honorable gentleman. Admirable. Praiseworthy. Utter perfection. Wasn't that how she'd thought of him?

What would she think, Huntington, if she knew what you hid under those gentlemanly manners of yours?

A dull little laugh escaped her.

Only a child would think that now.

Chapter Four

"More tea, Lord Huntington?"

Finn shifted to the end of the stiff silk cushion, his spine rigid with the effort it took not to lean back. He'd called on Miss Somerset dozens of times since he began courting her at the start of the season, and by now he knew better than to attempt more than a precarious perch on the edge of any of Lady Chase's overstuffed settees. No doubt the old woman chose uncomfortable furnishings on purpose, to fluster her granddaughters' suitors.

Today, however, it wasn't Lady Chase's damnable settee causing the dull ache between his shoulder blades.

No, today it was Lady Chase's granddaughter.

Miss Somerset had maintained a ladylike silence during his previous calls, preferring to leave the social niceties to her grandmother. Her reserve had never troubled Finn much, because she looked at him a good deal, her cheeks coloring prettily when he caught her gaze. He found it rather charming, and in any case, what sort of fool objected to a quiet wife?

Today, however, something was different. Today, Miss Somerset wasn't pleased.

She'd abandoned the shy, sweet glances in favor of a piercing stare, and her silent admiration had been replaced with something far less flattering, and far more speculative. One slim eyebrow was quirked over stormy blue eyes, and an odd, tight smile played over her lips, as if the tea had left a sour taste in her mouth.

Had her eyes always been such a dark blue? He couldn't recall having noticed it before, but then he'd never seen them narrowed on him with such intense scrutiny either, as if he were a bird caught in the sights of her hunting rifle.

Finn tried to remember if he'd ever known her to be displeased with him before the unfortunate incident in Lady Fairchild's garden yesterday, but he couldn't recall a single instance of it. If she'd been displeased in the past, she'd taken care to keep it to herself.

But not today. Today, something writhed and twisted beneath her scrupulous politeness. It grew more restless with every moment that passed, and it would only grow worse by the time he took his leave, because he had an unpleasant matter to discuss with his betrothed.

Lord Wrexley.

It was Wrexley who'd let Lady Beaumont into the garden yesterday.

He should have suspected it at once, but even Finn, who knew what Wrexley was, was shocked he'd gone so far beyond the bounds of gentlemanlike conduct. Once Finn arrived home that afternoon and recalled Lady Beaumont's parting words, however, he realized she'd as much as confessed to Wrexley's part in the scheme.

No doubt Wrexley had hoped Lady Beaumont would spill her ugly secrets to Miss Somerset. It hadn't quite worked out that way, but whatever his intentions, Wrexley had proved beyond any doubt he'd do whatever it took to have Miss Somerset, no matter how devious, and she was far too innocent to question his behavior. Worse, Wrexley was Lady Honora's beloved cousin, and Miss Somerset actually trusted the scoundrel.

She wasn't going to care for what he had to say, but Finn couldn't rest until he'd put her on her guard against Wrexley. It had to be done at once. Not only for her sake, but because he had to offer some sort of explanation for his regrettable behavior when he'd found her alone with Wrexley in the garden yesterday. Otherwise he was likely to meet an angry, scowling bride in the church four weeks from now.

"Yesterday, in Lady Fairchild's garden, Miss Somerset," Finn began. "That incident with Lord Wrexley—"

"If you don't care for more tea, may I fill a plate for you?" She leaned forward to fetch a dish from the silver tray in front of her. "You're quite certain I can't tempt you with the sweets, my lord?"

Oh, she was solicitous, yes—excruciatingly so—but not pleased.

"No, I thank you. About that matter yesterday—"

"I understand you're a gentleman with a ravenous appetite." She gave him a gracious smile, but there was a hard glint in her eyes. "I wouldn't like to send you away unsatisfied."

Finn's eyebrows shot into his hairline. *Unsatisfied?*

Good Lord, it was unsettling to hear that word spoken in such suggestive tones from such sweet, innocent pink lips.

"But perhaps you don't expect satisfaction from your betrothed. I daresay you wouldn't be the only gentleman to feel that way. Courtship can't be terribly exciting for a man of your vast experience, but then perhaps that's why so many aristocratic gentlemen go elsewhere to satisfy their cravings."

Finn choked on the sip of tea he'd taken and had to resort to pounding his chest with his fist. When he recovered at last, he blinked at Miss Somerset through streaming eyes. "Cravings?"

She set the plate aside, her lips curved in a sweet smile. "Yes. But are you quite well, my lord? Perhaps you'd like some more tea, after all? As I said, I don't like to send you away without attending to your appetites."

Good God, was he really sitting on this dainty settee in the middle of Lady Chase's drawing room, speaking to his innocent betrothed about a gentleman's cravings and appetites? The ache between his shoulder blades had begun to fade in comparison to an unexpected ache in his breeches, but as intrigued as Finn was, whatever had provoked her sudden vivaciousness would have to wait until he'd warned her about Wrexley.

"No, no more tea, thank you, but there is something I wish to discuss with you, about that business in the garden yesterday, with Lord Wrexley."

She'd lifted the teapot to pour herself another cup of tea, but now she paused, her hand in midair. "Yes?"

Her tone was polite, but Finn sensed the way she stiffened, and he paused and reminded himself to tread lightly.

"You must allow me to caution you against such lapses in propriety, Miss Somerset, and remind you to be more vigilant in the future. I wouldn't like to think you'd make it a habit to wander off like that once we're wed."

There. Finn took a calm sip of his tea. *That should do.*

She froze for a long moment, but then went on to pour her tea without meeting his eyes. "You consider getting lost in the garden a lapse in propriety, Lord Huntington?"

"No, of course not. I refer to your lingering in the garden with Lord Wrexley. You did so for far longer than was proper, and it was your second lapse that day."

Miss Somerset went on preparing her tea, but once she was finished she seemed to forget about it, and left it untouched on the tray. "My second lapse?"

Something unpleasant crawled up Finn's spine at her tone—something he would identify later as foreboding—but he pressed on. "Yes. You lingered there with me earlier, if you recall."

"Surely there's nothing so wicked in that? You *are* my betrothed, Lord Huntington."

A small smile drifted across her lips, but Finn found it far from reassuring. "Nothing so wicked, no, but there was that other matter."

"Other matter?" she asked, in a tone that could have frozen the tea in her teacup.

Finn squirmed on the settee, but resisted the urge to slide a finger under his cravat. This conversation wasn't going at all as he'd planned. "It's not a lady's place to initiate a kiss, Miss Somerset. You need to take better care, especially with a man of dubious honor, like Lord Wrexley, who—"

"Are you implying, Lord Huntington, I engaged in some improper activity with Lord Wrexley in the garden yesterday?"

Finn stared at her, baffled. Had it sounded as if he were accusing her? "No! Of course not. It's not *your* behavior I question, but his. I only mean to warn you of the risk of encouraging such a man—"

Miss Somerset's teacup hit her saucer with a sharp crack. "Encouraging him! You seem to be saying because I invited my betrothed to kiss me, I must have engaged in similar behavior with Lord Wrexley when I came upon him in the garden later that day. Do you think I go about kissing every gentleman who happens to cross my path, Lord Huntington?"

"No. I didn't mean to suggest any such thing." Damn it, why had he brought up that kiss at all? The less said about that disaster, the better. "It's your safety that concerns me, Miss Somerset. That's all."

But her face had gone dark with anger, and she was no longer listening to him. "Yes, well, I have some concerns of my own. There's something private I wish to discuss with you, my lord."

He blinked at the abrupt change in topic, but God knew he was making a muck of this. Perhaps it was wiser to remain quiet and let her speak. "Yes, of course."

There was a brief, charged silence, then she drew in a breath. When she spoke she sounded rehearsed, as if she'd practiced her speech in front of the glass a dozen times. Her words emerged with smooth precision, but they nevertheless landed with the force of a fist to his jaw, sending him reeling.

"It pains me to say this, but I must. While I'm sensible of the honor you've done me with the offer of your hand, I'm afraid I must end our betrothal."

Finn stared at her, speechless. End their betrothal? She was *jilting* him?

Christ, he *must* have misunderstood her. Either that, or she'd gone mad. He was fully prepared to beg her pardon for offending her just now, but a few misspoken words hardly warranted a jilting.

In his case, very few things did. He *was* the Marquess of Huntington, after all.

"You must end it," he repeated.

"Yes." Her voice was steady enough, but she looked at the teapot, then down at her hands clenched in her lap—everywhere but at his face. "I'm sorry for it, my lord, but I must."

Finn waited, but when the silence continued to stretch between them without another word from her, he placed his teacup on the table at his side and leaned forward, his tight fists resting on his knees. "That's it? *You must?* May I remind you, Miss Somerset, you've spent the entire season encouraging my courtship?"

Faint color rose in her cheeks. "I'm aware of that."

"Are you? Then you're also aware not more than a week ago you accepted my suit, and today, for no apparent reason, you've changed your mind?"

He'd be damned if he'd allow her to dismiss him without an explanation. If she was bold enough to jilt him, then she should be bold enough to tell him why.

She flinched at his raised voice. "There's no need to be uncivilized. I realize this is unexpected, but…well, we just don't suit, Lord Huntington. It's as simple as that."

A short bark of laughter burst from Finn's chest. "We don't suit. Forgive me, Miss Somerset, but those three words are not sufficient to explain your sudden disinclination. I believe it's customary for a lady to give a gentleman a bit more of an explanation than 'We don't suit' when she jilts him."

Her chin rose at the word *jilt*. "I'm not jilting you. That is, I *am*, but it's hardly a jilting at all, really. We've only been betrothed for a short time. We haven't even called the banns yet."

"Yet it feels very much like a jilting, nonetheless." He crossed his arms over his chest and fixed her with a cool stare.

She heard the sarcasm in his voice and bit her lip. "I realize this isn't an ideal situation, but it could be far worse."

"Could it?" An incredulous laugh escaped Finn. "I don't see how."

"It's the end of the season, and most of the *ton* has already left London. Whatever scandal there is will die down quickly. Why, you could be betrothed to someone else before next season begins. Any young lady would be…" She faltered. "That is, *most* young ladies would be overjoyed to become your marchioness."

"Yes, they would. Very few young ladies would scorn that title. What makes you any different?" It was a fair question, since he'd chosen her thinking she was much like every other young lady on the marriage mart.

She let out a heavy sigh. "I told you, my lord. We don't—"

"We don't suit. Yes, I heard you, and yet I remain unsatisfied with your explanation. You did express some concern earlier at sending me away unsatisfied, did you not?"

Her eyebrows shot up at his insinuating tone, but she recovered quickly. "Well, as to that, I'd be delighted to pour you more tea."

Tea? He was well beyond being satisfied by a cup of tea.

"Where is your grandmother, Miss Somerset?" He should be relieved the old lady wasn't here to witness this humiliating conversation, but Lady Chase had remained in the drawing room every other time he'd called, glaring at him with her beady eyes as if she thought he'd debauch her granddaughter on the cursed settee if she left the room. "How odd she should be absent for this particular conversation."

Her brows drew together into a frown. "She, ah…she and my sisters are visiting my eldest sister, Lady Carlisle, this afternoon."

"It's rather curious she should happen to be missing today, of all days. But never mind. Now, I'll have your explanation about the jilting, if you please."

"And if I don't please?"

He gave her an indulgent smile. "Oh, then I'm afraid I'll have to wait here until Lady Chase returns, and make my enquiries of her. Tell me, Miss Somerset, how do you suppose that conversation will go? Of course, Lady Chase must know you're jilting me. You'd never do such a thing without her consent, I'm sure."

Finn had spent more than his share of time with women of questionable character, but never in his life had he seen a lady who looked guiltier than Miss Somerset did when he mentioned her grandmother.

Lady Chase was a cantankerous old soul—excessively fond of her granddaughters, but a despot just the same, particularly when it came to their securing respectable matches. If the old lady knew her granddaughter intended to jilt the Marquess of Huntington, there was no way she'd have merrily gone off to Lady Carlisle's and left Miss Somerset to settle the business alone. The house would be in a complete uproar.

He retrieved his teacup from the table and held it out to her. "Perhaps I will have more tea, after all, while I wait for your grandmother's return."

Miss Somerset snatched the teacup out of his hand and dropped it onto the tray. "No. The tea is cold."

"My, such a quick temper, Miss Somerset. I don't recall you ever falling into a temper before, but that angry flush is rather fetching." His gaze lingered on her hot cheeks with more than his usual degree of appreciation. "I must say, outrage suits you. But back to the matter at hand. The jilting?"

"Oh, what does it matter? I've jilted you, and that's an end to it. Truly, my lord, I fail to see why you're still here at all."

"I just told you why. Because I'm not satisfied, sweet."

She choked back a gasp of surprise as the endearment fell between them like a heavy stone dropped into water. They both sat there silently as the arcs rippled in ever-widening circles around them.

Sweet?

Where had that come from? He'd never called her that before, and it was highly improper for him to do so now, especially in that low, husky tone, as if he were caught between anger and amusement.

Damn it, he wasn't amused, not by any of this, and Miss Somerset wasn't his *sweet,* or anything at all to him anymore, so there was no reason for him to be stumbling over himself like a besotted schoolboy. The sooner he had her answer, the sooner he could put an end to this torturous discussion.

"Come, Miss Somerset. I haven't all day to devote to ladies who jilt me. Your explanation, please."

She threw her hands up in the air, as if she'd lost all patience with him. "Very well, since you demand it. Yesterday, in Lady Fairchild's garden, we walked together, and I…"

She hesitated, and her cheeks went red with embarrassment.

"Yes? Please do go on."

"I tried to kiss you. I've never been confident in your affection for me, my lord, and I suppose I thought a kiss would reassure me. It hardly matters now, except, well, they don't teach respectable young ladies how to kiss gentlemen in gardens, do they? I was clumsy enough about it, I daresay, but your reaction…."

She looked away from him, and Finn sucked in a breath at her voice, the slight tremor in it, and the proud lift of her chin, in spite of that tremor. "Miss Somerset—"

"It was a kiss, Lord Huntington. Such a simple thing. Innocent even, but you made me feel as if I'd done something terribly wrong. You acted as if it were unforgiveable in me to want it at all, and now you've cast aspersions on my reputation because I happened to meet Lord Wrexley in a garden."

Helpless anger spread through Finn's chest. He hadn't meant to imply anything of the sort, any more than he'd meant to cut her so deeply with his cold rejection yesterday. He should beg her pardon, and try and tell her he regretted his harsh words to her, but he wasn't accustomed to explaining himself or accounting for his behavior in any way, and he wasn't even sure where to begin.

No one ever questioned him. He was a bloody marquess, for God's sake, and had been since he was eight years old. He issued orders, and people followed them. He couldn't remember the last time he'd been refused anything, and he didn't think anyone but Lord Derrick had ever dared speak to him the way Miss Somerset had just done.

Not one lady in a hundred would jilt him—not for any reason—and he never would have dreamed she'd be the one who would, but here she sat with every hair in place, as if she made it a habit to jilt marquesses over afternoon tea.

"Let me see if I understand you, Miss Somerset. You're jilting me over a kiss?"

She sighed. "I'm jilting you, Lord Huntington, because we don't suit."

He sat for a long moment, staring at her, trying to trace everything he'd never known or suspected about her in the lines of her face, because all at once he had the oddest sensation he was looking at her for the first time.

No, not looking at her. *Seeing* her.

She hesitated, and when she spoke again, her voice had softened. "I never intended to... I'm truly sorry to disappoint you, my lord."

Was he disappointed? He wasn't pleased, certainly. He was angry, yes, and even now he was fighting off a surge of wounded pride, but disappointed, at losing her? Damn it, he hardly knew, but there was something, weaved in among the other dark threads tangled in his chest.

Something he hadn't expected, and didn't welcome.

Awareness.

He wasn't enamored of Miss Somerset. He'd chosen her because she'd make an admirable marchioness, and once he'd made that determination, he hadn't spared her much thought. It wasn't gallant of him, perhaps, but then marriage was a practical matter, not a romantic one.

But now she'd jilted him, she'd forced herself on his notice.

One didn't jilt the Marquess of Huntington on a whim. Her future marriage prospects, her sisters' prospects—they were all in question now, and that was to say nothing of her grandmother's disappointed hopes. All of London would think her capricious to indulge in a courtship and then decline to follow through with the marriage. There was no question her reputation would suffer for it.

It took courage to jilt him, especially for the reasons she'd given.

While he'd been congratulating himself for choosing a bride who'd never give him a moment's worry, Miss Somerset had been hiding a core of steel behind that agreeable smile.

A strange sensation swept over Finn as he studied her. He felt as if he'd read a page in a book, then realized only after he'd slammed it shut he hadn't understood a word of it.

Such a lovely face she had, with those long, feathery lashes and her soft, pale pink lips. Such a delicate beauty, the perfect English rose, but now he looked at her—*really* looked at her—he could see a hint of stubbornness in the curve of her lower lip, and determination in the line of her jaw that matched the hint of willfulness in her eyes.

He rose to his feet. "I regret it came to this, Miss Somerset. I beg your pardon if I've caused you any pain."

She rose as well, and surprised him by taking his hands. "As do I, Lord Huntington."

He opened his mouth to say something more, but then closed it again, because there was nothing more to say. He bowed, and left Lady Chase's drawing room without looking back.

But as Finn alighted on the street in front of the house, he felt as if he'd lost something— as if he'd turned out his pockets to find them empty of the treasure he'd hidden there—a treasure he wanted with an inexplicable yearning only now, after he'd lost it.

Chapter Five

A week later, in early August

"You're wasting your time, Huntington. Miss Somerset isn't here. She hasn't set foot on the promenade for the past week."

Finn had been scrutinizing the scattered groups of fashionably-dressed ladies prancing down Rotten Row, but at Lord Derrick's amused tone, he jerked his gaze straight ahead again. Damn it, how many fair-haired ladies in blue riding habits were there in London? There seemed to be dozens of them on the promenade this afternoon, yet not a single one of them was *her*.

He slid his watch from his waistcoat pocket, a rough sigh in his throat as he flipped open the lid and noted the time. Seven o'clock. He'd been here for three hours. There'd been no sign of her, and the crowd grew thinner by the moment as the *ton* abandoned the promenade to dress for their evening entertainments.

She wasn't coming.

Lord Derrick gave his reins an impatient flick. "For God's sake, this has been going on for days. If you want to see Miss Somerset, then why not just call on her? There's no use in skulking around the promenade, glowering at every lady who bears the faintest resemblance to her. Look at poor Miss Blanton, scampering off down the Row. You've frightened her to death with that terrifying glower of yours."

Finn grunted. If Miss Blanton didn't wish to be glowered at, she shouldn't have worn a blue riding habit. "I *have* called on Miss Somerset, any number of times. She refuses to see me."

Lord Derrick drew his horse to a halt in the middle of the promenade, ignoring the protests of the riders behind them. "Why should she refuse to see you? I believe it's customary for a lady to accept calls from her betrothed. Bloody hell, Huntington. What have you done *this* time?"

Finn slid his friend a glance from the corner of his eye and heaved a silent sigh. He'd hoped to have this whole snarled mess resolved before he had to say a word to Derrick about it, but Miss Somerset had become a knot he couldn't untangle on his own. He was going to need Derrick's help to put things right, and even then, it wasn't going to be easy. "We're not betrothed. Not anymore. She jilted me."

Lord Derrick jerked upright in the saddle. "The devil you say."

His horse whinnied in protest at the sudden tug on the reins as Derrick made a sharp turn off the promenade and rode north toward the open ground near the Serpentine. Finn followed, bracing himself for the blistering lecture he deserved as he brought his horse alongside Derrick's.

Lord Derrick didn't waste any time. "Why, Huntington, would Miss Somerset jilt you? Whatever you did, it must be awful indeed for her to sacrifice the chance to become the Marchioness of Huntington."

Finn stared at the river, watching as the last rays of the setting sun caught at the gentle ripples on the glassy surface. He'd done a number of awful things, any of which might have justified her jilting him, but none of them were the reason she'd actually done so.

No, she'd jilted him over a kiss, or more accurately, the lack of one. If he hadn't seen her face when she said it he would have suspected her of lying, but there hadn't been a trace of subterfuge in her clear blue eyes.

A kiss. She'd jilted him over a kiss.

"It's that bloody wager, isn't it?" Derrick's mouth pinched into the same thin line it always did whenever the wager came up. "She found out about it, and she's jilted you over it. I warned you, Huntington, but you insisted on acting the fool, and now the wager has turned into a curse on the three of you. Here's Harley, caught cheating at cards and forced to flee to the Continent to save his neck. He won't have Lady Honora after all, any more than you'll have Miss Somerset, and now two lovely, innocent ladies are caught up in the scandals."

"You forgot Lord Wrexley." Finn spat the name as if he couldn't get it out of his mouth quickly enough. "*He* hasn't appeared to suffer any ill effects from that wager."

"Wrexley lost. He's exempt from the curse."

"There's no curse, Derrick, though I'll grant you it's unsettling how quickly a win became a loss once we left the gaming tables."

"Or a loss became a win. Think of it, Huntington. Now Wrexley has his choice of both Lady Honora and Miss Somerset, though I suppose his cousin doesn't want him."

"He doesn't want her, either. He wants Miss Somerset." A hard ball of anger lodged in Finn's throat at the thought. He wasn't pleased with her for jilting him, but that didn't mean she should be saddled with a rogue like Wrexley for the rest of her life. No woman deserved such a fate.

Lord Derrick shrugged. "Wrexley knew going into the wager he could lose her just as easily as win her."

Finn thought of Wrexley's careless smile when he lost the wager. "Come, Derrick. You know Wrexley better than that. He knew if he won her I'd abide by the terms of the wager and step aside, but he isn't an honorable gentleman. As soon as the cards hit the table he was determined to have her, whether he won or lost."

"Maybe he loves her." But even as he said it, Derrick looked doubtful. He knew Lord Wrexley almost as well as Finn did.

"Wrexley doesn't love anyone but himself. He does want her, though, even if only to keep me from having her, and he wants her badly enough to sink to alarming depths to get her. That trick at Lady Fairchild's, with Lady Beaumont…"

Understanding dawned on Derrick's face. "Of course! He was the one who sneaked Lady Beaumont in. I can't imagine why we didn't think of it at once. He's been to that house dozens of times, and knows every hidden alcove and nook in the garden."

"Yes, and you and I both know he didn't do it on a whim. Either he intended for Lady Beaumont to find Miss Somerset and whisper secrets in her ear, or else he thought he could lure Miss Somerset off to the gardens alone with him while I was occupied with Lady Beaumont."

Lord Derrick looked appalled. "Dear God. You don't think he intended to compromise her, do you?"

Finn had no idea whether Wrexley would go as far as to hurt an innocent lady. He only knew he didn't trust him *not* to. "Whatever his intentions, they weren't honorable. He doesn't love her, Derrick. If he did, he'd never manipulate her like that, or involve her in such a devious scheme."

"Why, that bloody scoundrel."

Finn nodded, his mouth tight. "He's selfish, down to his very soul. Selfish, debauched, and reckless."

Derrick ran a rough hand through his hair. "Christ, Huntington. I can't understand how there's never a whisper of gossip about him, given what an utter villain he is."

"Oh, there are whispers. One just needs to know where to go to hear them. After that debacle at Lady Fairchild's, I paid Lord Greyson a visit."

"Greyson? Good lord, is he still alive?"

"Alive, and as sharp as ever. He doesn't leave his house now, but he's as cheerful and entertaining as always, and all his friends still come to him with the choicest bits of gossip. He was a dear friend of my father's, and happy to receive me."

"You asked him about Wrexley."

"I hinted, yes. Delicately, of course. We're both aware Wrexley's not as spotless as he appears, but he does a bloody good job of hiding it from his aunt and cousin, and from most of London. Still, Greyson had one or two tales about him."

Lord Derrick shot him a wary look. "What is it, then? Gaming? Mistresses?"

"Both. Neither would distinguish him from any other nobleman, of course, except the degree to which he indulges his vices, particularly the gaming. Wrexley is so near ruin he'll be following Harley to the Continent if he doesn't pay his debts of honor soon."

"He wants Miss Somerset's money, then?"

"That's part of it. She has a good deal of it, thanks to Lady Chase, but we both know the real reason her wants her, Derrick. It has far more to do with me than it does with Miss Somerset."

Lord Derrick stared out at the Serpentine for a moment, thinking, then turned back to Finn. "Do you suppose she has a preference for him?"

Finn frowned. If she did have a preference for Wrexley, he hadn't noticed it, but he'd missed a great deal when it came to Miss Somerset. "No, but Wrexley is Lady Honora's cousin, and Miss Somerset and Lady Honora are friends. She's likely spent more time with him than she has with any other gentleman, and may feel more comfortable with him for that reason. I do think she trusts him."

"It's not uncommon for an impoverished nobleman to marry an heiress for her fortune, Huntington. You'll have to do better than that, because aside from Greyson's idle gossip, Wrexley hasn't done a thing to justify interfering if he does decide to court Miss Somerset."

Finn let out a short, hard laugh. "Justify it? I don't intend to justify a damn thing to him, Derrick. He's not going to have her."

Lord Derrick's head jerked back in surprise. "Indeed? That's a black scowl, Huntington. A bit possessive of your former betrothed, are you?"

Finn's scowl deepened. "Not possessive, no, but I can't stand by and leave Miss Somerset to fall into whatever trap Wrexley has planned for her. You know what he is. The lady…well, she deserves better than that. Better than *him*."

Lord Derrick gave a derisive snort. "She deserves better than the whole lot of you, but I don't see how you have a damn thing to say about who she marries, now she's jilted you. You no longer have any claim on the lady. She may marry who she wishes."

"No, she may not. She's marrying *me*."

Lord Derrick's eyes nearly fell out of their sockets. "Does *she* know that?"

"No, not yet, but she hasn't any other…that is, I can't just stand by and let her…she jilted me, yes, and she made her choice, and while I can't be expected to…I could leave her to face the consequences, of course, but even if I *didn't* feel some concern, I wouldn't just—"

"Huntington." That was all Derrick said, but it was enough.

Finn met his friend's steady gaze, and blew out a long breath. "This is my fault, Derrick. All of it."

Finn didn't even want to *see* Miss Somerset again, much less marry her. He wanted to wait for the *ton* to return to London for the little season, so he could begin the search for his marchioness anew, and find a lady who was everything he'd thought Miss Somerset was. A quiet, modest lady, one who didn't stir anything dangerous in him, or tempt him to let the tight control he held over himself unravel.

But ever since she'd jilted him, she'd squirmed her way under his skin, and no matter what he did to dislodge her, she clung to him like a burr hidden under a saddle. She'd been prickling and poking at him for a week now. Once he married her he wouldn't have a moment's peace, but he couldn't stand by and do nothing while she tumbled headlong into Wrexley's arms.

"Why is any of this your fault? Because of the wager?" Instead of delivering his usual indignant lecture on that subject, Lord Derrick waited for Finn to speak.

"Yes." Bitter shame flooded Finn's chest, and he couldn't meet Derrick's eyes. "No doubt Wrexley admired Miss Somerset even before the wager, but once those cards hit the table, this became less about her than the pleasure he'll get from taking her from me. He'll do anything to have her now."

"You refer to that business with Wrexley and your former betrothed, Miss Hughes?" Lord Derrick shook his head. "That was five years ago, Huntington. Surely even a man as vindictive as Wrexley wouldn't hold a grudge for so long."

Finn tensed, just as he always did when anyone mentioned Diana Hughes. "He would, and he does. Wrexley may have seduced my betrothed, Derrick, but he's never acknowledged his villainy. The way he sees it, I stole his heiress. He went to all the fuss and bother of ruining Miss Hughes, and then I snatched her away before he could marry her and secure her fortune. He wants revenge on me, and after five long years he sees his chance to get it. What could be a more fitting punishment than taking Miss Somerset from me? And she's more vulnerable to him than ever, now she's jilted me."

Once the gossips found out she'd sent him on his way, the *ton*'s judgment would fall heavily on her shoulders. There was every chance she'd never receive another offer of marriage. He might go on to choose another bride, and to get just the kind of compliant lady he'd always intended to have as his wife, but Miss Somerset would be left to languish for the unpardonable sin of encouraging and then jilting a marquess.

Especially one with his spotless reputation, undeserved as it might be.

"Wrexley will pounce on her, like any predator." Lord Derrick's voice was faint. "He's charming, handsome. He'll convince Miss Somerset he loves her, and Lady Chase will approve the match, because she'll have no other choice now her granddaughter's reputation has been stained."

"Another suitor is the only way for her to escape a dreary fate, and Wrexley intends to be that suitor. As I said before, it's a clever plan. It may not have gone just as he intended, but he's accomplished his goal. Miss Somerset's jilted me, and the way is clear for him to pursue her."

"Once he's secured her, he'll...Jesus, Huntington. Who knows what he'll do? Steal her fortune, yes, but a man who'd risk a lady's reputation and potentially her happiness by destroying her betrothal? A man that selfish, that reckless—"

"He won't secure her, Derrick."

That despicable wager—that was his failure, not Miss Somerset's. Finn would do what he must to see she wasn't the one who suffered for it, and in this case, doing what he must meant making a trip to Hampshire.

"Wrexley's going to Lady Hadley's house party. He's escorting his cousin, Lady Honora, and Miss Somerset and her sister. Once they're there, he won't waste any time. He'll try and have the thing settled before they even leave Hampshire, no matter what it takes."

Derrick blinked at him. "Lady Hadley's house party?"

"Don't look so shocked, Derrick. You received an invitation, didn't you?"

"Yes, I received an invitation. What shocks me, Huntington, is *you* did."

"Oh? I don't see why it should." Finn didn't mention he'd been so shocked himself he'd accidentally dropped the paper into the fire. He'd burnt his fingers retrieving it, but it was worth a singeing, because he'd seen at once the invitation could only mean one thing.

Miss Somerset was keeping secrets from her family.

"Lady Hadley," Derrick said. "That is, the Marchioness of Hadley, sister-in-law to Lady Carlisle, who also happens to be Miss Somerset's sister? *That* Lady Hadley?"

"Do you know of another Lady Hadley?"

"No, but why the devil would Lady Hadley invite *you*, Miss Somerset's former betrothed, to her house party?"

Several mounted gentlemen were approaching them from the east end of the Serpentine, so Finn drew his horse closer to Derrick's and kept his voice low. "Because Miss Somerset and I *are* betrothed—at least, as far as Lady Hadley knows, we are."

Finn paused to let that sink in.

Derrick gaped at him for a moment, but then he burst into an unexpected shout of laughter so loud the riders ambling by turned to stare at him.

Finn waited with ill-concealed impatience until Derrick's burst of hilarity subsided. "You find it amusing Miss Somerset hasn't yet told her family she jilted me?"

Derrick was wiping his eyes on his coat. "No, but I *do* find it amusing a lady you chose for her steadiness has turned out to be about as predictable as a hurricane." Lord Derrick laughed at Finn's sour expression. "Oh, come now, Huntington. You must admit the irony is irresistible."

Finn didn't find it the least irresistible. He found Miss Somerset's actions to be imprudent and deceitful, both of which were damn unsettling qualities in a wife. "It's been a week, Derrick. What can she hope to accomplish by keeping the truth from her grandmother? It's bad enough she's jilted a marquess, but she's made the situation worse by hiding it. What if Lady Chase finds out before Miss Somerset tells her? She'll be furious."

Derrick gave him a curious look. "You almost sound as if you're worried for her."

Finn didn't answer, but his jaw twitched with annoyance.

"If Miss Somerset's family believes she's still betrothed to you, then Wrexley must think so too," Lord Derrick went on. "If her own family doesn't know she's jilted you, then how can he know it?"

"She hasn't told her grandmother, but it may be she's confided in her sister and Lady Honora. If she has, then Lady Honora will have told her cousin of it. In any case, we already know a small thing like a betrothal to another man won't stop Wrexley."

"You must write at once to Miss Somerset's brother-in-law, Captain West, to warn him about Wrexley."

"I can't do that, Derrick. I don't know Captain West, and when he discovers Miss Somerset's jilted me, he won't trust what I have to say about her other suitor. In any case, all we have against Wrexley is gossip."

Finn didn't expect an argument, since Lord Derrick was perhaps the only gentleman in London who never engaged in gossip, but to his surprise, his friend hesitated, then shook his head. "Unless you tell Captain West about Miss Hughes. That's not gossip."

"No," Finn said, his tone flat. "Not unless there's no other way."

Even after Wrexley's perfidy, Finn had still wanted to marry Diana, but she'd refused him. She'd claimed to be too ashamed, and insisted only the most spotless of ladies deserved to become his marchioness. But Finn knew the truth. Diana was wise enough to know a marriage to Wrexley would only lead to further heartbreak, but even after Wrexley ruined her and destroyed all her happiness, she'd loved him still.

She wouldn't marry Finn, but she'd begged him to help her leave London, and he'd done as she asked. Diana Hughes was now safely married to a former Oxford classmate of Finn's. She lived up north near Newcastle, far beyond the reach of the *ton's* vicious gossip, but she had two much younger sisters, both of whom were still unmarried, and who would remain so if that scandal should ever come to light.

"Very well. To Hampshire, then. To Lady Hadley's house party, to woo back your former betrothed."

Finn scowled at the word *woo*. He couldn't think of anything more tedious than a second courtship, especially for a lady who'd jilted him once. "I doubt she'll be happy to find me there, but I don't see any other way."

Derrick nodded, and by mutual consent they guided their horses around the west end of the Serpentine and continued east toward Finn's house in Grosvenor Square, a heavy silence between them as they each fell into their own thoughts.

"You'll need to go gently with her, Huntington," Derrick said, once they'd turned onto King's Road. "Your fortune and title won't be enough to coax Miss Somerset back. She's already shown she won't be swayed by them." Derrick paused to consider this, then. "Unusual lady, isn't she?"

"Unusual?" Finn snorted. "To say the least, yes. What sort of lady jilts a marquess? I haven't the faintest idea how to proceed with her."

"You know, you never said why she jilted you, Huntington."

Because I wouldn't kiss her.

Finn didn't say it aloud, in part because Derrick would fall off his horse in a fit of hysterical laughter, but also because it sounded ludicrous. A kiss, for God's sake. There had to be more to it than that, and as soon as he got to Hampshire, he intended to find out what it was. "It's complicated."

Derrick chuckled. "I have no doubt, but as far as proceeding with her, you'll go on as any suitor would. She may be unusual, but she *is* a lady still. Be gallant and agreeable, speak softly and sweetly to her—none of your usual detachment and bad-tempered commands, if you please—and you'll have the business settled before you leave the house party."

Finn raked a hand through his hair. Christ, if this thing depended on his agreeableness, there wasn't a chance of success, especially against Wrexley, who donned his false charm as easily as he did his perfectly-tailored Weston coats. He didn't have Wrexley's easy smiles, or his glib sophistication. Finn's words would sound right in his head, but somehow when he spoke them they would be all wrong, and he'd seem cold and detached, or too stiff and proper.

He always did.

"Don't look so glum, Huntington. When we're not taking Wrexley to account, perhaps we'll have a chance to shoot some birds while we're in Hampshire."

Finn didn't reply.

Hunting was all very well, as long as Lord Wrexley missed his shot.

Chapter Six

"I know very well you're not asleep, Iris. You may twitch and mutter all you like, but you're not fooling me, and you look quite ridiculous."

Iris raised one eyelid just far enough to peek through the tiny slit hidden under her eyelashes. Lady Honora was tucked into one corner of the carriage, her brow furrowed with worry. Violet was next to her, and her sister looked as if she were about to leap across the carriage and shake Iris until her eyes closed for good.

Oh, dear. Her sister didn't look pleased, and when Violet wasn't pleased, she could be—

"We've been trapped in this coach for hours, and in that time you haven't said more than a dozen words to either of us." Violet stuck out her foot and prodded Iris none-too-gently with her toe. "Well, I won't speak for Honora, but I've had enough of it. You *will* speak to us, and tell us what's made you so cross, or I vow I'll spend the rest of the ride to Hampshire singing as loudly as I can."

Singing? Dear God, not that. Violet was infamous in their family for her lack of musical ability. She could even make a pianoforte sound tone deaf.

Iris sighed, and opened her eyes. There was no use carrying on with the ruse. Even if she'd truly been asleep, Violet's shouting would have woken her, and someone had to save Honora before she burst into tears.

"What nonsense, Violet. Why should I be cross?"

Iris forced the corners of her lips to curl upwards, but Violet, who wasn't fooled in the least by the anemic smile, rolled her eyes. "I haven't the faintest idea. I thought you *wanted* us all to go to Charlotte's house party."

"No. I didn't object when Grandmother ordered us to go, but that's not at all the same thing as *wanting* to go, is it?"

"Well, why shouldn't you want to go, for pity's sake? It wasn't as if you were doing anything in London this past week but sulking and muttering darkly to yourself."

"You haven't been out of the house in days, Iris," Lady Honora added. "You refuse to walk or ride in the park, or make calls, or go shopping. One would almost think you're hiding."

Iris opened her mouth to deny it, but then closed it again. There was no point in trying to fool them, especially Violet, who seemed to know her thoughts even before she had a chance to think them.

Had it only been a week since she'd sent Lord Huntington on his way? It felt like years since he'd sat across from her in the drawing room, his hazel eyes growing darker and darker with every word out of her mouth. By the time he took his leave they'd gone such a deep green she might almost have imagined his heart was affected, if she hadn't known better.

That was provided he *had* a heart. She'd never seen any definitive proof of its existence.

That alone was reason enough to jilt him, and she didn't regret doing it. No, of course she didn't. It was more a matter of, well…what should she do now? She'd begun to suspect—oh, it was just a niggling doubt, mind you, not even a worry yet, and certainly not a panic—it might have been wise to plan her next steps *before* she'd jilted Lord Huntington.

Not for her own sake, of course, but for everyone else's.

Perhaps you should start by telling your grandmother what you've done.

Iris bit her lip, her stomach twisting into nervous knots that pulled tighter with every day she continued her deception. She'd half-expected Lord Huntington to complain of his treatment to Lady Chase. He hadn't, not even when Iris refused to receive his calls, but her grandmother would have to know eventually, and she wasn't going to be pleased when she discovered Iris had jilted the Marquess of Huntington.

Dash it, why couldn't he have been some inconsequential viscount, instead? She might have been able to reconcile her grandmother to *that*.

But it was done. She'd sent Lord Huntington away, and there was nothing left for it but to confess the truth. Well, most of the truth. Oh, very well, as little of the truth as possible. It would be preferable, for example, if the word *blindfold* didn't make it into the discussion.

Iris stared down at hands, her cheeks reddening with shame. She'd been so busy congratulating herself for her high principles in refusing to wed a hypocritical marquess, she hadn't spared a thought for how her actions might impact her sisters' prospects, or considered how disappointed her grandmother would be.

It was all Lord Huntington's fault, of course. He'd been so sure she was docile and predictable, he'd driven her to rebellion and recklessness, blast him.

Jilting him should have been the first in a series of thoughtful, judicious steps to secure her future happiness. Instead it was the *only* step, and now she'd taken it, she hadn't the faintest inkling what to do next. It was quite possible no other suitor would offer for her. One couldn't refuse a marquess without consequences, and especially not the Marquess of Huntington, who all of London revered as a perfect gentleman.

Iris's lips tightened. Perfect, yes, if one overlooked his lordship's fondness for blindfolds, and his appalling taste in mistresses. But then she was just as guilty as every other young lady this season who'd clamored for his attention. As recently as a few weeks ago she'd thought him as perfect as anyone else did, which just proved the entire lot of them were about as discerning as a flock of sheep.

I may never receive another offer, once word gets out—

"You're muttering even now, Iris, and you have that wrinkle between your brows again." Violet tapped her own forehead, right between her eyes. "Right here. If you keep scowling like that, it's going to become permanent, and I can assure you, it isn't attractive."

Iris gave her skirts an irritated jerk. For goodness' sake, she should have kept up the pretense of sleep. "I'm not muttering, or scowling—"

"Is this about Lord Huntington?"

"No!" Blast it, how did Violet always *know* everything? "I'm simply worried about Hyacinth, that's all." Their youngest sister, Hyacinth, had left for Brighton with their grandmother several days ago, a few days after Iris had jilted Lord Huntington. "Perhaps we should have gone to Brighton with them."

"There's nothing at all to worry about. The doctor says Hyacinth suffers from a depression of spirits as much as anything else." Violet gave her a shrewd look. "But it's not worry for Hyacinth that's troubling you."

Perhaps not, but Iris thought it was as good an excuse as any for her low spirits. "How can you say that, Violet? I'm a most attentive sister."

"So am I. That's how I know you're lying. So, back to Lord Huntington—"

"It's awful, that business with Lord Harley!" Iris blurted, cutting her sister off before Violet could worm the truth out of her. She'd have to tell them everything and find out what they thought it best to do, but she needed a moment to think of the proper way to put it so as not to enrage Violet, or send Honora into hysterics. "My goodness, Honora. Can you imagine Lord Harley's cheating at cards?"

"He's a perfect scoundrel." Lady Honora smoothed her skirts, a tiny smirk on her face. She never had an unkind word to say about anyone, but she couldn't quite hide her satisfaction at having escaped a marriage to Lord Harley.

"They say he fleeced Lord Akers, and now he's fled to the Continent to avoid a duel," Violet said. "You must call on Lord Akers and thank him, Honora, for offering to put a ball in Lord Harley's forehead. He's saved you from what was sure to be a miserable marriage."

They all laughed at this, but a bitter lump lodged in Iris's throat at the thought of Honora's narrow escape. There wasn't a sweeter-tempered lady in all of London, or one more deserving of a worthy suitor, and yet she would have been sacrificed to Lord Harley without a second thought.

Cheating, mistresses, scandalous dark desires…was there a gentleman left in London who wasn't a blackguard? And if there was, how was an inexperienced lady meant to distinguish him from the horde of cheats and debauchers? It wasn't as if knowing how to flutter a fan and dance a quadrille would be much help.

"I never liked Lord Harley. At one point I thought he would offer for you, Iris." Violet gave a little shudder of distaste. "Thank goodness he didn't. Both of you deserve far superior gentlemen."

Lady Honora would likely get a superior gentleman, too. Now Iris had jilted Lord Huntington, it was only a matter of time before he offered for Honora. He'd wanted her all along, and there was no question she'd make a lovely marchioness. As for Lord Huntington's, ah…proclivities, Iris doubted Lady Honora would ever find out about them. She was much too ladylike to lurk in the bushes and eavesdrop on her betrothed, and even if she did find it out, it wouldn't make any difference. Lady Honora was a conventional sort of lady, and would consider the title fair compensation for any, well…irregularities.

Iris sighed. If only she were also a conventional sort of lady. It would be so much easier that way, but she'd been raised in Surrey, by parents who believed a splendid match was one where the parties were in love with each other. It had led to all kinds of ridiculous notions on the part of their five daughters.

Iris could almost hear the gossips now. *Love? My goodness, dear. How provincial!*

"Yes, well, I'm pleased you were able to join us at the house party after all, but let's get back to the matter at hand, shall we? What do you think, Honora? Lord Huntington has called on Iris every day without fail since he began courting her, and yet I haven't seen the man once this past week." Violet gave Iris an accusing look. "It's as if he's disappeared entirely."

"How dramatic you are, Violet." Iris forced a laugh, but the knot in her stomach twisted tighter. Perhaps she'd wait to tell them after they arrived at Hadley House. Yes, that would be much better. One didn't deliver distressing news while trapped in a small carriage with no chance of escape. "It's no great mystery. He's only gone off to his country seat in Buckinghamshire for some sport."

Yes, that would do. Gentlemen were always dashing off to the country on a whim, weren't they?

"Sport?" Violet folded her hands in her lap. "Well, that explains it, I suppose."

"I wouldn't have thought Lord Huntington could bear to be separated from you for these last few weeks before your wedding, Iris."

Lady Honora said this with such sweet sincerity, Iris forced back her snort. Lord Huntington couldn't bear to be separated from *something*, certainly, but it wasn't her. Still it wasn't her place to shatter Honora's illusions. "Yes, yes—his devotion to me is truly unparalleled."

All these lies were also Lord Huntington's fault, of course. She'd never had to lie about a thing before she met him.

I don't have to lie now, either.

That was true enough, but it was too late to take it back, so she'd have to embellish on the lie instead, to make it believable. "He's gone off to Huntington Lodge, to shoot..."

Birds? Was it birds in August, or fox-hunting?

"Pheasants?" Violet offered helpfully.

"No, not—" Lady Honora began, but Violet silenced her with a look.

"Yes! Yes, of course. Pheasants. Just so." Iris settled back against the squabs. There, that should do.

Violet leaned forward, her eyes narrowed. "Pheasant season doesn't start until November."

Iris glared at her sister. Violet was as wily as the wiliest fox. "Well, as to that—"

"You're lying."

"No. He really did go to Buckinghamshire, to...to..." Dash it, what could Lord Huntington be doing in Buckinghamshire that made the least bit of sense?

Lady Honora gave a delicate cough of disagreement. "I saw him in Bond Street yesterday, Iris."

Iris froze for a moment, then deflated, slumping back against the squabs. Why could the truth never wait for the most convenient timing?

"Are you quite finished telling tales?" Violet asked.

It appears so. "Yes."

"Well, then? What's happened? Did he jilt you? Because the *ton* won't have it if he did. The Marquess of Huntington might be able to get away with quite a lot, but even he can't—"

"He didn't jilt me. He, ah…well, it's a bit more complicated than that."

"If he didn't jilt you, then why hasn't he called on you? It doesn't make any…" Violet hesitated, and then her eyes went wide. "Oh no. Don't tell me you—"

Iris squeezed her eyes closed. "I jilted him."

"You jilted the *Marquess of Huntington?*" Lady Honora let out an odd squeak, and collapsed against the squabs in a heap of pink silk skirts, quite overcome.

"I jilted him," Iris repeated. No, it still didn't seem real, even when she said it aloud. It would soon enough, however, once the *ton* swept in to persecute her with their vicious gossip.

"But *why?* I mean, the *ton* would have made things uncomfortable for him if he'd jilted you, but for you to jilt the Marquess of Huntington? Why, they'll have your head on a platter! My goodness, Iris. What have you done?"

Violet looked so horrified Iris's own heart gave an anxious lurch in her chest. "I—I—he doesn't care for me. Not at all."

There was more, of course, so much more, and part of Iris wanted to blurt it all out, then lay her head on the carriage cushion and weep. If she told them everything—about Lord Huntington's wager, and Lady Beaumont, and the cravats and insatiable appetites and desires—they would understand. Lady Honora would soothe her, and Violet would fall into a rage on her behalf, then they'd both stroke her hair and tell her she'd done the right thing, and she'd feel so much better.

But something made her hold her tongue. She wasn't trying to protect Lord Huntington, of course. He'd chosen his debaucheries, and he could live with them, but she hadn't even told *him* she knew his secrets. She certainly wasn't going to tell Violet and Honora.

His secrets weren't hers to tell.

"Oh, Iris." Lady Honora's face was the picture of dismay. "This isn't because he refused to kiss you in the garden, is it?"

Iris didn't answer, but turned away from Honora's anxious face to look out the window. Lord Huntington thought that was the reason, but of course the kiss was only the sharp point of the dagger, and everyone knew it was the blade that did the real damage.

Iris could have overlooked a great deal to secure the match her grandmother had gone to such trouble to bring about. Lord Huntington's wager with Lord Harley, his mistress, his disinterest in her—it was all quite distressing, but she would have gone through with the marriage, nonetheless. His lordship could blindfold his mistress with his cravat and tie her to London Bridge if he chose, and for her grandmother's and sisters' sakes, Iris would have done everything she could to ignore it.

But to imply she'd engaged in an indiscretion with Lord Wrexley? To cast aspersions on her virtue, and call her very character into question when *he* was the one guilty of so many secret sins?

No. It was too much.

Here was a man who'd hold his wife to absurd standards of propriety with one hand, while he tied his mistress to…to…well, whatever it was one tied a mistress to, with the other. Perhaps there were ladies docile enough to overlook it for the sake of becoming a marchioness, but Iris wasn't one of them.

And marriage—a lifetime of marriage, no less—to a gentleman who didn't care a whit for her, who'd dismissed her as dull and tedious before he ever troubled himself to know her at all? A gentleman who kept a mistress, and used his cravat for a purpose no cravat was ever intended to be used?

She thought of Lady Beaumont's cruel taunts, her catlike smile. That vicious woman didn't deserve the least bit of good fortune to fall in her path, but as it turned out, perhaps Lord Huntington would keep her as his mistress, after all.

Either way, she didn't have a thing to fear from Iris.

Not anymore.

"I warned you he might not kiss you, Iris," Honora persisted, twisting her hands together in her lap. "He's a gentleman."

A short laugh escaped Iris, and even she could hear the note of panic in it. "Yes, you did, and you were quite right. When I tried to hint a kiss would be welcome, he scolded me as if I were a naughty child."

"But he made you an offer." As far as Lady Honora was concerned, this settled the question of his affections. "Why should he do that if he didn't care for you?"

Iris couldn't bear to admit he'd chosen her because he thought her dull and predictable, or worse, that she'd begun to think it of herself, especially after she'd seen the way Lady Beaumont raged and teased and tempted. That moment, when she'd sunk to her knees in front of him…

Iris had only been able see her red, silk-swathed back through the gap in the branches, but whatever she'd been doing, it had to do with Lord Huntington's breeches.

Not just his breeches.

She cleared her throat. "I think he regretted his offer, so you see, it's really for the best if we don't marry."

Violet looked like she wanted to argue, but whatever she saw in Iris's face made her pause and bite her lip. "You haven't told Grandmother."

"No. I meant to, every day." Iris gave Violet a pleading look. "I should have done so at once. I've only made this worse by keeping quiet, but—"

"Oh, dear God, Iris. You have no idea how much worse you've made it!"

"What do you mean?" Iris sank her fingers into the velvet seat cushion to steady herself, because she was sure she wasn't going to like whatever Violet said next.

"Charlotte and Captain West invited Lord Huntington to their house party!"

"Oh, no," Lady Honora moaned, burying her face in her hands. "Oh, Iris. It's going to be dreadfully awkward for you."

"Why would they invite Lord Huntington?" It was a foolish question. No one knew she'd jilted him, so why wouldn't they ask him to come? As far as they knew, he was her betrothed.

"Grandmother suggested it to Charlotte. She thought you'd be pleased." Violet reached for Iris's hand. "I'm so sorry for it."

Iris gave her sister's hand an absent pat. "It would be awkward indeed if he were to come, but he won't."

Lady Honora frowned. "But why shouldn't he?"

"Think of it. Charlotte, Captain West, and Grandmother don't know I've jilted Lord Huntington, but Lord Huntington certainly does. Why would he accept an invitation to attend a house party with the lady who's just jilted him? I'm certain he'll stay far away."

"Yes, that makes sense." Lady Honora's face cleared. "He won't come."

Violet wasn't as hopeful. "Perhaps not, but what of the other problem? You've refused a marquess, Iris, and not just any marquess, but the Marquess of Huntington. Grandmother is going to be apoplectic, and that's to say nothing of your future prospects."

I have no future prospects.

"My prospects are bleak at best, but I'm willing to entertain brilliant suggestions, if either of you should happen to have one."

A long, grim silence followed, then Violet straightened against her seat. "I do have one idea."

Lady Honora leaned forward. "What is it?"

"Lord Derrick will be there. You could encourage him." Violet kept her gaze on her lap, suddenly absorbed with smoothing the wrinkles from her skirts. "It would go a long way toward soothing Grandmother's hurt feelings over the loss of Lord Huntington if you had another suitor to replace him."

Iris was fond of Lord Derrick. He had lovely brown eyes, and to look into them was to see into the heart of him. He might be the one gentleman left in London who wasn't harboring a shocking secret, if only because he couldn't hide a thing in those melting brown eyes.

But he was Lord Huntington's dearest friend, and even if he did happen to show an interest in her, Iris would discourage him despite her enjoyment in his company, because Violet *also* enjoyed his company, and with rather more fervor than Iris did.

Violet fussed with her skirts to avoid Iris's gaze, and Iris felt a rush of warm affection for her sister. How dear Violet was, to offer up the gentleman she herself favored. "No. Lord Derrick is a kind, charming gentleman, but I don't think we'd suit."

Violet said nothing to this, but she drew in a deep breath, and then let it out again in a sigh of relief.

"My cousin, then!" Lady Honora beamed at them, her dark eyes triumphant. "You'll become Lady Wrexley!"

All three ladies turned at once to look out the window. Lord Wrexley was escorting them to Hadley House, but he'd opted to take his horse rather than ride in the carriage, and Iris had quite forgotten about him. They were friends, and he wasn't grand or stiff like Lord Huntington. His relaxed manners and effortless charm put her at ease, but she'd never before considered him as a potential suitor.

Now, as she watched him from the carriage window, she wondered why. He was certainly handsome, and he handled his mount with an easy grace she couldn't fail to appreciate.

He caught her eye, and gave her a wide smile as he touched his riding crop to his hat.

Iris smiled back, then settled against the squabs. Her trust in her own judgment had suffered a severe blow after she'd so misjudged Lord Huntington's character, but she knew Lord Wrexley quite well, since he was always about when she visited with Lady Honora.

Of course, despite their familiarity, there was a chance he hid a dubious character under his gentlemanly exterior, just as Lord Huntington and Lord Harley did. He could well have his own secrets—a mad wife hidden in the attics at his country estate, perhaps—but he seemed to be exactly what he appeared to be, that is, a carefree young earl with open, easy manners and a handsome face.

"Lord Wrexley." Violet tapped her finger against her lips, considering. "He is an agreeable sort of gentleman, isn't he?"

"Oh, yes, he truly is. He'd make any young lady an enviable husband." Lady Honora squeezed Iris's arm, her smile giddy.

Iris hesitated, glancing at Violet. "Well, I've got to do something. I've behaved rashly, dismissing Lord Huntington with so little thought. It will hurt Grandmother, and there's the issue of yours and Hyacinth's prospects—"

"I would never want you to marry a gentleman who would make you unhappy because you're worried about my prospects, Iris, and neither would Hyacinth."

"I know you wouldn't, Violet, but—"

"I don't deny it would solve a great many problems if Lord Wrexley were courting you by the end of Charlotte's house party—not just to console Grandmother, but because it will help to silence the gossips' wagging tongues. But you have to have some affection for him, and he must feel the same for you, or else you may just as well have married Lord Huntington."

If she did encourage Lord Wrexley, and he wasn't what he appeared to be...

The *ton* wouldn't overlook two jilted lords. No, if she encouraged him, she'd have to see it through to the end, or else she'd be well and truly ruined, and her sisters right along with her.

But surely Lord Wrexley was safe enough? Honora would never adore him as she did if he were a villain, and Iris herself had never seen any reason to doubt his character. "Well, I've always been fond of him."

"Oh, it's perfect!" Lady Honora clapped her hands together with delight. "He's so natural and easy, particularly for a gentleman of fashion. I'm sure you'll adore him, Iris, just as I do."

Violet was a bit more circumspect. "Shall we see how you feel when we arrive?"

The knots in Iris's stomach were twisting tighter and tighter, but she pasted a smile on her face for her sister's sake, and nodded. "Yes. I think that's a good idea."

But she'd already made up her mind, because she no longer had the luxury of consulting her feelings. If Lord Wrexley showed the slightest interest in her, she would encourage him. If all went well, she could be betrothed to him by the end of the house party.

They didn't speak much after that. Lady Honora lapsed into a happy silence, Violet ceased her scolding, and Iris stared out the window, watched

Hampshire roll by, and tried not to think of either Lord Wrexley or Lord Huntington.

Several hours later, when the roof of Hadley House peeked through the tops of the trees at last, Iris straightened in her seat. "We're nearly there."

Violet leaned to look out the window. "Charlotte says it's an odd house. Very large, with a maze of hallways leading in every direction."

Iris smiled. "Captain West wasn't as kind as that. He told me once Hadley House makes the London rookeries look organized."

"I suppose we'll find out soon enough. Now, don't look so grim, Iris. You adore Charlotte, and Lady Tallant will be here, as well. You've always longed to make her acquaintance." A sly grin drifted over Violet's lips. "I doubt our grandmother knows *she* was invited."

"Lady Tallant? Oh, dear." Honora bit her lip. No doubt she was imagining what her own mother, Lady Fairchild, would say if she knew her daughter was attending a house party with one of London's infamous wicked widows.

Of course, Charlotte herself had been a wicked widow, but she also happened to be the Marchioness of Hadley, so the *ton* was inclined to forgive her colorful past, particularly now that she was married to Captain Julian West, a celebrated Waterloo hero.

Lady Annabel Tallant, however, remained as wicked as ever. She was a dear friend of Charlotte's, and the *ton* thought her *so* wicked, Lady Chase had forbidden her granddaughters the acquaintance, even after Iris begged for an introduction. She'd always been rather taken with Lady Tallant, despite her wickedness.

Or perhaps because of it.

"It's bound to be a lively party, with—" Violet's voice was swallowed by her sudden gasp, and she reached out to grip Iris's arm.

"Violet? What is it?" Dread slithered up Iris's spine.

"For goodness's sake, Violet, are you ill?" Lady Honora went pale. "You're frightening me!"

Violet didn't answer, only pointed out the widow, toward the front of the house, where a small knot of people were gathered to welcome them. Charlotte, of course, and her husband, Captain West. Lady Tallant— oh, so elegant! And Lord Derrick, so handsome in his dark blue coat, and next to him—

Iris groped for Violet with one hand, and for Lady Honora with the other, her heart leaping into her throat.

Next to him, his mouth pulled into a stern line, his hazel eyes fixed on their carriage as it rolled up the drive, was Lord Huntington.

Chapter Seven

Finn didn't care much for fair-haired ladies. Porcelain skin, rosebud lips, and tall, slender figures didn't make his breath short, and he wasn't likely to get lost in a pair of blue eyes—no matter how deep a blue, or how heavily-lashed they might be.

Miss Somerset wasn't at all to his taste.

He could see why other gentlemen admired her, of course. Those heavy, silky curls made a man imagine what it might be like to pull loose every pin, tangle his fingers in it, and tilt her head back so he could press his mouth against that long neck and nibble a path down to the delicious curve of her shoulder. She'd be soft there, fragrant, and her pale skin would flush so prettily, warming his lips—

"Close your mouth, Huntington. You're distressing Miss Somerset."

Finn dragged his gaze away from her to scowl at Lord Derrick. "What the devil do you mean, Derrick? I wasn't—"

"Looking at her the way a wolf looks at a lamb, right before he devours it? Certainly you were. Every time she so much as twitches, your legs tense, as if you're preparing to leap over the settee and take a bite out of her. Why do you think she looks so agitated?"

Lord Derrick raised his teacup to his lips to hide a faint smirk, but Finn saw it, and his teeth snapped together. "Nonsense. I'm not looking at her at all. I was looking at Lady Honora."

At least he *should* be looking at Lady Honora, because with her glossy dark hair and wide brown eyes, *she* was the one who possessed the kind of gentle beauty he'd always admired. Miss Somerset's slender figure—no matter how graceful—was nothing next to Lady Honora's lush curves, and then there was Miss Somerset's coloring, which was all wrong. Her delicate, blush-pink lips couldn't compete with Lady Honora's red ones, even if they did look like a swollen rosebud, the lower lip a tempting curve, equal parts wickedness and vulnerability—

"Then I beg your pardon, Huntington. I've just never known Lady Honora to inspire such a predatory gleam in your eye."

"You've never known Miss Somerset to inspire it, either." Finn scowled down at his teacup. Anyone could see she wasn't at all to his taste—anyone but Derrick, that is, who seemed determined to believe Finn was gaping at her because he couldn't stop thinking about tasting the curve of her neck—

"No, but then she's never jilted you before. I think this sudden preference for the classic English rose is a direct result of her rejection. We all want what we can't have, eh, Huntington? Such an unexpected rebellion on her part, too. I think the lady has earned your admiration at last. Damned inconvenient timing, isn't it?"

"This whole business is inconvenient, and the timing is the least of it." The secrets, the potential for scandal, the lady herself—it would become a bloody mess before it was resolved, and Finn detested messes.

Lord Derrick chuckled. "That's not a gallant sentiment for a gentleman about to embark on a courtship." Lord Derrick smirked again, and this time he didn't even have the decency to hide it behind his teacup.

"Damn it, Derrick, this isn't some romantic courtship, it's—"

"…and I couldn't be happier to see you all." Lady Hadley beamed at her guests as she passed Lady Honora a plate of refreshments. "It's such a long journey from London, but I daresay you found a pleasant way to pass the time."

"Very pleasant, indeed, my lady. Beautiful ride." Lord Wrexley's dark gaze slid from Lady Hadley to Miss Somerset, and a slow smile curled his lips. "I can't recall ever being so captivated by the scenery before."

Finn slammed his plate down on a side table with a rude clatter. "Beautiful, yes, but I doubt you'll have an opportunity to see as much of it as you wish to, Wrexley."

Lord Wrexley didn't spare him a glance, but kept his gaze on Miss Somerset. "You're kind to be concerned, Huntington, but I assure you I intend to make the most of my visit. You see, I've made it a point to see as much as I possibly can in the fortnight I'm here."

"Ambitious of you, but you can't hope to accomplish much in such a short time. I'm afraid you'll be disappointed with your progress."

Lord Wrexley dismissed this concern with an idle flick of his fingers. "Oh, not to worry, Huntington. A fortnight is more than long enough for my purposes."

"We'll see. Tell me, Miss Somerset. Did you find the journey as diverting as Lord Wrexley?" Finn pinned her with a hard look meant to communicate his intentions.

I'm here for you.

Her blue eyes widened with alarm. "I, ah—it was a pleasant trip, my lord, but I find myself rather fatigued. Perhaps a rest before dinner would help."

Lady Tallant, who'd been watching this exchange with sharp interest, now let out a sigh and rose to her feet. "Come along then, Miss Somerset. I'm going up myself, so I'll take you. Otherwise you'll be wandering about for hours, and never encounter another living soul. It's like an Egyptian tomb up there, with dozens of dim passageways all leading precisely nowhere."

"Thank you. That's kind of you, my lady. I'll see you all at dinner, then?" With one last furtive glance at Finn, Miss Somerset followed Lady Tallant from the room.

Finn waited for a moment or two after they'd left, then rose to his feet. "My horse was favoring his left front foot on the ride here. I believe I'll go out to the stables and check on him."

Captain West, who was a former cavalry officer and knew his horses, turned to Finn with a frown. "I'd be happy to come out and take a look—"

"No, that's not necessary, I thank you. I believe it's just a loose shoe. It won't take long." He bowed and smiled at the ladies, then strode out into the entryway just in time to see Lady Tallant and Miss Somerset turn left at the second floor landing.

Finn didn't give himself time to reconsider, but went up after them, the thump of his boots muffled against the thick carpets. Damn foolish, following her into her bedchamber. Captain West would toss him out at once if he heard of it, and it wasn't as if Finn wouldn't have another opportunity to speak to Miss Somerset later this evening. And did he really need to see where she slept? She already haunted his dreams, for God's sake. He'd woken in the dark last night, half-smothered in his blankets, with the stubborn tilt of her chin and the blue flash in her eyes floating around in his fevered brain. Wasn't that bad enough?

None of these logical arguments did a thing to slow his steps, however. He continued down the hallway, cursing himself the entire way, a burning urgency in his belly driving him forward.

"...dine early because Lady Hadley and Captain West keep country hours."

A door opened, and Lady Tallant's voice drifted down the hallway.

"I'll see you at 7:00, Miss Somerset. Enjoy your rest."

Finn ducked around a corner at the end of the corridor until he heard the soft shuffle of Lady Annabel's slippers move past, and then he crept to Miss Somerset's door. He didn't knock, but turned the knob, slipped inside, and closed it behind him.

She was standing at the basin, dabbing at her face and neck with a damp cloth, but she caught sight of him in the glass and let out a small gasp. "Lord Huntington!" She whirled around to face him, her hand going to her throat. "You shocked me half to death! My goodness, what are you doing in my bedchamber?"

He leaned back against the door, trying not to notice the tiny droplets of water glistening on her skin. "I beg your pardon for the disturbance, Miss Somerset, but we have something to discuss."

He'd told himself he'd stay by the door, and he didn't recall having moved, but somehow he was standing in the middle of her room. She'd tossed aside her light traveling cloak and hat, her cheeks were pink from her ablutions, and damp tendrils of her hair curled in a riot of little ringlets around her face and the back of her neck.

So angelic, rather like a child.

Lady Beaumont's voice had dripped with scorn when she'd said it, and Finn hadn't contradicted her, but now, with Miss Somerset facing him, her back stiff and that contrary tilt to her chin, he saw how wrong he'd been. No lady who could calmly face off with a marquess who'd burst into her bedchamber was a child. Looking at her now, he didn't know how he'd ever thought her one.

"I can't imagine what's so urgent you think it appropriate to risk my reputation to get it. You know very well we can't be alone in my bedchamber, Lord Huntington. Shocking behavior, especially for a gentleman who wouldn't even kiss his betrothed in a private garden because he deemed it improper."

Finn's gaze dropped to her pink mouth, and he ran his tongue across the inside of his lower lip. It drove him mad to think about that kiss now—a kiss that should have happened but hadn't, and perhaps now never would.

"No one saw me enter, but if they had, we could simply claim that enthusiasm for each other's company so common among betrothed couples."

Her chin shot up. "I don't recall you being enthusiastic about my company when we were betrothed. It's one of the reasons we no longer are. I jilted you, my lord. Since you seem to be confused, let me explain what that means. No betrothal, no wedding, no marriage, and certainly no surprise visits to my bedchamber."

God, that stubborn little chin. He was coming to think of that maddening gesture as utterly hers. "It's kind of you to clarify for me. I do recall something about a jilting, and yet there's some lingering confusion on the matter."

She tossed her cloth into the wash basin and jabbed her hands onto her hips. "Indeed? I was certain I made my sentiments regarding that situation perfectly clear."

Finn fought back a sudden, absurd urge to grin at her show of pique. He'd never cared much for ladies with quick tempers, but he liked the flash in her blue eyes. "To *me*, yes, but not to your grandmother. Tell me, what will distress Lady Chase more? That you've jilted a marquess, or that it was weeks before you told her the truth about it?"

Her face paled. "I—what do you mean? She…that is, I did tell her—"

"No, I don't think so. You see, jilted fiancés make tedious house party guests. Initially I was surprised to receive Lady Hadley's invitation, but then I realized how things were. You're keeping secrets, Miss Somerset. Do you think that's wise?"

"I think, my lord, it shouldn't matter one way or another to *you*."

She pressed her lips together, but it didn't make them look anything less like rosebuds. "It wouldn't matter to me, only look at what a mess your lie has caused. Here we are, trapped together at your sister-in-law's house party for the next two weeks. Rather awkward, really."

"I never lied—"

"A lie by omission, Miss Somerset, is still a lie."

"Forgive me, Lord Huntington, but you're hardly one to lecture me about lies of omission, considering our betrothal."

Finn frowned. "What do you mean, considering our betrothal?"

She didn't reply, but went on as if he hadn't spoken. "And despite what my family believes, *you* know well enough I jilted you. You should have declined the invitation. Indeed, under the circumstances, I can't account for your being here at all."

"I told you. We have something to discuss." Finn closed the distance between them with two long strides. "I came to tell you I reject your dismissal, Miss Somerset. I *will* marry you, just as I planned."

He winced at the note of command in his voice. It wasn't *quite* the charming proposal Derrick had recommended, but at least there could be no doubt as to his intentions.

Her mouth dropped open in shock, but then a flush of angry color bloomed on her cheekbones. "But *I* won't marry *you*, Lord Huntington. Hence the jilting. That's rather a grave flaw in your plan, wouldn't you say?"

"Oh, but I think you will marry me. Come, Miss Somerset. If you really intended to jilt me, you'd have told your grandmother about it at once.

You didn't, so some part of you must still want this match. I may not be charming or gallant, but your other prospects are grim enough for you to overlook my more grievous flaws."

"I—you…" She was so furious she had to take several deep breaths before she could speak. "You're mad! Do you truly believe I jilted you because you're not *charming*? How dare you sneak into my bedchamber and presume to order me to—"

"Why *did* you jilt me, Miss Somerset?"

"You know why! We don't—"

"No. Don't tell me we don't suit."

"You asked for the reason, my lord. I jilted you because we don't—"

"No." Finn's hands were shaking with the need to press his palm to her lips to keep her from saying it again. "That's not a reason. It's an excuse, a way for you to dismiss me with as little bother as possible. Now, let's try again, shall we? Why did you jilt me? Have you fallen in love with someone else, and wish to be rid of me?"

Don't say Lord Wrexley.

Finn waited, but she didn't say Wrexley's name—she didn't say anything, but simply stood there, her eyes enormous in her pale face.

The silence stretched long enough for Finn's nerves to snap. "Miss Somerset? I asked you a question. Why do you wish to be rid of me?"

"It's you who wishes to be rid of me, I think," she muttered under her breath. Then, "Were you aware, my lord, Lady Honora is no longer betrothed to Lord Harley? He's fled to the Continent in disgrace. Pity, but that's what comes of wagering, isn't it?"

Finn frowned. What the devil did Lady Honora have to do with it? "Lady Honora? Why should I—"

"She'd make a lovely marchioness, wouldn't she? Before you insist upon marrying me, you should consider you now have options that weren't available to you when you first offered for me."

"Perhaps I don't admire Lady Honora."

She shrugged, but her gaze slid away from his. "Why shouldn't you admire her? Lady Honora is lovely. You couldn't choose a sweeter, kinder lady than her."

An incredulous laugh slipped through Finn's lips. "Are you so determined to be rid of me, you've chosen me another bride?"

Her face went whiter still, and when she spoke her voice was so low Finn had to take a step closer to hear her. "You chose her yourself, Lord Huntington, long before you chose me."

For the briefest moment he was baffled by this response, but then understanding slammed into him, and shock rendered him speechless.

She knows about the wager.

"And I *do* wish to be rid of you, my lord, because when I marry, I will be that gentleman's first choice, not his second."

That odd conversation on the day she'd jilted him, her preoccupation with his *satisfaction*, and the day before, when he'd found her in Lady Fairchild's garden, and she'd looked so lost and so defiant at once...

She'd overheard him that day, in the garden, arguing with Lady Beaumont.

There was no other explanation, either for her strange behavior the rest of that afternoon, for the jilting the following day, or even for the mutinous gleam in her eyes right now. She'd heard every word of it.

He thought back to the conversation with Lady Beaumont that day, every ugly word like another blow raining down on him, each more punishing than the last.

Blindfolds and silk scarves, his exotic appetites, his insatiability, and...

Jesus. Lady Beaumont on her knees before him, her busy fingers on his falls.

Finn's hands clenched into fists as he fought for breath. The wager, as despicable as it was, paled in comparison to the rest of what she'd heard. Lady Beaumont had said more than enough to terrify an innocent virgin like Miss Somerset.

The wager, his mistress, his mysterious dark desires—those were the sins he had to answer for, and he'd answer for them now, right here, in her bedchamber, with her furious blue eyes on him, piercing through his every lie and his every defense.

"Why, Miss Somerset, should you think you're my second choice? Tell me."

She let out a bitter laugh. "Come now, my lord. Let's have honesty between us, shall we? You chose me only after Lady Honora was betrothed to Lord Harley."

He wanted to look away from her, but instead he took a step closer, because if he looked away now, he'd never look her in the eyes again. "But how could you possibly know that? Supposing it's true, of course."

"Do you deny it's true?"

It took courage to look him in the eye and demand an answer she must not want to hear. "I don't deny it. But you didn't answer my question. How do you know you were my second choice, after Lady Honora?"

Say it. Because you were there, and you heard every word.

Her chin rose. "Because I heard your mistress Lady Beaumont say so, Lord Huntington, that day in Lady Fairchild's garden."

Finn flinched, but this was the truth he'd wanted, as ugly as it was.

"You have appalling taste in mistresses, you know," she went on, with a little toss of her head. "I don't suppose she was at her best that day, but even so, she's...well, she's a bit of a viper, isn't she?"

Despite his shame and embarrassment, a reluctant smile rose to Finn's lips. "I didn't choose her for her estimable character."

"Yes, Lady Beaumont is quite...well, I won't say I admire her, precisely, though I suppose I can understand why a gentleman who *did* admire her might find a less, ah, experienced lady"—she gestured to herself with a wave of her hand—"not as intriguing."

He'd made more than one disparaging comment about the tediousness of innocent maidens, but now she'd echoed his sentiments, Finn couldn't fail to hear how unfair it was. "Are you making excuses for my disgraceful behavior?"

"Oh no, my lord. I think you're awful enough. But I'm not as naïve as I appear. I'm well aware aristocratic gentlemen keep mistresses. On reflection, I wasn't terribly surprised to find you have an arrangement with Lady Beaumont."

"I don't have an arrangement with Lady Beaumont, Miss Somerset. Not anymore."

It was true enough, but the fact that he'd broken with her felt a bit like neatly coiling the noose after hanging an innocent man. That one feeble decency didn't make him any less guilty.

"Yes, I gathered as much. I confess it surprised me you'd dispensed with her, though perhaps not as much as it surprised Lady Beaumont."

"It wasn't the only thing that surprised you. There's more, I think." *Much more.* "What else did you hear?"

"I won't pretend I wasn't surprised by the—the...well, the business about the..." Her voice trailed off, and her cheeks went scarlet, but she straightened her shoulders, and her gaze met his. "Dark desires."

Surprised by it? It was a wonder she hadn't toppled headlong into a rosebush in a shocked swoon. For an innocent lady who'd overheard his mistress describe in salacious detail how he'd taken her against her dressing table, Miss Somerset was remarkably composed. He wasn't sure whether to be impressed with her stoicism, or appalled by it.

"But what Lady Beaumont said, my lord, about the cravats and blindfolds and such, and your, ah...insatiability?"

She squeezed her eyes closed, and in the next breath he was next to her, close enough to inhale the faint scent of soap clinging to her skin. "Look at me." He waited, his fingers hovering under her chin.

Don't touch her.

But when she wouldn't meet his gaze, he let one finger slide along her jaw, tipping her head gently until she looked up him. "Were you frightened by that? Disgusted by it?" She should be both. She should tell him she couldn't bear to look at him, that she was afraid of him. "Do you think I would hurt you? That I hurt Lady Beaumont?"

Her warm breath drifted over his face as she let out a little sigh. "Why do you want to know? What difference can it possibly make now?"

All the difference in the world, or no difference at all. Finn didn't know which, he only knew he had to *know*. "It makes a difference to me."

She did look at him now, her eyes a darker blue than he'd ever seen them. "No. I don't believe you'd ever hurt a lady, Lord Huntington. I never would believe it. But you don't care for me. Not in *that* way. Lady Beaumont was right about one thing. It's a mistake for you to marry a lady who won't be able to satisfy you. A mistake for you, and for the lady in question."

Finn caught his breath. "You think I don't want you?"

Wasn't it true? It had been, at one time, yes, but now…he was still touching her face, and her soft, warm skin under his fingertips dulled each of his other senses, and made everything else in the room fade away.

"If you did, Lord Huntington, you would have kissed me in the garden that day, without ever considering whether it was proper or not."

His gaze drifted over her face, narrowing on the telltale flush on her cheekbones. He wanted to tell her the truth about why he hadn't kissed her that day, but what if it became garbled somewhere between his brain and his mouth, and he said it wrong? What if he tried to describe the panic he'd felt when he'd found her in the garden in her torn gown, with Wrexley looming over her, and made a mess of it?

But he looked into her face, at the proud jut of her chin, and the next thing he knew, he was speaking. "Propriety had nothing to do with it." He traced a finger over her jaw, his voice soft. "I didn't kiss you because I knew Lady Beaumont was there, just on the other side of the hedge, listening, and I…I couldn't let her hear that."

Surprise flitted over her features, and then, for the first time since he'd entered her bedchamber, her face softened.

"If I had kissed you that day, would we still be betrothed? Would you really jilt a marquess over a single kiss? Because even if I kept dozens of mistresses and wagered on every lady in London, not a single one of them would jilt me for it."

She shrugged, but her throat moved in a nervous swallow. "Any one of those things is sufficient reason to jilt someone, isn't it?"

As far as society was concerned, wagering and debauchery didn't disqualify a man either as a gentleman or a husband, especially if that man also happened to be a marquess. "I don't care if it's a sufficient reason. I only care if it's *your* reason."

Her eyes searched his, making his breath stop in his chest, but then she pulled back. Not far, but far enough to let him know he'd gotten too close. "No. I jilted you, Lord Huntington, because I can't...I don't want to be a marchioness."

Finn stared at her, once again shocked into silence. She didn't want to be a marchioness? It was the last thing he'd expected her to say. His preference for Lady Honora, his mistress, his shocking preoccupation with silk scarves and blindfolds—she could have given any number of reasons to justify jilting him he would have no choice but to accept, but *that?*

"Doesn't every lady want to be a marchioness?"

She let out a heavy sigh. "No, they don't. But even if I did aspire to the title, I wouldn't...I don't want to be *your* marchioness. I won't be—that is, I don't think I can do justice to it, or to you."

Finn continued to stare at her, amazed. She was beautiful, accomplished, clever—a diamond of the first water. Why should she think she wouldn't make a worthy marchioness? "I don't understand. I chose you because I believe you'd bring honor to the title."

"No. That isn't why you chose me. I heard you say it yourself, Lord Huntington. You chose me because you want a lady with no inconvenient passions, no troublesome temper, and no surprises hidden under the surface. At one time I thought I could be that lady, but now...well, that's not me, and it never can be. I can't be the perfect marchioness, and I'll only make us both miserable if I try."

"What kind of lady are you?" It wasn't what he'd meant to ask, and even as the words left his mouth a part of Finn hoped she wouldn't answer. She wasn't *his*—not yet, and right now, that was the only answer that mattered.

"The kind that doesn't become a marchioness. If we marry, you'll regret me as your choice, Lord Huntington. Not today, perhaps, but someday."

Finn didn't argue, because he couldn't deny it was true. He wanted someone predictable, steady, who'd behave with propriety like a marchioness should, a lady who'd never surprise him, and never challenge him. That was why he'd chosen Miss Somerset in the first place. Because she was naïve, docile, predictable—

Except she wasn't, and she never had been. She was intelligent and complex, intriguing and spontaneous, and in Finn's eyes, it made her a less suitable choice for a wife, not more so.

They stood there in the middle of the room for a long, silent moment after that, until Finn roused himself, and cleared his throat. "These ladies who don't become marchionesses, Miss Somerset. What do they become?"

But he already knew the answer. The *ton* wasn't kind to young ladies who flouted the rules. Waywardness led to gossip, and gossip led to ruined reputations.

She shrugged, but the gesture looked forced. "Spinsters, I suppose."

A strange feeling coursed through Finn then, something more hopeless than anger, or even regret, because whether she ended up a spinster or the wife of a man who didn't care for her, it would be less than she deserved.

But she'd have him, because she had no other choice, and neither did he. "A spinster, ridiculed and sneered at by the *ton*. Such a sad fate, for a lady who could be a marchioness."

A smile drifted over her lips, but it was a sad one. "I'm willing to take that risk."

Finn turned away from her, but when he reached the door to her bedchamber, he looked back, and his gaze caught and held hers. "I'm not."

Chapter Eight

"There's something shocking going on, and I demand to know what it is at once."

Lady Annabel stepped from the breakfast-room onto the back terrace and gave Charlotte and Julian, who were seated at the table, an expectant look.

"What is it this time?" Charlotte was pouring more tea, and Julian was turning over the pages of *The Times*. Neither of them bothered to look up.

"Whatever do you mean, *this time?*" Lady Annabel dropped into a chair and held her teacup out to Charlotte. "This is the first interesting thing I've seen since I arrived in Hampshire. Goodness, the country is dull."

Charlotte raised an eyebrow at her. "You only arrived yesterday, Annabel."

Julian peered over the edge of his paper, his lips quirking into a grin. "Shocking events seem to sprout from the ground at your feet, Lady Tallant, so I can't say I'm surprised to find you've already stumbled across one. Go on, then. What is it? Did you see the butler kiss the housekeeper?"

Lady Annabel's eyes widened hopefully. "No, indeed, but if they're having a scandalous liaison, I'll be sure to watch more closely."

"Not so much a liaison as a marriage. Ten years now, I believe." Julian gave Lady Annabel a teasing smile.

Lady Annabel rolled her eyes. "No talk of marriage if you please, Captain West. The only thing duller than a happy marriage is a country house party, and I refuse to suffer both at once. But back to this shocking development I've witnessed. Aren't either of you the least bit curious to know what it is?"

"No." Julian straightened his newspaper with a brisk snap, then retreated behind it.

"Go on, then. I'll hear it." Charlotte waved a desultory hand at Annabel, clearly more tolerant than she was interested.

Lady Annabel nodded toward the wide lawn just off the terrace, then leaned toward Charlotte and lowered her voice. "They're all out there together, playing at *bowls*." She whispered the last word as if it were too scandalous to speak aloud.

"That *is* scandalous." Julian lowered a corner of his newspaper and squinted at the group assembled on the lawn. Violet was speaking to Lord Derrick, who was standing near the green, balancing a bowl in his hand as he waited his turn. Lady Honora was wandering at the edge of the garden with Lord Huntington, her arm in his, and Iris was laughing at Lord Wrexley, who was engaged in all manner of wild antics, tossing his bowls in every direction, and falling into melodramatic fits of despair when they invariably flew wide of the jack.

"Lovely day for bowls," Julian said. "Pity we'll have to put a stop to it, but we can't let them carry on like that right on our back lawn, Charlotte. The servants will gossip."

Charlotte watched her guests for a moment, then turned back to Annabel with a puzzled expression. "Is that all?"

"Well, it looks perfectly innocent at first glance, but there's something strange—"

"Why, it's indecent!" Charlotte interrupted with a gasp. She patted her fingertips against her chest in feigned shock. "My goodness, Annabel. The next thing I know you'll be telling me they're all taking tea together in the drawing room."

Lady Annabel frowned at Julian, who was chuckling from behind his paper. "This is Hampshire, Charlotte, not London. I'd be delighted to offer a more salacious scandal, but I'm afraid this is the best I can do. But I assure you, it's the most suspicious game of bowls I've ever seen. I tell you, something odd is going on."

Charlotte shrugged. "I don't see what. It all looks ordinary enough."

Annabel tossed her head. "Fine. If you insist, Charlotte. I just find it curious Lord Huntington should be sneaking about the hedges with Lady Honora, when he's meant to be betrothed to Miss Somerset."

Julian folded his paper with a sigh, and tossed it onto the table in front of him. "Miss Somerset is engaged with Lord Wrexley at the moment."

"At *every* moment, Captain West."

The three of them watched in silence as Lady Honora and Lord Huntington disappeared into the garden together. Iris didn't spare them a glance, but carried on with her game with Lord Wrexley, who made no secret of his admiration for her, or his satisfaction at having her full attention.

"Lord Wrexley has been flirting with Miss Somerset all morning, and there goes Lord Huntington on a private jaunt with Lady Honora, and neither of you find that the least bit odd? Because it seems to me as though more than one party has misplaced their betrothed."

"Now you point it out, it does look a little strange." Julian's eyes narrowed as Lord Wrexley slid his palm under Iris's elbow.

"I'm sure it's nothing," Charlotte began, but then her brow furrowed. "Though I'll grant you Lord Huntington and Iris don't behave as if they're betrothed. I don't think I've seen them exchange more than five words since they arrived, and there's something...not quite comfortable between them."

Lady Annabel snorted. "No, indeed. They act as if each believes the other has the pox."

"Annabel! Hush, will you?"

"Well, it's the truth, Charlotte. I've seen barnyard cats who are friendlier than those two. What do you suppose is the matter? Perhaps Huntington has jilted her now Lady Honora is free of that odious Lord Harley. Dear God, what a scandal that would be. Did Lady Chase say anything about it?"

"Not a word, except Iris had been suffering from low spirits ever since Lord Huntington came up to scratch. She suggested the house party, thinking it would soothe Iris's nerves if she became better acquainted with Lord Huntington before they wed. Lady Chase is anxious to see the business finished without any difficulties."

"Yes, well, it looks as if it might be finished, indeed."

"Oh, dear." Charlotte gave her husband an anxious look. "Julian, do you suppose there's anything we can—"

"Miss Violet! A word, if you please?" Lady Annabel called, rising to her feet and beckoning to Violet. "There's how you'll get your answer. Whatever the trouble is, you may be sure Miss Somerset confided it to her sister."

A few moments later, Violet mounted the shallow steps to the terrace, and greeted them all with a smile. "Good morning. How may I help, Lady Tallant? Perhaps you'd like to join us for a game of..." She trailed off as she noticed three curious pairs of eyes fixed on her. "What is it? Why are you all staring at me?"

"Oh, it's nothing at all, really. Do have a seat, dear." Charlotte waved Violet into a chair, and passed her a cup of tea. "It's just we were wondering—"

"Whatever is going on between Lord Huntington and your sister?" Lady Annabel interrupted. "Has he jilted her?"

Violet's head jerked toward Lady Annabel, the becoming pink color draining from her cheeks.

"If Huntington's jilted her, then he has no business being at Hadley House." Julian rose from his seat. "I'll have an explanation from him this very minute—"

"No, Captain West!" Violet held out a hand to stop him. "It's not...Lord Huntington didn't—"

"I'm telling you, he's jilted her."

"Annabel!" Charlotte gave Lady Annabel a warning look, then reached out to touch Violet's hand, her voice softening. "Violet, dear, we're meant to be their chaperones during the house party. If something's changed between them, you must tell us at once."

Violet bit her lip as her gaze moved between them. "Oh, dear. I don't like to tell Iris's secrets, but I suppose you'll have to know sooner or later. It's rather drastic, I'm afraid."

"How drastic? As drastic as being jilted by London's most sought-after marquess mere weeks before your wedding? As drastic as that?"

Violet shook her head. "Lord Huntington didn't jilt Iris, Lady Tallant, though in the end the result is the same. *She* jilted *him*."

There was a dumbfounded silence as they all looked around the table, as if each of them expected the others to offer some explanation for this shocking development.

Lady Annabel was the first to recover. "You mean to say after weeks of courtship, the Marquess of Huntington—a *marquess*, mind you—made Miss Somerset an offer of marriage, she accepted him, and now she's jilted him? But *why?*"

Violet gave a helpless shrug. "I don't know. Iris refused to say."

"Violet," Julian began. "If you know more than what you're saying—"

"Truly, Captain West, I only know what I've told you. Iris hasn't ever kept secrets from me before, but the rift with Lord Huntington happened a week ago, and she only told Lady Honora and me yesterday, in the carriage. She wouldn't say anything other than she jilted him."

"Oh, dear." Charlotte wrung her hands. "She's encouraged his suit for weeks, and agreed to the match! What would make her jilt him now, and with no explanation?"

"I wish I could tell you, but Iris said only Lord Huntington didn't care for her, and she's jilted him. She wouldn't say anything more."

"She jilted a marquess because *he didn't care for her?*" Lady Annabel's voice was incredulous. "Oh, you can be sure there's more to it than that. No lady refuses the chance to become a marchioness on such a flimsy excuse."

"Yes, I think that's true of most young ladies, but then Iris has never been much like most young ladies." Violet paused, considering this, then added, "At least, she never was before we came to London."

Charlotte exchanged a look with Lady Annabel. "What do you mean?"

"The shock of our parents' deaths, then the move to London a year later...well, it wasn't easy for any of us, but it was particularly difficult for Iris. She became a celebrated belle almost overnight, with all of London scrutinizing her every move, and, well...there are so many rules for unmarried young ladies, aren't there? She's been so terrified she'd make a misstep and disappoint our grandmother, I think she's quite lost herself."

Charlotte made a sympathetic noise, but then raised a hand to her forehead as if to hold off a sudden headache. "But Lady Chase must not know Iris has jilted Lord Huntington, or she never would have suggested I invite him to Hadley House."

"No, Iris hasn't told her. I don't excuse Iris—it's very wrong of her to keep it secret—but as much as our grandmother loves us, she can be a rather stern taskmistress." Violet shook her head. "She'll go mad when she finds out."

There was another silence, then Lady Annabel sighed. "Jilting a marquess with no explanation? This will end badly for Miss Somerset, I'm afraid."

"Iris told us yesterday she plans to encourage Lord Wrexley."

"Lord Wrexley?" Lady Annabel asked, her tone sharp.

Violet glanced at her, her brow furrowing when she noticed Lady Annabel's sudden frown. "Yes. It will help smooth things over with our grandmother if she has another suitor to replace Lord Huntington, and Lord Wrexley admires Iris."

A tense silence fell over the table, then Charlotte forced a smile and laid her hand over Violet's. "Thank you for telling us the truth. You may return to your game now. It looks like Lord Derrick is waiting for you."

Once Violet had gone, Charlotte turned to her husband with a groan. "Goodness, what a muddle. Iris has broken with Lord Huntington, and now Lord Huntington looks as if he's chasing Lady Honora, and Lord Wrexley is chasing Iris, and she's encouraging him!"

"Yes, it looks as if she is, doesn't it?" Lady Annabel was watching Iris and Lord Wrexley, a frown still marring her brow.

Charlotte exchanged a look with Julian. "You look as if you don't approve of Lord Wrexley, Annabel."

Lady Annabel jerked her gaze back to Charlotte. "Nonsense. I never met him before yesterday. Miss Somerset's best chance now is to make another match. Lord Wrexley isn't a marquess, of course, but in such desperate circumstances, an earl will have to do."

"I only hope Lord Wrexley will do for Lady Chase," Charlotte muttered. "She was so delighted Iris was to become a marchioness."

"Well, I daresay two countesses are nearly equal to one marchioness." Lady Annabel nodded at Violet. She'd accepted Lord Derrick's arm, and the two of them were walking toward a folly at the far side of the garden. "There's something afoot with those two, as well."

"What?" Julian gazed after Violet with a look of dawning panic. "Don't tell me Lord Derrick is enamored of Violet?"

"Oh, no. Not to worry, Captain West. He isn't."

Julian blew out a relieved breath. "Good, because two complicated love affairs is more than enough for one house party—"

"I said *he's* not enamored of *her*, Captain West." Lady Annabel took a calm sip of her tea. "I didn't say *she's* not enamored of *him*."

Julian stared at her with horror, then covered his eyes with his hand. "Bloody hell."

Charlotte groaned again. "It's like a game of blind man's bluff, with all the players bumping into each other."

"Or a game of chess." Lady Annabel's gaze drifted back toward Iris and Lord Wrexley. "Perhaps this house party won't be as dull as I feared, after all."

* * * *

"You bounder!" Lord Wrexley exclaimed as his ball once again flew wide of the jack. "Why won't you do as you're bid?"

Iris watched as the ball spun off the edge of the green. "You're throwing it too hard, my lord."

"It's not my throw, I assure you. It's the jack. It keeps moving, and I've no idea how, because I haven't yet tossed a ball that's gotten anywhere near it."

"I noticed that, Wrexley. I don't think this is your game. Perhaps you should leave the green before you hurt someone."

Lord Huntington's tone was unforgivably rude, but if Lord Wrexley were irritated, he hid it under a lazy smile. "I think I'll have another go, if you don't mind, Huntington. Here, Miss Somerset—is this how you hold the ball?"

Iris moved closer to study his grip, then shook her head. "I believe you're holding it too tightly, my lord. Mind the curve, as well. It controls your direction. Do you feel the curve, just here?" She took his other hand and placed it on the ball.

"Indeed I do. Is my palm meant to cradle the curve?"

"No. The ball should rest on your fingertips, like this." She slid the ball forward in his hand, then moved his fingers into the proper place. "Haven't you ever played bowls before, Lord Wrexley?"

Iris glanced up at him, but he wasn't looking at her. He was staring over her head at Lord Huntington, an odd smile twisting his lips. Something about that smile made gooseflesh rise on Iris's neck, but in the next instant his usual charming smile was back, and she was left wondering if she'd imagined the other one.

"It's been a long time since I played. I've forgotten some of it, but at one time I was quite good at it. Unbeatable, even."

"Oh, well, then you don't need my help."

"Men who believe they're unbeatable invariably lose, Wrexley."

Iris frowned at Lord Huntington, then turned back to Lord Wrexley and gave him a half-hearted smile. He'd been trying to divert her with a constant stream of nonsense since their game began, and he was great fun, but as much as she wanted to encourage his light flirtation, she couldn't.

It was all Lord Huntington's fault, of course.

He'd been glowering at her all morning, his fierce brows lowered over his hazel eyes in a way that could only be described as menacing. It was like playing bowls with a half-rabid guard dog threatening to pounce at any moment. At one point, when Lord Wrexley touched her hand, Iris would have sworn she heard Lord Huntington growl.

This wasn't the grand marquess who'd so coldly dismissed her that day in Lady Fairchild's garden. This was the man who'd burst into her bedchamber yesterday and demanded she marry him—the man whose cool hazel eyes had gone a dark, mossy green when he caressed her jaw.

Iris didn't recognize *this* Lord Huntington, and she didn't know what to make of him.

"Will you take me for a turn in the gardens, my lord?" Lady Honora took Lord Huntington's arm. "They're rather like a vast maze, aren't they? I'm afraid I'll get lost if I go alone, with all those twisting pathways."

Lord Huntington's gaze narrowed on Lord Wrexley for a heartbeat, as if in warning, but when he glanced down at Honora, his face softened. "Yes, of course. I'd be delighted to escort you for a short walk, Lady Honora."

Iris watched from the corner of her eye as they strolled toward the garden, stifling the overwhelming urge to hurl her ball at Lord Huntington's broad back. He hadn't wasted any time taking her advice about Lady Honora, had he?

Well, it was nothing to her. She just hadn't imagined he'd fling himself headlong into a new courtship when just yesterday he'd burst into *her* bedchamber and demanded *she* marry him.

But he'd already ruined her morning, and she refused to spend her afternoon wondering what he and Honora would get up to in the gardens. Not that she cared one bit what Lord Huntington did, but he'd made rather a muck of his stroll in the garden with *her*. Perhaps he meant to do better this time.

And if he didn't intend to kiss Honora in the garden, then why should he look so eager? No one wanted a walk that badly.

Honora's arm was tucked securely into his and she was looking up at him, her dark eyes alight, a sweet smile gracing her lips. He was speaking to her in low tones, a smile hovering at the corners of his mouth as he gazed down at her. Whatever he was saying, Honora seemed to find it fascinating. She seemed to find *him* fascinating.

Honora, and every other lady in London.

Every other lady, that is, but Iris.

He never smiled at me like that.

No, he hadn't, and she'd jilted him for it. It was done, and now Lord Huntington might court whoever he wished. After all, Iris had meant every word she'd said about Honora making a splendid marchioness. Indeed, it was as if she'd been born to the role, and if Lord Huntington was satisfied with treating young ladies as if they were interchangeable, that was all very well.

Iris didn't have a word to say about it. Not one word.

But if she did have a word, that word would be—

"...Offensive. I beg your pardon, Miss Somerset, for my foul temper. I'm ashamed of my poor sportsmanship." A warm hand cupped her elbow, and she looked up to find Lord Wrexley grinning down at her, not looking ashamed in the least.

He really had the most charming grin. Oh, perhaps it wasn't as mesmerizing as Lord Huntington's slow curve of the lips, but if it didn't quite steal her breath away, at least Lord Wrexley didn't hoard his smiles, as if giving one away would leave him with one fewer, instead of earning him one in return.

"Oh, I don't blame you, my lord. It's the game, I think. It tries one's patience, doesn't it?"

He sighed, and let the ball in his hand fall to the ground with a dull thud. "I haven't played bowls in ages, but I don't recall ever finding it so tedious before. Has it always been?"

Iris, who preferred much more energetic exercise to the sedate games deemed appropriate for ladies, let out an answering sigh. "I believe so, yes. We could play at shuttlecock, if you like, but it's just as dull."

"No, let's not. I'm frightened of shuttlecocks."

A laugh bubbled up in Iris's throat. "No, you're not. What nonsense, my lord."

"No, indeed. One flew right into my face when I was a boy, and the feathery end poked me in the eye. Nearly blinded me. I stay far away from the wretched things. What about you, Miss Somerset? No devastating shuttlecock injuries in your past?"

"No, but we didn't play shuttlecock much when I was a child. Bowls, either. My father was an avid sportsman, you see. If he'd had a son, perhaps my sisters and I would have had to content ourselves with lawn games, but as it was, we were forever dirtying our frocks with climbing trees and running races, or charging about the countryside on horseback."

Iris's throat swelled a little. She tried not to think about those carefree days now. She couldn't recall the last time she'd flown across the countryside on horseback, her eyes streaming from the wind and every pin scattering until her hair flew out behind her. It felt like another lifetime.

"The elegant Miss Somerset, in a dirty frock? How scandalous. I wish I'd seen it."

His pale blue eyes gleamed as he smiled down at her, and warmth flooded Iris's cheeks. "Oh, well." She gave him a shy glance. "Perhaps we should run a race, then."

She'd spoken in jest, but Lord Wrexley seized on the idea at once. "Yes, of course! That's just what we should do."

"But I can't. This gown..." Iris glanced down at her dainty, pin-tucked muslin gown.

Pink, of course. They were all pink.

"It's a pretty gown." Lord Wrexley's gaze drifted over her figure. "But if you tear it, you have others, don't you?"

"Yes." She did, dozens of others—a veritable regiment of dainty pink gowns. All at once Iris had a sudden, savage urge to rip into every sweet pink fold of this one, until she'd torn a gaping hole into each of the tiny gatherings.

"Well, then?" Lord Wrexley's lips curved in a most tempting smile. "Shall we race?"

"It's not proper." She glanced over at the terrace. Several ladies had come to call, and Charlotte had taken them out to the terrace for refreshments. "Lady Hadley's guests, and Lord Derrick, and Lord Huntington…"

"Lord Derrick never gossips. It's one of his most irritating qualities, I assure you, and Lord Huntington will never know. He's disappeared with Honora, and she told me you've jilted him in any case, so what does it matter what he thinks?"

Iris's mouth fell open. "She told you I jilted Lord Huntington?" For pity's sake, Honora hadn't wasted any time with that bit of gossip, had she?

"Of course she did. She tells me everything. Wise decision, Miss Somerset, to jilt Huntington. Who wants to marry a dry stick like him?" He didn't give her a chance to reply. "As for Lady Hadley's guests, we'll go around to the other side of the house. No one will see us there."

Iris bit her lip. She had no business tearing about the lawn like a wild hellion and scandalizing Charlotte's guests, but she was the one who'd suggested a race, and Lord Wrexley seemed quite keen on the idea. She didn't wish to offend him by refusing, and it was just a little race, after all. No one would see them on the other side of the house. What was the harm in it?

And it wasn't as if she'd got anywhere doing what she was told. She'd worn the gowns and danced the quadrilles and practiced the pianoforte until her fingers bled. She'd followed the rules, but no one had ever bothered to explain she was just as likely to be punished as rewarded for her efforts.

Well, she'd had her punishment. Didn't she deserve a reward?

Lord Wrexley leaned closer to whisper in her ear. "That only leaves me, and I swear I won't breathe a word of it."

He was a devil, whispering in her ear, tempting her with a moment of freedom.

"Come, Miss Somerset. Don't you want to run?"

Oh, I do. I do want to run.

Chapter Nine

Miss Somerset had been wrong to try and kiss him in Lady Fairchild's garden. She'd been wrong to eavesdrop on his argument with Lady Beaumont, wrong to let Lord Wrexley escort her to Hampshire, and certainly wrong to devote all her attention to the scoundrel this morning.

Finn's jaw tightened. She'd been wrong to jilt him.

Twice.

In short, she'd been wrong about everything, with one notable exception. She'd been right about her friend. Lady Honora *would* make an ideal marchioness.

"How does your horse do, Lord Huntington?"

"My horse?" Finn groped blindly for the last two minutes of their conversation, but aside from a stubborn image of blue eyes that insisted on lingering in his head, his mind was a blank. Had they been talking about his horse?

She gave him a sunny smile. "Oh, I'm sure it's nothing, but you mentioned yesterday he'd been favoring a leg on your journey to Hampshire."

Yes, he had said that, hadn't he? Right before he burst into Miss Somerset's bedchamber and caught her at her wash basin, with damp tendrils of fair hair curling about her flushed cheeks, and silvery droplets of water clinging to her skin.

"Is he quite all right, then?"

Finn dragged his attention back to Lady Honora. "He is. It was just a loose shoe. You're kind to enquire, my lady."

She was always kind, to everyone. It was her distinguishing characteristic, and it was true kindness, not the affectation of it so common among ladies of the *ton*. One had only to look at her to see it, for every line in her face bespoke sincerity.

She was everything he wanted in his marchioness, and by some miracle every obstacle preventing a betrothal between them had vanished. If he wanted to initiate a courtship, this was the moment to do it. They were alone in a garden, the sun bright over their heads. Her sweet brown eyes were fixed on him with a look of admiration that could be tipped over into adoration with only a modest effort on his part, and he...

He was fantasizing about drops of water clinging to the neck of a lady who'd jilted him.

Twice.

"I'm relieved to hear it. Do you intend to ride much while you're here? I haven't ridden anywhere but on the promenade for ages now, and I confess riding in Hampshire quite intimidates me."

"I'd be pleased to escort you." He smiled down at her. He'd always favored brown eyes, and Lady Honora's eyes were just the right shade of brown, that is, not too dark or too light, too lively or too dim, and without that troublesome spark hidden in their dark blue depths.

No, not blue, damn it. Brown. Lady Honora's eyes were *brown*.

Every other gentleman in London might turn poet over Miss Somerset's sparkling blue eyes if they wished, but he wasn't moved by them. Now he thought of it, the placid expression in Lady Honora's eyes had been the reason he'd chosen her over Miss Somerset from the start. Something about that blue spark made him uneasy. One never knew what mayhem a spark might lead to. Burns. Conflagrations. The fire that burned half of bloody London to ashes had started with a single spark, for God's sake.

Sparks weren't to be trusted.

"My goodness, the Hadley House gardens are large, aren't they, my lord? Confusing, as well. I vow we've been walking in circles this past half hour."

Despite his admiration for her, Finn found himself leaping at the chance to rid himself of Lady Honora's company. "May I escort you back to the house? I don't want to exhaust you on the first day of the party."

"Yes, of course. Whatever you think is best."

Finn was guiding her around the circular pathway and hurrying her back toward the house before the words had even left her lips.

Miss Somerset had made it clear she couldn't distinguish an honorable suitor from a rogue, and someone had to keep an eye on Wrexley. Or perhaps it made more sense to keep an eye on Miss Somerset. An extremely close eye—

"Oh, my goodness. I don't think that's quite..."

They'd just emerged from the garden, and Lady Honora had come to an abrupt halt with a little cry of dismay. She was staring at the wide expanse of lawn on the south side of Hadley House. "Oh, dear. I daresay this was my cousin's idea."

Finn followed her gaze, expecting to see Wrexley and Miss Somerset still at bowls, but what he saw instead made him freeze.

Miss Somerset was dashing across the lawn, heavy handfuls of her skirts clutched in her fists to free her legs, her feet bare. Half of her fair hair had slipped from its pins and was tumbling down her back. Even from this distance Finn could hear her shrieks of breathless laughter as she ran toward Wrexley, who was standing at the other end, leaping in the air, cheering her on, and making a great deal of noise. When she drew closer, he held out his arms to catch her, and she flew into them with one last gleeful cry.

Lady Honora made a distressed sound in her throat. "Oh, dear. My cousin can be...he means no harm, Lord Huntington, but sometimes he forgets propriety."

Finn's lips pressed into a hard line. Wrexley hadn't forgotten a damn thing. Miss Somerset might be hidden from the ladies assembled on the terrace, but anyone who happened to be walking the grounds or in the garden could see her easily enough, and it was no bloody accident. If Lady Hadley's guests were shocked by Miss Somerset, it was because Wrexley meant for them to be.

"Shall we go see what they're about?" Finn took care to keep his voice even, but behind his lips his teeth were clenched.

Lady Honora murmured her assent. Finn escorted her across the lawn, but he hardly spared her a thought. His attention remained fixed on Wrexley, who'd released Miss Somerset as soon as he'd steadied her on her feet. Damn good thing, too, as it might be the only thing that kept Finn from dragging the man back to London by his neck.

But Wrexley still stood far too close to her, and as Finn and Lady Honora came up behind them, Finn could hear him speaking to Miss Somerset in a wheedling tone. "Oh, go on, one more race, and I'll run against you this time. I'll even give you a start on me."

"You insult me, my lord, if you think I need a start to beat you." Miss Somerset attempted to speak in a stern tone, but she was laughing, and it came out flirtatiously, as if she were teasing him. "Anyway, I'm not worried about losing. I'm worried about someone seeing us. I must look a fright."

"Not at all. Just the opposite, I assure you. I've never seen you look as fetching as you do right now." Wrexley's voice dropped to a husky murmur. "Besides, who's to see us? There's no one about—"

"Look again, Wrexley. *I'm* about. I hate to interrupt your game, but you and Miss Somerset have run your last race for today. Or any other day."

"Oh, Honora, and…Lord Huntington." Miss Somerset's eyes went wide when she saw him. She touched a hand to her hair, her eyes sliding closed when she discovered it had come almost entirely loose. She tried to tuck the long curls back into the pins, but she soon realized it was beyond repair and gave up, biting her lip with mortification.

Wrexley, however, didn't look in the least concerned. "Good afternoon, cousin. Huntington. Where did you two disappear to? You've been gone for ages."

"We haven't been gone above half an hour." Finn's jaw ticked as he slid his gaze from Wrexley to Miss Somerset and back again. "Twenty-five minutes too long, from the look of things here."

Wrexley shrugged. "Pity you missed the races. It was grand fun, and I would have been delighted to offer you a start as well, Huntington. I'd wager it's the only way you'd catch me."

"On the contrary." Finn stepped closer, close enough so he loomed over the other man. "I've caught you already."

Both men fell silent, staring at each other, the tension between them growing thicker with every moment as each of them refused to look away.

"I'm fatigued, cousin," Lady Honora said at last, her voice unnaturally high. "Escort me inside, won't you?" When Wrexley didn't reply but continued to stare at Finn, Lady Honora grasped his arm and gave it a tug. "Now, if you please, cousin."

A beat of silence passed, and then another, but at last Wrexley broke the stare with Finn, and glanced down at Lady Honora. "Of course, Honora. As for you, Miss Somerset," he turned to her, took her hand, and raised it to his lips. "I can't recall ever spending a more enjoyable afternoon. We'll have to race again. Soon."

Wrexley shot one last parting smirk at Finn, then led Honora across the lawn, onto the terrace, and into the house.

"I, ah…well, I suppose I'll go make myself presentable before tea." Miss Somerset began to sidle toward the house, but before she could take two steps, Finn's hand closed around her arm. He didn't say a word, but he drew her aside, into the shade at the side of the house, where they were hidden from anyone who happened to be strolling in the garden.

"Keep still, if you please, Miss Somerset. This will only take a moment."
He held her arm and swept his gaze over her, from the bare feet he knew
she hid under her skirts to the top of her head, where her hair fell in wild
disarray over her shoulders. "Let me see. No slippers, skirts hiked to your
knees, cheeks flushed, and hair loose from its pins, hanging in a tangled
mess down your back. Have I missed anything?"

He almost laughed when her chin shot up. That hadn't taken long.

"Yes. I've also ripped the hem of my gown."

"Of course you have. Anything else?"

"Are you making a list, my lord? Very well, then. If you must know, I
believe I've bent my stays."

Finn's gaze snapped to her bodice, and once it was there, it took all his
concentration to tear it away. He cleared his throat. "Races are one way
to spend an afternoon, I suppose."

"Yes, and rather an enjoyable one, as it turns out. Bowls grow dull after
a while, but one can't say the same of racing."

"One can't say the same of Lord Wrexley, either. He's rather exciting
from beginning to end, isn't he?"

She shrugged. "He's great fun, yes."

Some of the tension in Finn's jaw eased. A lady didn't refer to a gentleman
she was enamored with as "great fun." Miss Somerset wasn't in love with
Lord Wrexley. Not yet, at least. As long as she remained indifferent to him
she was in less danger, but Wrexley's charm was insidious. He'd turned
more than one young lady's head, with disastrous results. By the time Miss
Somerset realized he was manipulating her, it would be too late.

"But you knew it wasn't a proper activity—no, don't bother to deny it,
Miss Somerset. I can see by your blush you did know it."

To Finn's surprise, a grin drifted over her lips. "Yes, I knew it, but
proper things are never great fun, are they? When was the last time you
ran a race, Lord Huntington? I daresay a bit of impropriety would do you
a world of good."

He frowned, taken aback by the question. "I don't recall." Had he ever
run a race? Surely he must have, when he was much younger, but if he
had, he didn't remember it. "I'm not sure I ever have."

"You've never run a race? *Ever*?" She stared at him for a moment, as if
she didn't know what to make of him, then she reached out her hand and
rested it on his arm in an almost comforting gesture. "That's not...well,
perhaps marquesses don't run races."

"Some do, I think. Just not me." Finn shrugged, but every nerve in his body strained toward the place where she touched him, his gaze fixed on her slender white fingers curled into his coat.

"You still could, you know." She swept her hand from his head to his boots. "You'd have to remove your coat, and loosen your cravat. Not quite the thing for such a proper gentleman, I suppose."

Finn blinked at her, puzzled. Was she teasing him? No one *ever* teased him. "Or a proper lady."

"Come now, my lord. It's not as if I raced down Rotten Row during the fashionable hour. This is a house party in the country, not Hyde Park. The *ton* will never know I ran across a bowling green, or that Lord Wrexley saw my ankles. My reputation isn't in danger here."

"You're wrong." As clever as she was, she was also as naïve as every other young lady of her limited experience, and Wrexley knew it well. "Don't think for a moment because Lord Wrexley encouraged you to race he'll hesitate to gossip to the *ton* about it."

She shrugged off the warning. "I don't believe he would, but even if he did, what's he to tell them? That I took off my slippers, and tore my hems? It seems a paltry thing to gossip about."

"Slippers, yes, but what if he gossiped about how you ran to him?" Finn's frown deepened to a scowl as he thought of the way she'd leapt into Wrexley's arms.

"He wouldn't do such a thing."

"Yes, he would, Miss Somerset. If he thought he could gain something by it, he'd do it without a second thought. He intentionally led you into an impropriety today because he believes he has something to gain from it. He has designs on you, and he wants you vulnerable."

"Designs on me?" She let out a short laugh. "That sounds quite ominous. I know you and Lord Wrexley don't care much for each other, Lord Huntington, but he's not the rake you make him out to be, any more than you're the perfect gentleman you pretend to be."

Finn's breath left his lungs in a painful rush. It was true, and yet her words wounded him far more than he would have thought possible. "You're referring to the wager?"

"Yes. It was a dishonorable thing to do. I hope you're not going to try and persuade me otherwise."

"No. It was despicable, and I regret it extremely." He paused, then said, "Do you suppose Lord Wrexley regrets it, as well?"

She stared at him, her eyes going wide as his meaning sank in. "Lord Wrexley? He—"

"He was there that night. He wagered on you, but he lost you to me. He tried to persuade me to wager for you a second time, but I declined him. If the wager is sufficient reason for you to jilt me, then it's sufficient reason for you to discourage Lord Wrexley."

"I—the wager wasn't the only reason I jilted you."

She was fighting to hold onto her composure, but Finn could see he'd shaken her, and he ran a rough hand through his hair. If he had even a drop of Wrexley's charm he'd know how to speak softly to her, to persuade her, but he'd never known how to shatter the hard, impenetrable shell that separated him from other people, and he didn't know now. He only knew it couldn't be done in one conversation.

Perhaps not even in one lifetime.

But he tried. He drew in a deep breath and spoke as gently as he could. "When I left to walk in the garden, you and Lord Wrexley were playing bowls. How did you end up running races with him?"

"He asked what my sisters and I used to play when we were children. When I told him we used to run races, he suggested we do that."

So clever of Wrexley, to discover what she wanted most, and then cajole her into taking it, regardless of the consequences.

"We used to run races at home, in Surrey," she added, a dreamy smile drifting across her lips. "My father, my sisters—even my mother, on occasion. We never thought about whether or not it was proper, only if it was good fun. It always was."

A strange, tight sensation gripped Finn's chest as he watched the smile flirting at the corners of her lips. There was so much joy in that smile it made his heart quicken until he felt dizzy with it.

What must it have been like, to run races with your family? To look back on your memories with joy? To recall moments of perfect happiness when you closed your eyes, instead of a lonely childhood, where one day unfolded after another, all of them the same, except each one was longer and emptier than the last?

What would it feel like, if she smiled like that for me?

She never had, because he would have noticed it. He would have noticed *her*.

Finn swallowed as his gaze moved over her face. Her cheeks were still pink from the exercise, and the fair hair escaping her pins fell in a long, heavy cascade of golden waves around her face and shoulders. Was it as soft as it looked? If he reached out and captured a lock of it, would it feel like strands of heavy silk between his fingers? If he brushed his fingertip against the corner of her mouth, would that dreamy smile disappear, or would it deepen? Could he catch it in his hand, and make it his?

"Keep still, Miss Somerset."

Her lips parted on a tiny gasp when he reached for her, the sound so quiet he felt it more than heard it, but she didn't jerk away from him, and his fingers closed around a hairpin still tangled in one of her curls. He slid it loose gently, and then, because he couldn't stop himself, he lingered, coaxing the silky strands of her hair to fall between his fingers.

He'd touched her before—her elbow, her arm, her gloved hand—but he'd never touched her like this. He waited for her to push him away, for her harsh laugh, and quick dismissal.

It never came. She only swallowed, then said, "You really never ran a race before? Not even when you were a child?"

His gaze darted to her slender throat, then back to her face, and a forlorn laugh tore from his throat before he could stop it. "I was never a child."

She gazed back at him without speaking, but her eyes went so soft for a single moment he wanted to say more—to tell her everything about himself—but then he noticed the sympathy in those blue depths, and the moment was gone.

I'm the Marquess of Huntington now. I don't need anyone's pity.

He released the lock of her hair and let it fall back to her shoulder. "Lord Wrexley, Miss Somerset. You need to be on your guard against him."

As soon as he spoke, her face closed. Her eyes snapped back into focus, her expression went from dreamy to wary, and everything inside Finn went colder, as if a dark cloud had obliterated the sun.

She shook her head. "He's my dear friend's cousin, Lord Huntington, and he's never been anything but kind and respectful toward me."

"Respectful? It was Lord Wrexley who let Lady Beaumont into Lady Fairchild's garden the day of the scavenger hunt. I think he hoped you'd discover her there, and it would cause a rift between us. Not quite the actions of an honorable gentleman, are they?"

"Forgive me, Lord Huntington, if I choose to treat anything you say about Lord Wrexley with skepticism. When you found me in the garden that day, after you left Lady Beaumont, Lord Wrexley was—"

Finn tensed. That tear in her gown...

"Did he touch you?" He gripped her shoulders. "Tell me the truth at once."

Her eyes widened, and in some distant part of his brain, under the sudden roar in his ears, he knew he must be alarming her. He managed to get a deep breath into his lungs, then another, and he forced himself to loosen his grip. "How long were you alone with him?"

"I told you already, it wasn't above five minutes. You keep accusing him of wrongdoing, and he's perfectly innocent of it."

A hard laugh tore from Finn's chest. "Wrexley is many things, but he isn't innocent. If I hadn't happened to come upon you in the garden that day, there's no telling what he might have done."

"Indeed? Maybe *he* would have kissed me."

The thought of a kiss between her and Wrexley made Finn rigid with fury. "He would have done whatever he could get away with."

"And he could get away with a good deal—at least, that was your opinion last week, when you implied I'd engaged in improprieties with him."

Finn didn't realize he'd moved closer to her until his face was mere inches from hers. He stared down at her, his chest heaving with each harsh, furious breath. "I misspoke. I never meant to suggest any such thing, but I mean what I say about Lord Wrexley. He isn't a man you can trust, and it's clear he's pursuing you. Stay away from him."

Her eyes went wide, as if she couldn't quite believe what she'd heard. "It sounds as if you're giving me an order, my lord."

Finn didn't blink. "I am."

Derrick would have my head if he could hear this conversation.

"You have no right to tell me who I may and may not see. I'll make up my own mind about Lord Wrexley."

"By the time you do, it'll be too late."

An angry flush rose to her cheeks. "You do him an injustice."

Finn's temper flared in response, because he knew she was angry on Wrexley's behalf, not her own. "I'm trying to help you—"

"I don't want your help. We're no longer betrothed, and never shall be again, so you may consider your obligations toward me to be satisfied, Lord Huntington. I thank you for your concern. Now, if you'll excuse me."

"No, I won't excuse you. Not on any count. You haven't any choice but to accept my offer. Your future, your grandmother's wishes—"

"Accept a man who will demand utter propriety of his wife, even as he indulges in every kind of debauchery himself? I know a proper marchioness would overlook such a thing, but I can't."

"You'd rather have a man who doesn't care if you ruin yourself, as long as he gets his greedy hands on your fortune?"

Her face drained of color, but she shook him off and turned away without another word. Finn went after her, determined to make her listen, but when they came around the side of house, he saw Lady Tallant and Lord Derrick standing on the terrace.

"There you are, Miss Somerset." Lady Tallant took in Miss Somerset's disheveled appearance with a raised eyebrow, then turned a curious look on Finn. "And Lord Huntington. Good afternoon."

"Lady Tallant." Finn bowed.

"Come along, Miss Somerset. Lady Hadley was asking for you."

Miss Somerset didn't look at him again, but disappeared through the terrace doors behind Lady Tallant.

Lord Derrick hung back. "You don't look pleased, Huntington."

"I found Miss Somerset alone with Wrexley on the green just now. They were running races, and she was—"

"Let me guess. Running straight into Wrexley's arms?"

"Among other things. He wants her, Derrick."

"Yes, I'm afraid there's no question of that, but it won't matter what Wrexley wants if she agrees to have you back."

"She didn't agree. She's refused me a second time." Finn dragged a hand through his hair, then let it drop to his side. "Perhaps you were right about that wager, Derrick. Perhaps it was cursed."

"Don't say Lord Wrexley told her about the wager?"

"Oh, no. It's a great deal worse than that. That day, in Lady Fairchild's garden? She overheard me arguing with Lady Beaumont."

Derrick's face fell. "Bloody hell. How bad is it?"

"It was Lady Beaumont, Derrick. On her best day she's a poisonous viper. I'm sure you can imagine how bad it was."

"Christ, Huntington. This changes everything. She'll never accept you now."

"She will." Finn's voice was hard. "I can't just let him have her, Derrick."

"You may not have a choice. You can't control everything, no matter how much you might wish to."

Finn let out a harsh laugh. "So you suggest I let Lord Wrexley control it, instead?"

"I know you feel responsible for Miss Somerset, but—"

"I *am* responsible for her, even more so than I first realized. Don't you see? Given what she overheard in the garden that day, she had no other choice than to jilt me, but that won't stop the *ton* from destroying her. Even if she manages to slip through Wrexley's grasp, her future and her sisters' prospects are all laid to waste. She *has* to marry me, or she's ruined."

Derrick didn't argue, but his breath left his lungs in a weary sigh. "She has to accept you first, Huntington, and under the circumstances, I don't see what you can do to persuade her."

"I'll do whatever I must. Wrexley's immoral, reckless—a man without principles or boundaries. He's out of control, Derrick."

Lord Derrick was quiet for a moment, then his gaze met Finn's. "Who do you suppose is more dangerous, Huntington? A man so out of control he risks everything, or one who's so tightly controlled, he risks nothing?"

Finn didn't answer, and after a moment Lord Derrick sighed, and followed the ladies into the house.

"The first man is a danger to others. The second is a danger only to himself," Finn muttered at last, but he may as well not have bothered.

There was no one there to hear him.

Chapter Ten

Iris went up to her bedchamber, threw herself down on her bed and lay there, staring up at the ceiling without seeing it.

Not once, during their brief betrothal and the long weeks of their courtship, had Lord Huntington ever looked at her like he had this afternoon. He'd never spoken to her in that soft, pleading voice, and he'd certainly never stroked a lock of her hair between his long fingers.

No, he'd waited until she'd jilted him for that.

Iris kicked her legs into the bed beneath her, giving in to the fit of temper squeezing her in its grip. He hadn't looked at all like the cold, grand Marquess of Huntington when he'd clutched her shoulders and begged her to listen to him, had he? Looking into his burning eyes, she'd felt as if they were at a masque ball, and he'd torn off his masque to reveal he wasn't at all the person she'd thought he was.

If he'd shown her even a hint of such passion before, they might still be betrothed, and she wouldn't be in this mess.

But in it she was. She'd jilted a marquess, lied to her grandmother, compromised her sisters, and now here was Lord Huntington, claiming no lady but *her* would do for his marchioness. He was determined to drive a wedge between her and her one chance at putting things back to rights.

Lord Wrexley.

She gave in to the urge to behave like a child having a tantrum and beat her legs against the bed again. He hadn't spared her any of his attention when they were betrothed, so how was it he couldn't bear the idea of living without her *now*?

How had he put it when he barged into her bedchamber yesterday afternoon? *I reject your dismissal.*

Gentlemen weren't even permitted to reject a rejection, were they? It was against the rules. It wasn't *done*, for pity's sake. And *why*, in the name of all that was just, did he have to look so absurdly handsome when he was in a temper—

"Miss Somerset?" A soft knock sounded on the door. "It's Lady Tallant."

Iris jerked upright on the bed. Lady Tallant? What could she want?

Another faint knock. "May I come in?"

"Yes, of course." Iris rushed to open the door. "Lady Tallant, this is a surprise."

"Yes, it's a day for surprises, isn't it?"

She strolled into Iris's bedchamber, closed the door with a firm click behind her, and regarded Iris in silence for a long moment.

Iris shifted from one foot to the other, her stomach fluttering with nerves under her ladyship's penetrating stare. "How may I help, my lady?"

"It takes quite a lot to catch my attention, Miss Somerset, but I confess you and your game of rotating suitors has piqued my interest. Now, suppose you tell me what was so awful it would make you jilt a gentleman like Lord Huntington?"

Iris's mouth fell open in horror.

Violet.

Before she could say a word, Lady Tallant held up a hand. "Now, don't blame your sister. She had no choice but to tell us. You can't truly believe you could hide this from Lady Hadley and Captain West for the next two weeks."

"I didn't intend to hide it. I—that is..." In truth, Iris hadn't even considered it at all. She'd been so busy running after Lord Wrexley, and running away from Lord Huntington, the jilting itself had faded to the back of her mind. "Oh, no. Of course not. I had every intention of telling them, my lady."

Lady Tallant raised a skeptical eyebrow at this, but she didn't pursue it. Instead she took a seat on the chair in front of Iris's dressing table, and waved a hand at the bed. "Do sit, Miss Somerset. I need to speak with you."

Iris sat. One didn't argue with a wicked widow.

"So, you've jilted a marquess. My, that's not a sentence one often has a chance to say. You're either the bravest young lady I've ever known, or the most foolish. Which is it?"

Iris tapped her finger against her lower lip, considering. "My courage has led me into foolishness, Lady Tallant. No, wait. That's not right. Perhaps it's the other way around."

"Yes, it's often difficult to tell the difference between the two, isn't it? All right, then. Let's start with something simple, shall we? Why did you jilt him?"

Iris's litany of vague excuses rushed to her tongue, but it seemed she'd only been waiting for a chance to unburden herself, because much to her surprise, when she opened her mouth, the truth came pouring out.

"Because he wagered with Lord Harley and Lord Wrexley over which one of them would have Lady Honora and which would have me, and he only offered for me because he *lost*. Because he has a mistress, or he had one, and she's *awful*. Because he wouldn't kiss me, or let me kiss him, and because of the other bit with the blindfolds and silk scarves, though I can't explain that because I don't entirely understand it, and because he's cold and detached, and he doesn't care for me at all."

Dear God, it sounds even worse when I say it aloud.

Iris sagged back against the bed, limp and exhausted.

Lady Annabel abandoned her seat at the dressing table, and sat down next to Iris. "Is that it?"

Iris turned to stare at her. "Isn't that enough?"

Lady Annabel laughed. "For many young ladies I'd think it was more than enough, but only you can answer that question, Miss Somerset."

Strangely, that laugh echoing in the quiet room soothed Iris. If Lady Tallant could laugh, then perhaps it wasn't as dire as she imagined. "Well, I've jilted him, so I suppose I've already answered it, haven't I?"

"Yes, one would think you had, and quite definitively, but there is one little matter still unresolved. If you've jilted Lord Huntington, what's he doing here? Why would he accept the invitation to Lady Hadley's house party?"

Iris gave the bed another half-hearted kick. "Oh, to save me from myself, of course. He's come to inform me he's 'rejected my dismissal,' which essentially means he's insisting we go ahead with the marriage, despite the small matter of my having jilted him."

Lady Tallant's eyebrows shot up. "I didn't realize gentlemen were permitted that option."

"Oh, well, it seems a marquess is permitted to do whatever he wishes, Lady Tallant. Or perhaps that's just the exalted Marquess of Huntington."

Lady Tallant's lips twitched. "Well, this is a rather fascinating state of affairs, and at a country house party, too. Who would have imagined? But Lord Huntington must be enamored of you, to chase you all the way to Hampshire."

Iris snorted. "He's indifferent to me, I assure you. Passion may not move Lord Huntington, but obligation does. He's here to save me from an unworthy suitor. I'd hardly had a chance to scrape the dust from my boots after we arrived yesterday before Lord Huntington was in my bedchamber, demanding I marry him, and that I stay away from Lord Wrexley."

Oh, dear God. She'd just told Lady Tallant Lord Huntington was in her bedchamber.

Iris waited in dread for her visitor to leap from her chair and rush to report this scandalous lapse in propriety to Captain West, but aside from a slight hardening of her features when Lord Wrexley's name was mentioned, her ladyship didn't react at all. "Lord Huntington doesn't care for Lord Wrexley?"

"I think it's safe to say they don't care for each other, my lady."

"Let me see if I understand you, Miss Somerset. Lord Huntington came all the way to Hampshire to insist you marry him, because he wants to protect you from a gentleman he thinks is unworthy of you? It doesn't sound as if he's as indifferent to you as you imagine."

Iris blinked. She hadn't thought of it in quite that way. "Lord Huntington is cold and detached, but he's a proper gentleman, despite that awful wager. He realizes he left me no choice but to jilt him, and I suppose he feels a responsibility for me, for that reason."

"He didn't look cold or detached just now, when he chased you onto the terrace. He looked quite wild, in fact."

He had.

Iris didn't know how to account for those odd moments with Lord Huntington. This other gentleman who seemed to have risen from the ashes of the man she'd been betrothed to was so different from the cold marquess who'd always been so blandly unaffected by her, she hardly recognized him. She could almost imagine she'd wounded him with her words today, and then there was that odd comment he'd made, about never having run a race before. It didn't make sense. Hadn't every child run a race at some time or another?

I was never a child.

What could he have meant by that?

Something she'd heard Lady Beaumont say came back to her then, something about what Lord Huntington hid under his gentlemanly manners. She'd been referring to the worst of what he hid—the cravats and blindfolds and such—but what if there was something more? What if those stiff, cold manners hid something warmer, some passionate side of himself he kept hidden away?

And if they did, how would a lady go about unleashing it?

"Miss Somerset?" Lady Tallant was studying her with narrowed eyes. "Do you care for Lord Wrexley? Are you in love with him?"

Iris felt a pang of sadness close to her heart. Love, it seemed, had very little to do with marriage. "No, but that hardly matters now. I've jilted a marquess. Twice. I have to find another suitor, or my sisters will suffer because of my folly."

"And you've chosen Lord Wrexley."

Lady Tallant's voice was inflectionless, but Iris sensed she didn't care for Lord Wrexley any more than Lord Huntington did. "He's lively and charming, but I confess it's more a case of Lord Wrexley choosing me. Given my situation, I'm very lucky *someone* has. Only…"

She trailed off, and Lady Annabel leaned toward her, her blue eyes intent. "Only?"

Iris grabbed a pillow and pressed it to her chest. "I can't trust myself to choose an honorable gentleman. I was mistaken about Lord Huntington, both in his character and in his affections for me. How can I be sure I won't make the same mistake with Lord Wrexley? How can I know if he's what he appears to be, any more than Lord Huntington was?"

Lady Annabel nodded, but she didn't speak, and as the silence stretched, Iris began to realize she was angry. With Lord Huntington, and with her grandmother. With all of London, and with herself. "It's rather unfair, isn't it? Instead of all that time spent practicing the pianoforte and learning to flirt a fan, why don't they teach young ladies something useful?"

"What would you suggest?"

"Things like how to tell if a gentleman's affection is sincere, or if he's even a gentleman at all. Even if a lady does manage to unearth a decent one among the rakes and fortune-hunters, how can she make him fall in love with her? To be truthful, Lady Tallant, a part of me understands why Lord Huntington would prefer Lady Beaumont to me."

"Ah, so Lady Beaumont is Lord Huntington's mistress?"

"Not anymore, but yes, she was, and I'm not a match for her, am I? No respectable young lady is a match for a courtesan, or a gentleman's mistress. I can't compete with Lady Beaumont, or anyone like her when it comes to the…well, that business with the silk scarves."

Iris glanced at Lady Tallant from the corner of her eye, but if her ladyship was shocked about the silk scarves, she hid it well.

"Yes, you said something about that before—silk scarves and blindfolds, I believe? Perhaps you should explain what you mean."

"Well, it seems Lord Huntington enjoys…" Iris could feel the heat rising in her face, but if a lady couldn't discuss silk scarves and blindfolds with a wicked widow, who could she discuss it with? "Blindfolds, and, ah... scarves and cravats and the like, for, um...binding."

"Ah. I see."

Iris waited, breath held, for Lady Tallant to ask her to explain how she could possibly know such a thing about Lord Huntington, but her ladyship only assessed Iris with a clinical eye. "That's why you jilted him, then? Because you were disgusted by it?"

Iris hesitated, but again, she had a wicked widow at her disposal. If she didn't confess the truth to Lady Tallant, she'd never confess it to anyone. "No. I should have been, but I wasn't. Only...curious."

There was a long silence, and before it was over Iris had squeezed her eyes shut, overcome with mortification. Oh, *why* had she been so forthcoming? Now Lady Tallant would feel compelled to tell Charlotte, and, dear God, if it should get back to her grandmother—

"May I call you Iris, Miss Somerset?"

Iris's eyes flew open. "I—yes, of course you may."

"And you must call me Annabel. Now, Iris, you've asked several astute questions—questions most young ladies never think to ask—and I believe you deserve some answers. I'm willing to provide them, if you like."

Iris stared dumbly at Lady Tallant for a moment, certain she'd misheard her, but as the words sunk in, she clapped her hands together, overwhelmed with relief. "Why, that would be wonderful! How kind you are, my lady!"

Lady Tallant brushed off the thanks with a wave of her hand. "I'm not kind, Iris, only ready to expire from boredom. I find country house parties tedious, and do this only for my own amusement."

Iris didn't care a whit about that. The offer was the important thing, not the motivation behind it. "May we start with garden seductions, my lady? I'm hopeless at them, and I'd rather not repeat the mortifying experience I had with Lord Huntington with Lord Wrexley."

Lady Tallant held up her hand with a laugh. "Perhaps we'd better work our way up to seductions. There are several books I'd like you to read first. Reading is not, of course, a substitute for experience, but it's a start."

"Books?" That sounded dull.

"These are special books—not like anything you've ever read before. I think you'll find them quite enlightening. Here, find me a pen and paper, and I'll write down the titles."

Iris fetched the supplies from her writing box, and Lady Tallant scribbled a few lines on a piece of paper, folded it, and handed it to her. "Here. If you can't find any of these, I have other titles, but I daresay you'll find one or more of them in the Hadley House library. Once you've finished them, come and see me."

"I will. Thank you, Lady Tal—that is, Lady Annabel."

An enigmatic smile drifted over Lady Annabel's lips. "Oh, no, Iris. It's I who should be thanking you."

* * * *

Iris spent the remainder of the afternoon in her bedchamber. By the time she joined the rest of the party for dinner, she'd been through all forty-seven pages of *Dialogues between a Lady and Her Maid*.

Twice.

She was prickling with heat, and worried the scorching blush that bloomed when she read the words "...for in his arms you will find such pleasures..." would never fade from her cheeks.

Those words were on page one. In the first paragraph. In the first sentence. The remaining forty-six pages were devoted to a detailed description of those pleasures.

Iris blotted some of the dampness from her forehead with the sleeve of her pale blue gown. Dear God, she could never wear another innocent pink gown again, now she'd read about Octavia and Philander's bedchamber antics.

She was too wicked for pink.

"Are you unwell, Miss Somerset?" Lord Wrexley, who was seated across the table from her, raised his wine glass to his lips, frowning as his gaze lingered on her red cheeks. "You look flushed."

Iris raised her fingertips to her face. "I'm quite well, my lord, only a bit warm."

"It's not overly warm in here." Violet, who was seated to her left, turned from her conversation with Lord Derrick to frown at Iris. "My goodness, Iris. You look like a teakettle about to boil over. Whatever is the matter with you?"

Iris stretched a ferocious smile over her gritted teeth and turned this frightening look upon her sister. "Nothing at all, dear, but you're so kind to enquire."

Nothing, that is, except she couldn't bring herself look at any of the gentlemen in the room, especially Lord Huntington, which wasn't right at all, since of the four gentlemen at the table, she was the least fond of him. Yet she caught her gaze wandering to him again and again, far more often than any of the others. The one small mercy was he was seated at the other end of the table, next to Lady Honora, and so absorbed with her conversation he hadn't spared Iris a glance all evening.

Just as well. If he *did* look at her, he might be able to tell she was thinking about his...breeches. Or not his breeches, precisely, but, well, something in that vicinity.

Iris twisted her napkin between numb fingers. Perhaps she shouldn't have read that book, but it was too late now. There was no going back to blissful innocence once a lady understood the particulars of the, ah...transaction.

"Shall we leave the gentlemen to their port?" Charlotte rose from the table and led the ladies toward the drawing room, but Iris didn't miss the fond look she cast her husband first, or his answering smile, and oh, dear God, *that* was why Charlotte was so taken with her husband! She never spared a glance for any other gentleman, no matter his attractions, and Captain West was equally smitten with his wife.

Don't think on it—not on any of it, particularly anything to do with Lord Huntington's breeches, or his long fingers, or the way his hazel eyes darkened when he'd touched her hair today.

"For pity's sake, Iris, do sit down. You look at if you're about to fall into a swoon."

Violet patted the space next to her on the settee, and Iris dropped into it before her wobbly knees could desert her completely.

Lady Honora took a chair opposite the settee and studied Iris, her dark eyes soft with concern. "I blame my cousin for your indisposition, Iris. He was quite wrong to coax you into racing with him. I believe you've had too much sun and too much exercise."

No, only too much reading.

"Oh, nonsense. Miss Somerset is perfectly well." Lady Annabel settled into a chair at the card table, and motioned for Charlotte to join her. "Isn't that right, Miss Somerset?"

Lady Annabel raised an eyebrow at her, and Iris straightened in her seat. "Yes, of course, my lady. I'm only a bit fatigued."

"You need some quiet time to yourself. Perhaps you should retire early with a good book. Have you been to the Hadley House library? It's an extensive one. I'm sure you'll find something entertaining to read there."

The mischievous smile playing at the corner of Lady Annabel's mouth was too subtle to be noticeable to anyone else in the room, but Iris saw it, and despite her embarrassment, her own lips quirked at the corners. "Yes, I daresay you're right, my lady."

Violet, who was too clever for her own good, glanced from Lady Annabel to Iris, her eyes narrowed in suspicion. "It's not fatigue, but agitation. You're preoccupied by this business with Lord Huntington."

"Business? What business?" Iris's voice was much louder than she intended, but if Violet thought she was preoccupied with the business of Lord Huntington's breeches—

"Why, the jilting, of course! Unless there's some other business I don't know about?"

"Oh, right. That." For pity's sake, how could she keep forgetting about the jilting?

"Yes, *that*. What's going on, Iris? Has something happened with Lord Huntington?"

"Or Lord Wrexley?" Lady Honora asked hopefully.

"I hope not," Charlotte put in. "Poor Captain West is confused enough as it is. He can't tell who's courting whom, and it puts him in a temper."

"Here are the gentlemen now." Lady Annabel shot a warning look at the ladies just as Captain West entered the room, with the other gentlemen trailing after him. "You didn't linger long over your port."

"No." Captain West took a seat at the card table next to his wife. "Lord Wrexley insisted we come at once. He was concerned about Miss Somerset."

"And rightly so." Lord Wrexley came toward her, his intention to sit with her unmistakable. "You still look flushed, Miss Somerset."

Before he could take the seat next to her on the settee, Lady Annabel called out to him. "Miss Somerset was just telling us she feels very well. Come, Lord Wrexley. We need a fourth for cards. You won't be so rude as to disappoint us, will you?"

"Of course not, my lady." Lord Wrexley's tone was polite, but he gave Iris one last lingering glance, his mouth turning down in a frown when Lord Huntington took the seat opposite her.

Lady Honora turned to Lord Huntington with a smile. "What time shall we ride tomorrow, my lord?"

Lord Huntington had been studying Iris's flushed cheeks with a puzzled expression, but now he jerked his gaze to Lady Honora. "Whenever you like, my lady. Do you fancy a long ride? If so, we should leave early to avoid the heat of the day."

So, Lord Huntington was taking Lady Honora riding tomorrow? Well, how lovely of him. But then he might do as he wished. It was nothing to Iris. Still, he'd been quite devoted to Lady Honora since they arrived at Hadley House. No doubt he'd given up on his mad plan to marry *her* and had chosen instead to initiate a courtship with Lady Honora before the season started, and she was surrounded by eager suitors.

Not that any other gentleman could compete with Lord Huntington.

Well, she wouldn't pay him the least bit of attention. She certainly wouldn't study the way his smooth, tight breeches hugged the long, lean line of his legs, or scrutinize the buttons of his falls, just peeking out from the bottom edge of his waistcoat.

A clever invention, falls. She'd never realized quite how clever until she reached page eight of her book, but just a quick twist of a button, and—

"I'm afraid you do look rather unwell, after all, Miss Somerset. The flush seems to be getting worse." Lady Annabel raised her gaze from her cards, and nodded at Lord Huntington. "My lord, won't you escort Miss Somerset upstairs? I don't like her to go by herself, in case she swoons."

Lord Wrexley leapt up from his chair. "I'd be happy to escort her—"

"No, no. We're in the middle of a game." Lady Annabel motioned for him to sit back down. "Lord Huntington isn't occupied. He can take her."

"Yes, of course." Lord Huntington rose and bowed to Lady Honora. "I beg your pardon, my lady."

"Do you fancy a game of chess, Lady Honora?" Lord Derrick gestured to the chess board on the other side of the room. "I warn you, though. I'm a hopeless strategist."

Lady Honora looked surprised he'd asked, but pleased. "Why, I'd be delighted, my lord. Shall we see what happens when two hopeless strategists have a game?"

She crossed the room, and soon their heads were bent together over the chess board.

"Miss Somerset?" Lord Huntington was standing beside the settee, his arm held out to Iris. "May I take you up?"

She stood on unsteady legs. "Thank you."

Touching Lord Huntington didn't seem a wise thing to do at the moment—not when she was so preoccupied with his falls—but she didn't have much choice, and it was only his arm, after all. Surely she could touch him *there* with no difficulty.

Her fingertips just grazed his coat, but the minute they did a bolt of heat raced over her skin, as if she'd shoved her arm into the fire.

Lord Huntington gave her a quizzical look, and drew her arm more firmly through his. "You're shivering. I'm afraid you're ill, Miss Somerset."

"No, I'm quite all right." But Iris could hear the note of uncertainty in her own voice, and she knew Lord Huntington heard it too by the way his arm stiffened under her fingers.

Neither of them said another word as he led her up the stairs, but when they reached the landing, she attempted to pull her arm free. "Thank you for your escort, my lord. I can make my way to my bedchamber on my own."

He didn't argue, but he didn't let her go, either—not until they stood in front of her bedchamber door, and even then he lingered, staring down at her with an expression that made Iris's heart thunder in her chest.

Why did one look from Lord Huntington make her pulse skip, and her breath come short? She didn't even like him much, and she certainly didn't trust him, so it wasn't possible she could...*want* him, was it?

Hard fingers touched her chin and tipped her face up to his. "Such a pretty flush," he murmured in a hoarse voice. "But I don't think you're ill, after all." His gaze drifted over her face, and then, without warning, he dragged his fingertips down her cheek, his hazel eyes flaring with heat as her flush deepened in the wake of those seeking fingers.

Or...was it possible he wanted her?

What would he do if she touched him? Philander and Horatio, the heroes of her book, had fallen into fits of wild passion on every page, sighing and gasping over their ladies' every touch. If she touched her fingers to his lips, would Lord Huntington lose control, as they had done?

You're rather intense when you're aroused...I've never know a more insatiable man...not many women could satisfy you.

If Iris could trust what she'd overheard Lady Beaumont say, it took very little to unleash the fierce passion Lord Huntington hid under his cool, stiff manners.

The part of Iris that was still wounded over his first rejection shrank back with fear at the idea of touching him, but the other part—the part that whispered this time it would be different—reached up slowly, so slowly, and touched a fingertip to his bottom lip.

He sucked in a harsh breath, and his lips parted on a quiet moan.

The desperate sound made heat surge into Iris's lower belly, so she did it again—her fingertip brushed gently across his warm lips, her touch so light she might have wondered if he felt it at all if his eyelids hadn't dropped half-closed over eyes gone black.

He felt it.

He didn't touch her, but his hot gaze traced every line of her face, lingering on her lips, and Iris could do nothing but stare back at him, mesmerized by the wild desire she saw in his eyes. His entire body had gone rigid as he strained to hold it back, but if he should let it go, unleash it...

Dear God.

Iris was innocent, yes, but even she understood the desire Lord Huntington now held so ruthlessly in check would sweep all before it.

Her heart gave a panicked leap in her chest, and she jerked her hand away from his face.

"No." He grasped her hand in his and brought her fingers back to his lips. "Touch me again."

Iris did as he bade her, because as much as she feared that powerful desire, she also wanted to drown in it. He held her hand as she did what he demanded and dragged her fingertip over his lips again. His eyes drifted closed, but he seemed to know what she would do without looking, because just as she drew her hand away, he opened his lips and pressed a tiny, damp kiss on her fingertip.

Neither of them moved, but stood there staring at each other, their panting breaths the only sound in the silent hallway, until at last he released her hand, and stepped away.

"Goodnight, Miss Somerset."

Iris watched him go, but long minutes after he'd disappeared around the corner, she still stood frozen by her bedchamber door.

She wanted him. There was no mistaking the way her breath caught when he looked at her, or the way her belly filled with liquid heat when he touched her.

She'd jilted him. Her entire future—and her sisters' futures—rested on her ability to convince another gentleman of her affections.

And still, she wanted Lord Huntington.

Chapter Eleven

"Well, Miss Somerset, what's it to be this morning? Slow and gentle, or swift and rough? Choose your pleasure, and we'll begin at once."

Iris's lips pressed together, and her fingers tightened on her riding crop. Lord Wrexley had invited her to take a ride with him this morning after breakfast, and he'd politely escorted her to the stable to help her choose her mount, but despite his gentlemanly attentions, she didn't miss the note of amusement under his polite tone, or the tiny smirk flirting at the corners of his lips.

As little as a day ago, she would have admired his easy manners, and returned his charming smile with a flirtatious one of her own, but today it was as if Lord Huntington were a devil perched on her shoulder, whispering in her ear.

He isn't a man you can trust. Stay away from him.

"That's quite a ferocious grimace, Miss Somerset." Lord Wrexley's smirk widened into a smile that was both angelic and suggestive at once. "I'm referring to horses, of course, and riding. But perhaps you thought I meant something else?"

Iris wasn't sophisticated—or, she hadn't been before she began her reading lessons with Lady Annabel—but she also wasn't an utter half-wit. She knew precisely what Lord Wrexley was insinuating, and her lips turned down in a stern frown. "You're not as subtle as you imagine, my lord. Indeed, you're rather wicked, I think."

He threw his head back in a hearty laugh. "And you're far more charming than *you* imagine, particularly when you scold. You get the most fetching little furrow, right here." He dragged a finger lightly between her eyebrows.

"Violet said the same thing, but she didn't think it was at all fetching." Iris touched her forehead, her fingers brushing his away, but she tried to shake off her uneasiness with him. It wasn't proper of him to tease an innocent young lady, but surely he couldn't be as bad as Lord Huntington made him out to be? Lord Wrexley wasn't licentious or debauched— only high-spirited.

"She's quite wrong. But come, we'll start over here." He took her arm and led her to one end of Captain West's enormous stables, stopping at the first stall. "This mare is a sweet, slow, gentle sort, and I don't know that I've ever seen a prettier horse. She's a perfect mount for a lady."

Iris ran her hand down the nose of the chestnut mare inside the stall. "She's beautiful, yes, and perfect for a certain kind of lady."

"But not for you?"

Iris shook her head. She should be in fits of ecstasy over such a lovely horse, but the mare wasn't any better suited to her than the pink gowns were. "No. Not for me."

"All right, then." Lord Wrexley led her to the next stall. "Another mare. Perhaps a bit livelier than the first, but still gentle and easy. She's the kind of horse a lady might ride on the promenade in Hyde Park during the fashionable hour."

Iris reached out to pat the horse's smooth neck and tried to hide her disappointment from Lord Wrexley.

"You must enjoy riding on the promenade?"

"I—" Iris began, but this time the lie she'd been telling all season lodged in her throat.

Much like gentle mares and pink gowns, the promenade was another thing she *should* enjoy, but secretly despised. She loathed mincing along with scores of simpering, tedious aristocrats. She couldn't say *that*, of course, because all fashionable ladies adored the promenade, and a gentleman like Lord Wrexley would expect her to adore it, too.

But her father had been a devoted horseman, and Iris had been riding from the time she was old enough to toddle to the stables. She'd ridden every day in Surrey, was exceptionally skilled with a horse, and preferred a challenging mount.

At least, she used to. Since she'd come to London she didn't ride much anymore. There never seemed to be time for it. She was forever at her modiste's for a fitting, or occupied with her dancing master, or practicing her music. When she did manage to steal an hour or so, her rambles were confined to Hyde Park during the fashionable hour, and always on a gentle mare like this one.

Iris watched the dust motes dance in the shaft of sunlight pouring through the open stable doors, and a heaviness that had become familiar to her since she came to London squeezed at her chest. Somehow, what she *should* want had become much more important than what she *did* want. How long would it be before she couldn't distinguish one from the other?

Despite her efforts to hide it, Lord Wrexley noticed her disappointment. "Not this mare, I think." He led her to the next stall, and then the next, pausing at each one to tell her about the occupant. Iris listened, and stroked her hand over one velvety nose after another, but by the time they'd made it halfway across the stables, she was still frozen with indecision.

The wisest course of action was to choose one of the mounts Lord Wrexley suggested. It was a compliment to his judgment, and it wouldn't do to irritate her potential betrothed by dismissing his recommendation.

"Perhaps you could tell me what kind of mount you prefer?"

Yes, one would think she'd be able to tell him that much. It was a simple enough thing to choose a horse for a day's ride, particularly in Captain West's stables, where each stall contained an animal more beautiful than the last. And yet all Iris seemed able to do was stare dumbly at one horse after another, her mind in turmoil.

Over a horse. A horse, for goodness' sake.

"Why don't I choose one for you?" There was a slight edge to Lord Wrexley's tone now, as if he'd grown impatient with her. "If the horse doesn't suit, we'll choose a different one tomorrow."

"Yes, all right." It was either that, or stand around the stables all day, gaping at horses like a half-witted child dithering over a tray of sweets.

"Very good. I think the chestnut mare, then, the one in the first stall. She's—"

"Good morning! Are you off on a ride?"

Iris turned at Lady Honora's voice, her smile stiffening on her lips as she watched her friend approach on Lord Huntington's arm.

Iris's gaze darted at once to his lips, her face flushing at the memory of their firm warmth before she jerked her gaze away. Dash it, why did the man have to show up *now*? She'd lain awake half the night thinking about how he'd pressed that tiny kiss on her fingertip. She'd finally managed to banish him from her thoughts and turn her attention to Lord Wrexley this morning, and now here he was again, his lips more distracting than ever.

It was too much. She couldn't even manage to choose a horse, never mind attract a new betrothed while the one she'd jilted stood there scowling at her, his brows lowered over his hazel eyes.

"Good morning, cousin. Huntington." Lord Wrexley tapped his riding crop against his boot. "We're off, yes. Miss Somerset had some difficulty choosing a mount, but I think we've settled on one."

"You don't know what kind of mount you prefer, Miss Somerset?" A mocking smile curled at the corners of Lord Huntington's lips. "I'm surprised to find you so indecisive. Indeed, I've known you to make crucial decisions on nothing more than the merest whim."

"Don't tease, my lord." Lady Honora gave him a chastising look, then smiled at Iris. "Miss Somerset spent most of her childhood in Surrey on the back of a horse, cousin. I daresay she can manage any mount in the stables."

"Indeed? I had no idea you were such an accomplished rider." Lord Wrexley's gaze sharpened as he turned to Iris.

"Any mount in the stables? Surely you exaggerate, Lady Honora." But Lord Huntington wasn't looking at Lady Honora. His eyes were a clear gray color this morning, and they were assessing Iris with cool disdain. "I don't believe I've seen Miss Somerset on the promenade more than once or twice this season."

Iris managed a sweet smile, but her blood began to heat with temper. "Surely you don't mean to suggest prancing about the promenade in the latest fashions is a measure of equestrian skill, my lord?"

His eyes darkened to slate, and Iris watched them with a strange mix of fascination and anger. Such a troublesome color, hazel—nothing like Lord Wrexley's pale blue. A lady might look into a pair of hazel eyes, and see nothing of the man behind the shifting colors, from a clear green to russet brown, and, when he was angry, to a forest green so dark it was nearly black. Why, a gentleman could hide anything behind such changeable eyes.

Any secrets and any sins, and Lord Huntington had plenty of both.

"The promenade is an adequate measure of horsemanship for a lady, yes."

"You underestimate the ladies, my lord. Ladies of an equestrienne turn prefer a hard ride in Richmond Park to a measured amble on the promenade, but then I suppose fashionable marquesses don't trouble themselves much with such *unpredictable* ladies, do they?"

Lord Huntington's jaw tightened, and Iris couldn't quite contain her satisfied smile. Not very ladylike, that smile, but it was difficult to care.

Both Lady Honora and her cousin were quiet during this exchange, but now Lord Wrexley cleared his throat. "What kind of horse did you ride when you lived in Surrey, Miss Somerset? It might help me to choose your mount today if I know."

"An enormous coal-black stallion with hooves nearly as big as my head." Iris laughed, thinking of her first horse. He'd been a heathenish creature, quite the worst-tempered horse she'd ever encountered, but she'd loved him with a fierce affection. "I christened him Typhon, in honor of his relentless bad temper, and his tendency to send riders hurtling to the ground."

"Typhon?" Lord Huntington frowned. "What, you named him after that deadly creature with the hundred dragon heads?"

"Yes, from the Greek mythology. He was stubborn and irascible, but I adored him nonetheless."

"My goodness." Lady Honora clutched at Lord Huntington's arm, her eyes wide. "He sounds quite menacing. How did you end up with a horse like that?"

"My father." Iris laughed at Honora's horrified expression. "He was a former cavalry officer, you see, and mad about horses, rather like Captain West. He gave Typhon to me when I was eight years old. Flying across the Surrey countryside on horseback with my father are some of my fondest memories of him."

Lord Wrexley leaned a hip against the stall door, his curious gaze fixed on her. "If you could ride a horse like that, then of course the mare won't do for you. What happened to Typhon?"

Iris bit her lip against the familiar ache that pressed behind her eyes whenever she thought of Typhon. It was foolish to cry over him after all these years had passed, but there were some wounds even a lifetime couldn't heal. For all his flaws, Typhon was the most perfect of animals to her, and she'd never since had a horse to equal him. "He escaped from the barn one night during a storm. He was running wild, and he fell and broke his leg. He had to be shot."

Iris heard the quaver in her voice, and no one spoke for a long moment after she fell silent, but then the rhythmic tap of Lord Wrexley's riding crop against his boot ceased. "I have something to show you, Miss Somerset."

There was an odd, calculating look in his eyes as he held out his arm to her. He didn't spare a glance for his cousin or Lord Huntington, but they followed as Lord Wrexley strode with Iris toward a dim corner of the barn.

Iris heard him before she saw him. A few irritable snorts, a warning nicker, and finally the slam of a massive body against the wooden walls of the stall.

"Stay back," Lord Wrexley warned. "Captain West says he has a wicked temper."

Iris hardly heard him. She took one cautious half step toward the stall, itching to reach her hand in to stroke that glossy dark coat, but she knew better than to get within biting distance of the horse's snapping teeth. "Oh, you're in a temper, are you?" she murmured. "But I'd wager you're the sort who's always in a temper. What's your name?"

"Chaos. Proper name for him, isn't it?" Lord Wrexley stood back from the stall, keeping a safe distance between himself and the horse. "Captain West keeps him in this corner of the stables for a reason."

Chaos tossed his head as if he knew he'd been maligned, and a shaft of sunlight fell on his neck. He wasn't black, as Iris had originally thought, but a dark, sleek gray, and even from the quick glimpse she got, she could see he was enormous. "What reason is that?"

Chaos jerked his head toward her and bared his teeth.

"He bites." Lord Wrexley chuckled. "Kicks, too, among other nasty habits. Captain West said he's the finest runner he's ever seen, but it seems Chaos here is particular about who rides him. He told me Chaos nearly threw Lady Hadley once and would have trampled her under his hooves if he'd managed to unseat her."

Lady Honora gasped. "My goodness! I wonder why Captain West keeps him at all."

"He's a remarkable animal, Honora, truly one of a kind, but he needs a firm hand." Lord Wrexley spoke to his cousin, but he was staring at Iris, his pale blue eyes gleaming in the dim light. "Do you suppose *you* could manage him, Miss Somerset?"

"What? Certainly not!" Lady Honora gasped again, and her voice had gone shrill with fright. "What do you mean, suggesting such a thing, cousin?"

Lord Wrexley ignored her. "Miss Somerset? Could you manage him?"

Iris took another cautious step forward, her breath held. Chaos kicked and whinnied and butted his head against the sides of his stall, but he was watching her, assessing her with those liquid black eyes, and everything inside her vibrated in response. Her body went rigid from the effort it took not to touch him, but she held back, because he wasn't ready to be touched by her.

Not yet. But he would be, and soon. She'd touch him, and she'd ride him.

"Miss Somerset?" There was a thread of impatience in Lord Wrexley's voice.

"He's not the kind of horse you manage, my lord, but if you want to know whether or not I could ride him…" Iris paused, and a small smile tugged at her mouth. "In the right circumstances, and given a chance to become more familiar with him, yes. I could ride him."

Lord Huntington hadn't said a word up to this point, but now he stepped forward, and the shaft of sunlight fell over his face.

A soft gasp escaped Iris's throat.

"A word, Wrexley?"

It was a low growl, dark and furious, and a shiver darted up Iris's spine. Lady Honora shrank back, away from him, her eyes wide.

His lips were white at the corners, and his eyes had gone black with suppressed fury. His powerful body shook with barely leashed rage as he approached Lord Wrexley, and Iris froze, her heart thundering in her chest as she stared at him.

He was beautiful—and terrifying.

She couldn't take her eyes off him.

* * * *

Finn jerked his head at Wrexley to follow him, then strode toward the stable door, where the ladies couldn't overhear them.

"What's the matter now, Huntington?" Wrexley sauntered after him, a mocking smile on his lips. "Christ, you haven't changed at all since school. Still fuming over one thing or another, aren't you? It must exhaust you to sustain that outrage day after day. Well, what is it?"

"What the devil do you think you're doing, suggesting that horse for Miss Somerset? He's not a safe mount for her, and you bloody well know it. Do you want to see her hurt, or worse?"

The light flooding through the stable door stabbed at Finn's eyes, and for a moment a horrifying image of Iris Somerset trampled under those enormous black hooves flashed through his mind.

"Why would I wish for that, Huntington? I think I've made it clear how taken I am with Miss Somerset. The lady likes a challenging mount."

Finn flexed his fingers to keep them from clenching into fists. He wanted to wrap his hands around Wrexley's throat until he'd squeezed that smirk right off the scoundrel's face, but he held back, his pulse throbbing with impotent fury.

"Challenging? That horse is more than challenging, Wrexley. With the wrong rider on his back, he's deadly."

Wrexley glanced behind him, and Finn followed his gaze.

Lady Honora had ahold of Miss Somerset's arm as if to pull her away from the stall, and her face was pale with fear. Miss Somerset, however, had inched closer, and even from this distance Finn could hear her murmuring to the horse in a low, soothing voice.

Wrexley turned back to Finn with a shrug. "She seems happy enough with him, and you heard my cousin. She assured us Miss Somerset can manage any horse in the stables. I can't see what reason *you* have to object."

Finn was taller than Wrexley, so when he stepped closer, his chin was right in Wrexley's face, and the other man was forced to back up. "I object to your putting Miss Somerset in danger. That horse is aggressive and much too big for her. If he chooses to bolt—and you only have to look at him to see he will—she won't have the strength to stop him, no matter how skilled she is in the saddle. Tell her you've made a mistake, and suggest a different horse."

"I'm afraid it's too late for that, Huntington. Look at her. She's besotted with the animal, and I wouldn't dream of disappointing a lady."

"You're all gallantry, aren't you, Wrexley? But gallantry will be of little use to Miss Somerset when that horse breaks every bone in her body."

"What a happy thought. One can always count on you to dampen the spirits. But I think you underestimate the lady. Tell me, Huntington. Is that why she jilted you?"

Finn didn't so much as twitch a muscle at Wrexley's jab. It took every bit of his control to keep his expression blank, but Wrexley saw something there that made his lips twist with a satisfied smirk. "Unfortunate, but your loss will be my gain. I expect Miss Somerset and I will be betrothed before the end of the house party. When the happy event occurs, I hope you'll be the first to congratulate me, Huntington."

Finn's jaw went rigid. It was just as he'd thought. Wrexley intended to take advantage of Miss Somerset's precarious situation with a whirlwind courtship. He'd already begun to ingratiate himself with her, and like most scoundrels, Wrexley was adept at feigning sincerity. He wasn't making an empty threat—there was a good chance he really could have the entire business settled before the end of the house party.

Finn's chest tightened with something that felt suspiciously like panic.

"As far as the horse is concerned," Wrexley went on, "you'll recall, Huntington, you're no longer betrothed to Miss Somerset. She may do as she pleases, and there's not a damn thing you can do about it."

"I think you're far more concerned Miss Somerset do what *you* please." Finn's voice was soft, menacing. "A naïve young lady with a substantial fortune, a recently broken engagement, and at a house party, no less, with all the freedom it affords. You're not one to let such an opportunity slip away, are you, Wrexley? She must be irresistible to you."

"Oh, she is. But then, I've always admired her. That's the difference between us, Huntington. You're the kind of man who doesn't value a jewel until you no longer hold it in your hand." Wrexley shook his head as if in regret, but his eyes gleamed with satisfaction. "I think you see your mistake now though, don't you? Pity it's too late."

Finn swallowed, but the bitter, acid taste of regret lingered in his mouth. There was nothing more galling than being taunted by a man with so little discernment as Wrexley, unless it was knowing he was right.

"But even considering Miss Somerset's many attractions, I don't deny I'm delighted to have the additional pleasure of taking her away from *you*. It maddens you, and that makes her infinitely more enticing to me. It's almost poetic, isn't it, how fate has offered me another chance to steal the heiress you'd chosen as your own?"

Wrexley saw at once he'd hit a tender spot and was quick to follow up his advantage with another blow. "I suppose it's difficult for a controlling man like you to find such a prize has slipped through your fingers, but I must say I'm relieved, for Miss Somerset's sake. What a pity it would be for such a passionate lady to be wasted on someone as cold and emotionless as you. I wonder, do you think she knows how narrow her escape was?"

Wrexley's smiled widened when Finn didn't answer. "I daresay you wouldn't have known what to do with her, but perhaps it will comfort you to know, Huntington, I intend to keep her very much in hand when she's mine, and I can think of quite a few things I'll do to her, and even more I'll have her do to *me*."

Things happened quickly after that.

A roar echoed in Finn's ears, and he grabbed Wrexley by his coat and yanked him off the ground. "She may not be mine, but she'll never be *yours*, either. You're very much mistaken if you think I won't look out for Miss Somerset's interests. I'll be damned if I stand by while she falls victim to a scoundrel like you."

"Take your bloody hands off me, Huntington." Wrexley tried to pry Finn's fingers loose from his coat, but Finn tightened his grip until his knuckles were white. Wrexley kicked and squirmed, his face and neck flushing a dull, angry red, but there was nothing he could do except dangle like a ragdoll until Finn chose to let him loose.

Finn took his time.

When he dropped Wrexley to the ground at last, he shoved past him without another glance, and strode to the back of the stables, forcing himself to smile at Lady Honora as he approached. "Will the chestnut mare your cousin chose for Miss Somerset do for you, my lady?"

Lady Honora was still pale, and she gave him a blank look. "The chestnut—oh, yes. Of course. She'll do very well."

"Fine. Your cousin will have the groom saddle her and bring her out to the yard for you. I'll join you in a moment."

"All right." Lady Honora cast one last worried look at Miss Somerset and the dark gray stallion; then she followed her cousin out into the yard without further argument.

Lady Honora never argued.

Finn doubted he'd be as fortunate with Miss Somerset. It seemed incredible he ever could have overlooked the obstinate thrust of that chin, or the dark blue flash of temper in her eyes.

Christ, what a fool he was.

Chapter Twelve

Finn had meant to take her arm at once and move her away from the horse before Chaos tried to knock her over or bite her, but he stilled when he caught sight of her leaning over the edge of the stall, her bright hair illuminated by a beam of sunlight.

Her head was bent toward the horse, one of her hands curled around the stall door, the other caressing the horse's neck with slow, easy strokes. She was murmuring to him, and the horse's ears were twitching with pleasure at the sound of her low, sweet voice.

Finn leaned a hip against the door of the stall and crossed his arms over his chest. She was so preoccupied with the stallion she didn't seem to realize he was there, and the scene was so tranquil he couldn't bring himself to interrupt them.

He'd watch her for a moment only, and then he'd—

"Oh, just look at you, you beauty." She let out a soft laugh when Chaos butted his nose roughly into her shoulder. "Oh no, indeed. There will be none of that. When I ride you, you'll act the gentleman, sir."

She continued to stroke the horse with long, steady sweeps of her hand, again and again, slow and rhythmic, crooning to him all the while. Finn couldn't hear all of what she said, but it didn't matter.

She could be saying anything, or nothing at all.

His eyes slid half-closed as he let himself fall deeper under the spell of her hypnotic voice, but even as his brain was lulled into quiet the rest of his body surged with awareness. She didn't look at him, but it was as if he were taking her inside him, each syllable sinking in and becoming invisible, like water disappearing into sand.

"There. That's it, Chaos. You can be sweet when you choose, can't you?"

She laughed again when the stallion nosed her cheek, and Finn's own lips curved in response. Had he never heard her laugh before? Or was it another thing he'd failed to notice about her? Her laugh, the stubborn lift of her chin, her voice like the stroke of a hand over him, a lullaby and a seduction at once.

He would have stood there all day and listened to her.

"You're both sweet and wicked, aren't you? Ah, such a soft mouth, like velvet."

Finn's breath grew short, his chest heaving with each inhale. Even here, in the stables, with Lady Honora and Wrexley right outside the door, every inch of him strained toward her, his cock rising and pressing against the front of his falls, his body desperate for more of her voice, her fingers stroking his lips. What would it be like to lie next to her, with her mouth pressed to his ear as she whispered to him, each word no more than a warm breath of air?

"No, I can't believe you're truly wicked, not with that mouth."

And the horse—damned if the horse wasn't just as fascinated with her as Finn was. Chaos was a devil. One look into those black eyes and anyone could see it, but she seemed to know just the right way to touch him and just how to speak to him.

"There now, Chaos. Shall we go for a ride?"

Her spell dissipated into the dust motes floating in the shaft of sunlight above them, and a pang of regret pierced Finn's chest. He couldn't let her ride that horse—not without speaking to Captain West first. Chaos might seem tame enough now, in his stall, but there was no telling how he'd behave once she was mounted and riding him across open country.

He opened his mouth to tell her she'd have to choose a different horse for today, but when he spoke, that wasn't what he said at all.

"He likes you."

"Yes, I think he does." A delighted grin flirted at the corners of her lips, and Finn's knees weakened.

They were both quiet for a moment, then he surprised himself again by asking her a question he didn't know he needed answered until the words left his mouth. "You never spoke to me about Typhon, or about your life in Surrey. All those weeks I courted you, and even after we were betrothed, you never spoke to me about your father. Why?"

She glanced at him, surprised. "I don't speak of him much, and I—I didn't think you were interested."

"But you believe Lord Wrexley is?"

Wrexley was utterly unworthy of her confidence, and yet she'd chosen to share a part of herself with *him*?

"I told Lord Wrexley the story about Typhon because he asked, my lord. You never did. If you recall, we didn't talk much, despite the many weeks we spent together."

Finn's brows drew together in a frown. "I don't recall that, no. We spoke as much as any betrothed couple does."

They'd spoken at suppers and musical evenings, and when they danced together at balls, or walked in Lady Chase's garden. When he'd called on her, they'd sat with her sisters and grandmother and spoken of… they'd spoken of…

Well, whatever they'd spoken of, he'd thought it perfectly acceptable at the time, and he'd never noticed any dissatisfaction on her part. But perhaps that was the problem. Now she'd jilted him—*twice*—he was noticing all kind of things about her he never had before.

She ran her palm down the horse's nose, avoiding Finn's gaze. "We spoke, of course, of the things any courting couple speaks of, such as dancing, mutual acquaintances, and the latest scandals, but we never spoke of anything of consequence, and certainly never of anything personal. I can't think of a single instance in which I openly shared my opinion with you during our courtship, or our betrothal."

There was a dejected note in her voice that startled Finn. He tried to recall their courtship—what he'd said, and what she'd said—but all he could remember was he'd always come away from their time together with a vague feeling the courtship was going as he intended. He hadn't bothered to consider it, or her, beyond that.

It had been a mistake, but surely it wasn't only *his* mistake? "I beg your pardon. I should have asked, or talked to you about my own—"

Family.

That was what he'd been about to say, but he bit the word back before he spoke it. What was there to say about his family? That his mother had run off to Scotland with her lover when he was six years old and left his heartbroken father behind to struggle with his grief? That his father had lost that battle when Finn was eight years old, and he'd been left to the care of an indifferent guardian, his headmaster at Eton, and a houseful of distracted servants? He never talked about his family, because beyond that grim tale and the empty void that followed it, there was nothing to say.

He cleared his throat, and tried again. "I should have talked to you, but you could have talked to me, as well. You never did."

She'd reached over the stall door and was stroking the stallion's chest, but her hand stilled at his words. "I wanted to at first, but…well, I was afraid I'd say the wrong thing, and after a while I was afraid to say anything at all. It just seemed easier to remain quiet."

Finn almost laughed. A few minutes ago this woman had nearly brought him to release with her voice alone. What did she need with words? "You don't seem to have any trouble finding the words to speak to Lord Wrexley."

"He's easier, somehow."

A muscle twitched in Finn's jaw. "Why? Because he's an earl and I'm a marquess? Or is it because Lord Wrexley is such *great fun*? After all, he's the sort of man who'll run races with you, whereas I'm the man who refused to kiss you in a sunlit garden."

There was so much resentment in his tone he couldn't deny the truth to himself any longer. He was jealous. Of *Lord Wrexley*, for Christ's sake, and angry with himself, because he'd been fool enough to squander the chance to kiss her.

A faint flush rose in her cheeks. "It has nothing to do with that, and even if it did, I don't wish to discuss it here. Lord Wrexley and Lady Honora are right outside the door, and they're waiting for us."

"Let them wait. It sounds as if you're saying you were afraid to talk to me, and I want to know why. I may be a marquess, but I'm not a brute."

She sighed. "I don't think you're a brute, Lord Huntington."

This sounded more promising, and some of Finn's tension eased, but before he could draw another breath, she added, "But at the same time, I never got the impression you cared much about what I thought, whereas I believe Lord Wrexley asked about Typhon because he truly wanted to the know the answer."

"Yes, he was quite keen, wasn't he? I doubt his curiosity is as innocent as you think it is." Wrexley was a villain, but he wasn't a fool. He had a reason for everything he did, and Finn had no doubt whatever reason he had to suggest she ride Chaos, it benefitted no one but himself.

She turned away from him, back toward Chaos's stall, but when she spoke she was watching him from the corner of her eye. "Innocent or not, I prefer his curiosity to your indifference, Lord Huntington."

She'd gone back to stroking the horse, but Finn wasn't about to let her avoid his gaze. If they were going to speak truthfully to each other at last, she was going to look him in the eyes.

He caught her wrist and drew her away from the stall. "Look at me. I'm not as…easy with people as Lord Wrexley is, but if you'd tried to talk to me, I would have listened to you. Did you think I'd reproach you, or dismiss your wishes?"

"We'll never know now, will we?"

"Why shouldn't we? You have my undivided attention right now, Miss Somerset, so if you've something to say to me, then say it."

She met his gaze with unflinching steadiness. "Very well, my lord. If I had told you about Typhon, if I'd said I wanted a beast of a horse just like him once we were married, what would you have said?"

Finn hesitated. Part of him wanted to insist he'd have been delighted to hear his future marchioness rode like a cavalry officer, but he'd asked for this, and he wasn't going to lie to her. "I might not have liked it, but I wouldn't have forbidden it. I would have insisted we get you a second horse, however."

"Why should I need a second horse? Surely one horse is enough for any lady."

"Not for a marchioness. Several horses, a carriage for your exclusive use—these things would have been yours as a matter of course, but a horse like Typhon or Chaos wouldn't be appropriate for a ride in Hyde Park during the fashionable hour."

She raised an eyebrow at that. "Oh? I don't see why not."

"Because a marchioness doesn't get into a tussle with a headstrong mount in the middle of the promenade with all of the *ton* watching."

"Ah." She smiled a little. "What if I told you I've never in my life gotten into a tussle with *any* horse, and even if I did, I wouldn't care a thing what the *ton* thought of it? What would you have said to that?"

Finn opened his mouth, then snapped it shut without speaking.

Now she'd found her words at last they poured out of her, as if she'd kept them behind her lips for far too long, and a dam had suddenly given way. "What if I said I didn't want to ride on the promenade at all, but preferred a hard ride in Richmond Park to a mindless simper with every other aristocrat in London riding on my heels? That even if I did take a gentle mare out for sedate rides along the promenade, and everyone who saw me thought me a proper marchioness, I would have been wishing I was flying over the open ground of Richmond Park the entire time? Somehow, Lord Huntington, I don't think any of it would have pleased you."

Finn stared at her. He wanted to argue with her, to deny her assumption, but he couldn't say a word, because it was true. He wouldn't have been at all pleased to hear that, not so much because he gave a damn if she paraded around Hyde Park on the mare, but because it was the last thing he would have expected her to say, or to feel.

A lie by omission.

He'd lied to her. The wager, his mistress, his past—he'd hidden it all from her, and those were lies of omission, and as devious as any other kind of lie. But she'd lied to him, too. She'd pretended to be someone she wasn't, just as he had.

"Yesterday you accused me of not being the perfect gentleman I pretend to be, but neither are you the quiet, docile lady you pretended to be, Miss Somerset. A great many lies were hidden in our silences, weren't they?"

She stiffened, going unnaturally still. "I think...I think we preferred each other's silence. It's easier that way—easier to be what you're expected to be, rather than what you are. If we'd been honest with each other, we might not have made it as far as a betrothal. It's a pity we did, but we can be thankful we escaped the marriage, at least."

Anger pulsed through him, and his fingers tightened around her wrist. "We've escaped nothing. It's much too late for that now. We *will* marry, because people will be hurt if we don't."

You'll be hurt.

"But we'll be hurt if we *do*." She tugged to free herself from his grip. "Now, if you'd be so good as to tell the stableboy to saddle Chaos, I'd be grateful."

Damn it, he'd forgotten all about the horse. "No, Miss Somerset. You can't ride this horse. You'll have to choose another."

"I beg your pardon? Did Captain West say he couldn't be ridden?"

"No, but *I'm* saying it. You need a safer mount. Chaos may look quiet now, but he's as temperamental as they come, and he's too much horse for you. Choose another, and then we can be off."

She studied him for a moment with narrowed eyes, then, "You've never seen me ride anywhere but on the promenade, so you can't have the faintest idea what I can or can't manage, and I'm afraid this isn't your decision to make, Lord Huntington. I can ride Chaos, and I will."

She spoke politely enough, but the cool determination in her tone told him she wouldn't give up easily, and it lit a spark inside Finn's chest. He kept his temper under tight control at all times, but this wasn't just anger. Oh, he was angry enough, but the anger was tangled up with other, more complicated emotions.

Admiration, disbelief, and a pulsing, restless excitement.

"No, Miss Somerset, you won't. Not until Captain West approves it, and not until you've taken him out in the stable yard and convinced me you can manage a horse of that size."

She stared up at him with mutiny in every line of her face. Her lips pressed into a thin, tight line, and...

Ah, yes. There it was, that stubborn chin.

"Convinced *you*? I don't think so, my lord. Now, if you'll excuse me, I'll find the stableboy myself."

She went to brush past him, but he still held her wrist, and he pulled her against his chest. "You'll do no such thing. You will not ride that horse, Miss Somerset. Not today."

His voice was low and rough, and he felt a slight shiver go through her.

Finn went still as his senses leapt in response. Her stared down at her, into eyes such an endless blue he felt as if he were hurling himself into an ocean, willingly, even though he knew he might never surface again. She was so close he could see the quick rise and fall of her chest under her riding habit, and caught the soft, delicate scent of her hair. Jasmine, perhaps, but with something else, too, something unexpected and exotic.

"How do you intend to stop me, Lord Huntington?"

An unmistakable challenge sparked in her blue eyes, and then, somehow, his lips were mere inches from her ear, so close the springy tendrils of hair that seemed to be forever escaping her pins brushed against his jaw, and he had to bite back a sudden, unexpected groan at the teasing caress of those curls.

"Look around you, Miss Somerset. I already have."

Another lady would have shuddered at his rasped command. Another lady would have submitted to him, or pushed him away and fled the stables. *But not her.*

She drew closer, until her lips were a breath away from his ear. "For now. But Chaos will be waiting for me tomorrow, and so will Lord Wrexley."

The moment she said Wrexley's name, the tight control Finn held over his emotions snapped. His riding crop landed on the floor of the barn as he caught her other wrist, then pulled her harder against his chest before his mouth crashed down on hers.

She let out a startled squeak at the first touch of his lips, but within seconds her mouth went soft under his, and when the tip of his tongue darted out to trace the seam of her lips she made another sound—a sigh, or a quiet moan—and her mouth opened to him without a hint of resistance, her breath a warm drift across his tongue.

And oh, God, she was sweet, sweeter than he could have ever imagined. Was this why he'd resisted kissing her? Because he'd known, even before his lips touched hers, he wouldn't be able to get enough of her?

His mouth clung to hers, coaxing her to open wider with a single gentle stroke of his tongue, and then another. He still held her wrists, and he lifted her hands to his chest. Her warm palms pressed flat against him and her fingers curled into his waistcoat. He released her wrists then and slid his fingers into the mass of silky hair at the back of her neck and drew her tighter against him, a low groan tearing from his chest as his tongue darted over the delicious curve of her bottom lip.

Finn tried to pull air into his heaving lungs, tried to remember that Wrexley and Lady Honora were just on the other side of the stable doors and could walk in at any moment, but he couldn't breathe or think. He could only taste her, his mouth growing more desperate with each eager stroke of her tongue, his hands rough in the heavy silk of her hair. He wanted to pull each pin loose until it spilled over her back as it had yesterday, so he could tangle his fingers in it, pull her head back and devour the soft, white skin of her neck and throat.

He nipped at her bottom lip, and a strangled moan escaped her as he trailed his fingers over her neck and down her back to palm the curves of her hips. He dragged her body tighter against his so the soft warmth of her belly cradled him, and he thought he'd go mad, *was* going mad, his brain clouding with frantic desire.

"We can't...this isn't..." She was breathless, her whisper a soft, warm breath against his neck.

Finn could almost pretend she hadn't said the words, that she hadn't gripped his forearms to pull his hands away.

Almost.

But he was still close enough to feel her trembling, and the thread of panic in her voice cleared some of the fog of desire from his brain. For the briefest moment he let his cheek rest against the top of her head, let himself bury his face in her hair, desperately inhaling her warm scent one last time before he forced himself to release her.

He dropped his arms to his sides.

They stared at each other, both of them breathing hard, neither of them moving, until at last he took a step back, away from her.

"Do you still think I'm a child, Lord Huntington?" There was a flicker of triumph in her eyes.

Finn stared down at her in a daze. "No."

She was no child. She was a woman who needed to be kissed, often, by him, and only him. Her mouth was made for his, and no one else's. He dipped his head toward hers again. Her taste was still on his lips, and all he could think about was getting more of it.

But she pressed her hands against his chest and held him back. "I'm not a child, and I'll decide what horse I'll ride and who I ride with. If I choose to spend time with Lord Wrexley, that's not your concern."

But it was, because he'd made it—*her*—his concern. "You think I'll just let him have you? You may think Wrexley is a wise choice, but he's—"

"He's my *only* choice. Nothing has changed since I jilted you, my lord. Both of us know I'm not the kind of lady you'd willingly choose for your marchioness. You don't want me, not really, and I don't..." She stopped, her throat working, then said, "I don't want you."

Liar. I can still feel you trembling, still hear your breathlessness.

She did want him, and he wanted her, so much he was dizzy with it, but he couldn't deny the thought of making her his marchioness filled him with both longing and dread at once. She was defiant and willful, tempting and beautiful, and he'd never wanted a wife who made him lose control. A wife who made him want her, who drove him mad with fury and desire.

He'd never wanted someone extraordinary.

But he didn't say any of this, and when he spoke, his voice was cold. "It doesn't matter what either of us wants anymore."

Finn got one final glance at her pale face in the weak sunlight coming through the door before she stepped into the deep shadows of the stables and hurried down the row of stalls, the skirts of her dark blue riding habit dragging across the floor.

He leaned down to pick up his riding crop, and when he straightened again, she was gone.

Chapter Thirteen

"If you must spend the entire evening gaping at Lord Huntington, Iris, the least you can do is stop nibbling on your lip. You look as if you wish you could take a bite out of him."

Violet, who was seated next to Iris on the settee, nodded subtly toward the other side of the drawing room where Lord Huntington sat, his rapt gaze fixed on Lady Honora, who was playing the pianoforte for the assembled company.

I already bit him, and he's delicious.

Iris's body flooded with unwelcome heat at the memory, and she gave her pink silk skirts an irritated twitch. "I haven't the least intention of biting Lord Huntington, Violet. I just had dinner."

That is, she'd been *served* dinner. Halfway through the meal she'd abandoned her plate in favor of her wine glass. Had the wine been unusually good tonight? Iris frowned, trying to recall.

Yes, yes. It must have been. Otherwise she wouldn't have had so much of it. Perhaps a trifle too much, but if she had overindulged, it had nothing to do with Lord Huntington.

Or his kiss.

Especially not his kiss, no matter if her blood was still humming with pleasure, and her knees were still weak, hours later. "But if I *were* going to bite Lord Huntington, it would be nothing less than he deserved."

Violet had forgotten Iris entirely in favor of gaping at Lord Derrick, who was seated next to Lord Huntington, his face aglow with pleasure as he watched Lady Honora, but now she turned her attention back to her sister, her brow creased with a frown. "What's Lord Huntington done to you this time?"

He's kissed me, and now I can't stop thinking about his mouth.

"Not a thing, it's just...well, he isn't as perfect as he pretends to be."

She sounded like a fretful child, but Iris didn't dare tell Violet about Lord Huntington's kiss. It would lead to all sorts of awkward questions, none of which she could answer unless she also told her sister he'd "rejected her dismissal" and was demanding she go forward with the marriage.

"Well, he's been a perfect gentleman tonight."

Yes, he had, hadn't he? His fashionable dress, his manners, his air of polite attention as Honora played—it was all impeccable. He was every inch the exalted Marquess of Huntington tonight. Looking at him now, Iris could almost believe that wild, passionate kiss in the stables had never happened.

"My goodness, he looks handsome in his blue coat, doesn't he?"

Iris darted a sour look at him. He looked handsome in every color coat, or no coat, come to that, but the effect was spoiled by his captivated expression as he gazed at Lady Honora. Indeed, both Lord Huntington and Lord Derrick seemed unable to look away from her, as if they'd forgotten anyone other than Lady Honora was in the room.

"Certainly, if you think cold, stiff gentlemen are handsome. He hasn't so much as twitched since we entered the drawing room. Why, just look at him! He looks as if he's sitting for a painting."

"Well, what do you expect him to do? Dance a jig? He's listening to the music." Violet stared hard at Lord Derrick for a moment, as if she could will him into looking at her, but he appeared transfixed by Honora, and his gaze never wavered.

Violet sighed. "Honora plays wonderfully well, doesn't she?"

She did, and she looked lovely, her cheeks flushed with pleasure as her elegant fingers flew over the keys. "She does. She does everything beautifully."

Iris glanced down at her pink skirts with a sigh. Honora was wearing a pink gown tonight too, one nearly the same color as Iris's pink gown, and as soon as Honora finished playing, Iris would be called upon to play. She played well—quite as well as Honora—and her pink gown flattered her, just as Honora's pink gown did.

Pink perfection, as far as the eye could see.

A lie, swathed in layers of expensive silk.

You're not the quiet, docile lady you pretended to be.

Iris squirmed against the settee, but no amount of squirming or denial would change the fact Lord Huntington was right. She'd been pretending to be someone she wasn't, just as he had, and if she hadn't quite realized how far she'd taken it until he said it aloud, it didn't make her any less guilty.

That cursed wager—her blood boiled every time she thought about it, not only because Lord Huntington had chosen Honora over her, though that was enough to offend any lady. No, what truly galled her was he'd thought she and Honora were interchangeable, as if it hardly mattered if he lost one lady on the turn of a card, since the other lady would do just as well.

Despicable, of course, except for one small thing.

He wasn't entirely wrong. That is, he was only right in a miniscule, shallow, and insignificant way, but still—he wasn't entirely wrong. She and Honora might be nothing alike in character or temperament, but they were so alike in their manners, their dress, and their accomplishments, it was a wonder anyone could tell them apart.

If all of London thought her a pale shadow of Honora, then it was her own fault. Somehow, over the course of the season, between the suitors, the balls, and the flirtatious flutters of her fan, Iris had realized plain Iris Somerset, the simple country miss from Surrey, wasn't going to be good enough for fashionable London society.

So she became Lady Honora instead.

Not consciously, of course, but now, looking back on it, Iris could see how it had happened. It made perfect sense, really. Her grandmother wanted a match with Lord Huntington, and Lord Huntington wanted Lady Honora. Well, Lady Honora, or Lady Beaumont. Iris wasn't sure which, but it hardly mattered, because she wasn't either of them.

The truth was, if he'd known what she hid under those layers of pink silk, he never would have offered for her at all.

Iris sighed and wished for another glass of wine.

"My goodness," Violet murmured as Lady Honora neared the end of her piece with a dramatic display of ringing notes. "How awful it would be to have to play after Honora does. You play beautifully, of course, so you'll have no trouble, but think how it would be for any lady less skilled than you are, Iris. I'd be quite terrified."

Iris snorted. "Yes, well, nothing motivates a young lady more effectively than terror. Why practice the pianoforte at all other than the threat of humiliation? It's no wonder the gentlemen expect such docile, predictable wives. The *ton* terrorizes us into compliance, and then marries us off."

"My, that's cynical."

Cynical, but true nonetheless, and young ladies who didn't comply— well, they had every reason to be terrified, didn't they?

The moment she'd jilted Lord Huntington, Iris had ceased to be compliant.

Her gaze wandered back to him, and her breath caught. He was so handsome, so perfect, with his snowy white cravat and that charming dimple in his chin. He'd transformed effortlessly from the fiercely passionate man who'd kissed her in the stables this afternoon to the flawless Marquess of Huntington this evening.

He could be both of them, it seemed.

But I can't.

She couldn't pretend anymore. The pink gowns, the perfect quadrille, the pianoforte—it wasn't who she was. She was the lady who hiked her skirts to her knees and ran races, the lady who wanted to tear across the countryside on a half-wild horse, with her hair streaming out behind her. All the things she wanted to do, like kiss a gentleman in a garden, or wear a royal blue gown, or ride Chaos—every single one had been denied her, and she could no longer pretend it didn't matter.

She could never be the perfect marchioness Lord Huntington wanted, and all the knee-weakening kisses in the world didn't change that. This afternoon, in the stables, she'd told him Lord Wrexley was her only choice, and it was still true. Lord Huntington's kisses, that hint of vulnerability in his hazel eyes—they would distract her from her goal, and then what would become of her and her sisters?

It wasn't the time or place to get into a panic, but within seconds Iris's heart was thrashing and her hands were trembling with it, and just then Lady Honora's fingers crashed down on the keys, and the music rose to an emotional crescendo, and Iris's head jerked toward the pianoforte, and all the fear in her chest tightened into a cold, hard ball of dread and lodged in the back of her throat.

Iris stared at the despised pianoforte. "I don't want to play."

Violet gave her a puzzled look. "What do you mean, you don't want to play? Everyone expects it. You have to play."

"No, I don't. I don't have to do anything I don't want to do."

"But...but then they'll ask *me* to play!" Violet was far from shy and retiring, but her one fear was public musical performances, and it was such a deep and abiding one it teetered on the irrational.

"Refuse, then." Iris gave her sister's hand a distracted pat as she glanced around the drawing room for a possible escape route. Now she'd made up her mind not to play, she couldn't bear to sit here another minute.

Violet was wringing her hands. "But I can't refuse. Can I?"

"Why not? I am."

Violet continued to mutter and fret to herself, but Iris didn't have the energy tonight to soothe her, and as it happened, she didn't have to. A movement in the hallway outside the drawing room caught her eye, and her gaze met Lord Wrexley's.

He'd been mysteriously absent at dinner this evening, and he seemed to prefer to stay hidden now. He'd positioned himself so he could see her, but he was just out of sight of the rest of the party. When she met his gaze he gave a beckoning tilt of his head, and an inviting smile drifted over his handsome face.

Iris didn't think about how rude it was to leave the drawing room while Honora was still playing. She didn't think about how she was abandoning her sister, or the impropriety of wandering off alone with Lord Wrexley.

She was thinking about pink gowns, and pianofortes, and Lord Huntington's hot mouth on hers, his commanding voice telling her she couldn't ride Chaos and ordering her to choose another horse.

It doesn't matter what either of us want. Not anymore.

But it did matter. It mattered to *her*.

She clutched her skirts in her hands and rose to her feet.

"Iris!" Violet hissed. "Where do you think you're going?"

"I need some fresh air. I'm going for a walk."

Violet caught hold of a fold of her skirts to stop her, but Iris yanked it away, and in the next breath she'd crossed the drawing room and joined Lord Wrexley in the hallway. He held out his arm as she approached, and she took it, and let him lead her into the darkness beyond the terrace doors.

* * * *

"Good Lord, it was as dull as a tomb in there, wasn't it?"

"Don't tell me you don't care for the pianoforte, Lord Wrexley."

"I'm utterly indifferent to the pianoforte, Miss Somerset, though I grant you my cousin plays very well." He smiled down at her. "Nearly as well as you, I believe."

"Much better, I think. Lady Honora truly loves to play, whereas I—"

"Don't? The *ton* has spent the entire season raving about your skills on the pianoforte, and you mean to say you've been fooling them all this time? How shocking."

He sounded more amused than shocked, however. Iris raised an eyebrow at him. "Technical skill isn't love, my lord."

Oh, dear. Perhaps she shouldn't be speaking of love to Lord Wrexley, especially not when she was out here alone with him on a dark terrace.

But he only laughed. "No, it isn't. But tell me, did you enjoy our ride today, Miss Somerset?"

"I did, only…" She hesitated. It wasn't proper to reveal the details of the argument she'd had with Lord Huntington to Lord Wrexley.

"Only you wanted to ride Chaos. I confess I was surprised to see you'd chosen another horse. I suppose Lord Huntington insisted?"

"He did." In the end she'd chosen one of the mares, but she hadn't any intention of giving up her plans to ride Chaos. After all, Lord Huntington couldn't watch her all the time, could he? No matter what Lady Beaumont might think, she wasn't a child on leading strings, her straps caught in Lord Huntington's fist, her every step dependent on his whim and pleasure.

A little shiver chased up her spine at the thought of being bound to Lord Huntington, his hazel eyes following her everywhere, uncovering her secrets, but Iris shrugged it away. It was hardly anything to shiver in pleasure over.

"Ah, well. We'll have to leave Lord Huntington behind next time. Shall we try again tomorrow morning? I spoke to Captain West, and he's given his permission for us to take out Chaos. We should go early in the morning, I think."

Iris hesitated. It was one thing to walk on the terrace alone with Lord Wrexley, but quite another to dash off into the countryside with him.

"Good Lord, Miss Somerset. Don't tell me you've let Huntington's blather about Chaos dissuade you from riding him. When anything pleasant is afoot, Huntington's always the first to disapprove of it. He was the same way at school."

Iris looked up at him, surprised. "You knew Lord Huntington in school? What was he like?"

Lord Wrexley snorted. "The same spiritless, dry old stick he is now, though I'll grant you the other boys didn't give him an easy time of it, what with that scandal about his mother."

Scandal? Both of Lord Huntington's parents were dead, and Iris had never heard a breath of scandal about either of them, but then today, in the stables, she'd been certain he'd been about to say something about his family before he'd stopped and abruptly changed the subject.

"Now I think on it, Miss Somerset, perhaps Huntington is right, after all, and you can't handle a horse of Chaos's temperament. My cousin assures me you're an excellent rider, but Chaos is a challenging mount. He may prove to be too much for you."

Iris's lips thinned with irritation. First Lord Huntington doubted her equestrienne skills, and now Lord Wrexley did, as well? The minute she'd touched that horse, she'd felt an instant connection to him she'd never had with any other animal aside from Typhon, and she ached to ride him.

"I haven't yet found a horse I couldn't manage, Lord Wrexley."

"You know, I believe you haven't." He grinned down at her. "You're rather a remarkable lady, Miss Somerset."

She forced a laugh. "Oh, not at all, my lord. I assure you, I'm quite dull and ordinary."

Except there had been a time, when her father was still alive, when she'd felt as if she were—well, if not remarkable, then utterly and completely herself. Every now and then she felt a trace of it again, but holding onto it was like catching fog in your hand. As soon as her fingers closed around it, it vanished into the air.

"Remarkable, and quite beautiful," Lord Wrexley murmured.

Iris's gaze lifted to his. They were strolling across the terrace, and there was just enough light for her to admire his smooth, dark hair and the confident smile toying with his lips. They didn't make her ache like Lord Huntington's lips did, but Lord Wrexley was very handsome, and it was foolish to ache over a gentleman who wanted someone else.

This afternoon, in the stables, it hadn't felt as if he wanted someone else, but tonight it couldn't be clearer his admiration for Honora hadn't waned.

"Miss Somerset." Lord Wrexley drew her closer to the edge of the terrace, toward the garden, and away from the light from the house.

Iris froze, unsure what to do. She shouldn't let him kiss her, but if she didn't, then she'd have only the memory of Lord Huntington's kiss when she was alone in her bedchamber tonight.

Lord Wrexley's face was lowering to hers, his gaze on her mouth. "May I—"

"Iris! There you are. I've been looking for you this age."

Iris jumped, and a low growl tore from Lord Wrexley's throat. He was staring over her shoulder, his full lips turned down in a frown.

Iris whirled around to find Lady Annabel standing at the top of a shallow flight of stairs, one of the terrace doors standing open behind her. The fire behind her toyed with the folds of the delicious flame-red gown that had rendered Iris nearly speechless with envy at dinner this evening.

Lord Wrexley cleared his throat. "You startled us, my lady. I didn't realize you were there."

"Yes, that's clear enough, my lord. Come with me at once, Iris."

She held out an imperious hand, and Iris didn't even think to disobey her. Before she could mount the stairs, however, Lord Wrexley caught her hand and pressed a kiss to her gloved fingertips. "Good night, Miss Somerset." He bowed, then leaned toward her and whispered, "Don't forget our ride tomorrow. Meet me in the stables before dawn."

He cast one inscrutable look at Lady Annabel, then bowed once more to Iris, and melted into the shadows of the garden behind him.

"Well, thank goodness he's gone. Come along." Lady Annabel didn't wait for an answer, but disappeared into the dim room beyond. Iris followed her, her breath catching with pleasure when she entered the tiny sitting room. It wasn't grand, but so cozy, with a rich blue and gold carpet, plump leather chairs, and a fire burning low in the grate.

"It's lovely, isn't it?" Lady Annabel sauntered over to the desk to fetch a carafe of wine and two glasses and motioned Iris into one of the chairs. "It's Charlotte's favorite room."

"I can see why it would be."

Lady Annabel poured a generous measure of rich red wine into one of the glasses and passed it to Iris, then sat down with her own glass. Iris expected a scolding, but Lady Annabel only traced one finger over the rim of her glass and observed her with a thoughtful expression.

The silence went on so long Iris began to squirm. "Lady Annabel, I—"

"Not yet. After you finish your wine."

The wine was as delicious as she remembered, but Iris gulped it down with haste, anxious to end the unbearable silence.

"Lady Annabel," she began again when her glass was empty. "I—"

Lady Annabel beckoned with her fingers for Iris's glass, filled it again, and handed it back. Iris's head felt a bit wobbly on her shoulders, but she took the glass and brought it to her lips.

By the time she'd half-emptied it, she felt quite a bit more cheerful about the situation. It was just a little walk on the terrace, after all, and nothing improper had occurred. He hadn't even kissed her. Why, it was nothing—

"Now, suppose you tell me what you were doing alone on the terrace with Lord Wrexley."

Lady Annabel was watching her, so Iris tried to arrange her face into a properly scandalized expression and opened her lips to plead ignorance, or beg for forgiveness, or do whatever it was a lady did when she was caught on a dark terrace with a gentleman.

"Well, I was going to let him kiss me, to see if I liked it as well as I did when Lord Huntington kissed me, but—"

Iris slapped a hand over her mouth. Oh, dear God. Had she said that aloud? Goodness, this was humiliating. Perhaps more wine would help. She raised her glass to her lips and peeked over the rim to find Lady Annabel watching her with an amused expression on her face.

"Well? Did he kiss you?"

Iris took a few more sips of wine to loosen her tongue. "No, but he was about to. I don't mind saying, my lady, I was relieved to find him so eager."

"I don't know many gentlemen who wouldn't be eager in that situation."

"But indeed there are such gentlemen. Lord Huntington, for one."

"Lord Huntington?" Lady Annabel looked surprised. "You mean to say he had an opportunity to kiss you, and he didn't take it?"

Iris covered her mouth to disguise a tiny hiccup. "Yes, but to be fair, he was in rather a rush. His mistress was hiding behind the rose bushes at the time, you see, and she was listening."

Lady Annabel's eyes went wide. "Lord Huntington had Lady Beaumont secreted away in the bushes while he was meant to be kissing you?"

He wasn't precisely *meant* to be kissing her, but it was too difficult to explain that to Lady Annabel, so Iris nodded. "Yes, something like that. Lady Beaumont is rather unpleasant, isn't she?"

"Oh, no. No more unpleasant than a nest of poisonous vipers, that is. But you mentioned Lady Beaumont the other day, when we spoke in your bedchamber. Is she the reason you jilted Lord Huntington? Because many aristocratic gentlemen keep mistresses, Iris. I don't suppose their wives like it much, but I'm afraid the only acceptable response for a lady is to look the other way. It's not sufficient grounds to jilt him."

Iris waved a hand in the air, then frowned down at the splash of red wine she'd spilled on her skirt. "No, no. I realize aristocratic gentlemen often have mistresses. No, it wasn't that, or even that awful wager he made, though I do think I would have been well within my rights to jilt him for that."

"Ah. The wager." Lady Annabel leaned forward. "You mentioned that before, as well. Well, let's have the worst of it, then."

Goodness, was her wine gone already? Iris held out her glass to Lady Annabel. "It was a very ungentlemanly business, but I suppose I ended up with the better end of it, since poor Honora only narrowly escaped a marriage to Lord Harley, that scoundrel."

Lady Annabel poured more wine into Iris's glass. "You mean to say Lord Harley, Lord Wrexley, and Lord Huntington wagered for the chance to court you and Lady Honora?"

"Yes. As I said before, Lord Huntington lost and got stuck with me, I'm afraid." Iris laughed a little, but she couldn't quite ignore the jab of pain in her chest.

"I wouldn't have thought that of Lord Huntington," Lady Annabel murmured, more to herself than Iris. "I confess I can see why you might wish to jilt him after that, but I doubt the *ton* will be so forgiving."

Iris held out her hand for her glass of wine, and Lady Annabel passed it to her. "No, but then that's not really why I jilted him."

"This is much more complicated than I anticipated. Why, then?"

Iris thought hard. There'd been a reason—something rather heartbreaking, actually, but she couldn't quite recall it now...

"Oh! Oh yes, I remember. I jilted him because Lord Huntington doesn't care for me. I just happened to be the season's belle when he made up his mind to marry, and I suppose one young lady is a good as another, isn't she? I daresay he spends a great deal more time and care choosing a horse at Tattersall's than he did his marchioness. Well, the wager shows that clearly enough. But I was wrong to jilt him. I see that now. My grandmother, and my sisters..." Iris stared down into the bottom of her wineglass. "It was foolish and selfish of me."

What had she expected from a marriage, after all? Love, devotion, faithfulness? Passion, even?

Yes. It was exactly what she'd expected.

No. It was more than that. It was what she deserved, not that it made the least bit of difference now.

Lady Annabel placed her wineglass on the silver tray in front of her and turned a penetrating gaze on Iris. "I confess you surprise me, Iris. I must say, I admire your courage. Not many young ladies in your position would trouble themselves much about anything other than becoming a marchioness."

Iris smiled over the dry ache in her throat. "Yes, well—just as I said, it was foolish, but it was more than just the wager, Lady Annabel. He refused an innocent kiss from me when we were betrothed, but not half an hour later he was skulking around the rose bushes with his mistress, reveling in his past debaucheries with her."

That wasn't *quite* fair, since he'd been trying to disentangle himself from Lady Beaumont more that he'd been reveling in his debaucheries, but Iris didn't feel like being fair, and she'd had enough wine she didn't have to be.

"I just...everything inside me swelled with fury at the injustice of it. For pity's sake, he tied Lady Beaumont up with silk scarves, then balked at a simple kiss from his betrothed!" Iris drained the rest of the wine in her glass. "I never even had a chance with Lord Huntington. He'd dismissed me before we were even betrothed. He would have made me his marchioness, and in return for that honor, he would have expected utter propriety from me at all times. Unquestioning obedience, as well. I never would have gained his love, or even his respect. I realize I'm meant to settle for the title—to be grateful for it, even—but I knew it was never going to be enough for me."

Iris fell back against the settee, a little surprised at herself, but as soon as the words came out, she realized she'd wanted to give herself permission to speak them for a long time.

"It's *not* enough, or it shouldn't be. Not for anyone. But you said earlier Lord Huntington did kiss you, so at some point his insistence on propriety must have given way to passion. Unless it wasn't a passionate kiss?"

Iris's belly gave a wild little leap as she remembered the way he'd looked at her when she'd challenged him about Chaos, and the feel of his mouth on hers, hot and demanding, his short, ragged breaths. She could have kissed him for hours, days—even now she hadn't the faintest idea how she'd managed to pull herself from his arms.

It seemed she had some dark desires of her own.

But how could she confess such a thing to Lady Annabel? Proper ladies didn't have dark desires. At least, Iris had never heard any lady of her acquaintance confess to them, but then a notoriously wicked widow wasn't just *any* lady, and Iris had come this far without Lady Annabel falling into a shocked swoon.

"Well, if I can't confide in a wicked widow about my dark desires, who can I confide in?" As soon as the words slipped past her lips, Iris could have bitten out her tongue. "I mean, not *wicked*, of course. I don't think you're wicked in the least, Lady Annabel. What I mean is—"

She didn't get any further, because Lady Annabel threw back her head and laughed. "It's quite all right. I reconciled myself to my wickedness a long time ago." She leaned forward, her blue eyes alight with humor. "And really, my dear, being wicked is far more amusing than being good."

Iris snorted. "Lord Huntington knows that well enough."

Lady Annabel's lips twitched. "You're referring to the silk scarves?"

"Yes!" Iris beamed. Lady Annabel was terribly clever. "That same day, when Lady Beaumont was hiding in the garden—well, this was rather bad of me—but I overheard her argument with Lord Huntington. That's how I discovered the truth about his *dark desires*."

Just saying those words made a shiver run down her spine.

"I see." Lady Annabel cocked her head to one side, studying Iris. "Speaking of desires, tell me, Iris. How are you getting on with the reading I recommended?"

"It's, ah...been quite enlightening, just as you promised."

Lady Annabel chuckled. "Yes, I daresay it has been. Do you have any questions about anything you've read?"

Iris raised her hands and pressed her palms to her burning cheeks. Goodness, that fire was hot. "I've finished *Dialogues between a Lady and Her Maid.* Violet interrupted me when I was searching for *School of Venus*, but I thought I'd look again before I retire tonight. Perhaps I'll save my questions for after I've finished them all."

"Very well." Lady Annabel hesitated, a frown creasing her brow. "You may find as you read that you learn as much about yourself as anything else. Every young lady should have such knowledge, but sometimes discovering truths about yourself makes things a bit more...complicated. Are you prepared for that?"

Iris nodded. Wasn't it a good thing if she learned about herself? "Yes, I think so."

Lady Annabel rose from the sofa. "Very well, then. Come to me when you've finished with the books."

"Yes, I will. You're very kind, my lady."

"I'm not kind at all. I assure you, I do this only for my own amusement."

"Yes, very well." Iris bit her lip as a thought occurred to her. "The house party ends in just over a week. That will be enough time to learn everything I need to know, won't it?"

For some reason, this made Annabel laugh. "Why don't we wait and see?"

Chapter Fourteen

He'd meant to be civilized about it. Gentlemanly.

Finn knocked quietly on Miss Somerset's door, but when there was no answer, and the knob turned easily in his hand, his fingers clenched until his knuckles cracked.

She'd left her bedchamber door unlocked.

Apprehension made him fling open the door with more force than he'd intended, and he winced as it crashed into the wall behind it. Damn it. He only wanted to see if she was in her bedchamber and out of Wrexley's reach, not frighten the wits out of her.

He needn't have worried. The room was dark, and even in the dim light from the hallway he could see it was empty. She wasn't here, and it looked as if she hadn't been here yet this evening.

"Bloody hell, Huntington. There's no need to tear the house down." Lord Derrick, who must have heard the crash, rounded the corner at the end of the hallway and joined Finn outside Miss Somerset's bedchamber.

"She's not there."

Derrick peered over his shoulder into the silent bedchamber. "Are you sure you have the right room? Christ, this house is worse than a puzzle maze. I feel like a rabbit who's scurried down the wrong hole."

"I'm sure. It's her room. It has her scent."

Derrick's eyebrows shot up. "Her *scent*?"

"Jasmine." Finn pulled the door shut and turned back toward the staircase. "We're wasting time."

"Just a moment, if you please." Derrick leaned a hip against the wall and crossed his arms over his chest with the air of a man who wasn't going anywhere. "You're acting like a bloody Bedlamite. Why are you so agitated?"

"*Why?* For God's sake, Derrick. Do you suppose it's a coincidence both Miss Somerset and Wrexley are missing? She's gone off alone with that villain. We haven't seen a glimpse of her since she left the drawing room, despite an hour's search through the house and gardens."

"Yes, I'm aware of the circumstances, Huntington. I didn't ask for a summary of them. I asked why you're so agitated."

Finn's back teeth snapped together. "I just told you."

"No, I don't think so. You know as well as I do Miss Somerset can't have gone far. She'll turn up, and in any case, I would have thought it would take much more than one misplaced young lady to shake the Marquess of Huntington's icy composure." Derrick gave him an innocent look. "Unless, of course, you've grown fonder of her than you're willing to admit. Have you?"

Fond of her? Finn didn't know whether to marry her or turn her over his knee. Did that mean he was *fond* of her?

Derrick arched an eyebrow at him, waiting.

"I don't care for fair-haired ladies," Finn muttered at last.

"Yes, I believe you've said so before."

"Or dark blue eyes, even if they are the toast of London."

Derrick shrugged. "A lot of fuss over nothing, if you ask me."

"She's a menace, as well. Did I tell you she tried to ride a half-wild horse this morning? She would have marched him right out the stable doors and jumped onto his back if I hadn't stopped her."

"Shocking behavior."

"I'm the injured party here, Derrick. *She* jilted *me*."

"Twice, even."

"She said we didn't suit, and now I know her better, I couldn't agree more. I don't want a wife who chases after every whim as it happens to strike her, without a care as to who she might trample under her feet as she goes."

"Troublesome thing in a wife, I daresay."

"Lady Honora was my first choice, you know, and I'm free to court her now if I wish. I should be thanking Miss Somerset for jilting me."

"You really should. Why don't you do that, once we find her?"

"Steady, peaceful, and predictable—that's Lady Honora. She's just the kind of lady I've always imagined would become my marchioness. *She* wouldn't insist on riding a wild horse, or be so rude as to leave the drawing room without playing the pianoforte, and she would *never* vanish into the night with a rake like Wrexley."

"She'd never dream of it."

"If Miss Somerset chooses to throw herself away on a scoundrel, what business is it of mine?"

"Why, none at all."

"She's caused me enough trouble to last me into my dotage, Derrick, and that's only in the last several days. God only knows what mayhem tomorrow will bring."

"God only knows."

"I don't even *like* the scent of jasmine."

"Why would you? Sickly sweet stuff. Cloying, even."

"I'm the Marquess of Huntington, for God's sake, and I've been tearing around this house like a fool all night, chasing after some unruly chit who's jilted me."

"Twice."

"Well, then. Miss Somerset may do as she pleases. I'm retiring to my bedchamber." Finn turned on his heel and marched down the hallway. He was scowling—he knew he was, because his brow was so low he could feel his eyelashes brush his forehead with every blink.

Damn it, where was she?

He stopped at the top of the staircase and turned back to Derrick, who was still leaning against the wall outside Miss Somerset's door.

Derrick raised an eyebrow at him. "Something the matter, Huntington?"

"I'll just go through the first floor one last time, only because I'll sleep better knowing I've done all I can to find her. Not for any other reason."

"All right, then."

"Perhaps I'd better search the terrace and garden again, too. I've been out there once, but there are a great many places to hide in a garden, especially one of that size."

Derrick straightened from his slouch against the wall and sauntered toward Finn. "I'll search the first floor, if you like. I'm going down in any case, for another game of chess with Lady Honora. The search will go more quickly if I help, and I know you're anxious to conclude this business with Miss Somerset."

"I am, only..." Only he hadn't the faintest idea anymore whether concluding the business meant leaving Miss Somerset to her fate, or dragging her off to his bedchamber and kissing her senseless until she agreed to marry him.

"Only?" Derrick gave him a look of polite inquiry.

Finn dragged both hands down his face without replying, because when it came to Miss Somerset, he hadn't the faintest idea how he felt, much less what to say. Christ, how had things gone so awry in just a few short days? It should have been a simple enough matter to persuade her to marry him, so how did he come to be chasing all over Hadley House, his stomach in knots over a woman he'd dismissed easily enough when he was betrothed to her?

"You know, Huntington, it wouldn't be the worst thing in the world if, despite her fair hair, blue eyes, jasmine scent, and air of general menace, you should find yourself fond of Miss Somerset, after all. If that should prove to be the case, allow me to offer you a few words of advice."

Finn blew out a breath. "Very well. What is it?"

"Tell her you're fond of her, instead of making her feel as if you're marrying her only because it's the honorable thing to do, as if you have no choice. Women are odd creatures, you see, Huntington. They like to think their betrothed has some affection for them. Rather foolish, but there it is." Derrick thumped him on the back, then brushed past on his way down the stairs.

Finn watched him go until Derrick melted into the shadows on the first floor, then he followed after him, taking the stairs two at a time and muttering to himself the entire way.

But when he emerged onto the terrace he found nothing but silent darkness, and the anxiety that had started as a pinch in his chest deepened to dread. His boots rang against the stones beneath his feet, the sound fading to a faint crunch when he reached the loose pebbles on the main garden pathway.

But the garden was as silent as the terrace, the only sound his gasping breaths as he turned this way and that, searching for someone who wasn't there.

Who wasn't…anywhere.

"She's in the library, Lord Huntington."

Finn whirled around to find Lady Tallant standing on the terrace behind him, her red gown fluttering in the breeze, and behind her, a flickering light, just visible through the glass door that led from the terrace to the library. He hadn't noticed it before.

"Miss Somerset, that is," Lady Tallant added. "I assume you're looking for her?"

"I—yes. Thank you." Finn came down the pathway and mounted the stairs to the terrace door. He'd checked the library earlier in the evening and found it empty, but the light was indeed coming from there.

It was her. It had to be.

Finn bowed to Lady Tallant and started for the door, anxious not to waste any more time, but she stopped him with a touch to his arm.

"Miss Somerset is your betrothed, I believe, Lord Huntington? At least, I understand you intend to marry her?"

Finn frowned. He wasn't sure why it should matter to Lady Tallant what his intentions were in regards to Miss Somerset, but for the sake of getting away, he inclined his head politely. "I've offered for her, yes."

Twice.

"I see. It may interest you to know I found her alone in the garden with Lord Wrexley earlier this evening. Perhaps you should keep a closer eye on her, Lord Huntington."

The moment she mentioned Wrexley's name Finn's eyebrows lowered in a scowl, but Lady Tallant didn't stay to hear his reply. She simply gave him a cryptic half-smile, and retreated into the house, leaving him alone on the terrace.

He didn't pause to make sense of this odd exchange but moved to the door that led into the library. He took care to enter quietly, but he needn't have bothered, because whatever Miss Somerset was doing, she was so absorbed with it she didn't notice him, not even when he closed the door behind him and crossed the room.

Not even when he was so close he could have reached out and touched her.

She was sitting at a long table with a book open before her and her back to him, with the feeble light from her lamp picking up the golden strands in her hair.

Finn drew closer still, his breath catching as the urge to touch her, to run his fingertips over her silky curls nearly sent him reeling. He had the strangest notion that if he did touch her, if she felt his hands in her hair, she'd tilt her head back until it touched his chest, and she'd smile up at him, her eyes darkening to deep cobalt as his mouth descended to her arched neck. It was so real, that image in his head, he reached out as if in daze, and let his fingers settle on her shoulder.

That was the moment his dream disintegrated into painful, ear-splitting reality.

She let out a strangled cry and leapt from her chair, which toppled backwards and would have crashed to the floor if it hadn't hit Finn's legs first.

"Lord Huntington! Dear God, whatever are you doing, sneaking about in the dark like that? You scared the wits out of me." She choked in a few gasping breaths and patted her chest. "For goodness' sake, you certainly make it a habit to appear where you're least expected."

Finn set the chair to rights, an unfamiliar heat suffusing his face. Had he actually just sneaked up behind her and touched her? She wasn't the only one who'd lost her wits. Good Lord, he must have gone mad.

"I—I beg your pardon. I didn't mean to frighten you. I was…"

Was *what?* Christ, he hadn't the least idea how to finish that sentence. *Hypnotized by you? About to stroke your hair? Frantic with worry over you, and so relieved to find you at last I lost my head?* "I'm, ah…" *Fond of you?*

He was fumbling for a convincing lie when he noticed she wasn't even listening to him. She'd turned to lean against the table, or rather, to sit on top of it, and she seemed to be greatly preoccupied with arranging her skirts.

"Miss Somerset? Is something wrong?"

"No, no. Nothing at all." She offered him an unconvincing smile, but she was biting her lip, and her eyes had gone huge in her flushed face. "What, ah…what brings you to the library so late at night?"

She darted a quick look behind her and gave her skirts another twitch. When she met his gaze again, her cheeks had gone from pink to scarlet.

What the devil was the matter with her? Finn took a step toward her and peered around her. The moment he moved, she shifted to face him, but he got enough of a glimpse to see she'd sat down right on top of her book.

Ah, so that's what was troubling her. Whatever she was reading, she didn't want him to see it. "Reading, so late at night? It must be a fascinating book. What is it?"

Her eyes widened with alarm. "Oh, it's just—it's nothing that would interest you, I'm sure, my lord."

"I think you'd be surprised at what interests me, Miss Somerset." It must be something suggestive, to have her in such a flutter, but Finn doubted he'd find whatever it was as shocking as she did. "What is it? A novel, or—"

He didn't get any farther, because to his surprise she leapt up, snatched the book off the table, thrust it behind her back, and began to back away from him.

All this fuss, over a novel?

Finn went after her, his eyes narrowing. "What have you got there, Miss Somerset?"

"Nothing that concerns you." She backed into a bookshelf and began to edge sideways, her gaze darting from his face to the door on her right that led to the hallway.

"Oh? But I find myself quite concerned, given you seem to be so intent on hiding it from me. What it is you find so fascinating you've abandoned your bed for it?"

"Nothing! That is, it's nothing to do with you."

No, it didn't have anything to do with him, but he'd wager it had something to do with Wrexley. It couldn't be a coincidence she'd spent time alone with that scoundrel, and now she was in the library, alone, after midnight, reading something she didn't want Finn to see.

"It does now." He held out his hand. "Let me have it, if you please."

"No. It can't matter to you what I choose to read. You have no right to pry into my affairs."

Her chest was heaving, and she looked to be in an utter panic, which only made him more determined to see what she was hiding. He edged around the table, shifted to his left to block her path to the door, and held out his hand for the book. "Come now. What could be so terrible it has you this agitated? Show it to me."

She didn't answer, but darted another desperate look at the door. Finn could see she was one breath away from bolting, and every muscle in his body tensed to go after her.

I'll chase her right into her bedchamber if I have to.

She worried at her lower lip and swept her gaze over him, as if trying to determine how quickly he could move.

Very quickly—much more quickly than Miss Somerset, as it turned out. Finn saw her shoulders tense right before she made her desperate leap for the door, and he was there in front of her before she was more than two steps from the table. She crashed into his chest and he wrapped his arms around her and eased her backwards until her spine met the bookshelf behind her.

"Let go of me at once!" She squirmed against him, trying to land a blow on his shin. "How dare you manhandle me in this shameful way! I insist you release me!"

"No kicking, if you please, Miss Somerset. Now, I'll let you go, of course. Just as soon as you hand over the book, that is."

"I will not hand it over! I thought you were a gentleman, Lord Huntington." *I did, as well.*

Apparently things had changed. He'd come to Hampshire, and lost his mind.

"I don't like to restrain you when you so clearly wish to be free." It was true enough, though he didn't mention he'd be delighted to restrain her *with* her permission. "But I will see what it is that has you so distressed."

He reached around her and managed to grab a corner of the book she still hid behind her back, but she began to thrash in his arms again, so Finn just held her, careful not to hurt, but determined to keep her there until she either gave up or exhausted herself. When she loosened her grip on the book at last and sagged against him, he slid it out from between her limp hands and released her.

No doubt all the fuss was over a copy of *Tom Jones*, or at worst, Richardson's *Pamela*. He held it up so the light from the table fell on it.

When he read the title, he froze.

School of Venus.

He'd read it. Every boy who'd gone to public school had read it. It regularly made the rounds at Eton. It was a provocative bit of erotic literature presented as a book of instruction for a lady's sexual edification, and Finn couldn't deny any lady who read it would find it...edifying.

To say the least.

To say it was blunt was like saying water was damp, and fire was tepid. Lewd, vulgar, crude? Finn avoided judgments of that sort, given his own proclivities, but was it proper reading for an innocent, unmarried young lady like Miss Somerset?

God, no. Lady Chase would have an apoplexy if she knew her granddaughter had even got a glimpse of the frontispiece.

He raised his gaze to her flushed face, then looked back down at the book. His knuckles had gone white. "Where did you get this?"

She could have fled as soon as he let her go, but she hadn't stirred a step. She still stood with her back pressed against the bookshelf, a defiant expression on her face. "I don't choose to explain myself to you, my lord."

He braced his hands against the bookshelf on either side of her shoulders, the offensive book still clutched in his hand, and leaned forward until his mouth was mere inches from hers. "I asked you a question, Miss Somerset. Where did you get this?"

But he already knew. There was only one person in this house so debauched he'd carelessly destroy a young lady's innocence.

Wrexley.

Chapter Fifteen

Her chin rose in the air, but her throat rippled in a nervous gulp. "It was here, in Lady Hadley's library."

A rough, impatient sound tore from Finn's throat. It was an enormous collection, and every Marquess of Hadley had no doubt had a hand in shaping it. It was likely true enough she'd found it here, but that didn't answer his question.

"You would never have known to look for this particular book if someone hadn't told you to do so." Finn took her chin between his fingers and held it until she looked at him. "You think to protect him? It's far too late for that, Miss Somerset. Wrexley's fate is sealed."

Finn didn't give a bloody damn if Wrexley was Lady Honora's much-beloved cousin, or if he was a guest in Captain West's home. Wrexley's smooth lies and charming smile wouldn't save him this time.

But Miss Somerset was shaking her head. "No, you don't understand—"

"No. It's you who doesn't understand." Finn's temper was fraying at the edges, and he couldn't bear to stand here and listen to her make excuses for Wrexley's perfidy. "My God, are you so naïve you can't see what he's doing? He's trying to ruin you."

"Ruin me, by directing me to read a book? That's absurd, and it wasn't even Lord Wrexley who—"

"No, by directing you to read *that* book. Don't play with me, Miss Somerset. I saw your face when I walked in here tonight. You were so flushed I thought you were on the verge of a swoon."

"*A swoon?* Is that what you think, my lord? That a proper lady should be so timid she falls into a swoon after reading a few salacious words?"

"Oh, Wrexley didn't send you after that book because he wants a proper lady. If you bothered for even a moment to consider his motives, you'd see he's trying to lure you into an indiscretion."

She grabbed his wrist and jerked his hand away from her face. "So a man like Lord Wrexley lays a snare, and a silly, naïve chit like me must fall into it? Is that what you're saying, Lord Huntington? Dear God, you really do think me an utter fool, don't you?"

"No. I think you're an innocent, and you may trust me when I say Wrexley thinks it, as well. He relies on it."

"Innocent, yes, but perfectly capable of making my own decisions, despite what our courtship and betrothal may have led you to believe. In any case, Lord Wrexley doesn't have anything to do with—"

"You think to compare my courtship with Wrexley's reprehensible scheme?" Finn clenched his hair in his fists, so frustrated he was ready to pull it out by the roots. "Wrexley isn't *courting* you—he's *seducing* you. That you don't seem to recognize the difference shows you aren't able to make a reliable decision. Not about this."

Miss Somerset hadn't the faintest idea how easy it would be for a man like Wrexley to manipulate her into a seduction. Tonight it was some titillating literature to put pictures and words to the vague ideas in her head. By tomorrow it would be an innocent kiss, and then another, the second one not so innocent. He'd work on her by degrees until he'd stolen her virtue, just as he'd done with Miss Hughes.

Once he'd ruined her, she'd have no choice but to marry him, and God knew what would happen to her then. Someone as debauched as Wrexley wouldn't settle quietly into a respectable marriage. He'd very likely install Miss Somerset in his moldering country estate and leave her there alone while he traipsed off to London to squander her fortune on whores and wagering.

Finn ran a shaking hand down his face. Wrexley was leading her into an abyss, without her ever realizing she stood with one foot hovering over the edge.

It will be your fault if she falls.

If he hadn't all but forced her to jilt him for his despicable behavior, they'd be betrothed even now, and she wouldn't be vulnerable to the machinations of a man like Wrexley.

"Go to bed, Miss Somerset." He stepped back so she could pass by him. "We can discuss this tomorrow."

"There's nothing more to discuss, my lord." She held out her hand. "I'll have my book back, if you please."

He let out a short laugh. "I think not. You have no business reading it, and you know it yourself, or you wouldn't have tried to run away before I could get a look at it."

"If you think I ran away from you because I'm ashamed of it, you're very much mistaken, Lord Huntington. I ran because I knew you'd disapprove and would do just as you have done—try and take it away from me."

"You're damn right I don't approve, and I don't think your grandmother would, either." Finn tried to speak calmly, but dear God, this woman drove him mad. "And I haven't *tried* to do anything. I *have* taken it away from you."

"And now I'll have it back." She wiggled the fingers of her outstretched hand. "As I reminded you today in the stables, Lord Huntington, we're not betrothed anymore, so what I choose to read, or what horse I choose to ride, is none of your concern. I shouldn't have let you order me away from Chaos to begin with, and it was the last time you'll issue commands to me. Now, my book, please."

He stared into her furious blue eyes, his breath coming short. Christ, he couldn't remember ever being so livid in his life. "So it's to be ruination, is it?"

"Ruination?" She laughed, but she looked so enraged Finn half-expected her to leap upon him, knock him down, and snatch the book from his hands. "No, I thought I'd settle for a bit of reading for tonight."

He turned the book over in his hands, but he didn't offer it to her. "Very well, Miss Somerset, if you insist on having it, I suppose I can't stop you. As you say, we're no longer betrothed. Before I give it to you, however, a question, if you would. What kind of man sends an innocent young lady in search of something like this?"

"I don't know, my lord. Perhaps the same kind of man who'd blindfold a lady with a cravat."

Her voice was low and clear, but the silence echoed so profoundly after those words fell between them it was if she'd shouted them. But here it was at last, the part of the conversation she'd heard between him and Lady Beaumont she hadn't dared to mention since that afternoon in her bedchamber.

She dared now. She dared all manner of things now, whether she should or not, because she didn't know enough to be wary.

But wariness could be taught.

Finn moved closer to her and slid his thumb across her jaw in a light caress. "Ah, but the two things aren't the same at all, sweet."

Her eyes went wide, either at the caress or the endearment, or perhaps just at the look in his eyes. "No, they're not. One is much worse than the other."

"I agree. There's no sin in blindfolding or binding a lady who's aware of what she's doing and consents to it for her own pleasure."

His tongue curled on the word *pleasure*, lingered over it, and a small smile lifted the corners of his lips as she tried to suppress a shiver.

Tried, and failed.

"But a man like Wrexley, a man who'd use a young lady's innocence against her, or prey on one who doesn't yet understand her own desires? That man is a villain. But you don't need me to tell you that, do you, Miss Somerset? You'd have me believe you know all about men like Wrexley, and men like me, as well. Isn't that right?"

She didn't quite meet his eyes. "I know enough."

No, you don't. Not yet. But you will.

"Once you read your book, you'll know even more." He held out the book to her, but when she tried to take it, he refused to let it go. "Go ahead, then. Read it."

She gave him a suspicious look, but when she tugged on it again, he let it go. "I—ah, thank you. I wish you a pleasant evening, my lord."

Finn hadn't moved out of her way, and now he braced his hands against the bookshelf on either side of her shoulders, looked down at her and slowly shook his head. "No, Miss Somerset. Read it *here*. Now."

"Here? But—"

"Yes, right here. To me."

She blinked down at the book in her hands, then back up at him, and color swept from her bosom to her neck in a heated rush.

"You look warm, Miss Somerset. Whatever is the matter? You did say you weren't ashamed of reading it, and why should you be? I've read *School of Venus*, you see. It was some time ago, but I remember it clearly enough."

He moved closer and let his body brush against hers. "As you said, there's nothing shameful in it. It's just a forthright discussion of what happens between lovers, though without the cravats, of course." Finn dipped his head toward her neck to breathe in her scent before he pressed his lips to her ear. "It's quite detailed, if I recall, and contains some rather provocative drawings. Shall we look at those together?"

She'd refuse, of course, and once she did, he'd take the book away.

There was a brief, charged silence, but then Miss Somerset cleared her throat. "Very well, my lord." She flipped through the pages, then stopped and looked up at him, her gaze fierce with challenge. "Shall I start where I left off when you came in?"

Finn went still with shock—everything but his stomach, which leapt with a confusing mix of anger and anticipation.

"My lord?"

He didn't answer, but stared down at her, into that delicate face, at the sweet curve of her mouth, and wondered how he could ever have imagined she wasn't anything more than she appeared to be, as if her story began and ended with her face.

She waited, but he remained silent, and after a moment, she bent her head and began to read.

"Hadn't we better enjoy our pleasures? Truly I did not care how soon I parted with my maidenhead, and nobody be the wiser, which I believe may easily be done, if according to your advice some young fellow be employed in management of the secret affair?"

She paused and raised her eyes to his, but whatever she saw in his face made her gaze dart back to the book spread open in her hands. But when she began to speak again, her voice was different—lower, huskier, with a note of breathlessness.

"You cannot imagine the satisfaction you will take, when once you have gotten a friend fitted for your purpose, you may carry on your designs and order private meetings with your friend, who will secretly give you all of pleasure imaginable."

Finn remained frozen, listening to her, his skin burning, his muscles tensing and releasing as her soft voice rolled over him.

"To pass away the time till he comes, pray tell me what your Husband does to you when he lies with you, for I would not willingly altogether appear novice, when I shall arrive to that secret happiness—"

"Enough." He was shocked to hear the rough rasp of his own voice, but it didn't matter—nothing mattered but making her stop. She had to stop, or he'd touch her—

"I will briefly tell you all, first, he comes up a private pair of stairs, when all the household is in bed..."

Finn couldn't take his eyes off her. His lips parted when her breathing began to quicken, and her color deepened and rose higher in her cheeks.

"...he finds me sometimes asleep and sometimes awake, to lose no time he undresses himself, comes and lies down by me, when he begins to warm he lays his hands on my—"

"Damn you, I said stop!" He tore the book from her hands and threw it aside.

There was a long, tense pause, then she said, "Isn't that what you wanted, my lord?" Her voice was quiet. "For me to read to you?"

Christ, was he shaking? "I didn't think—" Finn grabbed the back of his neck, dug his fingernails into the hot skin there, his gaze on the floor.

I didn't think you'd do it.

Now she had, he'd forever have those words, in her soft, breathless voice, whispering inside his head.

"You thought to teach me a lesson." She gave an awkward little laugh. "Well, it was a good deal more interesting than the pianoforte lessons, at least. But allow me to ease your mind, Lord Huntington. Lord Wrexley didn't recommend the book. He has nothing to do with this."

Finn dragged both hands down his face. "If not him, then who? Please tell me the truth. I can't be easy until I know you understand it's not safe for you to trifle in this way with a man like Wrexley."

Her face softened. "Lady Tallant. She and I have struck up a... friendship of sorts."

A friendship? He couldn't imagine what Miss Somerset and Lady Tallant had in common. He didn't begrudge Lady Tallant her pleasures—from what he'd heard of her deceased husband, she'd earned them—but she wasn't a proper choice of companion for an innocent young lady like Miss Somerset.

Then again, Miss Somerset wasn't like most young ladies, unless every debutante in London had the courage to linger in a dark library and blithely read erotic passages from *School of Venus* to a dangerously aroused marquess. "Lady Tallant recommended you read *that* book? May I ask why?"

"She's helping me with something."

"With what? What sort of help could she be giving you that includes reading *School of Venus?* Unless..." Finn wrapped his hands around her shoulders. "Is she teaching you how to seduce a gentleman?"

"No!" She squirmed loose from his grip. "Not seduction. That is, not *only* seduction, but about gentlemen, and how to judge a man's character, and engage his affections. About...well, about marriage, and love."

"Love?" Family connections, compatibility, fortune—these were all things one considered when embarking on a marriage, but *love?* It only got in the way of making a wise choice, and in the end, the best one could say of it was it didn't last. At worst, it ripped families apart and left nothing but pain and destruction in its wake.

She frowned at him. "Yes, Lord Huntington. Love."

An awful thought occurred to Finn then. "Are you in love with Lord Wrexley?"

She tried to laugh, but it was a hopeless sound. "My situation is such that I no longer hope for love. I'll have to make do with friendship and affection, but as our courtship clearly shows, I can be easily misled as to a gentleman's true feelings. From the very first I suspected you lacked affection for me, but if I hadn't overheard you with Lady Beaumont, I never would have trusted my own instincts. I don't wish to repeat that mistake."

She said it quietly, and without a trace of accusation, but her words landed with such painful impact Finn staggered under them.

I made her doubt herself.

When he spoke, his voice wasn't quite steady. "Even if there isn't a deep affection, a proper gentleman will always be kind and respectful to his wife, Iris."

Her eyes widened at his use of her given name. "And if a lady should end up marrying a man who isn't a proper gentleman, Lord Huntington? Young ladies aren't trained to be discriminating. Look at poor Lady Honora. She hadn't any idea she was betrothed to a cheat and a villain."

"I don't pretend to defend Harley, but Lady Honora's is an unusual circumstance—"

"It is, my lord? You've spent the better part of a week trying to convince me Lord Wrexley is a similar kind of scoundrel."

He wanted to argue with her, but as soon as he opened his mouth, Finn found he didn't have a word to say that wasn't an utter falsehood. The truth was, Wrexley *was* a scoundrel, and if he hadn't intervened, it was doubtful Miss Somerset would have realized it before it was too late.

She was shaking her head. "You see the trouble, my lord. Ladies are expected to find a suitor, someone with a fortune and a title, and once we've accomplished it, no one seems to care much about anything else. It's almost as if we cease to exist once we become a wife."

Finn's chest went tight at the dejected look on her face, but before he could give in to the strange urge he had to press her head against his chest, the look was gone.

"None of this explains why Lady Tallant recommended you read *School of Venus*, Miss Somerset."

She regarded him in silence for a moment, then reached behind him and retrieved the book from the table. "Those ladies you mentioned earlier—the ladies who don't understand their own desires. What happens to them?"

Finn frowned. She was naïve, but she must understand at least the basics of what happened in the bedchamber. "They marry, and their husbands teach them."

"I see. So once a gentleman marries, it's his duty to attend to his wife's desire and pleasure?"

"Yes." It was his duty to get an heir on her, at least. That was nearly the same thing, wasn't it?

"The gentlemen—husbands, that is—generally have a great deal more experience in those matters than their brides, I believe?"

"One hopes so, yes."

"And their brides have less experience than courtesans and mistresses as well, I imagine? A lady of birth and connections in particular—the sort of lady who might marry a marquess, for instance—I think she must be among the most ignorant of brides when it comes to matters of the bedchamber."

"If you're asking if such a lady is a virgin when she first comes to her husband, then yes. That is, again, one hopes so."

"But an experienced gentleman—the sort of gentleman with mysterious *dark desires* and handfuls of cravats—mightn't he find such a lady quite dull? Predictable, that is."

Finn couldn't prevent a faint smile. She'd chosen that word deliberately. "Do you mock predictability, Miss Somerset? Some would say it's a desirable quality in a wife."

"Yes, I believe I've heard gentlemen say so, but as much as they pretend to want it, they scorn it, as well. One can't blame them entirely for it, I suppose. Such a lady can't be terribly exciting."

No, but then neither was marriage, and it wasn't meant to be. "As to excitement—"

"Exciting in the bedchamber, I mean. That's what the mistresses are for, isn't it, my lord?" A sly smile curved her lips. "For the gentleman with more exotic tastes, or those with insatiable appetites? I've heard such gentlemen can be most demanding."

Was she flirting with him? She never had before, and he'd never encouraged her to, but it was a far more pleasant sensation than Finn would have anticipated, like having a playful kitten bat at his nose.

Unable to resist, he caught a loose lock of her hair between his fingers. "Tell me, Miss Somerset. What sort of tastes do you imagine a demanding gentleman indulges in the bedchamber? Now you're so well read, I'm certain you can enlighten me as to the details of a gentleman's satisfaction."

"*Me*, enlighten *you*, my lord, on the matter of *your* satisfaction? No, I think not. I don't like to bore you, and we can both agree I know very little about it."

"Oh, I think you know more about it than you're letting on. Please, explain it to me."

"Well, I suppose it varies by the gentleman. I imagine some are more determined to satisfy their desires than others, as dark as those desires might be. It must be rather difficult to please that kind of gentleman, but there are ways to do so, I'm sure."

Finn blinked. It was midnight, she'd just read aloud to him from a book that would make a sailor blush, and now they were discussing the myriad ways in which a lady could please a demanding gentleman in the bedchamber. His cock was harder than he could ever remember it being, and they were alone in a dark library. He couldn't imagine anything more improper.

Or more arousing.

He should put a stop to this at once, but he couldn't imagine *that*, either. "Yes, I believe there are ways to please a more challenging gentleman. What do you suppose they are?"

If she had any notion of what this conversation was doing to him, she didn't let on. She cast him a demure look from under her lashes, and then, without a trace of embarrassment in her voice, said, "Restraints, my lord. Blindfolds, perhaps, or a chase around the bedchamber?"

Restraints. Blindfolds. Chasing.

He swallowed back a moan as his entire body exploded with heat. "I…well, those would be very…but a gentleman doesn't expect his wife to know—"

"Ah." She looked up at him, the tiny smile still curving her lips. "That, Lord Huntington, is what the book is for."

Finn didn't often find himself speechless, but all he could do now was stare at her with his mouth open, like a fish dangling on a hook.

She went on before he could answer. "But most wives can't provide such amusements, can they? I would think a gentleman accustomed to those things would much rather spend time with his mistress, and if a gentleman should be so preoccupied with his mistress he neglects his wife, what becomes of the wife's desires then? I ask, my lord, because I imagine it happens all the time in aristocratic marriages. After all, a proper wife—and most gentlemen *do* want a proper wife—must look dull indeed in comparison to a mistress or a courtesan."

Well. She'd paid close attention to the argument she'd overheard between him and Lady Beaumont, and she hadn't forgotten one word of it. "I suppose a marriage like that might prove a lonely one for the wife. Is that what you wish to hear me say?"

"I don't wish for anything at all from you." She blew out a soft sigh. "You're not to blame for this, Lord Huntington. You've only done what's expected of you, just as I have. You found a proper lady, engaged in a respectful courtship, and became betrothed to her. Nearly every lady in London would have been delighted to receive your addresses and felt themselves amply compensated for any lack of affection in the marriage by the title of marchioness. You simply chose the wrong lady."

Something inside Finn howled with rage at that. He tried to force it back, to shove it down into the deepest recesses of his chest, because she *was* the wrong lady. Everything about her was alive, and vibrant, and different. She was extraordinary, and extraordinary was dangerously unpredictable.

But the harder he shoved, the louder that part of him roared and clawed to get loose, and he was tired, so tired of keeping it down, holding it back—he'd never understood how tired, until he found her.

If I set it free for a moment, just a moment only...

"Tell me about your book, Miss Somerset," he murmured, sliding his hands around her waist. "Tell me what you've learned about gentlemen."

She stiffened slightly, but she didn't move, or push him away. "I—what I've learned?"

"Yes." He dragged his hands from her waist to her hips, then moved closer—close enough to feel the outline of her thighs through her skirts. "What do gentlemen like?"

She sunk her teeth into her lower lip, torturing the tender pink flesh, and he reached up and gently pulled it free. Did she know what it did to him when she bit her lip like that?

"Do gentlemen like to be touched?" he asked, his voice low, husky.

She slicked her tongue nervously over her lip where she'd nibbled on it. "Yes."

Finn bit back a groan. "Where? Show me."

His skin heated, every inch of it straining toward her, aching for her touch. It didn't come for a long time—so long he thought she would deny him—but then she reached a trembling hand toward him, and brushed her fingertips against his lips. "Here."

His eyes drifted closed. "Yes."

Her fingers stroked lower, and she pressed the pad of her index finger into the dimple in his chin. "Here. Or maybe that's more for me."

He opened his eyes, gazed at her flushed face, her parted lips. "It's for both of us."

She dragged her fingertips down the length of his throat, slowly, torturing him with the light caress. "Here."

This time Finn couldn't hold back his soft moan. "Yes."

She hesitated when she reached his cravat, as if unsure what to do, and he knew they should stop, that he should send her away before this went any farther, but he couldn't bear to give up her sweet caresses and the innocent wonder on her face as she touched him.

He took both her hands in his and brought them up to the knot in his cravat. "Take it off."

He didn't move while her fingers worked on the knot, or when she loosened it at last, reached up, and pressed her warm hands on either side of his neck.

"Here," she whispered.

Finn let his head fall back, offering her his throat again. His lips opened on a guttural moan when she took his offer, and traced her fingers over his throat. She slid her hands under the opening of his shirt to caress his collarbones, then let them dip lower to stroke his chest.

"Yes. God, yes."

He wanted her mouth, her beautiful pink mouth, hot and open, moving over every inch of his skin, biting at him, sucking and licking—

"Here." Her warm hands slid lower on his chest, moved over his belly, then lower still to the waistband of his breeches, and he was so hard for her, and her hands were so close, and he wanted her hands on him everywhere, more than he'd ever wanted anything, but if she touched his erection he'd lose control, and he wouldn't be able to stop...

He took her wrists in gentle fingers and moved them away from his body. "No, sweet."

"But..." Her gaze darted down to where his cock was straining against his breeches. "I thought...don't gentlemen like to be touched there, too?"

A half-laugh, half-groan tore from his throat. "Yes. Too much."

"Oh." Her brows drew together, and he couldn't help but kiss her then, softly, just the lightest touch of his mouth against her warm lips. Her body melted into his and her breath caught, but Finn didn't let himself taste her deeply, because if he did, there was no way he'd leave her alone tonight, and that would make him no better than Wrexley.

"It's late. I should let you go to bed." He dragged his thumb across her lower lip one last time and then forced himself to back away, but he couldn't keep from turning at the door to catch one last glimpse of her.

She was leaning against the bookshelf, watching him, one hand clutching the book to her chest, the fingers of the other pressed against her mouth.

Chapter Sixteen

As soon as Iris slid her foot into the stirrup and swung herself onto his back, she knew she'd been right about Chaos. She might have been wrong about everything else, but when she laid her hand on the horse's sinewy neck, she felt as if she'd come home.

"Very pretty, Miss Somerset. I don't know of any lady in London who is as skilled in the saddle, and your seat puts half the gentlemen of the *ton* to shame."

Iris turned and blinked at Lord Wrexley, who cantered along beside her on his gray stallion. She'd nearly forgotten he was there.

"Thank you, my lord," she called back with a quick smile, but she turned away from him to discourage more conversation. She only had time for one gentleman this morning, and it wasn't Lord Wrexley, or Lord Huntington.

It was Chaos.

Lord Huntington, of course, had no intention of allowing her to banish him from her thoughts. Just when she managed to forget him for a brief moment, he'd sneak past her defenses and batter his way back in. It was his hazel eyes that caused her the most trouble—his eyes, and those sensuous lips, and that delicious little—

No! For pity's sake, not the dimple again.

She didn't want to think about her former betrothed, or her future betrothed, or indeed about any gentleman at all this morning, so she'd simply have to ride harder and faster to dislodge Lord Huntington.

She tightened her knees and leaned forward in the saddle, just the tiniest shift of her body, but Chaos stretched his neck forward and lengthened his gait in response, as if he knew before she did what she wanted and had only been waiting for her to realize it and issue the command.

Oh, it was glorious to be running wild again, riding toward the glow of pale orange light just emerging over the horizon. It was early enough the dew was still fresh on the grass. The rising sun illuminated each tiny droplet of water, and it felt to Iris as if she were riding through a field of glittering diamonds.

She laughed aloud at the fanciful thought and lifted her face to the wind. She couldn't remember the last time she'd ridden like this, with the rolling hills flying by her in a blur of spring green, on a horse who was so attuned to every twitch of her muscles his body was like an extension of her own. She couldn't remember the last time she'd felt like this, so filled with joy she thought her heart would burst out of her chest.

When was the last time I felt like myself?

Several years, ever since she'd left Surrey for London. Or had it been longer than that? Long enough to lose the girl she used to be, when she'd raced across the countryside on Typhon, with her father by her side shouting his encouragement, the wind teasing his fair hair, and his eyes, so like her own, alight with pride and love, and that joy he'd always known how to coax out of life, like coaxing a tender green shoot in the ground to blossom into a flower.

It was the same kind of joy she felt now, but more poignant, and more beautiful, somehow, from the loss of him. Grief was strange that way, like a violent storm that was both terrible and exquisite at once.

A single tear leaked from the corner of Iris's eye, but she didn't bother to wipe it away, and the wind took it before it could stain her cheek.

That had been another lifetime, hadn't it? A time before her parents died, before she'd become a London belle and let herself be wrapped so tightly in yards of pink silk she hadn't known how to fight her way free of it. How had she drawn breath, with the weight of so many expectations upon her?

Despite her vow to banish him, an image of Lord Huntington as he'd looked in the drawing room last night crept into her thoughts. He'd been so still and perfect as he'd listened to Honora play, his face arranged into a proper attitude of attentive appreciation, but otherwise expressionless—nothing at all like the man who'd watched her with burning eyes as she'd traced her fingers over his lips.

Did he struggle against the same smothering weight of expectation she did? If he could heave it away with one mighty shove and crawl free of it, what kind of man would he be underneath? That man with the gentle voice, and the world of longing in his soft hazel eyes?

I could love that man—

"I see the summerhouse just ahead. Do try to keep up, Miss Somerset!"

Lord Wrexley grinned over his shoulder at her just before he shot forward with a triumphant shout. Iris shook the confusing thoughts of Lord Huntington from her head and charged after him, heading for the tiny summerhouse at the crest of the hill in front of them.

She reached it just before him, and Lord Wrexley gave her an admiring look as he drew his horse to a halt beside her. "Ah, very good. Shall we rest here for a bit? Spectacular view. I can see why Lady Hadley enjoys it."

"The property seems to go on forever." Iris shaded her eyes and gazed down at the panorama spread out below them. "I daresay we could ride for hours and never reach the boundary."

"I hope you aren't suggesting we ride for hours." Lord Wrexley gave her a sly grin. "No, no, it wouldn't be at all proper. We'll have to return before the rest of our party rises for breakfast as we planned, or I might find Lord Huntington's pistol pointed at my heart at dawn tomorrow."

Iris knew better than to encourage his nonsense, but he'd twisted his face into such a comical look of despair she couldn't resist a laugh. He glowed with good-humor, and his cheeks were ruddy from the wind and exercise. He was so handsome and charming, it would be easy to dismiss Lord Huntington's warnings about him.

But charm could hide any number of sins, just as the lack of it could hide a heart overflowing with tenderness.

"You're rather hard on Lord Huntington. Why is that, my lord? You're not still angry about that wager you lost, are you?"

Lord Wrexley went still, and a long, tense silence fell between them. Iris patted her gloved palm with her riding crop and waited.

"You mean the wager over…"

"The one between you, Lord Harley, and Lord Huntington, over which of you would offer for me, and which for Lady Honora."

Lord Wrexley shot her an apprehensive glance, saw at once he was caught, and to his credit, he didn't try and deny it, but gave her a sheepish grin. "Well, I did wager for *you*, you know."

Ah, so it was true, then. Now Lord Wrexley had confessed it, Iris was surprised to find she'd believed Lord Huntington all along. Perhaps that was why she hadn't asked Lord Wrexley about it sooner—she'd already known the truth.

"How very flattering, my lord. Though I suppose one could argue Lady Honora is rather like a sister to you."

He shrugged. "First cousins often marry, as you know, but I never considered offering for Honora."

"You weren't reconciled to your loss, I think, or else you would have honored the terms of the wager, instead of resorting to that trick with Lady Beaumont."

Another long silence followed. Iris held her breath as it stretched between them, but even before Lord Wrexley turned to her with guilt written plainly over his handsome features, she knew it was true.

"I'd reconciled myself to the courtship, but I suppose I never thought you'd accept him. Once you became betrothed, well...I didn't think you'd be happy with Huntington."

He didn't say anything more, or explain himself further, and Iris didn't ask him to. She knew very well he'd been motivated by her fortune, but then many gentlemen married for money. It didn't disqualify him as a husband, any more than Lord Huntington's mistress disqualified him. Lord Wrexley was selfish, yes, and careless, but he'd been one of her first friends in London, and in his own way, he cared for her.

He simply cared for himself more.

Sadly, that also didn't disqualify him as a husband, especially in her present circumstances.

"Well, what do you plan to do then, my lord? About Lord Huntington's pistol, I mean. Perhaps you'd better have an excuse in mind, in case our scandalous secret ride this morning is discovered."

He gave her a relieved grin when he realized she wasn't going to pursue the discussion about the wager or Lady Beaumont. "I'll simply explain I couldn't rest until I'd discovered if you're as skilled a horsewoman as my cousin claims you are."

She arched an eyebrow at him. "Well, what's your conclusion?"

"I'm afraid I can't say with any certainty."

He shrugged as if the subject didn't interest him and looked away to fiddle with his glove, but Iris saw the grin hovering at the corners of his lips. "You can't say? We've been out for an hour, and you haven't yet made a determination?"

"My dear Miss Somerset, anyone with adequate equestrienne skills can plod along as we've done all morning. We haven't gone above a canter. Forgive me if I question whether you can handle such an enormous beast with equal expertise in a flat run."

"Are you challenging me to a race, my lord?"

His brows rose in feigned horror. "Certainly not. A gentleman doesn't encourage a lady to risk her safety in such a way, and that's to say nothing of my *own* safety. If Huntington discovers I've encouraged you to race, he'll shoot me twice."

Iris was confident in her ability to handle Chaos at a run, but that didn't mean it was wise to go tearing across unfamiliar terrain on his back. She'd only ridden him this one time, after all.

But the moment Lord Wrexley mentioned Lord Huntington, she swept her doubts aside.

She might dream of dipping her tongue into that dimple in his chin, but that didn't mean she'd allow Lord Huntington to control her every move, as if she were nothing more than a chess piece he maneuvered around a chessboard.

He'd behaved with unbearable presumption toward her since they'd arrived at Hadley House. Even if she hadn't jilted him she wouldn't tolerate that kind of nonsense, but the fact that they weren't even betrothed any longer made his behavior that much more infuriating. First it had been the footrace with Lord Wrexley, and then Chaos, and last night, when he'd come upon her in the library and found her with that book…

Heat washed up her throat. She'd spent half the night squirming against her damp bedsheets, lost in memories of his smooth, warm skin under her fingertips, his quiet groans.

Had she really read those passages from *School of Venus* aloud to him? She'd never done anything so scandalous in her life.

When he begins to warm he lays his hands on my…breasts.

He'd stopped her before she could finish it, but the next word in the last sentence she'd read aloud to him was *breasts*.

She'd almost said the words *my breasts* to Lord Huntington.

By the time she'd gotten as far as the breasts, his hazel eyes had gone black, and he'd had such a…well, primal was the only way she could think to describe the way he'd looked at her. But however one described it, it made her shiver every time she thought about it.

If she'd gone ahead and said *my breasts* aloud at that moment, anything could have happened. That is, quite a bit *had* happened, but she knew from her reading there was a good deal more to it, and if she had said the word *breasts*, perhaps he wouldn't have stopped her when her hand slid close to the edge of his breeches. Another shiver fluttered down her spine at that thought, but this was no time to indulge in illicit fantasies about Lord Huntington.

She forced her attention back to Lord Wrexley. "Lord Huntington isn't here, and even if he were, I don't need his permission to race, or indeed, to do anything at all."

"Very well, then. Shall we race?" Lord Wrexley took care to sound bored, but there was a thread of tension underlying his words.

How odd. Was he afraid she'd best him in a race?

Before she could determine if she'd imagined it, his sweet, sly grin was back. "I'll give you a start on me, if you like."

Iris shot him a disdainful look and drew herself up in the saddle. "No, indeed. Where shall we race, my lord? We'll start from the bottom of the hill, I think." She wouldn't risk Chaos's legs by taking him down the hill at a flat run. "A sprint, to that tree line in the distance?" She pointed with her riding crop toward a thick line of trees about a half mile away.

"Yes, all right." Lord Wrexley nodded his agreement and followed her down the hill. "You're certain you don't want a few seconds start, Miss Somerset?" he asked, when they were side by side at their mark.

"Are you in the habit of offering your competitors a start in a gentleman's race, Lord Wrexley?"

"No, indeed."

"And didn't you just tell me not half an hour ago I have a better seat than half the gentlemen of the *ton*?"

He grinned. "I did, and it's true enough."

She gave him a sweet smile. "Then why would I need a start?"

He threw back his head in a laugh. "Well said. On my count, then?" He pulled his horse into position beside hers and raised his riding crop. "Ready? Set? Go!"

They took off in a flurry of damp grass and flying hooves. As it happened she did get a start, because Lord Wrexley's horse hesitated for the barest fraction of second before he registered the command, whereas Chaos leapt into motion almost before Iris's fingers had a chance to tighten on her riding crop.

They shot forward, Iris low over her horse's neck, her hands firm and steady on the reins. Lord Wrexley was right behind her, so close she could hear his harsh breath and feel the earth shake with each of his gray's pounding hooves, but they hadn't taken more than a dozen strides before she knew she and Chaos couldn't be beaten.

Not by Lord Wrexley, and perhaps not by anyone.

They were so seamless, so completely in sync it was as if Iris had been born on Chaos's back, or he'd grown into place beneath her. She could see his every stride forward in her head, anticipate the bunch and release of the muscles in his powerful haunches, and she made constant, minute adjustments in position with every ripple or jerk of his body beneath her.

Iris reached the tree line five or six seconds before Lord Wrexley, an unquestionable victory. Chaos twitched restlessly underneath her as she slowed. He wanted to keep running, but she brought him to an easy, gradual halt, and leaned over to murmur in his ear. "Next time, all right?"

Wrexley came up beside her in a whirl of pounding hooves. "Astonishing, Miss Somerset. Truly."

Iris smiled at him and stroked her hand down Chaos's sweaty neck. "Chaos deserves the credit, my lord. Did you see how smooth his gait is?"

"It's the two of you together that are so remarkable. I don't know that I've ever seen a more natural match between horse and rider. It seems incredible you've only ridden him this once."

"I know. It's feels like I've been riding him for years. He loves to run. He was born to race, I think."

"Yes, I think so, too." Wrexley gave her a strange, speculative look, and there was an odd light Iris couldn't decipher in his pale blue eyes. "But the sun has risen, and our friends will be at breakfast soon."

He wheeled his horse around and began an easy trot toward Hadley House. Iris rode beside him, but they were both quiet. She was absorbed with Chaos, and Lord Wrexley seemed to be lost in his own thoughts.

When the stables came into sight, however, he cleared his throat and turned to her. "If you and Chaos ever raced, you'd stand a fair chance of winning."

Iris's brows drew together. It wasn't unheard of for ladies to race, of course, but still unusual, especially for ladies of quality. Public races could attract large, unruly crowds, and they generally included a great deal of wagering. No respectable lady would attend, particularly not as a participant. "A fair chance of being injured, as well—both my person, and my reputation."

"I would never risk either, I assure you." He didn't quite meet her eyes. "I refer to a private race. Just you and Chaos, and two gentlemen of my acquaintance from London."

"I doubt Captain West would approve of such a thing." Iris didn't mention Lord Huntington, but it went without saying he'd have Lord Wrexley's head for suggesting such a dangerous scheme, despite the fact that he didn't have any claim on her.

None at all.

"Yes, well, if you did choose to race, it would be best to keep it between us. We could sneak away just as we did this morning, and I would attend you the entire time. No one else need know about it."

"If we have to hide it, my lord, then it can't be at all proper."

That should have ended the discussion, of course, but a familiar flutter of excitement tickled behind Iris's breastbone. She'd loved racing since she was a girl, and she and Typhon had won many races together in Surrey. How wonderful it would be to race again, especially with a horse like Chaos.

"Propriety is a matter of opinion, Miss Somerset. If you asked me, I would say it was proper enough, but if you asked Lord Huntington, I have no doubt he'd disapprove." His tone implied it would be absurdly rigid of Lord Huntington to do so. "It would be good fun though, wouldn't it, and such a great triumph if you won."

Iris bit her lip. Lord Wrexley was the very devil to suggest such a thing, but like the devil he was most persuasive, and Iris was tempted in spite of her better judgment. "Well, I suppose I don't see any real harm in it. It's not as if it's a public race."

"No harm at all, since I'll be with you the entire time. No one else can know of it, however, or they'll forbid you to go."

Iris shifted uneasily in the saddle. She didn't like to lie, and if her friends would forbid her, it meant she shouldn't be entertaining the idea at all, but it seemed like a lifetime since she'd raced, and really, it wasn't so *very* shocking, or so much different than the races she used to run in Surrey. Lord Wrexley would be there the entire time, after all.

"Very well, my lord. I'll race, as long as I can ride Chaos."

He'd been watching her with narrowed, glittering eyes, but now his face relaxed into a smile. "Of course. I'll arrange everything just as you wish. What good fun you are, Miss Somerset! I confess I'm rather besotted with you."

His forwardness, and the look of undisguised admiration he gave her, made a flush rise in Iris's cheeks.

He let out a soft laugh. "What a charming blush. It flatters you. I don't think I've ever seen bluer eyes than yours."

They were approaching the stables, and Iris was saved from having to reply as they both looked to see if anyone was about.

"I think we're safe. Quickly, before someone sees us."

Lord Wrexley kicked his horse into a trot and headed for the stables, and Iris followed, letting out a sigh of relief when she darted inside and found them empty but for the stableboy, who came at once to attend Lord Wrexley's horse.

"I'll assist the lady." He dismounted, tossed the boy his reins, and held out his hand to Iris as the boy led the gray off. "May I help you?"

Iris frowned a little as Chaos tensed underneath her and sidestepped nervously, away from Lord Wrexley. "I'm perfectly capable of dismounting."

"Of course you are." Even as he agreed, Lord Wrexley reached up and wrapped his hands around her waist. "But you must be tired after our race, and famished, as well. I'd hate for you to fall."

She put her hands on his shoulders to steady herself as he lifted her easily from the saddle and lowered her until her feet touched the floor. "Thank you, my lord."

"My pleasure, Miss Somerset." He should have released her then, but instead his fingers tightened on her waist, and his eyes warmed as he looked down at her. "I'll set the race for the day after tomorrow, but shall we sneak out again tomorrow morning? It will give you another chance to ride Chaos before the race."

Iris nodded, aware as she did she was far more tempted by Chaos than she was by Lord Wrexley.

He didn't seem to notice. He lifted a hand and smoothed a tendril of hair away from her cheek. "I've always found you lovely, but more so today than ever before. I didn't realize you were a lady of such spirit." He trailed a gloved fingertip over her cheek. "It shows here, in the curve of your face."

He was gazing down at her with the same look in his eyes he'd had last night when they'd walked together on the terrace.

She knew what it meant. Lord Wrexley wanted to kiss her, and she was going to let him, because she wanted something from him, as well.

To know if another man's kiss could devastate her the way Lord Huntington's did.

Iris drew a deep breath and forced herself to remain still as Lord Wrexley's mouth drew closer, but just as he was about to touch his lips to hers, the memory of a pair of hazel eyes drifted through her mind.

She gave a tiny shake of her head to knock it loose, to focus on Lord Wrexley's blue eyes, which were really quite nice. Why, any lady would be thrilled to gaze into those eyes as he lowered his head for a kiss.

Except the hazel eyes were still there. Iris closed her own eyes to shut them out, but she could still see them, a cool gray brown at first, darkening to a warmer green, and then going darker still, a forest at midnight, the long, thick lashes growing heavier as she ran her fingertips over his lips and throat and inhaled the warm, fresh scent of his skin.

A sigh escaped her, and she just had time to see Lord Wrexley's lips curve in a satisfied smile before his face was so close it grew blurry, and the voice in her head spoke then, so clearly, as if the words had been whispered in her ear.

I don't want to kiss Lord Wrexley. I only want to kiss Lord Huntington.

And then, as if she'd conjured it from her fevered imagination, another voice, low and vibrating with fury.

"Take your hands off her *now*, Wrexley, or be prepared meet me at dawn."

Chapter Seventeen

"Calm down, Huntington." Lord Wrexley took care to sound bored, but he didn't waste any time stepping away from Miss Somerset. "Nothing improper took place."

Not yet, but it would have.

Finn didn't bother to voice the reply, and he didn't spare Wrexley a glance. "Get out."

"Now look here, Huntington. You can't just—"

"Does Captain West know you took that horse out?" Finn pointed his riding crop at Chaos. "Did you get his permission before you hoisted Miss Somerset into the saddle and tore off into the countryside with her, alone?"

"Of course he did! Didn't you, my lord?" Miss Somerset appealed to Lord Wrexley, but he remained silent.

Finn let out a harsh laugh. "I didn't think so. Get out, Wrexley."

Wrexley shot a questioning glance at Miss Somerset, who gave him a curt nod, then he turned and left the stables without another word, leaving her there alone to manage a large, enraged marquess.

Bloody coward.

Miss Somerset, however, looked more than equal to the task. Lips pressed into a tight line, stubborn chin thrust into the air and jaw tight—yes, those were the telltale signs.

The lady was about to succumb to a fit of temper.

Despite his jealous fury, anticipation sparked low in Finn's belly.

She crossed her arms over her chest and gave him a bland look. "Good morning, Lord Huntington. What can I do for you?"

One, two, three, four...

Finn tapped his riding crop against his boot and tried to gather himself together, but even after several minutes of tapping, he didn't speak. As soon as he opened his mouth ugliness would pour out of him—a dark, writhing mass of jealousy, anger, and unjust accusations.

Had she been testing her newfound knowledge of a gentleman's anatomy on Wrexley? The villain had been about to kiss her—Finn had seen that much when he entered the stables. Wrexley's hands had been on her, his mouth lowering to her upturned face.

Snap, snap, snap...

His riding crop slapped harder against his boot, the smack of cane against leather deafening in the quiet stables.

Had she encouraged him? Had she run her fingertips over his lips, as she'd done to Finn in the library last night? Had Wrexley given her the kiss Finn had failed to give her in Lady Fairchild's garden?

Christ, jealousy was a foul emotion, especially when it was tangled with fury and panic, and all of it was crushing his chest at once. He'd sealed himself off from strong emotions for most of his lifetime, but his feelings for her swept him up in a whirling vortex, and no amount of kicking and struggling would free him. She'd set them all loose, and jealousy swarmed him now, picking and jabbing and jerking him about like a flock of buzzards with a rancid carcass.

"Lord Huntington? Do you have something you wish to say to me?"

Yes. An entire lifetime of words, but I don't know how to say any of them.

"I take it you rode Chaos this morning." He gestured toward the horse, but then his hand fell back to his side in a helpless gesture. "You're not hurt?"

She looked down at herself, then back up at him, one eyebrow raised. "As you see."

Finn nodded. Jesus, he was bloody awful at this. "It seems I underestimated your equestrienne skills after all, then. I beg your pardon."

His words were so stiff and awkward one would never guess at the turmoil roiling under the surface. Before her, he'd never realized how treacherous words could be. Relying on them was like seeing a glimpse of a face in a mirror's reflection, and believing it revealed the entire person.

"I thought we had Captain West's permission to ride him." Her cheeks reddened, but she didn't say she'd trusted Wrexley only to find out he'd lied to her.

At any other time, Finn would have said it himself—he would have seized this opportunity to rail about Wrexley's deceitful nature, his selfishness, the way he manipulated every situation to his advantage—but this time, he didn't say any of that, because this wasn't about Wrexley anymore.

"No harm was done. Captain West will understand, once you explain the situation to him."

"Yes, I...yes, of course I will." She hesitated, her face uncertain, but when he didn't speak again she took a few steps toward the stable doors.

Now. It had to be now. He'd find the words, once he started speaking.

"Wait, please." He laid a hand on her arm when she tried to brush past him. "I want to speak to you first. I have something to tell you. I—I should have told you days ago, as soon as we arrived at Hadley House."

She searched his face, and whatever she saw in his eyes made her pause. "All right."

Finn never talked about what had happened with Diana Hughes—not just to protect her and her sisters' reputations, though that was part of it. Very few people knew he'd been betrothed to her, and even fewer knew about the scandal with Wrexley, and that was for the best for all concerned.

But there was another reason he didn't speak of it.

Shame.

He was ashamed he hadn't seen what Wrexley was about from the start—ashamed he hadn't protected the lady he cared for from ruination at the hands of a merciless rake.

He tried not to even think about his doomed betrothal to Miss Hughes. He'd locked that year of his life down tight in his chest, and he'd kept it there for seven years. It would have remained there forever, if it hadn't been for Iris Somerset.

A game of bowls, a race across the gardens—perhaps those things were harmless enough, but this morning she'd gone off alone with Wrexley, without telling anyone. Not even her sister knew where she'd gone. She'd returned unharmed, yes, but what if she hadn't returned at all? What if Chaos had thrown her, and she'd been hurt? What if Wrexley had forced her to run off with him?

Finn had to make her understand Wrexley wasn't her friend, but his commands and threats, his warning and bluster—none of it moved her. She wouldn't be intimidated, or controlled, or coerced in any way.

It was why he'd fallen in love with her.

Ever since he'd inherited his title, the fact that he was the Marquess of Huntington had been enough to make people scurry to do his bidding. He'd never had to offer anything more. To be anything more.

Until her.

From the moment she jilted him, she'd demanded more of him. More than anyone else ever had, and more than he'd ever thought he was capable of giving.

He'd come to Hadley House for *her*. Not because he had an obligation to her, or to protect her from Wrexley. He'd told her once there was a difference between a reason and an excuse.

Those were his excuses.

The truth was he'd come here because he wanted her for himself.

She'd told him they didn't suit, and he'd agreed with her at the time. Maybe it was still true. Maybe they didn't suit.

But that didn't mean they weren't perfect for each other.

"What did you want to tell me, Lord Huntington?"

He raised a hand and brushed his knuckles over her cheek. "Will you...I want you to call me Finn."

Her eyebrows shot up. "But we didn't even call each other by our first names when we were betrothed."

"No, and that was a mistake. Don't you agree?"

Her gaze caught and held his. "Perhaps it was."

Some of the anxiety drained from Finn then. If she would just help him a little, he could do this—he could tell her the truth, and make her understand. "There's something you don't know about Lord Wrexley, Iris. I want...I need to tell you."

He half-expected her to refuse to hear him, to pull free and march into the house without letting him speak a word, but she didn't. She simply stared up at him and waited.

Finn drew in a deep breath. "I've known Lord Wrexley for a long time. We went to Eton together, and later to university. We've never been friends, but we were never enemies, either—not until the year after we left Oxford."

"Something happened to turn you into enemies?"

"Yes. There was a lady, Miss Diana Hughes. She was the sister of a schoolmate of ours, Lord Farrington, a viscount. Their father had died years before, and his death had left their mother feeble in both mind and body. Miss Hughes was sweet and lovely, and her brother doted on her. He was fiercely protective, as well, and took great care to keep her safe from the rakes and fortune-hunters attracted by her generous dowry. But Lord Farrington died of a fever the year after we left university, and Miss Hughes and her younger sisters were left quite alone in the world aside from their mother, who, as I said, was feeble."

"How awful."

"Yes. Lord Farrington was a good man, and a friend of mine. After he died, I offered for Miss Hughes. Her mother approved my suit, and we became betrothed."

Something flickered in her eyes. "You, ah…you were betrothed to another lady?"

"Yes. Briefly."

"But you never married."

"No, I didn't, because Lord Wrexley, tempted by her dowry, lured her into a love affair, seduced her, and then tried to force a marriage between them on the grounds he'd ruined her."

Iris's face drained of color. "No. No, he wouldn't do anything so wicked."

She swayed, and Finn wrapped his fingers more firmly around her arm to steady her. "He did, Iris. If you doubt me, you may ask Lord Derrick. He knows all about it."

"But Honora…" She looked up at him with a stricken expression. "She would never have suggested I encourage Lord Wrexley if she knew of this."

"She doesn't know. Very few people do. Miss Hughes never came out in society, and she was married off quietly. The story hardly does Wrexley credit, so he never speaks of it, and aside from Derrick, I've never told a soul. Certainly Wrexley's family doesn't know. Do you think Lady Fairchild would allow him in her house, around her unmarried daughter, if she knew the truth?"

"No, I—no. Of course not. What became of Miss Hughes?"

"She confessed the whole thing to her mother, and Lady Farrington came to me. I was Miss Hughes's betrothed, remember, and Wrexley knew I'd find out, so he was insisting on an immediate marriage by special license. But Miss Hughes was underage, so he needed her mother's permission. I begged Diana to marry me at once to put her out of Wrexley's reach for good, but she refused me. I won't go into her reasons, but by then all she wanted was to leave London and never see Wrexley again, so I arranged a hasty marriage between her and another of our university classmates, a gentleman with a comfortable estate in northern England. He'd been in love with Miss Hughes throughout our entire four years at Oxford, and he was happy enough to get her, despite the circumstances. We put Wrexley off, and by the time he realized what had happened Miss Hughes had been bundled off to Newcastle. I hear she and her husband are very happy together."

"Dear God." Iris pressed a hand to her forehead. "So Lord Wrexley—"

"Has despised me ever since, and would be delighted to avenge what he sees as a wrong I've done to him."

Her face went even paler. "By marrying me, you mean. You came to Hadley House out of a sense of obligation, to keep me from making a match with a gentleman who only wants me so he can have his revenge on you."

"Wrexley has many reasons to want you, Iris, just as any gentleman would." Finn's voice softened. "But the wager was what made him decide to pursue you in earnest, and he's since admitted to me it would give him great pleasure to take you from me."

She was quiet for a moment, then, "And what of you? Would it give *you* great pleasure to take me from *him*? Did you love Miss Hughes? You must have if you still wished to marry her after Lord Wrexley ruined her."

Finn hesitated. How to answer that question? He'd cared for Diana Hughes, but his feelings for her had been a faint echo of the feelings he now had for Iris. "I loved her as much as I could love anyone at that time, yes."

"Then you have as much reason to want revenge as Lord Wrexley does. Perhaps more." Her blue eyes were bright with pain. "How arrogant I was, to imagine myself the queen of this game, when all this time I've only been a pawn."

"No!" He gripped her shoulders, desperate to make her listen. "I'm not like Wrexley, Iris. I'd never use you like that, or marry a lady for revenge."

"But you'd marry a lady from obligation." Her voice was dull. "You're an honorable man, Lord Huntington—so honorable you'd sacrifice your own happiness to protect me from Lord Wrexley."

"No. You don't understand. From the moment you jilted me, I've—"

"Huntington."

Finn and Iris both whirled around to find Lord Derrick standing at the stable door.

"I need to speak with you." Lord Derrick's tone was grim.

Finn dragged a hand through his hair. "Can't it wait?"

"No. Now, Huntington." Derrick's face was gray and set, and his tone allowed no room for argument.

Finn nodded to his friend, then turned back to Iris. "Go and find Lady Hadley, and explain to her what happened with Chaos. I'll come find you when I've finished with Derrick, all right?"

She nodded, but her gaze was unfocused, and she wandered out the stable doors as if she were in a daze. Finn watched to make sure she entered the house, then turned to Derrick. "What's happened?"

Derrick shook his head. "I'm not sure, but I was walking the eastern side of the grounds with Lady Honora just now, and I saw Wrexley go tearing by on his horse as if the hounds of hell were on his heels. Wherever he's going, he's in a damn hurry to get there, and this isn't his first mysterious errand this week."

Finn was already motioning to the stableboy. "Perhaps we should follow him, and see what has him in such a hurry."

"My thoughts exactly, but we'll need to move quickly, Huntington. He has a solid start on us."

"I want Captain West with us." This business with Wrexley would end now, today. Finn would make sure of it. It was time to confess the whole of it, and ask Captain West to forbid Wrexley from returning to Hadley House.

"I saw him in the breakfast parlor not five minutes ago. I'll fetch him."

Lord Derrick hurried off toward the house, and a few minutes later he met Finn in the stable yard, accompanied by a puzzled-looking Captain West.

"What the devil's all this about, Huntington?" Captain West demanded, mounting one of the three horses Finn had waiting. "Something about Lord Wrexley?"

"We'll tell you on the way. What's the closest town to the east, Captain?"

"Cheriton is within three miles."

"We'll start there, then." Finn kicked his horse into a run, and Derrick and Captain West fell into place beside him.

Finn didn't mince words as they made their way to Cheriton, and by the time they reached the small village, Captain West looked as if he were ready to toss the entire lot of them out of his house.

"Bloody hell, Huntington. It never occurred to you to mention this to me a week ago? Lady Chase will have my head if she discovers one of her beloved granddaughters has been trifled with under my roof. As it is, she's going to have an apoplexy when she discovers Iris won't become a marchioness."

"She *will* become a marchioness, Captain. I'll marry her tomorrow, if I can persuade her to have me again."

Captain West's gaze narrowed on Finn, and after an intense scrutiny, he nodded. "Ah, so that's how it is. Very well, Huntington, but you'd better make this right. Lady Chase may get my head in the end, but not before I get *yours*."

"One thing at a time, Captain. You can decapitate me after we take care of Wrexley."

"Well, now, what have we here?" Derrick interrupted, jerking his head toward the one inn on the main street of Cheriton. "I don't see Wrexley, but isn't that Lord Claire coming out of the George and Dragon?"

"It is, indeed. Lord Claire, and Lord Edgemont with him. What do you suppose those two scoundrels are doing in Hampshire?" Finn watched as the two men left the inn and stumbled down the street.

"I know Claire well enough. The man never stirs a step out of London unless he thinks he can make a coin from it." Captain West made a disgusted noise in his throat. "They're in their cups already, not two hours after the sun's risen. Bloody wastrels."

"But convenient, for our purposes. Drunken men are more forthcoming. Shall we go and welcome them to Hampshire?" Finn didn't wait for a response, but urged his horse down the street at a trot and stopped in front of the two men, blocking their progress.

Lord Claire squinted up at him. "That you, Huntington?" He shaded his eyes from the sun. "By God, it is. Look, Edgemont. Huntington's here."

Lord Edgemont raised his head and fixed his bleary gaze over Finn's shoulder. "Derrick, too. Who're you?" he asked, peering at Captain West.

"West."

Captain West didn't offer anything further, but a dim look of recognition crossed Lord Edgemont's slack features. "What, that Waterloo bloke? For God's sake, Claire. Half the bloody *ton* is here. Wrexley said it was just the three of us."

"Just the three of you for *what*?" Derrick asked, not bothering to hide his revulsion.

Lord Edgemont belched, then, "Race, of course. Wrexley's wagered high on some chit he's got he says can best the two of us in a race. Damn fool, Wrexley, but it's his coin, and I'm happy to take it from him."

Both Claire and Edgemont guffawed, and Finn, Derrick, and Captain West exchanged looks.

"When's the race?" Finn took care to keep his voice calm, but it took every bit of his control to keep from grabbing one of the scoundrels by the neck and shaking him until the truth fell out.

So this was why Wrexley had been so fascinated to learn of Iris's skills in the saddle, and so determined to see her ride Chaos. He'd sneaked her out on the horse this morning so he could judge her speed, and lay his wagers accordingly. Lords Edgemont and Claire had deep pockets, and both would scoff at the idea that a woman could beat them in a race. The purse must be enormous for Wrexley to take such a risk.

"Now look here, Huntington," Lord Edgemont said, his tone belligerent. "If you want in, then hand over your coin like the rest of us. Claire and I aren't fools, you know."

Finn raised a skeptical eyebrow at that, but there was little point in arguing with a fool. "I know the rules of wagering, Edgemont. But you didn't say when the race was to take place."

"Day after tomorrow, in the morning, a few miles from here. Wrexley's coming to fetch us. I don't know what we're supposed to do in bloody

Hampshire until then." Lord Claire looked around the small village, scorn curling his lip. "No whores about. Nothing else for it but to get sotted."

Lord Derrick rolled his eyes. "Yes, what a wonderful plan, and it looks like you're well on your way. But where's Wrexley, in case we decide to wager?"

Lord Edgemont looked confused for a moment, then he turned to Lord Claire. "Damn good question, Derrick. Where is Wrexley? He was supposed to meet us at the George and Dragon. We came out to look for him, but I don't see him, and now I'm parched again from standing about in the sun."

"Perhaps he came in while you were out here. You'd better go check, hadn't you?" Finn glanced at Derrick and Captain West. "We'll wait right here for him, and if we see him, we'll tell him where you are."

"Damn good idea, Huntington." Lord Edgemont turned and staggered back toward the inn, and after a moment Lord Claire shrugged and followed after him.

"The other side of the road if you please, gentlemen," Captain West said. "If Wrexley sees us waiting here, he'll bolt."

Finn and Derrick followed him across the street and the three of them took up positions in the shade of a tree, where they were partially obscured from anyone coming down the main road from Hadley House.

They didn't have to wait long. Wrexley came sauntering along not ten minutes later. Now he was out of sight of Hadley House, he dawdled as if he had all the time in the world. He brought his horse to a halt in front of the George and Dragon, but before he could dismount, Finn, Derrick, and Captain West crossed the street and surrounded him.

"Good morning, Lord Wrexley." Captain West gave him a pleasant smile. "Busy day for you already, and here it is about to get busier."

"No, don't bother to dismount," Lord Derrick added. "You won't be able to meet your friends, after all. I doubt they'll notice. They're both already halfway to unconscious."

Lord Wrexley didn't spare either of them a glance, but fixed his gaze on Finn. "So it's to be this way, Huntington? You must be worried indeed about where the lady's affections lie, if you're willing to chase me out of Hampshire."

"Whatever it takes to get rid of you, Wrexley."

"It won't be so easy to get rid of me in London, and I'll be waiting for Miss Somerset when she returns."

"I doubt she'll agree to see you. I told her about Miss Hughes."

Wrexley's expression didn't change, but his fingers went tight on the reins. "I'm surprised it took you this long, though I know you don't like to talk about poor Miss Hughes and her unfortunate ruination. But you know, Huntington, Miss Somerset and I have been friends for some time now, and of course I'm her dear friend's cousin, as well. I'm sure I can explain away any lingering doubts she has. So you see, this is hardly a victory for you. More like a temporary suspension in play."

"For God's sake, Wrexley. Don't you know when you're beaten?" Captain West's voice was heavy with disgust. "Lady Chase won't let you within ten paces of her granddaughter when she finds out what you are, and you can be quite sure she *will* find out. I'll make certain of it."

"Lady Chase will do whatever it takes to make her granddaughter happy, and it's not as if Miss Somerset is still the belle of her season with an array of suitors kneeling at her feet. Now she's just the foolish chit who jilted a marquess." Wrexley swept a disparaging look over Finn. "She has few options left to her, and besides, the lady loves me."

Finn's mouth went dry as crippling doubt threatened. Perhaps Iris really did love him. She wouldn't be the first lady to succumb to Wrexley's practiced charm.

Wrexley must have seen the uneasiness on his face, because his lips stretched in a triumphant smile. "Don't tell me you actually thought she loved *you*, Huntington."

"Enough," Lord Derrick growled, before Wrexley could say another word. "Let's go. We'll see you on the road toward Alton, just to be polite, of course."

"My things—"

"Don't worry, Wrexley. I'll send a servant with them." Captain West's tone was clipped. "I'd just as soon you never set foot in my house again."

Chapter Eighteen

Iris didn't go look for Charlotte, as Lord Huntington had bade her. She didn't enter the breakfast parlor either, though she could hear the low murmur of feminine voices and knew she'd find Violet and Honora there.

She couldn't confide in her friends without first offering some sort of explanation for the snarled web of secrets she'd become enmeshed in, and she couldn't do that. Not yet. She'd only just begun to untangle the fragile threads of the truth from the lies, and she couldn't explain to them what she didn't understand herself.

Only one thing was clear in her head.

She'd been wrong about Lord Wrexley.

A part of her wanted to believe Lord Huntington was lying—about the wager, and the reason Lady Beaumont was in Lady Fairchild's garden that day, and now about Miss Hughes—but she knew he wasn't. Perhaps he could hide some secrets behind the shifting colors of his eyes, but he wasn't a liar. There'd been nothing but naked truth in those hazel depths just now.

She'd been wrong about Lord Huntington, too.

About Finn.

"Good morning, Iris. Where have you been off to so early?"

Iris was standing at the bottom of the stairs, staring at them without seeing them, but she turned at the sound of Lady Annabel's voice.

"I wondered why I didn't see you in the breakfast parlor—" Lady Annabel began, but as soon as she saw the look on Iris's face, she took her arm and hurried her down the hallway. "Come with me."

Iris didn't resist, but let Lady Annabel tug her along toward Charlotte's private sitting room.

"Sit." Lady Annabel turned to ring the bell as Iris sank into one of the plump chairs in front of the fireplace.

"Tea, please, if you would, Mary," Lady Annabel said, when the maid appeared. Once the servant had gone again, Lady Annabel took the seat opposite Iris, but she didn't say a word until Mary had returned with the tea tray and disappeared again, closing the door behind her.

"I gather from the expression on your face this isn't about *School of Venus*." Iris shook her head.

"Pity. I have a suspicion it would be much easier if it were." Lady Annabel fetched a teacup from the tray, poured Iris some tea, and then set the cup down in front of her. "Drink some tea, Iris. You need a restorative."

Iris took an obedient sip of her tea. "I was wrong, Lady Annabel."

Lady Annabel didn't look in the least surprised to hear it. "Yes, I imagined that would happen at some point. Love affairs are complicated enough with one gentleman, and you've had to manage two of them. Your rate of error rises accordingly, I'm afraid. Who were you wrong about? Lord Wrexley, or Lord Huntington?"

Iris opened her mouth to say Lord Wrexley, but she bit the words back before his name could leave her lips. She'd been wrong about him, yes, but Lord Huntington was the man she'd truly wronged.

Shame made her avoid Lady Annabel's eyes. "Both of them."

Lady Annabel sighed. "Look at me, Iris."

Iris looked up to find Lady Annabel's steady, calm gaze on her face. "If you recall, I did warn you this could become complicated."

"But...I thought you meant the other part, about the...the..." Iris's face heated. "Well, you know."

"Oh, no. The physical part is fairly straightforward, though if one is lucky, not lacking in variety. But love—well, I'm afraid that's much more complex."

Iris stared at her. Love? Which of the two gentlemen in question did Lady Annabel suppose she was in love with?

Not Lord Wrexley.

The thought came out of nowhere.

No. Surely not—

"I suppose you've discovered what a scoundrel Lord Wrexley is?"

Iris choked on the sip of tea she'd just taken. "You knew Lord Wrexley was a scoundrel, all this time?"

"Of course. I'm a wicked widow, Iris. I know a scoundrel when I see one."

"But why didn't you just tell me, then?" Iris dumped her teacup on the tray with a clatter. "It would have saved me so much fuss and bother."

Lady Annabel arched one blond eyebrow. "Would you have believed me?"

"I…well, of course I would have at least listened, even if I didn't—"

The eyebrow inched up another notch. "Didn't Lord Huntington tell you Lord Wrexley was a scoundrel?"

Iris's lips turned down in a sulky frown. "Yes."

"Did you believe *him?*"

Goodness, it was unpleasant to admit it when one was wrong. "Not entirely."

"No, you wouldn't, would you? No one can convince a lady a gentleman is a scoundrel. It's the sort of determination she must come to on her own, and it sounds as though you have. I suppose Lord Huntington's told you about Miss Hughes?"

Iris's mouth fell open. "Miss Hughes! He said only a few people knew her story. Why, even Lady Honora doesn't know, and Lord Wrexley is her cousin!"

Lady Annabel sighed, and set her teacup aside. "Diana's story isn't widely known, and Lord Huntington isn't aware of my connection to her family. Her mother, Lady Farrington, and I grew up together. We were dear friends, and Miss Hughes was something of a niece to me, though not by blood."

Dear God, what a tangle. How had a simple house party turned into a drama worthy of the London stage? "But neither Lord Wrexley nor Lord Huntington act as if they know you."

"They don't. Miss Hughes's unfortunate association with Lord Wrexley took place after I'd married. I was living in Derbyshire and heard of it all through letters from her mother. I can assure you, Iris, Lord Wrexley is as guilty as Lord Huntington claims he is."

Iris fell back against her chair, shaking her head. "What a fool I am. Lord Huntington tried to warn me about him, but I didn't believe him."

"You're not a fool. Lord Wrexley is a skilled dissembler who exploited your innocence for his own gain. But scoundrels like Lord Wrexley don't interest me much. Once their perfidy has been revealed, they become nothing more than tedious caricatures of themselves. I think we've said all we need say about him."

"I hope I can forget him as easily as you can."

"You will. But I'm pleased Lord Huntington has told you the truth about him at last. I've been waiting for him to do so all week. I'd begun to worry I'd have to tell you myself."

Iris lapsed into a pensive silence as she stared into the fire. When he'd told her he'd been betrothed before, and that he'd loved Miss Hughes, the strangest sinking sensation had squeezed her heart. Perhaps he loved her still. Perhaps a lingering loyalty to Miss Hughes was the reason he wanted to marry a lady he didn't care for.

"He told me he never talks about it."

"No, he doesn't. Otherwise such a scandal couldn't have been kept secret for so long. Lord Huntington has his flaws, just as we all do, but he's an honorable gentleman, Iris. Not a simple gentleman, or an easy one, but an honorable one."

"Perhaps, but he's distant and difficult to talk to."

"Yes, I've heard people say so, though I find him to be a touch awkward and shy more than anything else."

"*Shy?* He's a marquess!"

"His title is irrelevant, Iris. When all the trappings are stripped away, he's simply a man, just like any other."

"He's cold and detached. Don't you think he's cold and detached?" Iris was beginning to feel quite desperate.

Lady Annabel leaned forward in her chair and gave Iris a long, stern look. "Tell me, Iris. How many gentlemen do you know who'd marry a lady who'd been ruined by another man? Who'd go to the trouble to arrange a marriage for that lady, after she'd betrayed his trust in such a hurtful way? Miss Hughes committed a grave offence against Lord Huntington, and he would have been more than justified in letting her suffer the consequences of it. He didn't—he saved her instead. Does that sound like something a cold, detached man would do?"

It didn't. Of course it didn't. "No."

"And what of you, Iris? You jilted him. Perhaps you were justified in doing so, but he would have been equally justified in never giving you another thought after that. What must it have taken, do you suppose, for a proud man like Lord Huntington to chase you to Hampshire, and offer for you a second time to protect you from a scoundrel like Lord Wrexley? Again, do those sound like the actions of a cold, detached man?"

"No." Iris's cheeks burned with shame. "I've been unbearably selfish, haven't I?"

"No. You've been unbearably young and inexperienced, and there's nothing to be ashamed of in that, but now it's time for you to behave like a woman, Iris, not a girl. As I said before, Lord Huntington isn't an easy man. Do you understand what I mean by that?"

Iris was beginning to understand, but her intuition whispered when it came to Lord Huntington she'd hardly peeked under the surface. "He's strong-willed."

"Yes, he is. But then so are you. You're well-matched in that way."

"He's overbearing and domineering. Controlling."

Lady Annabel smiled. "Both in and out of the bedchamber, if Lady Beaumont can be believed. He needs a lady who can manage him, certainly."

Iris thought of his flashing hazel eyes, his low, commanding voice, his stern jaw, and a shiver ran down her spine. "I haven't the vaguest idea how to manage such a man."

"I'm surprised to hear you say that, Iris, since you've been managing Lord Huntington since you arrived at Hadley House."

Iris's mouth fell open, and she regarded Lady Annabel in shock. "Why, what have I done to manage him? He lectured me for running races with Lord Wrexley, and he forbade me from riding Chaos, as if he had a right to forbid me anything, and—I didn't tell you this, Lady Annabel—but he tried to take *School of Venus* away from me last night, as well."

"And did he?"

"No. I, ah…I took it back from him." Iris didn't explain *how* she'd gotten it back. Lady Annabel was a wicked widow, yes, and likely wouldn't be shocked, but Iris was still a bit shocked herself over what she'd done.

"What about the horse?" Lady Annabel swept a meaningful look over Iris's riding habit.

"I rode Chaos this morning."

"Ah. And the race?"

A hesitant smile touched Iris's lips. "I told him it would do him good to race himself, and then I said…I believe I told him I'd bent one of my stays."

Lady Annabel laughed. "It's no wonder he's so enamored of you."

Iris's smile faded. "I don't know that he is."

Lady Annabel moved to the edge of her chair, reached over, and took Iris's hand. "He's here, isn't he? He's here, and he's made it clear he wishes to marry you."

"Out of obligation, Lady Annabel, not love."

"Do you truly believe that?"

Iris shook her head. She wasn't sure what she believed anymore. "I don't know. I'd ask you to help me untangle it, but you'll say this is one of those decisions only I can make, won't you?"

"Yes, I'm afraid so, but I will say this. It would be something special indeed to have the heart of a man like Lord Huntington entrusted to your keeping. I believe you're strong enough to understand the value of it, and to do justice to it, but you'll have to help him, Iris. He didn't grow up surrounded by love, as you did. His childhood was a lonely one, and he won't always know how to go on."

Iris frowned, remembering something Lord Wrexley had told her. "Was there some scandal—something to do with his mother?"

"Yes. She left him when he was a boy—ran off with a Scotsman and never came back. There are rumors he has half-brothers there, a pack of wild Scots born on the wrong side of the blanket. His father died a few years after his mother left, and Lord Huntington was left to the care of a distant guardian, who promptly sent him off to Eton and left him there. It couldn't have been easy on him. Boys are cruel. I'm sure you can imagine what he endured, given the scandal about his mother."

Iris thought about what he'd said that day, when she asked him if he'd ever raced as a child, and her throat closed.

I was never a child.

For a moment she couldn't speak, or catch her breath, because of the fist squeezing her heart.

Because he *had* been a child, just a child, left alone—

"It's remarkable, really, he became the man he is." Lady Annabel's voice was quiet.

"Yes. It is."

Lady Annabel patted her hand, then rose and walked to the door. "You have a decision to make. I saw Lord Huntington ride off with Captain West and Lord Derrick before I left the breakfast room, and Lady Honora and your sister went for a walk. I'll tell Charlotte you need a bit of quiet in here, shall I?"

"Yes, thank you. You're very kind, Lady Annabel."

Lady Annabel made an impatient noise in her throat. "No, I'm not kind. I do this only for my own amusement, Iris."

Iris smiled at that, but once the room was still, she wondered if all the quiet in the world would be enough, and her smile faded.

* * * *

It was dark by the time Finn made it back to Hadley House. Captain West and Derrick had returned hours ago, but he'd followed Wrexley all the way to Alton before he turned his horse's head back toward Winchester.

He couldn't rest easy until he was certain Wrexley was gone for good.

His steps were weary and his heart sank as he made his way into the house and stopped in the silent entryway. He could think of nothing but Iris, but she'd have gone to bed long ago, and all the things he wanted to say to her—all the words he'd rehearsed on his solitary ride back to Hadley House—would have to wait until tomorrow.

"She's in Lady Hadley's sitting room."

The hair on Finn's neck rose in warning, but when he turned he saw it was only Lady Tallant. She appeared to be waiting for him.

"I've done all I can to help you, Lord Huntington." Her slender figure detached itself from the deep shadows surrounding the stairwell. "I do hope I haven't wasted my efforts."

Finn was unable to account for her sudden appearance, and too exhausted to make sense of her words. "I don't understand you, Lady Tallant. Help me with what?"

"With Miss Somerset, of course. I consider myself indebted to you on Lady Farrington's account, you see—she was a dear friend of mine, and I always settle my debts." She cocked her head, her eyes narrowing as she studied him. "But despite my best efforts you've managed to make quite a mess of things, haven't you?"

Finn stared at her, still not sure what to make of this strange conversation. "You knew Lady Farrington?"

"Lady Farrington, her daughter, and the part you played in saving Miss Hughes from ruin. I've related the story to Miss Somerset." She pointed down the hallway, in the direction of the library. "You'll find her behind that closed door, and I believe she's ready to listen to whatever you choose to say. A word of advice, Lord Huntington? Make the most of this opportunity. I can't do everything for you, after all."

She began to mount the stairs, but turned back to face him again before she reached the landing. "Miss Somerset is a remarkable young lady, but I suppose you know that already. It's why you're in love with her, isn't it?"

It didn't occur to Finn to deny it, or refuse to answer, or to tell Lady Annabel it was none of her concern how he felt about Miss Somerset. He simply told the truth, without hesitation. "Yes. She's...extraordinary."

His quiet voice was nearly swallowed into the silence of the still, empty space, but Lady Tallant heard him. "Ah. Perhaps there is hope for you after all, Lord Huntington." With that, she resumed her climb until she disappeared into the darkness at the top of the stairs.

Finn didn't waste any more time, but hastened down the hallway and eased open the door to Lady Hadley's sitting room. He half-expected to find Iris asleep, but when he entered the tiny room she was curled into a corner of a large sofa, her legs tucked beneath her, eyes wide open. A book lay in her lap, but she wasn't reading. She was staring into the fire.

He stood for a moment to admire the way the dying embers cast a glow around her and turned her hair a deep gold before he came the rest of the way into the room and closed the door behind him.

The soft click made her turn, and when she saw him her breath caught in her throat, and Finn closed his eyes for a moment to savor that tiny gasp. It was the most beautiful sound he'd ever heard, and his heart leapt with hope.

"It's late." He settled onto the other end of the sofa, leaving plenty of space between them. He already ached to touch her, and he was determined not to tempt himself further by sitting too close to her. "I didn't expect you to be awake."

She kept her eyes on her lap as she fiddled with the pages of her book. "I was worried about—that is, I couldn't sleep."

Finn hesitated. He needed to tell her Wrexley was gone and wouldn't return to Hadley House, but if Iris really did love the villain, as Wrexley claimed she did, she wouldn't thank Finn for his interference, and he didn't think he could bear to see any coldness in her blue eyes when she looked at him.

Not now. Not tonight.

Finn cleared his throat. "Lord Wrexley is—"

"I wasn't worried about Lord Wrexley."

This time it was Finn's turn to catch his breath. Had she been worried about *him*?

"After our talk in the stables today, I spoke with Lady Tallant, and she told me...I was wrong about him. The wager, and his part in Lady Beaumont's appearance in the garden that day. You tried to warn me, but I wouldn't listen to you. I was wrong about you, and I—I beg your pardon, Lord Huntington."

Relief rushed through Finn then—a relief so powerful he felt dizzy with it—but there was one more thing he had to know before he could put the question of Lord Wrexley behind them forever. "Do you...are you in love with him?"

Her blue eyes were soft as they rested on his face. "No."

Finn's eyes drifted closed as her whispered word washed over him. With that one small word, she'd managed to fill that lonely, cold space inside him he'd despaired of ever reaching.

She didn't love Wrexley, and that meant there was still a chance for them. "Iris, I need...I want to..." He trailed off, because whatever he said, whatever words he chose, he knew they wouldn't be enough, and in the next moment he was beside her, so close his knee brushed against hers when he reached for her.

Finn wanted nothing more than to take her in his arms, but she held him back with a gentle hand on his chest. "I've been in here all day, thinking about our betrothal, and how I jilted you, and I need to tell you—"

"It doesn't matter anymore." He wrapped his fingers around the hand on his chest and leaned forward to rest his forehead against hers. "None of that matters now."

"It does matter. I need to tell you the truth, Lord...Finn. I lied to you when I told you I jilted you because of the wager, and because of Lady Beaumont, and because you didn't kiss me that day in Lady Fairchild's garden. Those were never the reasons. I thought they were, but they were excuses, just as you said the day we first came to Hadley House. I lied to myself, just as surely as I lied to you."

She looked into his eyes, and the pleading look in hers nearly broke his heart in two. He wanted to tell her it didn't matter, that she didn't have to say anything more, but if they were going to move forward from this moment, they had to do so with nothing but the truth between them.

Finn cupped her cheek in his hand. "All right, sweet. I'm listening."

"I was afraid—" Her brows drew together and she broke off with a slow shake of her head.

He stroked her cheek. "What were you afraid of?"

She drew in a deep breath, as if to help her push the words out, but when she did speak, her voice was a whisper. "I was afraid if I married you I'd become the lady I pretended to be during our courtship. I was afraid..." Her voice caught, and her gaze dropped to her hands. "I was afraid I'd lose myself, and I'd never become anything more than who I am right now."

Finn's throat went thick with words, with denials, because she said it as if who she was now was nothing special.

Didn't she know? Didn't she see how remarkable she was?

No, she didn't, and why would she?

He hadn't.

But now he did, and there was no going back from it.

"I've never admired fair hair." He reached for a loose lock of her hair and tucked it behind her ear, then brushed his fingertips across her cheekbone. "Blue eyes, either. I've always preferred ladies with dark coloring."

She blinked once, twice, then her brows pulled down in a frown. "Yes, ah....well, every gentleman is different."

"Or pink lips." He touched a finger to the center of her bottom lip. "Especially when they hide such a sharp tongue, as yours do. You've a temper, for all that your lips look like rosebuds, and I've never wanted a lady with a temper."

The rosebud lips pressed into an irritated line, and she wrapped her fingers around his wrist to pull his hand away from her face. "If you've quite finished—"

"I haven't." He slid his fingers to the back of her neck and held her, a half smile on his lips as his gaze touched every part of her face, and this time, he didn't think about it before he said it. This time, he didn't worry he'd stumble over his words, or say the wrong thing. He didn't try to deny it, or reduce it to something less than what it was. "I never wanted any of it, until you. I want *you*, and it's not because of Wrexley, or because the *ton* will gossip about us, or because I feel an obligation toward you. I want you because I'm in love with you, Iris."

Her fingers went slack around his wrist, and she stilled.

He brushed a gentle kiss against her mouth, then trailed his lips across her cheek to whisper in her ear. "You're everything I never knew I wanted, and everything I can't live without."

Chapter Nineteen

Finn held his breath and waited with burning lungs as a dozen different emotions chased each other across her face. Shock, confusion, doubt, even anger, until at last something soft emerged and turned her eyes a dark, midnight blue.

Tenderness.

She raised herself to her knees so her face was level with his and she could look him in the eyes. He waited for her to speak, but she didn't. She remained silent for so long, in fact, the back of Finn's neck began to burn with embarrassment. Why didn't she say something? He didn't expect her to say she loved him in return—he hadn't earned her trust yet—but surely he was owed more of a response than resounding silence.

Finn's nerves were on the verge of snapping like taut violin strings when at last she made a pleased humming sound in her throat, and touched her finger to the middle of his chin. "I like touching you here."

Finn was shocked to hear a low groan break from his chest when she dipped the tip of her finger into the tiny dimple. It was his *chin*, for God's sake, not his *cock*, but it seemed her hands on any part of his body were enough to make him wild with desire.

"I thought about touching it when we were betrothed. Touching it, and tasting it," she murmured, her gaze fixed on her own finger caressing his face, as if she were mesmerized. "May I?"

She didn't wait for permission, which was just as well, because Finn couldn't have spoken a word as he watched her draw closer, her thick lashes dropping to half-mast over burning eyes.

He drew in a sharp breath when her warm lips touched his chin, but his gasp turned into a moan when the tip of her tongue—*dear God, her tongue*—darted into the small indentation.

"Iris." His hands shot to her hips, but before he could ease her away— yes, of course, that's what he intended to do—she pressed a final kiss to his chin and slid her mouth higher, so her lips brushed against his.

It was a shy kiss, an innocent kiss, but it felt to Finn as if an entire lifetime had passed since he'd kissed her in the stables, and as soon as her mouth touched his, his blood raced in his veins, and his body shuddered with pleasure. He dug his fingers into her hips to pull her closer and opened his mouth under hers.

Not a demand, but an invitation.

She hesitated, and Finn forced himself to keep still and wait for her to decide, but he couldn't restrain his groan of triumph when her tongue crept out and traced his lower lip, then slid deeper inside his mouth to meet his in a slick, hot stroke that left him panting for breath.

One kiss, and he was ready to devour her.

A dim warning penetrated the fog of desire in his brain. Her scent, her sweetly curved body, her mouth against his, the taste of her—she was driving him mad. He was one stroke of her tongue away from losing control and taking her on Lady Hadley's soft leather sofa.

She was *his*, but she was also an innocent, and he was an honorable gentleman.

Most of the time.

"Iris. Listen to me, sweet." He slid his hands from her hips to her waist to ease her away from him. "We can't—"

She let out a protesting growl that made his cock strain against his falls, wrapped her arms around his neck and pressed closer, so her breasts were crushed against his chest. "I know gentlemen enjoy kisses, Lord Huntington."

He touched his fingertips to her mouth to hush her, a grin curving his lips. "Not Lord Huntington anymore, Iris. Finn. I can't be Lord Huntington to a lady who's kissed my dimple."

"I'm vastly relieved, then, that I've never heard another lady call you Finn." Pink colored her cheeks when she said his name, but she looked pleased.

"Now, tell me about these gentlemen who enjoy kisses." He shouldn't encourage her to talk about kisses when he had a full, eager erection, but he couldn't bring himself to send her off to bed, either.

"Philander and Horatio, you mean?"

Finn blinked. Philander and Horatio? Who the devil were Philander and Horatio?

Iris laughed at his puzzled look. "The heroes of *Dialogues between a Lady and her Maid*. Then there's Roger, from *School of Venus*, and Charles from *Memoirs of a Woman of Pleasure*."

Finn's eyebrows shot to his hairline. "You've read all three?" Jesus. She might be an innocent, but she was a remarkably well-educated one.

"I haven't finished the third one yet, but it...well, it's more of the same, I think." She peeked at him. "Isn't it?"

"I—ah, the same as what?" He stifled a groan when her fingers sank into the hair at the back of his neck. He couldn't think about the books, or about anything but burying his face in her throat and drowning in her subtle jasmine scent.

She gave his hair a gentle tug, a tiny admonishment. "The other two books are about relations between men and women, and, ah...well, about how to make a gentleman...how to give him pleasure. Isn't that what *Memoirs of a Woman of Pleasure* is about, too?"

Finn closed his eyes and let his head fall back against the sofa. He was treading on dangerous ground. He was so aroused his thighs were shaking, and the woman he loved—a woman whose simplest touch hurled him headlong into a vortex of desire—was gazing at him with her enormous blue eyes, her lips still swollen from his kisses, calmly asking about erotic literature.

"Lord Hunt—that is, Finn?"

Her soft, warm palm landed on his neck, and Finn opened his eyes and raised his head to find her nibbling on her plump lower lip.

A defeated groan fell from his lips. He intended to marry her, and soon. She was curious and eager, she'd read enough about a man's body and lovemaking not to be shocked when certain things, ah...sprang up, and damn it, he wasn't a saint. He wanted her, and he could see by her flushed cheeks and breathlessness she wanted him, too.

He let his hands drift down her back, his fingertips stroking her spine before his palms came to rest on her waist. "What about a lady's pleasure? Don't your books say anything about that?"

Her eyebrows pinched together. "Now you ask it, her pleasure does seem to be rather incidental to the gentleman's. That is, she has pleasure—after the initial pain—but the point of the business seems to be more his pleasure than hers."

"And therein lies the cause of frustration of ladies all across England," Finn muttered, with a disgusted shake of his head. "Ignorance—or worse, laziness—on the gentleman's part."

"I don't understand."

Finn leaned forward to kiss the tiny frown between her eyebrows. "Did you feel any pleasure when you read the books, Iris?"

Her wide-eyed gaze met his. "I—yes."

His mouth went dry as he watched the color rise from her chest to her throat until it bathed her cheeks in a tempting wash of bright pink. "Where did you feel it? Show me."

She stared at him, her lips parted, but he saw the uncertainty at war with her desire before her heavy lashes swept down and hid her eyes from him.

Too much, too fast.

Finn shed his coat and tossed it onto one end of the sofa, loosened the buttons on his waistcoat, and then held out his arms to her. "Come here, sweet." His hands were firm on her waist as he lifted her onto his lap. He turned so his back was against the side of the sofa and arranged her legs on either side of his thighs, with her skirts covering her. "My pleasure is tied to yours, as surely as yours is to mine. Will you let me show you?"

"Yes." No hesitation.

He trailed a single finger down her cheek and across her bottom lip in a slow caress, then dipped lower to trace her neck before coming to rest at the pulse fluttering at the base of her throat. "You like my touch." He stroked her soft skin, his breath catching at the wild throbbing under his fingertip. "I can feel how much, right here."

She was still dressed in the riding habit she'd been wearing this morning, but she'd removed the jacket and hat. Finn's heated gaze traced the curves visible under her thin muslin shirt, pausing on the cravat at her neck, and the bow tied in a simple knot under her breasts.

A faint gasp left her lips when he tugged on the end of first one bow, then the other, loosening them both. Finn hesitated, his gaze darting back to her face. She was watching him with dark, feverish blue eyes, her shallow breaths hard and quick between her parted lips.

"Untie it," she whispered.

His hands shook as he loosened the knots, slid the cravat free, and then grasped the hem of her shirt and raised it over her head. She wore only a corset underneath, and his heart nearly leapt from his chest when her bare skin met his hungry gaze.

"So pale and fine." He dragged his fingertips across her delicate collarbones and down her chest, greedy for the feel of her silky skin.

When he reached the edge of her corset he paused, but she didn't stop him, and he moved lower and cupped her breasts in his palms. His cock surged against his falls at the breathy whimper that tore from her throat as he dragged his thumbs over the straining peaks of her nipples.

"Unlace me." She took his hands and brought his fingers to the top lace of her corset.

Finn's eyes dropped closed as he struggled to remind himself he was an honorable gentleman, but the pretty pink flush on her skin, her whimpers and sighs and the pleading note in her voice—it was all too much. He fumbled with the laces of her corset, his fingers desperate and clumsy, but she helped him, and within seconds the corset was hanging loose, and he caught a maddening glimpse of the smooth skin between her breasts, and before he could think at all or reason with his cock, he'd dragged the corset away and tossed it aside because he couldn't wait another second to see her, and...

Ah, God. She was perfect.

Pale, flawless skin, her nipples the same blush pink as her lips, and they were hard for him, pouting for his touch. He couldn't tear his gaze away from her. "Oh, Iris. You're so beautiful, sweetheart."

She made a soft noise when he trailed a finger between her breasts, as if she'd waited forever for him to touch her, and the sound broke him. Any illusions he'd had that he could send her back to her bed alone vanished with that one breathless sigh.

"Did you ache here when you read your books?" He circled his thumbs around her nipples, his gaze locked on her flushed face as he stroked her.

"Yes." She grabbed his shoulders to steady herself as his relentless caresses made her squirm in his lap.

Dear God, he was going to come just from watching her. "Did these pretty peaks get hard, sweet?"

"Yes." She looked down at where he caressed her, staring at his fingers as they toyed with her nipples, which had turned a deep pink from his attentions.

"Did you touch them? Did you stroke them, as I'm doing now?" Finn trailed soft, open-mouthed kisses over her throat, and felt it move in a nervous swallow under his lips. "Tell me."

"I—" she began, but her voice trailed off, and when Finn raised his head from her throat, her cheeks were scarlet.

"It's all right, Iris." He nudged her chin up so he could look into her eyes. "It's natural to touch yourself when you're aroused, and nothing to be ashamed of. It felt good, didn't it?"

"Yes." It was more a sigh than a word.

God, he wanted to watch her fingers stroking her breasts and playing with her nipples, but she wasn't ready for that, and his mouth was watering to taste that beautiful pink flesh. He lay one hand flat against her back and leaned forward to pull a hard peak into his mouth.

She moaned when his tongue darted out to stroke her flesh. "Oh, that's...it feels..."

He sucked her nipple, then bit down gently on the tender nub. She cried out, and he went back to slow, tender strokes with the tip of his tongue. When he felt some of the tension ease from her body, he sucked and nipped at her again.

"Oh." Her head fell back and her spine arched, and she sank her fingers into his hair to hold his mouth to her breasts. "Finn, please...more."

So much more, and I want to give it all to you.

He teased one nipple, then the other, alternating between light, caressing strokes of his tongue to gentle bites and rough sucking until she grew restless and her hips began an unconscious, rhythmic movement against his lap.

God, she was so beautiful, innocently seeking her pleasure. Her sinuous glide against him was the most erotic thing he'd ever seen, and if he hadn't wanted to touch her so badly, he could have watched her all night.

But he did want to touch her, and he couldn't wait another moment.

"Where else did you feel pleasure, sweetheart?" He slid a hand under the hem of her skirt and traced his fingers over her thigh, then inched his hand higher to caress the bare skin above her garter. "Here?"

Her legs stiffened on either side of his hips. "I—not there."

"Higher then, I think?" He teased the tip of one finger between her folds. He didn't do anything more, but kept his finger still while he continued to kiss and lick her breasts.

For a long moment she didn't move, but at last she gave a tiny thrust of her hips, and an involuntary moan tore from her throat when his fingertip stroked over her clitoris with the movement.

Finn groaned at the sound, and his mouth grew more frantic against her breasts. "Yes, sweetheart. It feels good when you move against my hand. Did you touch yourself here when you read your books? Did you stroke your pretty fingers between your legs?"

"Yes," she gasped, all embarrassment gone as she pressed down hard and jerked her hips, desperate for more friction against his hand.

Finn's head fell back against the sofa. Dear God, she was going to kill him. The thought of those long, white fingers caressing her damp, flushed skin was enough to make him spill into his breeches like some overheated schoolboy.

He slid one finger into her narrow passage, a tortured groan leaving his lips when he felt how wet she was. "So hot and wet for me, Iris." He thrust gently and made lazy circles with his thumb around the tender bud hidden between her folds. "You feel so good. God, I can't wait to feel you come on my hand."

Her cheeks were flushed and her eyes unfocused as she met each of his gentle thrusts, her hips working faster now as she chased her pleasure. "Ah, I can't...please..."

"Do you need more, sweet?" He pressed his thumb more firmly against her clitoris and quickened his strokes, then carefully slid a second finger inside her. He was immediately rewarded when her back arched and her body stiffened against his.

"Finn..." She writhed against him, panting his name as she came in a flood of wet heat, her head thrown back and her body shuddering with pleasure.

When the spasms ceased and she went limp against him, Finn drew his hand out from under her skirts and urged her down onto his chest. She lay against him, breathing hard, a fistful of his silk waistcoat clenched in her hand.

Christ, was he still *dressed*?

He pulled what was left of the pins from her hair and watched the firelight play against the long golden strands as he sifted them through his fingers. He held her and couldn't remember another time in his life when he'd felt more joy than he did right now.

He thought she'd fallen asleep, but after a while she raised her head. "It's not at all the same thing to read about it, is it?"

He let out a startled laugh. "Not at all, no. Most things aren't, but perhaps this more than any other."

"Yes. A book can't touch you, after all, and touch seems to be a rather important part of it, doesn't it?"

Finn dropped a kiss on her forehead, grinning at her as he played with a lock of her hair. "You could even say it's the most important part."

She was quiet for a moment, then she braced her hands against his chest and sat up.

Finn frowned as she pulled free from the circle of his arms. "What—"

"Hush." She rested her fingers against his lips for a moment, then she loosened the knot on his cravat, unwound it from around his neck, and dropped it to the floor next to her shirt. His waistcoat followed, then she sat back on her heels, studied him, and shook her head. "No."

He raised an eyebrow at her. "No?"

"I've never seen a gentleman in only his shirtsleeves, and it's quite… that is, you're very…well, I like it." She leaned down and pressed her lips to the expanse of skin left bare by his shirt, making his breath catch. "But I want you to take it off."

Finn hesitated. If he took his shirt off, he was one step closer to taking his breeches off, and once they were off, he'd take her. He was painfully aroused after watching her come, and every one of his masculine urges was demanding he make her his.

But not here, in Lady Hadley's sitting room. He wanted her safe behind his locked bedchamber door, naked on his bed, her hair spread across his pillow, both of them free to give voice to their pleasure without fear of being overheard. He wasn't looking forward to staggering up the stairs with a raging erection, but there would be no hurrying, and no half measures in this.

Not in anything. Not with her.

"Not here, sweet." He scooped his waistcoat and cravat off the floor, then fetched his coat from the end of the sofa. She'd struggled back into her shirt and was attempting to straighten her skirts, but there was no hiding her flushed skin, her swollen lips or the mass of tangled curls tumbling over her shoulders. She looked like just what she was—a woman who'd just come to a trembling, shattering release in the arms of her lover.

My arms.

He draped his coat over her shoulders, grinning as it engulfed her. "You could wear it as a gown."

She smiled up at him. "Does it suit me?"

"Everything suits you."

He couldn't resist cradling her face in his hands so he could kiss her again. He brushed his lips over her forehead—surely that was safe enough—and took just the briefest of moments to bury his face in her hair. He was a grown man, after all. He could control himself, and…dear God, she smelled good, especially the sensitive skin behind her ear. He could go mad from the warm silk of her skin under his lips, the flutter of her pulse against his tongue, her quiet moan when he bit down gently on her earlobe…

"Finn." Her arms stole around his neck, and then his mouth was crushed against hers, his tongue hot and demanding as he surged inside, and he was wild to be inside her everywhere, her damp heat enveloping him, pulling him deeper—

But not here.

He tore his mouth from hers with a pained groan. "Upstairs, sweet. My bedchamber."

He took her hand in his and led her to the door. He paused before leading her into the hallway, but it was late. The house was dark and silent. They stole up the stairs and slipped into his bedchamber without encountering a soul.

Finn turned the lock and leaned back against the door, watching her. He could still take her back to her bedchamber, drop a chaste kiss on her cheek, and vow to himself he wouldn't touch her again until they were wed. He was an honorable gentleman, after all.

Most of the time.

She slid his coat from her shoulders, dragged her shirt over her head, climbed onto his bed, and leaned back against the pillows. Her rosy nipples were hard, and a wicked half-smile curled her lips as she beckoned to him with her fingers.

This isn't one of those times.

He tossed the clothes in his hand aside, kicked off his boots, and dragged his shirt over his head, a needy growl rising from his chest as he stalked toward the bed. The flickering light from the fire fell over her face, revealing her gaze as it moved over every inch of him—his shoulders, the bare skin of his chest and stomach, lingering on the trail of dark hair that started just under his belly button and vanished into the waistband of his breeches.

She swallowed, her tongue darting out to moisten her lips as her gaze moved over the bulge of his stiff cock pressed against the front of his breeches.

Finn groaned as his cock twitched. "I like it when you look at me."

"I, ah...I see that."

A faint grin crossed his lips, then he placed one knee in the middle of the bed and reached for her. "Give me your hand."

She scrambled across the bed and offered her hand. He drew it toward him, and pressed her palm flat against the front of his breeches.

Both of them gasped when her fingers instinctively wrapped around his hard length.

"Touch me, sweet. Like this." Finn moved her hand in a slow, steady caress from his base to his tip.

She was hesitant at first, careful, but after a moment her fingers tightened around him, her eyes widening when a helpless groan tore from his lips at her rougher strokes. "Is that...am I hurting you?"

"God, no. You're driving me mad." Another low moan slipped past his lips as she continued to tease her hand over his aching cock. She seemed to know just what he wanted, her fingers lingering at his tip until his hips were jerking to increase the friction of her hand against him.

She watched his face as if fascinated, her lips parted, a sigh escaping her when he reached out to cup her breasts and tease her nipples.

"I want to see you." She rose to her knees and tugged at the buttons of his falls. Once she'd loosened them she slid her warm hand past the crumpled fabric to draw him out, uttering a surprised, pleased sound when she held his throbbing cock in her hand. "Oh, my. You're…oh, my."

Finn sucked in a deep breath and threw his head back when her warm palm met his bare flesh. If he let her continue, he was going to come like this, and he was dying to be inside her, to make her his.

He gripped her wrist to still her hand, and she let out a surprised squeak of protest. "But…I want to touch you, and I've hardly begun."

He slid his fingers over her jaw, unable to prevent the smile that rose to his lips at her indignant expression. "But I'm about to finish, sweet, and neither of us wants that."

Her brows drew together. "Finish what?"

Finn dragged his breeches off and kicked them aside, then joined her on the bed. "I'll show you in a moment. Well, hopefully a bit more than a moment."

"But I wanted to—"

He silenced her with a fierce kiss, his lips and tongue demanding a response until she fell back against the bed with a moan of surrender. Finn reached for the buttons on the side of her skirt, tore them open, and dragged it and her petticoat over her hips and down her legs until at last she was bare before him.

"Beautiful." He propped his head on his hand as he lay beside her, his gaze memorizing every inch of her body. "I've dreamed of you like this, spread out across my bed, but I never imagined…" His voice grew thick, and he trailed off and brought her hand to his mouth, pressing a warm kiss into her palm.

She leaned over and brushed her lips over the center of his chest, over his wildly beating heart. "I didn't, either."

He rolled her onto her back and came over her, lowering his head to suck at a nipple while he slid a hand up the inside of her thigh.

She arched against his mouth as he kissed and licked and sucked at her breasts for long moments and teased his fingers through the curls between her thighs. He brushed his thumb against her sensitive knot of flesh until she grew hot and slick, and he felt it harden and rise for him, begging for his touch.

"Are you wet for me still?" He dipped a finger inside her and had to clench his teeth to hold back his orgasm when his hand came away covered in her sweet honey. "Ah God, yes." He slipped a second finger into her and thrust gently until her hips rose to meet his fingers, and she couldn't hold back her desperate whimpers.

"Is this what you want, Iris?" He cupped her cheek in his hand and held her until her hazy eyes focused on his. "Do you want me inside you?"

She looked up into his face with those eyes that could break his heart, and she didn't hesitate. "Yes."

He dropped a tender kiss on her lips. "And you're going to be mine?"

"Yes." She urged his mouth back down to hers, and her kiss was a promise.

Finn slid one knee between her legs to open her, then settled between her thighs, his eyes squeezing closed when he felt her wet warmth against the tip of his cock. He eased partway inside, stopping to kiss her lips and her breasts when he felt her tense beneath him.

"It's going to hurt a bit." He brushed a few loose strands of her hair from her eyes. "But I'll be as careful as I can with you."

"I know you will be." She gazed up at him, and Finn's heart burst in his chest at the trust he saw in the deep blue depths of her eyes.

His gaze never left her face as he eased into her, as far as he could go before he felt the barrier of her innocence against his cock, then he drew back and surged forward again with a powerful thrust, not holding back, because it was best done quickly, so the worst of the pain was over with a single stroke.

She gasped, and her body went rigid under his.

Finn went motionless. He was seated deep inside her now, and God, she was so hot and tight and wet his body urged him to thrust into that seductive heat again and again, but he remained still and prayed for the control to stay that way until her pain faded.

"Iris? I'm sorry, love." He let his head rest in that sweet space between her neck and shoulder. He stroked her hair and kissed her throat, whispering soothing words in her ear—broken words of love and desire—until at last she sighed, and the tension began to drain from her body.

"That, ah...well, that also wasn't the same as reading about it," she murmured.

Finn placed a tender kiss on her lips. "No, I'm afraid not. I hate that I hurt you—"

"Hush. It's over now." She paused, then gave him an uncertain look. "I mean, that part is over. There's more to it, isn't there? There seemed to be more in my books, but—"

He let out a soft laugh, then slipped a hand down to stroke between her legs. "There's more."

"Oh, I thought there must be, but...*oh*." She squirmed under him as he teased his fingertip over her again.

"Spread your legs wider, sweet," he whispered, nibbling on her earlobe. "I'm going to stroke you so you're wet and slick for me."

She opened her legs to him, her moans growing increasingly desperate as he teased and played with her. When he felt slippery heat gather between her legs, he moved his hips in a small, experimental thrust.

She cried out, but it wasn't a cry of pain, so he thrust again, gentle still, but even that was enough to make his eyes roll back in his head and pleasure pound through him.

"Finn." His name was a breathless plea on her lips, and when she met him on his next thrust, he began to move inside her in slow, steady strokes, his fingers still toying with the slick bud between her legs.

A jolt of pure, masculine triumph surged through him when her fingernails dug into his back, and she wrapped her legs around his waist.

"Does it feel good, love?" His thrusts were more frantic now, faster, and he could feel his powerful release edging closer.

"Ah, yes. So good. Please, I want...please."

"Do you want to come?" He was working her hard now, dragging his fingertip over her clitoris again and again, his hips tight against hers as he thrust his cock into her, then drew almost all the way out before thrusting again.

Her only answer was an incoherent moan. Her head thrashed against the pillow, and then she cried out as her body clenched around him, sucking him deep inside her, and she cried out again, her fingernails biting into his shoulders as her release swept over her.

Finn groaned as the telltale tingling began low in his back, and his spine drew tight, and God, he was going to come, explode inside her—

A guttural moan tore from deep in his chest when his release hit him, his back arching and his legs shaking with the astonishing pleasure. He held her tight against him as his cock jerked inside her, his mouth open against her neck, harsh, panting breaths tearing from his throat as his orgasm went on and on, shaking him like a ragdoll until at last it released him, and he went limp against her.

He didn't release her when he was spent, but rolled onto his side and gathered her close to his chest, his heart thundering against her back as they both caught their breath.

When they'd calmed and the only sound in the room was the crackling of the fire, Finn brushed her hair over her shoulder and nuzzled his face into her neck. "Iris? Are you all right?"

"Mmmm." She drew his arm into the curve of her waist, a long sigh of sleepy contentment escaping her when he curled a possessive hand around her breast.

He stayed awake for a long time after her breathing turned deep and even, his arms wrapped protectively around her and his face buried in her hair. Just before he drifted off to sleep she murmured something, but her whisper was so quiet he wasn't sure if he'd dreamed it or not.

I love you. I love you, Finn.

Chapter Twenty

There was nothing but darkness outside Finn's bedchamber window when Iris untangled herself from his warm embrace, crept across the room and began to gather her clothing.

It proved to be a daunting task.

Coats, shirts, stockings, and cravats were scattered from one end to the room to the other. She stumbled about in the dark, stifling a hiss of pain when she tripped over Finn's boots and hit her shin against the bedframe. She found her petticoat twisted in her riding skirt in a heap under the bed, and her shirt and cravat were hanging over the wash basin on the other side of the room.

Dear God. It looked as if they'd fallen on each other in a wild frenzy and torn each other's clothes off as soon as the bedchamber door closed behind them.

Iris's cheeks heated. In other words, it looked like precisely what it was.

She glanced at the bed and a yearning sigh escaped her. Finn was asleep on his back, his long limbs flung in every direction. The sheets rode low on his hips, and his powerful chest and taut stomach were on display, along with acres of smooth, bronzed skin.

And she'd thought his chin dimple was mesmerizing.

He looked sleepy and warm and utterly delicious, and every feminine instinct urged her to slide back under the covers and wake him by pressing kisses to every inch of that delectable skin, but she couldn't dally here all morning.

Could she?

No, no, of course she couldn't. There'd be no end to the uproar if anyone discovered she hadn't slept in her bed, especially if that person should happen to be Violet, who'd worm the truth out of her before Iris managed to struggle back into her corset.

Where *was* her corset?

Perhaps she'd left it by the bed. She'd just have a quick look, and while she was there it wouldn't hurt to take one last peek at Finn while he slept, and in any case, she couldn't leave him, ah...exposed like that. He'd take a chill. She'd just pull the blanket over him, and perhaps smooth the hair away from his face, and then she'd scurry off to her bedchamber.

Iris padded back across the room in her bare feet, her clothes in a bundle under her arm. She stood by the bed gazing down at his peaceful face for long moments, her heart both full and yet aching with a strange melancholy at once. He looked younger when he was asleep, almost boyish, the stern lines of his face softer in repose, and his golden-brown hair lying in disheveled waves across his forehead.

She reached out to trace his firm lips with one gentle finger. Just the lightest touch, so as not to wake him—

His hand snaked out and grabbed hold of her wrist. "Sneaking away in the dark, are you?"

A sound that was embarrassingly like a squeak left Iris's lips, and she dropped her clothes to the floor. "No! I never sneak. But I need to get back to my bedchamber before someone discovers I'm missing."

He raised himself up on one elbow and gazed at her with sleepy hazel eyes, his full lips curving in a lazy smile as he slowly shook his head. "Oh, no. I don't think so, sweet."

"If Violet finds us out, I'll be...Finn!"

Finn caught her in his arms, tossed her onto the bed, and came down on top of her in a tangle of warm limbs. "Now, what were you were saying?"

His lips hovered over hers, so close, a mere breath away. "I, ah..." What *had* she been saying? "Oh, that Violet will catch me out, and then you'll have to explain to Captain West a debaucher lurks under your gentlemanly exterior."

"Yes, but I only let him loose when I want something." He touched his thumb to her mouth, his eyes darkening when her lips parted for him. "And I want you, Iris."

"I see. Do you always get what you want, Lord Huntington?" She bit down gently on the tip of his thumb, making him moan.

"Always." He slid one long, muscular leg between hers and stroked a large hand over her belly, inching closer to the curls between her legs with each caress.

Iris caught her breath as wet warmth flooded her core. She was tempted to spread her legs and let him pleasure her as he had last night, but as delicious as that would be, there was one small matter she hadn't worked through.

How did he use the silk scarves?

"Tell me about these dark desires of yours."

Finn went still, and his body tensed. He was silent for a long moment, then he blew out a breath and flopped over onto his back, covering his eyes with one arm. "There's nothing so dark about them."

Iris propped herself on her side beside him and balanced her head in her hand. "I'm not asking you to explain yourself to me, Finn. I'm simply curious. My books described all manner of scandalous things, but Philander never blindfolded Octavia with a cravat."

She was only teasing him, but he didn't smile. "I would never hurt you, Iris. You know that, don't you?"

Iris's smiled faded. Did he truly believe she was afraid of him? She pulled his arm away from his eyes and turned his face toward her. "Of course you wouldn't hurt me. I never for a moment thought you would. That's not why I asked. It's just… I want to know you, and…" Her face heated. "Give you what you need in the bedchamber."

"I don't need it," he said, too quickly. "Not from you."

"If not from me, then who?" Iris winced at the jealousy in her voice, but blast the man, if he was going to bind anyone, it was going to be *her*.

"No, I didn't mean that. I meant I'll do without, sweet."

Iris might be a novice in the bedchamber, but it didn't take unusual perception to see there was a part of Finn who needed to take command, to dominate. "You like the control of it."

His jaw ticked. "It's complicated."

She ran her fingers over his raspy chin, then leaned forward to kiss away the tension in his jaw. "Explain it to me."

He ran a rough hand through his hair. "It's not just about control. That is, it does excite me to be in control of your pleasure, but it's also about taking care of you, and protecting you, even. It's difficult to explain."

Iris thought about that for a moment, then she got out of bed and sifted through the piles of clothes on the floor. When she found what she wanted, she crawled back into bed beside him and held up two cravats. "Show me."

He stared at her, horrified. "No, Iris."

"Finn—"

"*No.* You're an innocent—for God's sake, last night you were a virgin, and you've only recently decided I'm not a liar. Even if I were to agree to it at some point, it wouldn't be now. Not when trust is still so fragile between us."

Iris ran the long length of his cravat between her fingers. He was right. She wasn't quite ready for that kind of adventure, but perhaps there was another way.

"Do you trust me?"

"It doesn't work like that, Iris. I do trust you, but I don't permit my lovers to bind me."

"Have you ever had a lover you trusted, or have they all been like Lady Beaumont? Mistresses, or courtesans?"

He didn't reply, but his silence was her answer.

Iris placed her hand on his chest, over his heart. "Have you ever taken someone you love to your bed, Finn? Someone who…who loved you in return?"

He'd been staring at the ceiling, his lips tight, but now he turned to her, his eyes soft. "No." His voice was choked. "I haven't."

She leaned down and pressed a tender kiss to his lips. "Until now."

But Iris tossed the cravats aside. She didn't want to push him on this. He knew he could come to her if he changed his mind, and for now, that was enough.

She lay down beside him with her head on his chest, and Finn wrapped his arm around her. After a while his breathing became slow and even, and Iris thought he'd fallen asleep, but then he stirred against her, and his low voice rumbled against her ear. "Lay the cravat over my eyes, but don't tie it."

She rose up next to him, startled. "We don't have to, Finn—"

"I want to."

The first fingers of dawn had crept through the window now, and she studied his expression in the dim light. His jaw was still tense, but there wasn't a trace of doubt in his eyes.

Iris reached behind her and picked up a cravat. "Like this?" She laid the long strip of cloth over his eyes but left it loose, as he'd asked her to do.

"Yes. Now the other." He raised his arms over his head and crossed them at the wrists. "Bind my wrists, but loosely, so I can pull free if I need to."

Iris bit her lip as a wave of doubt assailed her. "Are you certain?"

"Yes. Bind my hands."

Iris grabbed the remaining cravat and looped it around his wrists. "I've left the ends untied, so if you need to get loose, you can easily slide it off."

"Well, then. I'm at your mercy."

That was when the reality of the situation hit Iris. He *was* at her mercy, laid out in front of her with every beautiful inch of him on display. His lips, that bronze skin, his hard chest, and that distracting line of hair low on his belly that led straight down to his—

"What are you waiting for, sweet? I thought you wanted to touch me."

"Oh, I do. I'm just, ah…well, I'm not sure where to begin."

Finn let out a soft laugh, and moved his hips. "I have a suggestion, if you like."

Iris glanced down the length of his body. The sheet still covered him from his waist down, but the thin white cloth was already rising over his hard length.

And all at once, Iris knew just what she wanted to do.

She pressed an open-mouthed kiss to the center of his chest. "That day, in Lady Fairchild's garden." She slid her hand from his chest over his stomach and felt his muscles tense under the caress. "I was peeking through the rose arbor at you and Lady Beaumont, and I saw something I didn't quite understand at the time, but now…"

I still don't quite understand.

But she did have a much clearer idea of the ultimate goal, and the rest of it, well…she'd work it out as she went along.

She stroked a finger over his nipple, surprised when he tensed, and the tiny nub hardened under her touch. "You like it when I touch you there, just as I do." She stroked him again, then leaned over his chest to trace it with her tongue.

The muscles in his stomach jumped at the caress. "I do like it. Do it again."

Iris smiled. He was terribly bossy for someone whose wrists were bound, but she had no intention of denying him. She nibbled at him and dragged her teeth over his nipple, then soothed the abrasion with gentle licks of her tongue.

He let out a strangled moan and threw his head back against the pillow. "Jesus, your tongue is so hot."

Heat built between Iris's legs at his panting breaths and the way he writhed under her hands. He didn't seem to even know what he was saying, and the idea she could make him lose control was so arousing, she wanted more of it.

"I saw Lady Beaumont sink to her knees in front of you that day." She inched the sheet down his body, a whimper of pure lust tearing from her throat when he thrust his hips against the cloth as it dragged over his length. "I couldn't see clearly, but I think she lowered your falls. Did she?"

"Yes," Finn moaned. "Touch me, sweet."

Iris squirmed closer to him so she could rub her hard nipples against his chest. "Oh, I will. In a moment. But first, tell me what she did to you after she lowered your falls."

"She took…" He tried to catch his breath. "Took out my cock."

"Like this?" She slid her palm down his stomach and wrapped her fingers around him, amazed at the way he pulsed in her hand. He was fully erect, his tip slippery from the bead of fluid welling there, and flushed a deep red.

"*Yes.*" His hips lifted off the bed so he could thrust into her hand. "Harder."

"Not yet." Iris kept on with her slow, gentle strokes, biting her lips at his tortured moan. "After she released you from your falls, you pushed her away."

"Yes." He thrust against her hand again, then growled in frustration when she drew back to keep him from getting the friction he needed.

Iris shimmied down his body so she was close enough he could feel her breath on his straining shaft. "What would she have done if you hadn't?"

"Ah, God. She..." He trailed off with a groan.

The ache between Iris's legs had grown unbearable. She was desperate for him to take her, to fill her with his hard length until she shattered around him, but she wanted this first, and she wanted him to ask her for it.

She tightened her fingers around his shaft and stroked faster to encourage him. "I saw her lower her head toward your lap. What was she going to do?"

"Suck," Finn gasped. "She was going to take me in her mouth and suck me."

"Do you want that now?" Her mouth hovered over his swollen tip. "Do you want me to take you into my mouth?"

He struggled with himself as she continued to stroke him, but he was moaning and thrusting his hips toward her mouth, and Iris knew his battle was over before it even began. The honorable marquess who was never far from the surface was no match for such wild, fierce arousal. "God, yes, sweet. Please. Suck me."

Iris wrapped her hand around the base of his shaft and slid her lips hesitantly over his swollen head. She hadn't any clear idea what to do, but he didn't seem to notice. He arched off the bed with a harsh groan. "Don't stop. So good. Your mouth is—"

She never found out what her mouth was, because whatever he was going to say was lost in another moan as she licked and teased, drunk on his clean, musky scent and the taste of him— soap, with a faint hint of salt. She sucked harder, amazed at the way his soft, thin skin slid so smoothly over the hard shaft underneath.

A guttural moan tore from his chest and his cock surged against her lips, as if it were begging for more of her mouth. So she took him deeper, and his hips jerked hard, as if to push deeper still, but despite his body's desperation, he was pleading for something, his words nearly incoherent between his breathless gasps. "I don't want to...ah, God, not yet, Iris. Don't make me come."

Iris released his shaft from her mouth with a wet plop, but she didn't stop. She pressed her lips to his thick base and slid her fingers over his slick tip, playing with the moisture there as she nibbled at him.

"*Iris.*" It was a plea, and a warning.

She might have continued to play with him, despite his command—after all, he was supposed to be at her mercy—but then she felt his strong hands sink into her hair, and realized he'd torn loose from the cravat binding his wrists.

"Inside you. Now." He wrapped her hair around his fist and eased her up the bed until she was sprawled on top of him. "Straddle me, with your legs beside my hips." He kept one hand in her hair, but pressed the fingers of the other into her hip to help her into position. "Take me inside you." His lips were pulled back from his teeth, his face nearly savage with stark desire.

I'm at his mercy now.

He hissed as she shifted to grasp him and her damp core brushed against his cock. "Spread your legs wider. *Yes.*" He nudged against her entrance and sucked in a breath when his tip slipped inside her. "Jesus, you're so slick and hot. Did it make you wet to bind and tease me?"

Iris's head began to fall back at the exquisite sensation of him slowly filling her, but Finn gave her hair a sharp tug. "No. Answer me. Why are you so wet, sweet?" He grasped her by the waist and raised her over him, then pulled her down onto his cock, a smile of pure masculine satisfaction curving his lips when she cried out.

But then he froze, his hazel eyes burning into hers. "You liked having me at your mercy, didn't you? Would you have sucked me to release if I hadn't stopped you?"

She whimpered and squirmed on top of him to try and make him move, but he let out a dark laugh and held her hips still. "No. Not until you tell me. Maybe this will loosen that busy tongue of yours."

He leaned forward and took one of her nipples into his hot mouth and sucked, devouring her, and any thought she'd had of resisting him fled as he nipped and teased her. "Yes!" She grasped his head to hold him to her breasts. "I wanted to keep going, to keep you in my mouth until you—"

"Came." He thrust his hips up, driving his cock into her once, and then, before she could catch her breath, he jerked his hips hard again, this thrust so powerful she nearly toppled off him.

Iris gasped, and her hands flew to his chest to steady herself as Finn, wild from her teasing, surged into her again and again, his hands guiding her hips down onto him with each upward stroke. He bit her earlobe, his whispers lost in his ragged breath as he begged her to come, to come for him...

Her release was hard and sudden, crashing over her like a wave and then sucking her deeper and deeper into the undertow, so deep she was gasping for breath and clinging to Finn as he toppled into his own release with a shout, his body going rigid for a long, heart-stopping moment before it let him loose at last.

Their skin was flushed and damp and they were both still breathless when he collapsed onto his side and tucked her against his chest, murmuring broken words of desire and love to her as she succumbed to a dreamless sleep.

When she woke again, weak morning sunlight was filtering through Finn's window. It was early still, just past dawn, but Iris shrugged off her delicious languor, tossed the covers aside, and struggled to a sitting position.

Finn wrapped an arm around her waist and pulled her back against him. "No."

"I have to, before Violet comes in search of me." She gently unwound his arm from her waist and slid from the bed.

"She won't be up for hours." Finn flopped over onto his back with a grumble, then shoved a pillow against the headboard and leaned back against it, watching her as she scrambled to find her clothes.

Iris tugged her petticoat over her hips and struggled into her skirt. "She rises early, and if she sees even the least sign a debauchery has taken place, she'll guess everything. I'd rather not be wearing a wrinkled riding habit when she finds me."

"Wrinkled, and inside out." Finn grinned and waved a hand at her. "The skirt, anyway. I'm not sure about the petticoat, but if you'll come over here and climb into bed, I'd be happy to examine it."

Iris scooped her shirt off the floor. "No, indeed, for you'll have it off me in a trice, and…where in the world is my corset? Have you seen—" She slapped a hand over her mouth, her eyes going wide. "Oh, dear God. We've left it in Charlotte's sitting room!"

Finn yawned and shoved his hands behind his neck. "You'll be all right without it. Your bedchamber is just on the other side of the stairwell, and no one will be in the hallways at this hour."

She bit her lip, her brows drawn with worry. "But what if someone should find it in the sitting room? They'll know at once what we've been up to! No lady happens to just leave her corset lying about in a sitting room, unless she's been up to something she shouldn't!"

"It's all right, love. I'll fetch it. Though if someone did find it, it wouldn't be so terribly shocking. We'll be married by the end of the week, after all."

Iris was struggling to tuck the ends of her shirt into her skirt, but her head jerked up at his words. "*What?*"

He looked taken aback at her incredulous tone. "I spoke to Captain West about it yesterday. We'll marry here, at Hadley House, before the end of the house party. We need to be wed before we return to London, Iris, to dispel any lingering rumors about you jilting me. I won't have every half-wit in London gossiping about my wife. Captain West and I discussed it, and we both agree its best this way."

"I see." Iris crossed her arms over chest. "And are you marrying Captain West?"

"No, I'm marrying *you*." Finn stared at her for a moment, then his eyes narrowed. "You look as if you're contemplating jilting me. *Again.* For the *third time*. I swear to you, Iris, if the words 'we don't suit' cross your lips right now—"

"Oh, hush. Of course I'm going to marry you. Do you think I would have permitted you to…" Her cheeks heated, and she tilted her chin at the bed. "To do *that* to me if I wasn't?"

"As I recall, you did that to *me*, as well." He gave her an inviting smile and pulled back the covers. "Now, come back to bed and do it again."

"I most certainly will not." She pressed her lips into a prim line. "You're incorrigible. What happened to the honorable, proper Marquess of Huntington?"

"I'll wear my cravat, if you like." His eyes gleamed with playful humor.

Iris fought back a smile, and gave him a stern look. "I'm simply saying I would have preferred you discuss wedding plans with *me*, rather than with Captain West. You'll keep that in mind with any future staggeringly important, life-changing events, won't you?"

"If you insist. I meant to discuss it with you last night, but I became distracted." His gazed roved over her, lingering on her unrestrained breasts. "I'm *still* distracted. I expect I'll be distracted for many years to come. I may never let you leave the house once we're wed."

Iris flushed with pleasure, and this time she didn't bother to hide her smile. "Go back to sleep, Lord Huntington. I'll fetch the corset myself."

Chapter Twenty-one

Of all the people who might have caught her sneaking around Hadley House with her clothes askew and her corset tucked under her arm, Iris would have chosen Lady Honora.

"Iris! Oh, thank goodness. I must speak to you at once!"

To be fair, she would rather not have been caught at all, but it could have been far worse.

It could have been Violet.

Iris turned with a sigh, trudged back down the stairs, and met Honora in the entryway. She hid the corset behind her back and sent up a quick prayer Honora wouldn't notice it, because there was no plausible explanation for it. For the corset, or the handful of buttons missing from her riding skirt, or her hair, which hung in tangled knots down her back, as if she'd been rolling about in bed with a marquess all morning.

Iris winced as another button came loose and hit the marble floor with a ping. Oh, dear God, there was no way Honora would overlook *that*.

But Honora didn't seem to notice. "Oh, Iris. It's such a dreadful business! He was very wrong to have done it, I know that, and you know how I despise wagering of any kind, but to involve a lady in such a sordid business! But he's like a brother to me, you see, and I'd forgive him anything."

Iris reached out and pulled a leaf from her friend's hair. "Forgive who? Have you been wandering around in the woods this morning, Honora?"

Honora raised a distracted hand to her hair. "I've just come from the wilderness beyond the garden. He couldn't risk anyone seeing him, least of all Captain West or Lord Huntington, and oh, Iris! I do hope you'll forgive me for meeting him after he's been so dreadfully unfair to you."

"Honora!" Iris grasped her friend by the shoulders. "I haven't the faintest idea what you're talking about. Who's been unfair to me?"

For one sickening moment Iris was afraid Honora was going to say Lord Huntington, but before her heart had a chance to sink, Honora burst into a flood of tears.

"Wrexley! He sent me a note this morning by one of the servants. I shouldn't have gone to meet him, of course I shouldn't have, but I couldn't say no, even though he's been so wicked, and—"

"Why should Lord Wrexley have to send you a note? Why not just see him at breakfast?"

Honora's mouth fell open. "What, you mean to say you don't know? Captain West and Lord Huntington have sent him away, on account of the race!"

"The race? What..." All of a sudden it dawned on Iris what had Honora so unhinged, and all the blood left her head at once.

The private horse race Lord Wrexley had arranged—Finn had found out about it.

Iris squeezed her eyes closed and tried to fend off her dizziness. Dear God, he must have been furious. He'd have gone to Captain West at once and the two of them—and likely Lord Derrick as well—must have hunted Lord Wrexley down and sent him back to London.

Last night. It had to have happened last night. That's why Finn had been so late returning to Hadley House. He'd known last night, and he hadn't told her.

I meant to discuss it with you last night, but I became distracted.

This time her heart did sink, right down to the bottom of her slippers. In the space of a single day he'd arranged the details of their wedding, put an end to the horse race, and chased Lord Wrexley away, all without breathing a word to her about any of it. What else had he been too distracted to tell her last night?

She hadn't time to dwell on it at the moment, however, because Honora was now sobbing in earnest. "Honora, calm down. It's upsetting, yes, but you'll see your cousin as soon as you return to London."

"No, I won't!" Honora wailed, crying harder. "He's collected the wagers for the race already, and he's used the money to pay off a debt to Lord Avery. If the race doesn't take place, he'll have to pay the money back at once. He doesn't have it, Iris, and he told me there's not a gentleman left in London who will accept his vowels. He'll end up fleeing to the Continent, and then he'll take back up with that odious Lord Harley and be ruined, and I'll never see him again!"

"How do you know all this, Honora?" Iris's head was spinning. "And if Captain West sent Lord Wrexley away, then how have you just seen him the garden?"

"He sneaked back." Honora took a deep breath, wiped the tears from her cheeks, and pressed a crumpled piece of paper into Iris's hand. "Here. He sent a servant to fetch me, and asked me to give this to you. I read it. Forgive me."

Iris unfolded the note, but aside from his apologies and pleas for forgiveness, Lord Wrexley's note said little more than what Honora had just told her.

With one exception.

His companions were still eager to race. If Iris wished to accommodate them, she could meet them tomorrow morning at a field to the east of the Hadley House property, and the race would go off as originally planned. If she won, Lord Wrexley could pay off his debts and remain in London.

"I don't ask you to do it." Honora's voice was quiet. "He was very wrong to involve you in this. Indeed, I don't know what to say to you. If I'd known of his wagering, I never would have suggested you encourage his courtship." Another tear slid down Honora's cheek. "I'm so sorry, Iris."

"There, now. Don't cry. You must know I don't blame you." Iris enveloped her friend in a tight hug, but even as she murmured comforting words to Honora, her mind was testing and discarding one idea after the next to find a way out of this new tangle.

By the time she'd soothed Honora into a semblance of calm, she had the beginnings of a plan. "Find Violet, Honora, and bring her to Lady Hadley's sitting room. I'll go fetch Lady Tallant and Lady Hadley."

There was only one thing to do that made the least bit of sense.

It was time to call in the ladies.

* * * *

"You don't owe Lord Wrexley a thing. You do realize that, Iris?"

Violet had been pacing in front of the glass doors that led from the sitting room onto the terrace ever since Iris, with some tearful assistance from Honora, told them the truth about Lord Wrexley.

"Let's put aside the question of the race for a moment. You might have *married* Lord Wrexley, Iris, and if you had, you can be sure your fortune would have ended in the pockets of every scoundrel in London. Forgive me, Honora," Violet added, her face softening when Honora began to weep again.

"I still can't quite believe it. Such a gentlemanly man. I never would have suspected this of him." Charlotte shook her head, her lips pulled tight.

Iris glanced at Lady Annabel, who was the only one who hadn't looked the least bit surprised to learn of Lord Wrexley's perfidy. She raised an eyebrow at Iris in an unspoken question, and Iris gave her a tiny nod.

Lady Annabel cleared her throat. "Lord Huntington, Iris. What of that matter?"

"He's...that is to say, we're both...well, it's all rather complicated—"

Violet, who'd never had much patience for equivocation, threw up her hands at this. "Oh, for goodness' sake, Iris. It's not as if anything you've said this morning makes the least bit of sense. Just say it, won't you?"

"Very well, then. We're betrothed."

"*What*?" Violet stared at her. "How can you be betrothed? You've jilted him!"

"Twice." Lady Annabel hid a smile behind her teacup. "But as they say, the third time's the lucky one."

"Twice? Whatever do you mean?" Violet looked from Lady Annabel to Iris, her eyes narrowed, but when neither of them answered, she threw up her hands and resumed her furious pacing. "Are you only marrying Lord Huntington because Lord Wrexley's out of the question now? I know you're worried about what Grandmother will say, and you want to avoid a scandal, but those are not sound reasons to marry. Grandmother will reconcile herself to the circumstances, and the scandal will fade, but a marriage is forever, Iris."

"Not always." Lady Annabel took a polite sip of her tea. "Just as well, too, in some cases."

No one seemed to know quite what to say to *that*, and a brief silence descended, but then Iris cleared her throat. "It's not the scandal, or Grandmother, Violet. It's...I was wrong about Lord Huntington. He's really quite...well, I know he might not seem so from a casual acquaintance, but he's nothing at all like I imagined he was."

"You're in love with him," Violet said, her tone both relieved and irritated at once. "Well, Iris. I'm happy for you, but you could have saved us all a great deal of fuss and bother if you'd realized that two weeks ago."

Lady Annabel laughed. "Ah, Miss Violet. I think you'll find when it's your turn love is many things, but convenient isn't one of them."

Violet darted a quick look at Lady Honora, then looked away. "I don't intend to take another turn."

"Well, I think it's lovely." For the first time that morning, Honora smiled. "I'm very pleased for you, Iris."

"Yes, it's a good match. I'll think they'll suit." Lady Annabel winked at Iris. "But of course Lord Huntington won't be at all pleased over this race business. I assume you're thinking of racing, Iris, or you wouldn't have called us here at such an ungodly hour."

"I'm considering it, yes."

Violet groaned. "Oh, no. Lord Huntington's going to go mad when he hears of this. Really, Iris, you do know how to ruin an otherwise perfectly lovely house party. Why in the world would you choose to race?"

"Because Lord Wrexley is Honora's cousin, Violet, and he'll be obliged to flee to the Continent if he has to forfeit the money from this wager."

He might simply turn around and wager it again, of course—wagering was a sickness, and it was made worse when one escaped the consequences of it, not better. But if Lord Wrexley stayed in England, there was at least a chance Honora and Lady Fairchild could help him, whereas if he fled to the Continent, he'd never return.

But there was more to it than that, and it had nothing to do with Lord Wrexley. Violet was right—Iris didn't owe him a thing. Quite the opposite.

And yet...

She couldn't quite forget it had been Lord Wrexley who'd encouraged her to run races with him on the lawn that day, and Lord Wrexley who'd arranged her first ride with Chaos. Oh, he hadn't done it for her, of course. His intentions toward her had been far from honorable. Finn had been right all along when he said Lord Wrexley was only concerned with his own satisfaction.

But however villainous his intentions, Lord Wrexley's feigned charm and wicked schemes had led to Iris finding a part of herself again. A part she treasured, and one she might have lost for good if he hadn't happened along. She no longer had any illusions about Lord Wrexley. He wasn't a good man, but this race wasn't about him at all.

It was about her.

Perhaps it didn't make sense, but this was something she felt compelled to do, with a kind of bone-deep certainty she couldn't dismiss. If she did—if she turned a deaf ear when her every instinct was screaming at her to race, then where would it end? She'd turn a deaf ear the next time too, and then the next, until she'd denied the truth to herself for so long she'd no longer remember who she was anymore.

Finn wasn't going to approve of this. That much was certain. But if he truly loved her, he'd never ask her to deny such an elemental part of herself, no matter what his objections might be. He'd want her to be who she was as much as she wanted it for herself.

"You'll want to race Chaos, I expect. Poor Captain West isn't at all ready for this new debacle, I'm afraid. He won't like it any more than Lord Huntington does, but I may be able to persuade him." Charlotte tapped her chin, considering. "He'll want to see you ride Chaos first, though, Iris."

"Chaos! What, that enormous gray beast?" Honora went pale. "Surely you don't intend to race *him*, Iris?"

"Yes, I do. But only with Captain West's permission."

"What of Lord Huntington's permission?" Lady Annabel raised an eyebrow at Iris.

Violet flopped down onto the settee next to Iris. "She doesn't need Lord Huntington's permission. Only Captain West's."

Iris smiled at that. Violet tended to see things in black and white. It would be fascinating indeed when her sister fell in love and found herself awash in shades of gray.

Lady Annabel chuckled. "You're quite right, but I doubt Lord Huntington will see it that way."

Charlotte sighed. "No, he won't. He'll want to manage everything. Men always do, and Lord Huntington more than most. And I warn you, Iris, they're particularly troublesome when they're in love."

"Well, as to that," Iris said, "I'll simply begin with Lord Huntington as I mean to go on with him."

Charlotte glanced at Lady Annabel. "Indeed? How is that?"

"I will always be honest with him and consider his wishes on every matter, but I will never *ask* Lord Huntington's *permission* to do anything."

Lady Annabel's lips quirked. "Ah. Well, Iris, I daresay your marriage will be an exciting one."

An image of Finn's stern face and changeable hazel eyes rose in Iris's mind. *Exciting, indeed.*

* * * *

Finn didn't see Iris again until the party assembled in the drawing room for tea, and then he was obliged to sit beside her, chat politely like a proper gentleman, and act as if he wasn't going mad with the need to touch her.

By the time tea was over, he was ready to devour her.

They both lingered in the drawing room afterwards and waited for everyone to wander off to their own amusements. Violet dawdled for what seemed to Finn an interminable time, fussing with the tea things and studying the chess board until she could no longer ignore Iris's glare, and left the room with a loud sigh.

It took every bit of Finn's patience not to slam the door behind her. "Good Lord, I thought she'd never leave." He caught Iris by the waist, pulled her tight against him, and eased her back against the closed door. "I've missed you. Where have you been all day?"

She slid her arms around his neck and rested her head against his chest with a contented sigh. "I missed you, too. I rode with Captain West all morning, then had a bath and fell asleep in my bedchamber. When I woke, it was already teatime."

Finn brushed his mouth over hers, a soft groan rising from his chest as she parted her lips and stroked her tongue against his. He buried his fingers in her hair to bring her mouth closer, and mumbled against her lips, "Come upstairs with me."

"What, right now? You're mad. I can't do that. Someone will see us."

He hissed a protest when she gently pushed him away. "What does it matter? We're betrothed."

She arched an eyebrow at him. "Betrothed, not married. You're aware there's a difference?"

He grinned down at her, then nuzzled his face into her neck. "I deserved that, I suppose, but it's a bit late for the distinction now."

"Ah, but I didn't say I wouldn't come upstairs with you, my lord. I only said not *now*."

Her blue eyes were teasing as she gazed up at him, and Finn couldn't resist taking her lips in another deep kiss. They were both breathless when he pulled away. "This is going to be the longest afternoon of my life."

She smoothed her hands over his shoulders, but her smile dimmed a little, and she looked away.

"Iris?" He turned her face back to his with a finger under her chin. "Is something wrong?"

"No, but I need to speak to you, and I'd just as soon get it over with."

A dark sense of foreboding Finn couldn't explain crept over him, raising the hair on his neck. "What is it?"

"I took Chaos out on my ride this morning. Captain West wanted to see how I did on him."

Finn tensed, but she'd never promised she wouldn't ride Chaos again, and he could hardly object to it if Captain West hadn't. "And what was Captain West's opinion?"

"He was satisfied with my skills. I have his permission to ride Chaos."

Every one of Finn's protective instincts bristled, but he forced a deep breath into his lungs. "I'd like to see you ride him myself, Iris, just so I can be easy about it."

"You can see me ride him tomorrow morning." She pulled a wrinkled piece of paper from her pocket and pressed it into his hand.

"What's this?" He looked at her, then down at the paper.

"It's...well, go ahead and read it."

Finn noticed the slight tremor in her voice, and he tore open the note.

He read it, and then he read it again, more slowly, and then a third time, but he still couldn't make sense of it. Wrexley wasn't even in Hampshire anymore. Finn had set him on the road to London himself, and unless Wrexley had turned back the moment he was out of sight, there was no way he could have—

Except he could. He *had*. The villain had returned to Hampshire. Jesus, the purse on this race must be staggering for Wrexley to risk returning to Hadley House for it, especially with such little hope of success. He must know Finn would never allow Iris to run the race. Or did he think Iris wouldn't tell him about it at all?

"I'm running Chaos in the race, Finn."

Finn froze, certain he must have misunderstood her. "What did you just say?"

She swallowed nervously, but she met his gaze without a trace of hesitation. "I said I'm running Chaos in the race."

Finn stared at her in silence, then he slowly crumpled Wrexley's note in his fist. "No, you're not."

Her chin lifted. "Yes, I am. Captain West isn't in favor of the idea, but he's granted his permission, and Lady Hadley has, as well."

She'd spoken to Captain West and Lady Hadley before she'd come to him? Finn's hands clenched into fists, and the calm he'd worked so hard for disintegrated. "I haven't granted *my* permission, and I don't intend to, so there's an end to it."

His low furious growl would have terrified a grown man into submission, but she only raised her chin another notch. "I didn't come to you to ask for your permission, Finn. But I didn't suppose you'd be pleased, either, so I've come to explain the reasons for my decision."

Finn gripped his hair in his fists. "What possible reason could you have that makes the least bit of sense? You know what Wrexley is—what he's done. Given half a chance, he would have ruined you, Iris. How can you even consider helping him?"

"This has nothing to do with helping *him*. Honora says he'll have to flee to the Continent to escape his creditors if the race doesn't go off. She's afraid she'll never see him again, and she's made herself ill with worry over it. She's my dear friend, and not to blame for her cousin's misdeeds."

Finn turned and tossed Wrexley's note into the fire, then stood for a long time with his back to Iris as he drew breath after breath to calm the explosion of emotions threatening to steal his reason. When he turned to face her again, he was calmer. "I'm sorry for Lady Honora, but if she really is your dear friend, she won't ask you to risk your safety and reputation for her sake. As for Wrexley, he may find his own way out of the mess he's created—one that doesn't require him to endanger my betrothed."

"I'm not just your betrothed. I'm also *me*." Iris's voice was quiet. "Don't you see? This isn't about Lord Wrexley, or even Honora. Riding Chaos, racing him to help my friend—that means something to *me*. I can't explain why, exactly, but it has to do with feeling as if I'm utterly myself, like I did when I was a child and rode with my father. I won't brush aside something that matters to me because you don't like it, Finn. Who will I become if I simply give way to you in everything? I can't do it, and you... you shouldn't ask me to."

Finn's throat worked. He wanted to tell her he heard her, that he understood, and that he'd never ask her to give up something she needed for him, but what if he said so, and then found he couldn't keep his promise? What if he said it, and it turned out not to be true?

No answer came.

She laid her hand on his chest, her eyes pleading. "You said...I thought this was what you loved about me, Finn."

It was. Wasn't it? Jesus, he hardly knew anymore. He only knew it was all coming at him at once—the anger, the fury, the jealousy and the fear—and he didn't know how to do anything but raise his fists and fight against it.

"I thought so, too."

Finn froze at the stark misery that clouded her eyes when those words left his lips, and he couldn't look at her, couldn't bear to see it.

Her hands fell away from his chest.

She crossed the room to the door, but before she went out, she paused and turned back to look at him. "I love you, Finn...so much, but this is who I am. I can't be someone else for you."

She paused, as if waiting for him to say something, but he remained silent.

After a moment the door clicked softly, and when Finn turned, she was gone.

Chapter Twenty-two

The next morning, when Iris emerged from Hadley House and stepped onto the drive, the one person she most wanted to see wasn't there.

"Lord Huntington won't attend the race?"

She'd spent most of the night awake, unblinking eyes fixed on her bedchamber ceiling, but the few times she'd fallen into a fragmented, troubled sleep, her nightmares had been about the moment when she'd need Finn, and he wouldn't be there.

And now that moment was here.

Iris's body went numb with shock. Even in the darkest part of the night, when the nightmares were at their worst she'd still believed he wouldn't abandon her, but now, standing here on the drive with the rest of her family and friends surrounding her, she saw how wrong she'd been.

"Miss Somerset." Lord Derrick stepped forward, his face haggard, and his brown eyes grim. "I beg your pardon on Lord Huntington's behalf. He wasn't in his bedchamber when I went to fetch him, and his horse is gone from the stables. It appears he's gone, ah… for an early morning ride."

Or he was on his way back to London, without a backward glance, and without a word of explanation to anyone. Iris sucked in a breath as pain unlike any she'd ever known sliced through her.

She didn't try to stop it. She let it tear into her flesh, let it cut her heart into shreds of bloody pulp, but only for a moment. Just a single, terrible moment, and then her chin lifted and she straightened her shoulders. She took one ragged breath, then another, and a third, the last one steadier, deep and steady…

"Shall we go, then?" Iris swung herself into Chaos's saddle. "Lord Wrexley awaits."

For a moment everyone stood about on the drive looking at each other blankly, as if they weren't sure what to do next.

"Will you ride, Captain West?"

Captain West snapped out of his trance at Iris's voice and mounted his horse. "Yes. The ladies will take the carriage. Derrick, if you would?"

Lord Derrick handed Honora and Violet into the carriage first, then offered his assistance to Charlotte and Lady Annabel. Once the ladies were settled he mounted as well, and Captain West led the party down the drive.

When they arrived at the designated meeting place, they found Lord Wrexley waiting for them. Two other gentlemen stood at one side of the field, checking their tack and fussing over their horses. Iris recognized them at once as Lord Claire and Lord Edgemont, two notable London scoundrels.

"I'd like to speak with Lord Wrexley alone, if I may. Perhaps, Captain, it would be best if you and Lord Derrick waited with the ladies?" Iris pointed with her riding crop at the carriage, which had stopped some distance away. "You'll be close enough to see the race from there, but not so close—"

"We're likely to get into a brawl? Yes, perhaps that would be best. I wish you luck in the race, Miss Somerset." Captain West tipped his hat, then made his way over to the carriage.

"Watch out for Lord Claire, Miss Somerset. He's not above trying to knock you aside." Lord Derrick paused. "Neither is Lord Edgemont, come to that. Watch out for them both."

Iris managed a strained smile. "I will, my lord. Thank you."

He looked as if he wanted to say more, but after a moment he sighed and joined Captain West and the ladies.

Iris kicked Chaos into a trot and came alongside of Lord Wrexley. They stared at each other without a word for a moment, then Lord Wrexley removed his hat. "You're very good to come, Miss Somerset."

Iris didn't say she was being much kinder to him than he deserved, because they both already knew it. "I'll ask for something from you in return, if I may."

He looked surprised, but he nodded. "Yes, of course. What can I do?"

Iris wasn't sure why she asked when she knew lies rose more easily to his lips than the truth, but she plunged ahead. "You can tell me the truth, my lord. There was a lady, a Miss Hughes. She was betrothed to Lord Huntington seven years ago, I believe?"

Lord Wrexley's face drained of color, but he must have seen at once there was no use denying it, and after a moment he nodded. "Yes."

"And you ruined her?"

"It wasn't as simple as Huntington makes it out to be," Lord Wrexley ground out through a jaw gone tight. "I loved her—"

"No, you didn't. A man doesn't destroy the happiness of a lady he loves, Lord Wrexley."

His face went dark with anger. "I suppose you think Huntington loves you? You're mistaken, Miss Somerset. He doesn't know how to love anyone. He's a—"

Iris held up a hand. "That's all, Lord Wrexley. Thank you for answering my question."

She breathed a sigh of relief when he fell silent. She didn't want to hear his excuses, or any of his hateful remarks about Finn. She'd made Lord Wrexley acknowledge his perfidy aloud, and that was all she wanted.

After a moment of strained silence, he closed his pocket watch with a snap. "It's time."

Iris followed him across the field where the other two gentlemen waited on their mounts.

"Well, Miss Somerset." Lord Claire swept his hat off to her in a mocking bow. "Are you to be our competitor this morning? I confess you're the last lady I would have expected. Pretty little chit, Wrexley, but I can't imagine we'll have much trouble beating a dainty London belle, can you, Edgemont?"

"Oh, she's not a belle anymore, Claire. Didn't you hear? She's jilted Huntington." Lord Edgemont leered. "She won't become a marchioness after all, and I'd say that makes her fair game. I'd be delighted to serve, Miss Somerset, if you're looking for a lover to replace Huntington."

Iris didn't bother to respond to these taunts, but ran a firm hand over Chaos's neck and raised her riding crop. "I'm ready, Lord Wrexley. I await your pleasure."

"Fifteen seconds from now, on my word." Lord Wrexley's gaze was fixed on his pocket watch. "Ready. Set…"

Iris drew in a quick, deep breath, closed her eyes, and let the restless energy coursing through Chaos's body flow into hers. A slight smile crossed her lips. This horse was made to race, and she was made to race him. Her worry and heartbreak would be waiting for her when she finished the race, but for now, everything else but Chaos fled her mind, and she savored the perfect rightness of the moment.

"Go!"

Iris hardly had a chance to twitch the crop before Chaos surged beneath her and shot forward, every sleek muscle and sinew working in such smooth harmony she might have believed they weren't moving at all if she hadn't heard the sudden roar of pounding hooves.

After that, she didn't see anything at all except the green blur of the ground beneath her, and Chaos's ears twitching with joy and excitement as they flew across the field, floating as if his hooves didn't even touch the ground. Iris imagined the sight of his long legs, each of his perfect, leaping strides, listened to the pounding in her ears, felt the reverberation of his hooves slamming into the earth in her body as she pointed him toward the tree line and gave him his head, her own head thrown back with a shout of pure delight that she should be gifted with this moment of perfect, incredible freedom.

Iris watched the tree line draw closer with each of Chaos's pounding strides as he devoured the ground beneath them. Lord Claire was a dozen paces behind her and rapidly losing ground, and by the time they were halfway across the field he must have realized there was no chance he could beat them.

Not by fair means.

That was when he made his move.

Iris's first warning was the hiss of a riding crop slicing through the air, and then Chaos stumbled—just the tiniest hitch, no more than an instant's break in his gait, so subtle a rider less attuned to her horse might not have even noticed it.

But Iris did. She noticed it the first time Lord Claire brought his crop down in a brutal blow against Chaos's flank, and again when he did it the second time.

Another tiny stumble, and a shout, a voice raised in fury—

Hers.

If Chaos had been any other horse, or Iris any other woman, it would have been the end—of the race, the horse, and very likely the rider.

But Chaos wasn't any horse. He was *this* horse, and Iris knew him down to his very soul.

As well as I know myself.

Neither of them would ever surrender to a coward like Lord Claire, and neither of them would ever settle for less than they deserved.

From the corner of her eye Iris saw Lord Claire raise his crop a third time, but he never had a chance to land the blow. She squeezed her knees around the massive body beneath her to steady herself, gripped the reins in her hands, and leaned so low over Chaos's head she could hear each of his heaving breaths in her ear.

Go, go, go...

She might have shouted it. She might have whispered it. She might not have said it aloud at all, but it didn't matter, because Chaos understood her, and in the next breath he plunged ahead in a powerful surge of clenched muscle and sheer stubborn will, out of the reach of Lord Claire's vicious riding crop.

One minute later, it was over.

Chaos raced past the tree line, with Lord Claire so far behind them by the time he arrived, sweating and panting, he was no more than an afterthought. Lord Edgemont came in last, his horse lathered with sweat, and his lordship red-faced and cursing.

It wasn't until Iris brought Chaos down to a walk to cool him that she felt it.

He was limping.

Her heart filled with dread as she dropped the reins, scrambled down from the saddle and knelt on the ground next to Chaos's right front leg. He was holding it aloft to keep his weight off it.

Then she noticed the blood. "Oh, no. Please, no."

There was an ugly, ragged gash between his right hoof and his knee joint, and even through the smears of dark blood, Iris could see the white of Chaos's bone.

Panic slammed into her chest with such pitiless force it threatened to crush her flat to the ground. "Oh, *please*, no. Not this horse."

"What's the matter, you silly chit?" Lord Claire snapped. He was still mounted and looming over her, his horse prancing nervously. "You won, didn't you?"

Tears burned Iris's eyes, but she cradled Chaos's leg injured leg in one hand and ran her fingers gently above and below the gash see if she could feel a break in the bone, her breath held, and broken pleas falling in whispers from her lips.

Please, please...

Chaos flinched, and Iris's hand froze.

There, on the front of his leg, midway between his pastern and knee joint, where the leg should be straight, was an asymmetry in the cannon bone.

Iris's heart gave a painful wrench and she stumbled back onto her heels, but even as despair gripped her, her mind was scrambling for a denial, a way to make it not be true.

It wasn't a bad break, was it? No, no, it wasn't. Of course it wasn't, because she wouldn't let it be. It was a minor fracture only, and Captain West would fix it. He wouldn't let anything happen to Chaos. He'd know what to do. He'd fix it, and Chaos would be fine, and all would be well...

Iris let her face fall into her hands as a deep, heaving sob wracked her chest.

I'm tearing apart...

"Iris!"

A feminine cry, high with panic, and then a deeper one—Captain West, or Lord Derrick—then the confusing sound of multiple hooves coming toward her at once, and the rattle of carriage wheels over the rutted field.

"My God, Iris." Gentle hands reached for her, helped her to her feet, and then warm arms wrapped around her. "Iris, oh, thank goodness." It was Violet's voice, thick with tears. "When he struck Chaos, I was sure you'd fall. If you had, I can't…I don't want to think of it. Are you hurt?"

Iris couldn't speak, but she shook her head, then buried her face in Violet's soft shoulder.

Another set of thundering hooves approached. An ominous silence fell, then was broken by the sound of heavy boots hitting the ground as the rider dismounted.

Violet stiffened against her. "Oh, dear God."

"Easy, Huntington." It was Lord Derrick, his voice tight with warning.

Iris jerked her head up and gasped at the stark fury on Finn's face as he advanced on Lord Claire.

Lord Claire paled. "Christ, Huntington. What's the trouble? You can see she's perfectly well, can't you?"

Finn didn't say a word, but prowled toward Lord Claire, his body taut with menace, and murder in his eyes.

Lord Claire gave his reins a desperate flick, but Finn got to him before he could flee and yanked the reins out of his hands.

"Now, Huntington. Be reasonable. You don't wish to do anything you'll regret—"

Lord Claire didn't get any farther, because Finn seized him by the neck of his coat, jerked him from the saddle with a single powerful wrench, and threw him on his back onto the ground. Lord Claire tried to scramble upright, but Finn didn't give him a chance to even twitch before he was over him, shoving his face into Lord Claire's. "I should kill you."

Captain West and Lord Derrick leapt down from their mounts and moved toward the two men on the ground, both of them tensed to haul Finn away if it proved necessary, but otherwise not interfering. Neither Lord Wrexley nor Lord Edgemont came forward to defend Claire, either, or even bothered to dismount, but watched the scene unfold from a safe distance.

"Julian?" Charlotte's anxious gaze met her husband's, but she fell silent when Captain West gave a nearly imperceptible shake of his head.

Finn twisted Lord Claire's coat into a tight knot around his neck and kept twisting until Lord Claire's eyes bulged with panic and his face turned a mottled red. "I could keep twisting, Claire, until the last miserable breath is choked from your body. It's one way to be sure you *never* endanger another rider again."

A desperate gurgle bubbled from Lord Claire's mouth. He clawed at Finn's hands and kicked and writhed to be free, but he couldn't tear himself loose from Finn's grip.

Finn jerked Lord Claire's head off the ground. "If she'd fallen—if she'd suffered so much as a single scratch—you'd be drawing your last breath right now." He slammed Lord Claire's head back to the ground and rose, his lip curling with disgust as the man rolled to his side, coughing and gasping for breath.

"Get out of my sight." Finn jerked his gaze to Lord Wrexley and Lord Edgemont, who were gaping at Lord Claire's prone body with open-mouthed horror. "All of you."

Lord Edgemont scrambled down from his horse, yanked Lord Claire to his feet and half-lifted, half-threw him onto his horse, and the three men disappeared in a flurry of pounding hooves.

When they were gone, Finn turned to Iris, his chest still heaving.

She stared at him for long moments, her face frozen, then she deliberately looked away from him. "Chaos is hurt. It's his right front leg, Captain."

"Iris." Finn stepped toward her, his voice pleading. "I—"

"I want to go home." Iris's hands were shaking as she reached for Violet's arm to steady herself.

Charlotte took Iris's other arm and led her toward the carriage. "Come, Annabel, Lady Honora. We'll ride back to Hadley House in the carriage, and the gentlemen can follow once they've—"

"No." Iris clutched at Violet and Charlotte as she stumbled on the carriage steps. "Not Hadley House. I want to go home to London."

* * * *

Finn was standing in front of the cold fireplace in the drawing room, staring at the empty grate, when Derrick found him several hours later.

"You'll escort them back to London?" Finn asked, without turning around.

Lord Derrick held his hat in his hands, his fingers worrying the brim. "Yes. Lady Honora goes, as well."

Finn nodded. "There's an end to the house party, I guess."

Derrick hesitated, then said, "When will you return to London?"

"Soon. Tomorrow, perhaps. I have a few things to discuss with Captain West first." Finn braced his hand against the mantel and let his forehead rest on his forearm. "She won't see me, Derrick."

"She's upset, Huntington. Chaos…Captain West isn't certain he can save him. Even if the bone can be set, there's the question of infection."

Lord Derrick stepped toward Finn and laid a hand on his shoulder. "Miss Somerset blames herself for it. She's saying she never should have raced at all. You simply need to give her some time. All may yet still come to rights."

"Yesterday afternoon, when she told me she intended to race, she begged for my understanding, and I…" Finn straightened and ran a weary hand down his face. "I denied her. I wasn't there for her when she needed me, Derrick."

"You *were* there—when it mattered, you were there. As for the rest, get down on your knees and beg her pardon. The lady is in love with you. I feel certain she'll forgive you."

"Perhaps I don't deserve her forgiveness."

"There's nothing unforgivable about being afraid for the woman you love, Huntington, but if you want her forgiveness, the best thing you can do is find a way to deserve it." Lord Derrick shoved his hat onto his head and turned for the door. "I'll see you back in London."

Finn stood still for a long time after Derrick left, thinking about what his friend had said, and about what Iris had tried to tell him yesterday, when he was too overwhelmed with his own fears to hear her.

This is who I am. This is what you love about me.

What he loved about her…

Her eyes. Her laugh. That she knew herself, and understood how rare and precious that was. The way she challenged him. Her passion.

Her courage.

The answer came to him so easily then, almost as if Iris had whispered it in his ear.

He found Captain West in the stables, his hands folded on the edge of Chaos's stall, his chin resting on his hands and his face grim as he watched the horse move awkwardly inside. "Miss Somerset managed to calm him when we first brought him back to his stall, but he grew agitated again at once. I'm damn grateful Lord Derrick has taken the young ladies away."

Finn stiffened. "What can be done for him?"

Captain West didn't answer but reached for the rifle propped against the wall next to him and lifted the latch on Chaos's stall door.

Finn grabbed the stall door, pushed it closed again, and looked Captain West in the eye. "No, West. What can be done for him?"

Captain West searched Finn's face for a long moment. Finn held his breath, his chest tight as he waited for West to make up his mind.

I'll do anything, whatever it takes…

At last the other man blew out a long sigh. "It looks like we're going to find out."

Chapter Twenty-three

"Iris? It's been four days, and I've had quite enough of this nonsense. Open this door at once."

Iris let out a low groan and threw her arm over her eyes. Had it really been four days since she'd locked herself in her bedchamber? One would think Violet would have given up and gone away by now.

"Grandmother is threatening to send for Dr. Graham if you refuse another meal. Do you really want him here, prodding at you with his cold hands? At least open the door, if only to prove you're still able to move."

Iris's mouth pursed with self-righteous indignation. Violet might be terribly clever, but she didn't know as much as she thought she did.

Iris *had* moved. Not ten minutes ago, she'd rolled from her left side to her right.

She sagged against her pillows and squeezed her eyes closed. If she'd spent most of the morning languishing in her bed—just as she'd done the day before, and the day before that—it was no one's concern but her own.

There was a faint thud, as if Violet had let her forehead fall against the door. "I know your heart is broken and you feel wretched, Iris, but you can't hide in your bedchamber forever."

Certainly she could. If a lady couldn't hide in her bedchamber when her heart was broken, then when could she? Heartbreak seemed a perfectly good reason to never rise from her bed again.

And she *was* heartbroken. It had been two weeks since she'd fled Hadley House, and each moment of that time she'd thought of nothing but Finn. She woke every morning with her foolish heart leaping wildly in her chest, certain he'd call on her, and retired to her bedchamber every night with every hope dashed.

Finn didn't come.

Her heart wasn't just broken. It was shattered.

She longed for him with a visceral ache that left her breathless and teetering on a precarious edge between hope and anguish. Each day he didn't come another piece of her heart splintered loose with a dry crack, until she was left with nothing but thousands of tiny shards.

So many shards there was no hope of it ever being whole again.

But just when she'd thought there was nothing left of her heart to break, Honora had paid her a visit and given her some news that had toppled Iris into an abyss of misery the likes of which she'd never known before and despaired of ever escaping.

Lord Derrick, who'd been paying Honora frequent calls since their return from Hampshire had told her Finn wasn't even in London. Honora had pressed him, but Lord Derrick had been either unwilling or unable to say where Finn was, or when he intended to return.

Or if he intended to return at all.

That had been four days ago. Iris hadn't left her bedchamber since.

She tried not to think of Finn, but he invaded her every waking thought, and when she did manage to fall into an exhausted sleep he haunted her dreams. She was tormented by the memory of his cool gray eyes as they'd looked that day in Charlotte's drawing room, when she'd told him she intended to race Chaos. He'd looked at her as he'd done early in their courtship, before he'd cared at all for her.

Before he told her he loved her.

The next day Chaos had been injured in the race, and she'd been so overwhelmed with guilt and grief she'd left Hampshire without a word to Finn. She'd fled like an overwrought child at the first sign of strife, and now, two weeks later, she bitterly regretted it.

Hiding in her bedchamber was hardly the answer, but here she was nonetheless, staring at the ceiling, her heart as heavy as a stone in her chest.

Her grandmother and sisters continued to lay siege to her locked door, but Iris had responded to Violet's threats and Lady Chase's scolding with a resounding silence. Even Hyacinth's gentle pleas had failed to lure her out again.

There was another quiet thud, and then Violet's voice came through the closed door again, shakier this time. "You're not the only one with a broken heart, Iris."

Iris's eyes flew open, and she struggled upright. "I'm not?"

"No, you're not."

Lord Derrick had called on Lady Honora every day since their return...

Oh, no. It couldn't be. "Is it...it's not Lord Derrick, is it?"

There was a brief silence from the other side of the door, then Violet sighed. "If you don't mind, Iris, I'd rather not stand in the hallway and shout about Lord Derrick through a closed door. Let me in."

Iris scrambled off the side of the bed and hastened to the door. As soon as she opened it and saw Violet's ravaged face, her heart sank. "Oh, Violet. I'm so sorry. I didn't realize, but I should have. What kind of lady is so selfish she doesn't notice her sister's broken heart?"

"A lady whose heart is also broken." Violet came in and perched on the edge of Iris's bed, her shoulders hunched in defeat. "Love makes us all selfish, I think. If it didn't, I'd be happy for Honora and Lord Derrick, but I'm not, Iris. I'm not."

"Oh, my dear." Iris sat next to Violet and opened her arms, and Violet fell into them.

"I don't know why I'm surprised at it. I'm not the type of lady a gentleman falls in love with. I've always known it, and I never expected to come to London and have some grand love affair. It's just...I suppose I thought Lord Derrick was different than other gentlemen. He's so kind, and...ah, well. It doesn't matter now."

Tears pricked behind Iris's eyes as she ran a soothing hand over her sister's back. "Is it quite a settled thing between Honora and Lord Derrick?"

"He's courting her, and she confided in me she believes he'll make an offer before long."

"She intends to accept him?"

"Yes. Why wouldn't she? He's...well, he's lovely, isn't he? I wonder we didn't foresee this would happen. I can't think of two people who are better suited."

Iris wanted to deny it, to reassure Violet no one could ever suit Lord Derrick as well as she could, but the truth was she'd wondered more than once whether Lord Derrick's easy calm was a good match for Violet's sharp, restless inquisitiveness.

Whereas Lady Honora and Lord Derrick...

Well, Violet was right. One had only to look at them to see they were as ideally suited as two people could hope to be. "Does Honora know you're—?"

"In love with Lord Derrick? No, and you mustn't tell her, Iris. If she knew, she'd likely try to discourage him, for my sake." Violet attempted a laugh, but there was a trace of bitterness in it. "You see how well-matched they are? She's every bit as lovely as he is."

Iris sighed. Dear God, what a muddle. "Love is dreadful, isn't it?"

Violet dragged her sleeve across her eyes, then managed a watery smile. "I'll take care to avoid it from now on, yes. I never planned to marry anyway, as you know. Why, in another month or so I won't even recall what I saw in Lord Derrick and will be quite reconciled to my original plan of becoming London's most infamous bluestocking spinster."

"Oh, dear. Grandmother won't like that."

"No, it'll drive her mad, I'm afraid. Hyacinth will have to land a duke to make up for our shortcomings."

Between Violet's disappointment and her own, Iris's heart was battered beyond repair, but she could see her sister was attempting to put a brave face on it, so she forced a smile. "Come, Violet. I've lingered in my bedchamber long enough, and I think we'd both benefit from some fresh air. Let's go for a ride in Richmond Park."

Violet brightened a little. "Yes, all right. I'll change into my riding habit, and meet you downstairs."

Before Violet could move, however, their grandmother hobbled over the threshold, and pointed her cane at Iris. "Well, miss, I'm pleased to see you've put aside this foolishness and risen from you bed at last."

As far as Lady Chase's rebukes went, it was a mild one. Their grandmother wasn't known for forbearance, but ever since Iris had returned from Hadley House and confessed to the disaster she'd made of her courtship with Finn, the old woman had shown remarkable restraint.

Violet gave her grandmother a cautious smile. "We thought we'd take a ride in Richmond Park this afternoon."

"No, no, that won't do, I'm afraid. Iris has a visitor waiting for her in the drawing room." Lady Chase swept a shrewd gaze over Iris, and her lips pinched together with displeasure at what she saw. "You look a perfect fright. Brush your hair and wash your face before you go down, Iris, and for pity's sake, change that gown."

With that she hobbled back out the door, leaving Iris and Violet staring at each other.

"A visitor?" Iris's heart began to race in her chest. "Do you suppose… could it be Lord Huntington?"

Violet gave Iris a gentle push toward the washbasin. "I don't know, but I hope so. Quickly, Iris. Wash your face, and I'll help you with your gown and hair."

By the time Violet had fussed and brushed and smoothed her into ladylike respectability, Iris was so breathless with nerves and anticipation her knees felt as if they would collapse beneath her. She stood outside the closed drawing room door for a moment with her palm pressed to her stomach to calm the flock of birds that had taken up residence under her ribs, then took a deep breath, grasped the knob with damp fingers, and pushed the door open.

And when she saw who it was, her heart plummeted right down into her slippers.

"Ah, Iris. How do you do? Your grandmother tells me you're out of sorts, so I've come to take you for a drive in my carriage."

"Lady Annabel." Iris tried to force a smile onto her stiff lips. "I—that's very kind of you. It's lovely to see you again."

"Is it, indeed? But you look a trifle disappointed, though of course I can't imagine why you would be. Did you expect someone else? No, I can only suppose your grandmother is right, and you're suffering from low spirits. Well, come along then. Fresh air will cheer you."

Iris was quite sure nothing less than a handsome, hazel-eyed marquess would ever cheer her again, but one didn't argue with Lady Annabel, particularly not when she had such a determined gleam in her eyes.

"There now. This is lovely, isn't it?" Lady Annabel asked, when they were seated in her phaeton and she'd taken the ribbons. "Well, Iris. Lady Chase despises me, as you know, and yet she put aside her dislike and asked me to call on you, and now I see why. You look unlike yourself—so pale and dispirited. Is something troubling you?"

Iris plucked at her skirts. She hadn't lived up to Lady Annabel's faith in her, and now she could hardly look her friend in the eye.

"Iris?"

If she said Finn's name she'd burst into tears, so Iris didn't say it. "Have you had any news from Charlotte, Lady Annabel? I've expected to hear from her every day since my return to London. She said she'd write to tell me how Chaos did, but she hasn't. I think Captain West must not have been able to save him, and Charlotte doesn't want to tell me."

Despite her vow to avoid another bout of pathetic sniveling, tears flooded Iris's eyes. She couldn't think of that race, or of Chaos, without a rush of unspeakable grief.

"Now, Iris. Why do you assume the worst has happened? Perhaps it's not what you think at all."

Iris didn't argue, but stared sightlessly ahead and watched one street blur into the next as Lady Annabel guided the phaeton through London.

"What of Lord Huntington?" Lady Annabel asked, after they'd driven for a while in silence. "Has he called on you since his return to London?"

"Lord Huntington is back in London?" For one moment Iris's heart burst with hope, only to be dashed again when it occurred to her Finn *hadn't* called on her. "When did he return?"

"Just last night. No doubt he hasn't had a chance to call on you yet, but no matter. We're very near Grosvenor Square, so we'll just call on him, shall we?"

"*What*? No, my lady! He won't want…I don't think he wishes to see… that is, it isn't proper for me to call on a gentleman!"

Considering what else she'd done with Finn, propriety was a thin excuse indeed, but Iris clung to it with both hands. What if she appeared on his doorstep, and he refused to see her? Her heart wouldn't survive the blow if he sent her away—

"Proper?" Lady Annabel waved that away with a tinkling laugh and turned onto Brook Street, where Finn kept a handsome townhouse at the north end of Grosvenor Square. "Oh, what nonsense. I'm certain he'll be pleased to see you."

Panic seized Iris, and she gripped Lady Annabel's arm. "He won't be, Lady Annabel. I left him in Hampshire without a word of explanation. I don't know that he'll ever forgive me."

"Why not beg his pardon and see? Ah, here he is."

Iris mouth went dry. Dear God, Finn was standing in the drive watching the phacton approach, an indecipherable expression on his stern face.

Iris fell back against her seat as every hope of escape evaporated.

"Lord Huntington—how convenient we should find you right here, waiting. I've brought you Miss Somerset, as promised. Do hand her down, won't you? She looks a trifle unsteady."

Finn's large hand enveloped Iris's, and he helped her to alight. He hadn't taken his eyes off her since he sighted the carriage, but now he tore his gaze away to bow to Lady Annabel. "Thank you, my lady. You're very kind to bring her to me."

Lady Annabel raised an eyebrow at that. "I assure you, I'm not kind in the least. I do this for my own amusement only." She set the horse in motion with a practiced flick of the reins, and disappeared down Brook Street.

Iris and Finn stood in silence for long moments, staring at each other, until at last Finn cleared his throat. "I hope you'll forgive me for bringing you to Grosvenor Square. The proper thing would be for me to call on you at your grandmother's house, but I, ah…I have something to show you I hope will please you."

Iris's throat worked. Oh, how she wanted to tell him she was pleased already—pleased to be near him, to inhale his clean scent and look into the beautiful hazel eyes she'd dreamed about every night since she'd left him, but a tight ball of emotion welled in her throat, and she could only nod.

He flushed a little when she didn't answer, and an anxious frown crossed his lips, but he held out his arm to her. "It's just this way."

Iris slid her hand into the crook of his elbow, her breath catching at the familiar feel of his muscled forearm flexing under her fingertips, and let him lead her through a garden still scented with lavender, despite the lateness of the season.

He didn't pause, but led her through the garden to the mews behind the house and into a spacious stable with a grand, wood-timbered ceiling.

"My lord?"

Iris searched Finn's face in the dim light, but he only tucked her arm closer against his side and led her down a long central corridor, past rows upon rows of stalls.

At last he came to a halt at the last stall on the left.

"He's not fully healed," he said in a rush. "His leg is fragile still, but the gash has closed, and there's no longer any risk of infection."

Iris peered into the stall, and for the second time that day, her knees went so weak they threatened to buckle.

Chaos. Finn had brought Chaos to her.

She tried to speak, but all she could manage was a choked gasp as she raised her shaking hand to cover her mouth.

The horse's sleek gray coat had been brushed to a glossy shine, and his liquid black eyes were as clear and alert as Iris remembered. As soon as he saw her he whinnied impatiently, as if he were scolding her for taking so long to come to him.

"Captain West said the bone is mending much faster than he expected." Finn shifted from one foot to the other, his uncertain gaze fixed on Iris. "There's quite a lot that can be done for a fractured cannon bone, it turns out, if one has the patience to see it through."

She remained silent, still too overcome to speak, tears gathering in the corners of her eyes. This was the reason Finn hadn't returned to London at once. He'd stayed in Hampshire with Chaos, to heal the horse and save him from having to be shot.

He'd done it for her.

"It was a neat trick getting him here from Hampshire without putting any strain on his leg. Have you ever seen a horse van?" The words began to tumble faster and faster from Finn's mouth when she still didn't speak. "The famous racehorse Sovereign was brought to Newmarket Racecourse in one last year, and Captain West suggested we try the same with Chaos.

It took five days to get from Winchester to London, but you see how fit he is, even after such a long journey..."

He trailed off into an awkward silence, and it was then Iris realized he was nervous. Lord Huntington, the grand marquess, the quintessential English gentleman, was nervous, because he wanted so badly to please her.

And after all, he wasn't Lord Huntington, was he? Not to Iris. To her, he was Finn, the man she loved, who'd given her the most precious gift she could ever hope to receive.

Himself.

"We'll have to be careful with him for the next several months, but after that you'll be able to fly over the ground on his back through Richmond Park, just as you told me you always wanted to."

Iris gazed up at him, still too dazed to speak. What could she say? How could she ever put into words what this meant to her?

"Iris." Finn's tone was pleading. "Say something, sweetheart."

"I—he's...this is..." She curled her fingers into his waistcoat and buried her face against his chest as her breath caught on another sob. "There's nothing you could have done that would mean more to me than this."

He groaned as his arms closed around her. "I'm so sorry, sweet. That day, in Lady Hadley's drawing room...I want you to know I never doubted you, Iris. I turned away from you because I doubted myself. It's haunted me, the sadness on your face that day, and the way I let you leave. I never should have—"

"Shhh." She touched her fingertips to his lips to hush him. "I turned away from you, too. I left Hampshire without a word, and I've regretted it every single day since. What you've done for me..." She gestured helplessly at Chaos as she struggled to find the words. "The two gentlemen I love more than anything else are here with me, and I couldn't ask for anything more."

He clasped her face in his hands and took her lips in a passionate kiss that left them both breathless.

"I can think of one more thing to ask for," he said, when he'd eased her away at last.

"Oh? Do you want me to read the rest of *School of Venus* to you?"

His eyes darkened, and he let out a husky laugh. "Two things, then."

She traced his lips with a gentle finger, then pressed a kiss to the dimple on his chin. "There's nothing I wouldn't give you, Finn."

His forehead touched hers. "I love you, Iris. I want you to be mine."

His. Not just a wife, and not just the Marchioness of Huntington, but *his.*

Iris rose onto her tiptoes and wrapped her arms around his neck. "I already am."

Epilogue

Three months later.

"If you don't stop that at once, my lord, you'll make me fall, and then you'll be sorry, indeed."

Despite Iris's protests, Finn's hands strayed further under her skirts, his warm palms sliding from her ankles up to her calves. "If you fall I'll catch you, sweet, and once I have you in my arms, neither of us will be sorry."

Iris wobbled on the library ladder, a little cry escaping her lips as his teasing fingers inched up the backs of her thighs. "If you'd just give me a moment I'll come down, and—Finn!"

"Hmm?"

"Did you just untie one of my garters?"

He let out a husky chuckle as his deft fingers plucked at the second bow. "It was an accident. Both times."

Iris craned her neck to glare over her shoulder at her husband, but as soon as his playful eyes met hers, her frown dissolved into a smile. Goodness, he was handsome, and he looked so much like a mischievous little boy it was impossible for her to stay cross with him.

"You're very wicked, Lord Huntington, and nothing at all like the scrupulously proper marquess I was led to believe I was marrying. Now, if you'll only behave for a moment, I'll come down, and I'll bring you something you'll like."

"I'd like a number of things right now," Finn murmured as he tossed aside her garter and teased her stocking down her leg. "And a book isn't one of them."

"That depends on the book. Under certain circumstances, I've known you to be quite fond of reading." Iris tucked a large, heavy book she'd pulled from the shelves under her arm, then stood on her tiptoes and stretched to reach a small tome half-hidden between two much taller volumes. "Ah. There it is! All right, I've got it. Will you help me down now?"

Finn wrapped firm hands around her waist and lifted her from the top rung of the library ladder and into his arms. "I missed you this afternoon." He cradled her against his chest and nuzzled his face into the loose hair at her temple with a soft groan. "Good Lord, you smell good. You're the only woman in England who still smells of jasmine after hours in a dusty library."

Iris slid her arms around his neck as he crossed the room and sat in one of the large sofas in front of the fire. She brushed a lock of silky hair away from his forehead and settled herself on his lap. "How was your ride today? Does Chaos continue to mend?"

She usually took Chaos out herself each afternoon, but the sky was overcast this morning, and her husband had objected to her riding in the rain. On any other day Iris would have balked at his high-handedness, but this time she hadn't argued with him, and as it happened, Finn and Chaos had been caught in a cold, relentless drizzle.

"He's as fit as I've ever seen him. It's remarkable, really. You'd never know he'd been injured. I think we should go easy with him for another month, just to be sure, but after that..." He tugged gently at one of her curls. "You can ride him like a hellion all over Richmond Park if you like."

A tiny, secret smile curled Iris's lips. There wouldn't be any wild rides for her for quite a few months to come. "I'm afraid you must have been soaked when you returned."

"I was. Wet, and freezing, too. Will you warm me, sweetheart?" He brushed his mouth against her throat as his hands slipped back under her skirts and dragged her remaining stocking down her leg.

Iris caught her breath at the tantalizing caress. "You're already warm."

He caught her earlobe between his teeth, tickling it with his tongue before he dropped a trail of open-mouthed kisses down her neck. "I intend to be warmer still, and you, sweet, will be wet—what the devil is that?"

He'd eased back against the sofa and grasped her hips to pull her on top of him, but now he jerked back up again and reached behind him. "*A Genuine Narrative of All the Street Robberies*?" He held up the book, a blank look on his face. "You thought *this* was something I'd like? An account of crimes in the London streets by..." He flipped to the title page. "James Dalton, prisoner at Newgate?"

"No, that one isn't for you. It's for Violet."

"Violet?" Finn's brows drew together in a frown. "Is she plotting a crime?"

"No, no. Of course not. She, ah…well, I suppose you may as well know. Violet's writing a book."

Finn raised an eyebrow. "What kind of book requires a study of criminal activity in London?"

"Well, it's a bit difficult to explain. She calls it *A Treatise on London for Bluestockings*. Or is it *A Treatise on London for Adventuresses*? I can't recall which, because she keeps changing her mind. The book is filled with stories, drawings and research about London for curious ladies, or any young lady who prefer books to ballrooms, and wishes to explore beyond the boundaries of Almack's. She has an entire chapter on ghost sightings. It's really quite clever."

Finn stared down at the book in his hand, then back at Iris. "Good Lord. Lady Chase approves of this?"

"Well…"

"Iris," Finn said in a warning tone. "You aren't encouraging Violet to deceive your grandmother, are you?"

"No! That is, not exactly. Grandmother knows Violet is writing *something*. She just doesn't know quite what. But there's no harm in it, and Violet needs the distraction, especially now Lord Derrick and Lady Honora will marry." Iris sighed. "I've never seen Violet so dejected."

Finn's face softened. "Ah. I'm sorry for her, though I never did think Violet and Derrick would suit. That's not much comfort when one's heart is broken, however."

"You're quite right. They *don't* suit, but Violet doesn't see it." Iris took the book from Finn and set it on a table beside the couch, then snuggled against him and laid her head on his chest. "I can't bear to think Violet won't find a gentleman she loves as much as I love you, but she swears she'll never fall in love again, and no matter how much Grandmother scolds, Violet refuses a second season, and insists she'll never marry."

Finn stroked a hand over her hair. "Time will change her mind, sweetheart, and until then, we'll do what we can to cheer her."

Iris lay quietly in his arms and listened to his slow, steady breaths and the reassuring beat of his heart, but after a long moment she raised her head and met his gaze. "I do know of one thing that might help to cheer her."

Finn was toying with the buttons on the back of her gown, releasing them one by one, his breath quickening as the thin muslin of her shift was revealed. "Hmm? What's that, love?"

Iris pressed a kiss to his chest, over his heart, then reached into a pocket of her gown, pulled out the small book and handed it to Finn, her heart pounding.

He frowned down at it in confusion. "*A Little Pretty Pocket Book*. Why should Violet want a children's song and instruction book?"

Iris laid a hand on his cheek and smiled up at him. "That one isn't for Violet. It's for us."

For a single, breathless moment he remained baffled, but then his face lit up, and his eyes went a softer green that she'd ever seen them. "Oh, my love." His hands were shaking as he took her face in his palms and kissed her with such tenderness Iris was certain her heart would break with happiness.

She turned her head to kiss his palm. "You like my surprise, then?"

He stroked a finger over her cheek. "Nothing in the world could make me happier, sweet."

Iris bit her lip to hide her grin. "Nothing? What a pity, because I do have one more book for you. I thought I'd read it to you this afternoon."

"You've another book secreted away somewhere?" He hooked a finger into the neckline of her bodice, a grin curling his lips as he peered into it. "No, it's not down there, and I've already explored under your skirts."

"Ah, but you haven't turned out my pockets, my lord." Iris burrowed into the folds of her gown. "Ah, here it is, but now I think of it, you told me once you've read this book before." She held it up so he could see the title.

Finn's lips parted, and his eyes gleamed as he gazed down at her. "*School of Venus.*"

"Yes, just so. I don't like to bore you by reading it to you again, though, so perhaps we should choose another—"

"I don't think so, sweet." He took the book from her, opened it to a random page, then handed it back and went to work again on the buttons of her gown. "Read."

Iris smiled at the note of command in his voice, and began to read.

"Kissing and feeling are two very good pleasures. Let us first speak of kissing; there is the kissing of our breasts, of our mouths, of our eyes, of our face. You must know then there are a thousand delights in love—"

"A thousand delights?" Finn brushed his lips over hers. "One..." He pressed his warm mouth between her breasts in a lingering kiss. "Two..." He touched his lips gently to one fluttering eyelid, then the other, and kissed her cheeks, her chin, and the tip of her nose. "Three, four, five, six..."

"You must speak to your gallant low, with little phrases, calling him your heart, your soul, your life, telling him he pleases you extremely, that he may perceive you love him."

Iris slid her fingers into his hair and tugged gently. Finn raised his face to hers, and she caught her breath at the exquisite tenderness in his eyes. "You're my heart, my soul—"

"And my life. You're my life, Iris."

"I think the minutes we spend in love are the sweetest of our life," she whispered, her gaze holding his. *"For there is nothing so pleasing as love."*

Notes

The School of Venus, or The Ladies Delight, by Michel Millot was translated from the French and published in England in 1680. All the lines of text that appear in the epilogue are in the original book, but I've taken bits of pieces from a series of different passages to fit the scene.

ABOUT THE AUTHOR

Anna Bradley is the author of The Sutherland Scandals and The Sutherland Sisters novels. A Maine native, she now lives near Portland, OR, where people are delightful and weird and love to read. She teaches writing and lives with her husband, two children, a variety of spoiled pets, and shelves full of books. Visit her website at www.annabradley.net.

Printed in the United States
by Baker & Taylor Publisher Services